FILE UNDER FAMILY

Geraldine Wall

Books in this series

For Izzy and Simona

1

Ambiguous Loss

1

The dead woman's house was not where it should have been. Anna parked on a double yellow line, cursed her satnav and snatched the ancient A-Z from the glove compartment. She checked the index and flicked pages over and back until it was clear that the vital page was missing, torn from its spine by too many similar frenzied searches. It was going to be one of those days. She took a deep breath and forced herself to calm down.

The day had started badly when Ellis had trailed into her bedroom while it was still dark announcing apologetically that he had just had to throw up in the kitchen sink because Harry was in the bathroom. He was white and sweating. She had wrapped him in her fleecy dressing gown and steered him back to bed with one hand on his forehead to test his temperature. He was clammy, not hot. Then the new order clanked into action. George was roused and brought the boy tea and dry toast and told Anna to see to herself since it was her first field job and she mustn't be late. Ellis would be fine, it would all be fine, not to worry, this would all work out. And so Anna had rushed through her own preparations to spend a few minutes before leaving to test Ellis with a proper thermometer and to kiss his fed-up face. She would phone George the minute this visit was over.

Anna re-programmed the satnav. It was all she could do and it was possible she had put in the wrong postcode since she'd been preoccupied with Ellis. It obediently suggested another route. She drove fast for two miles swearing at every traffic light and screeched to a halt behind a sleek silver hybrid crouched by the curb.

The man from the Coroner's Office was pointedly looking at his watch when Anna ran in. He was immaculately turned out and cool; she was flustered and sweaty and fifteen minutes late and couldn't stop herself from apologising profusely. He presented her with his card with the name James Proudie, and she gave him hers with the photo ID which made her look like a hung-over spaniel. He put the keys to the house and a piece of paper with the name of Margaret Clark's solicitor on the kitchen table and quickly summarised the situation, most of which she already knew although not that there had been a post-mortem. Anna was surprised and asked him why. There had been no signs of violence. James Proudie sighed the sigh of a man who resents having to deal with an inferior species but is too polite to say so.

'Well, her death ticked all the boxes for one, didn't it? She died suddenly and had not been having medical treatment and was alone. We like to do things professionally, Mrs Ames.' Implied – not like you turning up late.

'And what was it?'

'Heart attack the path lab said, probably brought on by acute thyrotoxicosis.' He seemed bored and embarrassed to find himself in this low-end property and kept skimming his phone with a long forefinger giving Anna scant attention.

'She was a bit young for that wasn't she? Fifty-three?' He just shrugged. She heard footsteps coming down the stairs. A heavy-set man in a creased black suit appeared carrying two cardboard boxes. 'Shouldn't I have a look through those, Mr Proudie?' she said. There could be all sorts of useful information if those were boxes of documents.

'They're just old files, nothing of use to you – and, of course, her jewellery and some little porcelain figures which I would imagine don't amount to much. We have to clear the house of valuables, Mrs Ames, until things are sorted out. You can look at them at her solicitor's if you find you need to. Can't imagine why.' He glanced round disdainfully. 'It's not exactly a mansion, is it?' He peered into the small back garden. 'She won't have left much and her heirs won't be hard to trace. I know the signs.' He turned back to appraise Anna with perfectly groomed eyebrows fractionally above their designated slot on his face. She instinctively straightened her back and then felt resentful and annoyed. 'I don't know why they've brought Harts into it. Normally relatives or friends deal with this sort of thing.'

Anna felt a spasm of dislike at his referring to Margaret Clark's early and sudden death as "this sort of thing" as well as his general attitude to herself. A cool part of her brain recognised this flush of antagonism as a danger signal and she took a moment to breathe. Not much point in getting a reputation as an easy wind-up. 'Actually,' she said, 'the heir does need to be traced. No-one has come forward.'

James Proudie waved an elegant and dismissive finger. 'Sad,' he murmured insincerely. 'I've left Mrs Clark's address book by the phone although, of course, we have had the landline disconnected.

You may find there are relatives listed. You'll have to phone everyone.' Do I have 'muppet' tattooed somewhere only other people can see, Anna thought in irritation.

'Yes,' she smiled, 'I do realise that. Was it your office that tried to contact the daughter?' She rapidly scanned the small, tidy kitchen in which they were standing and noticed a photo-collage over the radiator to examine later.

'It was the police, in fact, but no luck. You do know she's in America? Chicago I think.'

Anna reviewed her mental check-list. The funeral. 'So if the post-mortem is complete have you signed off the body for burial?'

'There's a cremation certificate – no more room in the ground even for a pauper's grave,' he said matter-of-factly. She shivered. Margaret Clark suddenly became real to her. This woman was not old, not that much older than herself, and had died alone with her daughter far away and it was possible, likely in fact, that she would be cremated before the young woman even knew her mother was dead.

'No mobile phone has been found? That's odd.'

'No phone, no lap-top, no tablet, no getting some people into the twenty-first century.'

Anna refused to be side-tracked. 'Was there no will at all and why a pauper's grave? This house must be worth around £200K.'

'If it's paid for, yes. But we can't wait to dispose of her until her beneficiaries are found so the council will pay for a plain service at the crematorium. No following car or flowers or anything like that, just a simple service. They'll recoup their expenses out of the estate in due course. There is a do-it-yourself will but it's useless.' The phone was still out like an electronic fetish and the finger hovered over it longing to play.

'Not witnessed?'

'No address for the daughter. It was all filled in apart from that. She plainly meant to leave everything to her but the solicitor doesn't have any contact details either. People are astonishingly careless about these things. No doubt you'll soon find a close relative who knows where, er,' he tapped and stroked, 'Briony Clark can be reached.' Slipping the phone into his coat pocket he began to pull on black leather gloves. Anna's dislike for his superior manner deepened.

She thought quickly. She hated the idea of a bleak service and a rushed disposal of the dead woman's body. Even though she was a stranger to her, Anna felt for her. She was a mother. Yes, that's what it is, Anna thought, I can't bear a *mother* to be treated like that. Not that I have any hang-ups, of course. She stopped the man as he put his hand on the front door knob to leave. 'I'd like a little time to try to contact people and tell them so that they can come to the service if they want to. Can you give me a few days?' He said he could and he'd let her know the details when the cremation was arranged. He was swiftly out of the door and across the short front garden. She could sense the relief in his erect spine as his Prius obediently unlocked itself at its master's approach.

So unsettling and weird, Anna reflected, that when you die strangers come into your house and do things to you and make decisions about you and you might have passed these people on the street and not known that they would handle your dead body and examine your stilled heart and sort through your private things. She shook the thought away and dialled George. 'I think he's feeling a bit better,' he said, 'I've got him wrapped up on the sofa watching a recording of Countryfile with Harry. He's kept some dry toast down – so far anyway.' He paused. 'Lucky you put that waste disposal unit in.'

Now that both men had gone Anna had a good look round the house. Someone had been in and tidied up the kitchen because there were no signs of cooking in progress such as Margaret Clark must have left. Anna glanced round the immaculate grey and white work tops and couldn't help a quick look at the floor. Nothing. Of course there would be nothing. In the corner away from the through draught there was a large wicker basket and a hairy wool blanket.

The short hall opened into a surprisingly light living room. There were windows on both sides so the room on this east/west orientation would be light all day. A modern wood floor had been laid and on top of this was a large cream flokati rug. At right angles to an alcove filled with framed photographs and books and an art deco lamp, was a blue velvet chesterfield, a purple chenille throw folded along its back. There was a framed studio photograph of two women on the chimney breast wall. Presumably Margaret and Briony. Anna studied both faces. The older woman had a pleasant, rounded face with a glossy bob of light brown hair and a fresh complexion. She looked as though she smiled often and easily. She was placed slightly above and to the left of the younger woman but Anna had the impression that Briony was the taller of the two. Briony had an incisive expression in her light blue eyes and her blonde hair was carefully arranged in an artful tangle of well-disciplined curls. Anna glanced around and saw no image of a man.

A television stood on a low table in the other alcove and beneath it was a digital box, a DVD player and a modest sound system. DVDs were stacked tidily against the wall and Anna noticed that the top one was a Clive Owen film, *Bring the Boys Home*, one of her own favourite weepies. Two deep chairs faced the sofa and between them was a square coffee table with boxes of games arranged neatly underneath. Nothing matched, very little was new, but the room was pretty, comfortable and welcoming. Margaret Clark wanted to make her house a home, not a fashionable showroom.

Anna was closing the door with a small smile when she turned back, a notion having struck her. There was something wrong with the room despite its pleasant look. What was it? She let her gaze roam over the perfectly aligned pictures, the cushions each on a diagonal point arranged symmetrically along the back of the sofa, the neat stacks of DVDs and games. Her own living room had much the same family clutter in it – pictures, games, movies, CDs and so on but there was a difference. It wasn't just that her house was almost never tidy like this, there was something else. The room felt forlorn. It shouldn't do, but it did. Anna shook her head thinking she was getting too whimsical. It was her dad's fault, of course.

Everything else in the house seemed much as expected except for a couple of oddities. There was a box, a shoebox, beside the bed in what was clearly Margaret Clark's bedroom with notes and cards and some letters all of which seemed to have come from her daughter. Anna sat on the bed and checked the postmarks on the envelopes remembering the inversion of day and month in US notation. They were tucked in as though it was a small filing cabinet in date order, the last one being December 2010. Well, there may be another box she hadn't found yet which continued with January 2011. They were a bit worn but all neatly folded along their original creases. It was as though Margaret read one each night before she went to sleep and then put it back in the right order. The addresses written on the top left corner of the envelopes changed several times but were now, very probably, out of date - she would check. She would need to try the latest one in case it was not the one the police had used. Anna knelt on the floor and peered under the bed. Nothing.

In the box there was a photocard with a digital image of a baby wrapped in a fleecy blue shawl which seemed to have been used to mark the place that she'd got to. The couple of notes Anna read seemed normal and affectionate – requests for items Briony couldn't get in America and questions about activities in Margaret's life. From the notes she discovered that Briony had had a baby, a boy called Donny, who was born in December, 2008. Clearly, the baby on the photocard. Anna looked around the small bedroom. The photos on the walls were of a baby and then a toddler who couldn't be more than two, if that. But he must be five now?

Another odd thing was that although Margaret had lived alone she had the smaller bedroom of the two. The bigger bedroom was furnished smartly and quite expensively. It had cream-coloured, deep-pile carpet, not the usual cheaper bedroom quality, and the latest style in mahogany bed frame for the double. A deep pink satin quilt lay folded back on the white duvet. There was a child's bed too with a Disney character duvet cover heaped with stuffed animals, and it all looked brand new. There were even, Anna noticed with a start, fresh flowers in a pretty vase on a white wicker stand by the double bed. It was as though Margaret had been expecting her family any minute. The candy pink carnations were still alive which felt spooky since the hand that had placed them there was now dead.

Beside each bed was a book: a pristine Lee Childs paperback thriller for Briony and a CBeebies annual for her son. Had she recently re-done it, Anna wondered, expecting them to visit very soon? For all she knew, they'd been coming often. All very normal.

Except for the fact that the police had not been able to trace Briony. Perhaps she had moved back to Britain? The address and phone number must be here. The snooty Mr Proudie was probably correct; this could all be cleared up by finding a simple piece of information which must be in the house somewhere.

She needed to talk to some people. Glancing out of the back bedroom window, Anna saw an opportunity to do just that. She ran down the stairs and out into the neatly arranged garden with its pruned shrubs and mulched roses ready for the winter. All very orderly and well-maintained. Margaret Clark was clearly no slouch.

There was a gap in the fence with a wrought iron gate which

she called through feeling slightly ridiculous. The white-haired woman next door stopped pegging out sheets and joined her at the gate unlatching it from her side. Anna showed her business card.

'Joan.' The woman put out her hand to shake Anna's in a firm clasp. Anna explained the situation and the difficulty over finding Briony. She asked when the neighbour had last seen her.

Joan looked down at her fingers and counted on them. 'It must have been Christmas 2010. Yes. Donny was just a toddler then.'

'So Mrs Clark didn't see much of them as they were living in America?'

'Oh no, she saw them quite often. They just didn't come here.' Joan pulled a tissue from her trouser pocket and blew her nose. 'She was a lovely woman, you know, Margaret. I still can't get over her not being around.'

'I'm sorry.' Anna paused for a moment. 'I wonder why Briony didn't come home more often?'

'Well, there wasn't a lot of money about by then so it would make sense for Margaret to go there because that's only one fare isn't it? And then it's a nightmare travelling long distances with a baby or a toddler.' Not moved back then. Anna hesitated to press further but risked wondering aloud why the money had got tight. She thought about the expensively furnished bedroom.

'Maggie took voluntary redundancy. The firm was having to make cutbacks and they asked some people if they'd be willing to go. She had a bit of a widow's pension and she'd got fed up with the commute. It was quite a way – over the other side of Birmingham, in the Black Country.' Anna wrote down the name from her - Aluminium Fixings. She would go over there and talk to someone in HR – see if there were any colleagues still around who could shed some light.

'So how was Mrs Clark discovered? Did the milk get left on the step or something?'

'Oh no!' Joan was shocked and Anna rebuked herself for sounding so cold. 'I found her. Well, it was the dog that came and got me.'

'Sorry?'

'Yes, he never was a barker but that morning he was up at this gate rattling it and shouting his head off. I came rushing out because I thought he'd finally got his paws on my cat but it was me he wanted. As soon as I came out he barked just once and then ran to the back door and barked and barked looking back at me and then into the kitchen, you know how they do when they want to tell you something. Luckily the back door was open but in any case I've got a key. We kept each other's keys for emergencies. It's like that round here – we're quite neighbourly but not,' she gave Anna a hard look, 'interfering.' Anna guessed she was a good fifteen years older than Margaret Clark with her hair in a short, no-nonsense style and a figure that was still trim. Her manner could be described as, what? Sprightly. What a lovely word. She wondered if Ellis would like it.

'So you found her? I'm sorry to ask this, but was she still alive?'

'Why do you want to know?' Why *do* I want to know? Anna thought in confusion. It's the sort of question they ask on TV dramas but of course she didn't need to know – bloody stupid.

'I just wondered if she had said anything before she died, before the police came.' That seemed to save the situation and Anna relaxed. Joan looked sad and thoughtful.

'No, she was dead when I found her. I've seen dead people before. I used to volunteer at a cottage hospital. She was in a heap on the floor with a wooden spoon in her hand. Just like Maggie, making a cake for someone or to raise money for something. All I did was turn the oven off and call the police and the doctor but it was just a formality. She was gone. Only just, though. I think the dog must have dashed out when she fell to the floor – she was still warm when I touched her. We have the same doctor, that's how I knew who to call.' Then her face gave way and Anna put her arm round her.

'I'm so sorry.' Anna waited until she had regained control before asking, 'What happened to the dog?'

'He's gone to Safe 'n' Sound. I phoned them and they came for him – the least they could do really after all the volunteering she's done for them and not only at the sanctuary, she worked in the charity shop as well. Always on the go, always doing things for others. She was mad about animals.' Anna made another note but didn't want to just pump for information and leave.

'So the dog would have been bought for Briony when she was a child?' she smiled.

'Oh, no. Jim, her husband, was a miserable bloke and wouldn't let her have animals. She made up for it, though, after he died. She had cat lodgers when people went on holiday or weren't well, you know. Only one at a time and I'm sure she didn't charge for it but most people would much rather their pet goes to a home and not a cage in a kennels, wouldn't they? Mostly they were animals from the people she worked with. She got a bit of a reputation I expect. Of course she had to stop the cats when the dog moved in.'

'He was a stray?'

'Oh that old dog. I think even my cat misses him!' Joan lightened up which was nice to see. It made her face look kind and much younger. 'The dog came from Mrs Kelly four doors up. She had to go into a home and Maggie said she'd have him for a bit.

Well, of course, Mrs Kelly never came out so the dog stayed. They were very fond of each other. Maggie had a jokey way of treating him like a person who didn't much approve of her. You know, "Can't stop, he's waiting for his tea – he knows I'm chatting to you and he'll give me a dirty look when I get in." '

Anna was struck by a thought. 'I'm sorry to seem as though I'm prying, Joan, but I have to. Did Margaret have any other relatives that you know of? It's hard to tell from an address book.'

'She did have a sister but I know she was a widow and I'm pretty sure they didn't have kids. I don't know her last name.'

'Do you know where she lives?'

'Lived. She died, oh, must be a couple of years ago. It really upset Maggie for ages which surprised me because I didn't think they were close. There's no other family I know of. People lose touch these days. No, I think Briony and Donny were all the family Maggie had. She never stopped talking about them.'

'Really?' Anna made a tell-me-more face.

'Yes. That was why she went so often. After she'd stopped work, of course - natural when Donny was small and I expect Briony needed the support.'

Anna thought about the shoe box. So, no need for lots of letters and cards in 2011 and 2012 if Mrs Clark was visiting them frequently. They probably just phoned each other. 'Donny must be about five now. Do you know if they're still in Chicago?'

'Oh yes, I think so. Maggie was always telling me the things he gets up to and all that. Apparently he's doing really well now he's started nursery, well, kindergarten they call it over there, don't they? But then Briony was a bright girl.'

'And the father?'

Joan wrinkled her nose. 'Karl. Maggie wasn't too keen. A bit selfish I think although she didn't say much. They met at university here but he was American. Took her back with him before she graduated. She would have liked it if they had got married first, you know, that he'd shown some commitment before the baby was born but for all I know Briony didn't want to marry him. They don't nowadays, do they? Bri told her mum about being pregnant when she came back for her dad's funeral. That must have been summer 2008. Yes, that's right.' She thought for a moment. 'He didn't come with her, the father, but as I say fares aren't cheap and being young they were struggling a bit for money I imagine.' She stopped herself and stood up straight, turning to look at the half-full laundry basket.

'Anyway, Ms ?'

'Mrs Ames. Anna.'

'Yes, well I have to get on now. You know where I am if you need me.'

'Thank you so much, you've been very helpful.'

'No date yet for the funeral I suppose?'

'No. It's going to be at the crematorium. I'll let you know as soon as I know.'

'You might want to tell them at Safe 'n' Sound too. They were very fond of her and shocked when I told them.' She latched the gate and went back to pegging out the washing and Anna went inside to think. For all the information, she was still no nearer to an address or a phone number.

2

Anna got to work on the address book. There weren't many personal numbers that hadn't been crossed off. Some people were very sad and wanted to be told about the service but said they hadn't seen her for years. No extant friends yet. (Mental note to teach Ellis that word.) Perhaps they're all to do with the sanctuary and the shop. That would make sense since she was so active there and it is true that when people leave a job they mean to keep up but don't.

There was an address and a phone number for Briony in Chicago. Impossible to tell when it had been written down. It was different from any of those on the envelopes. Anna tried it and got a furious brush-off from a man who said he'd never heard of her and suggested an obscene place where Anna might look next. Then she realised it was only 5.00 in the morning in Illinois.

She finished her inspection of the upstairs part of the house and noted that the large bathroom was also recently renovated. Redundancy money? She decided to look more closely into drawers and along shelves to see if any kind of financial records could be found. Patterns of spending could be a good indicator of events and there may even be a standing order set up for Briony which might yield a US bank account and address. She thought again about the documents the Coroner's Office took and wished she'd been more assertive about retaining them.

There was a box file on the top shelf of the alcove above the sofa. Anna climbed on to one arm and stretched. Why had she got the short gene? Must be from her mother. Harry, Faye and even Ellis these days towered above her. She stood on tiptoe and tried again, grabbing one. The sofa skittered away and tipped her on her back among the cushions. She giggled at herself in her smart suit and legs in the air but the box was, disappointingly, filled with recipes torn from magazines. When she had scrambled upright she saw a slim chrome oblong revealed by the angle of the sofa and pounced on it with joy. A laptop! And, she quickly discovered, it was not locked. Brilliant.

There was a whole folder in the Documents library which contained letters to Briony so, stupid me, Anna thought, of course there were no hand-written notes after 2010. They would have communicated by email like everyone else. Free and instantaneous. Probably Briony nagged her mum into getting a laptop when she was back at Christmas that year if Maggie hadn't bothered with one before. Anna started to read.

After some time, she raised her head and looked out of the window. What would she have done now if things were the same as a year ago? She would have phoned Harry. She wanted so much to talk to him but she couldn't, so she just had to pretend. Like an imaginary friend.

Darling Harry, her inner voice said, I just have to read you this email from Margaret to Briony. It was written in February, 2011, it's the first one in the folder. It's amazing how when you read someone's correspondence you feel as though you know them. Do you remember Uncle Bill used to send letters with multiple dependent clauses, semi-colons and perfectly indented paragraphs? I always used to expect him to end 'yours sincerely' instead of the rather nice 'fondly'. But then, I suppose that makes my point. He was like that in the flesh if that's not too indelicate a word for him.

Here goes -

Hi my darlings,

How are you both doing? Very cold I should think. I see that the weather over there is just freezing. I hope you're keeping warm and found the thermals I sent useful, especially Donny. He's probably having a great old time in the snow making snowmen and sliding about on the ice. I remember you doing that, Bri, and never wanting to come in even when your hands were blue with cold from the wet gloves. You had such rosy cheeks that Auntie Mand called you Apples, do you remember? And then the trick you played on me that went wrong! You'd heaped up snowballs on top of the back gate (I don't know how you did it thinking of it now) so that when I came out to call you I'd get an avalanche down my neck – you were a little monkey -but you forgot and came dashing in to go to the loo and got it all down your neck instead!

It was Colin on the 62 today when I went into town. It's so much better on the bus than in the car with all the parking expense and hassle. His little girl has just started school. I only had egg and mayo to give him because Bob made me give him the last of the ham and I haven't been to the shops to stock up. They do have such long shifts these drivers, all the way from Birmingham to Rednal and back again so they can do with a little snack.

I think Bob may have some arthritis although he doesn't complain – it's hard work getting him to take some exercise.

Well, I'm rabbiting on as usual. I'll let you go now, I just wanted to say hi and say how much I think of you all and wish you well. I'm wearing the sweater you gave me last Christmas and I've had lots of compliments. Thanks again. Drop me a line when you can, I know you're busy.

Your loving mum and gran XX

You see what I mean about her? Doesn't she sound lovely? Who would think of taking sandwiches for bus drivers? I know what you're thinking but there is no email address for Briony in the contacts list. There's no email history at all that relates to her either in the Inbox or in the Sent folder. Bob must be the dog, do you think? She doesn't sound the kind for a bit on the side.

In fact, all the addresses in the email contacts were impersonal organisations, charities and such. It was clear that Margaret had used the computer in only the most limited way. The history was no good either because that was just banking and general interest websites. So, she resolved, I'll go in and talk to Steve at work and see if he can push some magic buttons and retrieve something useful. There were also the people at Safe 'n' Sound to see and ex-colleagues at Aluminium Fixings.

When Anna got home Ellis and his dad were in the living room watching a documentary on the Hadron Collider. They were sitting next to each other on the huge old sofa and Ellis had his father's right foot balanced on a towel on his knee and was cutting his toenails. The other foot was in a bowl of soapy water. Anna stood at the door and watched, smiling. When Ellis wanted to look at the screen he conscientiously stopped clipping and raised the scissors clear of the foot. His father was semi-recumbent so that his feet were in the right position and his head was propped on one hand.

'How are you feeling?'

'OK. But Pops said I might as well have the day.'

'So what do you think? Something you ate?'

'Probably.' Ellis clipped a bit more off the awkward little toe nail. 'You cooked last night.'

'Nice. Tea?'

When she got back with three steaming mugs she gave them theirs and settled in the corner armchair sipping slowly. The coffee table was littered with remotes and sections from Sunday's newspaper and, she noted, wincing, an elderly apple core or two. She thought about Margaret Clark's tidy, sad room.

'They're looking for the Bosun-Higgs particle. It's infinitesimally microscopic.'

'Right.' She remembered this from her own childhood, this love of unusual and complicated words. Recently he had become very taken with the word 'quotidian' and, to tell the truth, had quite a few occasions to use it.

'The God particle – that's what it is. It's the ghost in the machine.' She looked at her husband fondly and crinkled her eyes at him over her tea mug. How similar they were, her husband and her son. It always shocked her mildly to see those two pairs of gold-green eyes, so rare and beautiful, fringed with dark lashes. A touch of the Ghengis Khans she used to tease – her own personal Golden Horde invasion. But while Ellis's face was as sharp as a fox under his clump of brown hair, her husband's was softening and fading. That's what happens with age, she thought, we fade like watercolours in the sun and our faces get rumpled and untidy.

She got up and picked up the mugs. 'Is Pops in?'

'He's in the shed.' She went into the hall. 'Mum?' She stopped and dropped her head to show she was listening. 'He's got Ashok with him.'

The kitchen was an old-fashioned rectangular one with plenty of room for the draw-leaf oak table they had found underneath a heap of bric-a-brac in a run-down shop the year they had married and bought the house. They had carried it home together through the streets and then she had stripped and sealed it. Pine was so popular then that the more substantial oak furniture which they loved was much cheaper. None of the chairs matched but with the leaves out there was room for all of them with spare space for a couple more. They had meant to use one end of the living room as a dining area but once the children arrived that idea was quickly abandoned and the space filled with a family piano and a nest of toys and generations of storage solutions which always turned out to be hopelessly inadequate. It was easier and much more pleasant to eat in the kitchen and, of course, nowadays they never had formal dinner parties. Anna couldn't remember the last one.

On the kitchen table, carefully placed on one corner, was a pile of post. Nothing of interest. The best you could hope for these days was that there was nothing alarming. Her assessment from the latest unit for the Diploma in Genealogy was there but she hadn't felt very good about the rushed assignment she'd turned in and decided that it could wait till she felt more robust. The rest of the kitchen was cheerily cluttered and she knew that this neat pile would be Ellis's work when he came home from school. The teenagers in the sitcoms on TV were all venal and selfish and exploited their parents in every way. Where had they gone awry with Ellis that he was such a great kid? But then, there was always Faye to make up for him. Anna smiled. There was no smell of anything cooking so she made her way down the narrow passageway out of the kitchen past the laundry room and outside up the short path to the shed.

'As the sour ashes of the blackening soul...' Ashok was declaiming. She waited to tap on the door until he had finished. The shed had been George's gift to himself when he decided to come to live with them a year ago. Saying he needed his own personal space, he had wanted to build it himself but gave in quite readily when she insisted on having professionals. In fact, it was a very nice shed and as large as some rooms in the house. He had moved his favourite bits and pieces in from his old terrace and stacked the shelves with his books and papers, tapes, CDs and the memorabilia of a lifetime. He had had a power line put in so that he could use his super deluxe photocopier and computer and printer to keep churning out his poetry magazines. Then he had let Faye loose with a paintbrush and the two of them had covered every bit of bare wall or ceiling with whatever took their fancy. Faye had been into Manga and graffiti but George had been inspired by the op–art he had liked as a young man so he had wild swirls of psychedelic colours making the walls look as though they were buckled and bent. Pushed up behind the desk was Harry's racing bike with an old rug over it. They had found out the hard way it was better not to let him see it.

Voices had now taken a normal chatty tone and Anna knocked at the door. 'Hi Dad, Ashok, everything ok?'

'Oh, Anna, you should hear this – do it again, Ashok, it's brilliant!' Hastily, Anna intervened.

'Actually, Dad, I was just wondering about dinner?' The animated features messily wrapped in a tangle of white hair and beard stilled.

'Is it me?'

'Tuesday. Yup.'

'I'll get fish and chips. I'll go now – sorry, angel.'

'That's fine. Get a couple of large peas and some curry sauce if you would. Ellis and Faye will be thrilled. But can you leave it for half an hour, I really want to have a shower and get changed. They're all right watching a documentary and I have no idea where Faye is anyway.'

She let the hot water gently pound her skin, turning and twisting voluptuously as it drummed on her breasts and back. Why would Margaret have no email address for her daughter? Who doesn't have an email address these days? Or if she did, why wouldn't she have it in her laptop address book? If, for some bizarre reason, it was confidential she could have put a lock on access to the computer. There was another possibility. Maybe the letters were not draft emails but draft letters. Maybe Margaret had horrible handwriting or some physical problem with her writing hand and had to type and then print them out. Or maybe she changed things a lot and needed to set up the letter the way she wanted it first and then write it out by hand. Anna certainly found handwriting anything extempore was difficult to do without errors. But Margaret's letters were so natural and informal that seemed unlikely.

And why did the notes and cards from Briony in the box by Margaret's bed only go up to December 2010? Almost three years old but still kept by her bed. Of course, on some the dates were illegible so it's possible that these were later, but then the others were all in careful date order. Even if they emailed each other, surely Briony sent birthday cards and so on? The dates on the letters to Briony had started on January 1, 2011. So 2011 up to Margaret's death seemed to be undocumented as far as getting mail back from Briony. She had managed to write regularly to her mum when Donny was a new baby which would be the time you would expect communication to be chaotic. Ok, they probably phoned each other between visits but it was odd to have nothing in writing of any kind. Margaret had kept every other bit of mail from her, it seemed.
Although, how could Anna know that? Of course it was more than likely that she hadn't found everything.

And then there was the main bedroom, so stylishly and comfortably set up with just the right decor for a modern young mum and a five-year old. But, possibly, never used.

What had seemed like such an easy case had turned out to be a bit more complicated. Unless. Anna turned off the shower abruptly and stood dripping and staring. Was Briony dead? The spooky shrine-like room and the unsent letters and the defunct American address and phone number could all be because her daughter had ceased to exist and Margaret couldn't bear it. Her letters and the room were all a fantasy to comfort a mother who had lost her only child. In a rush Anna remembered Joan's comment about how upset Maggie had been by her sister's death and yet they had not been close. Perhaps it was Briony's death she was upset about. It could have been about the same time. But why not tell Joan whom she seemed to be on friendly terms with?

And what about the grandson? Didn't Joan tell her she had seen Briony and the boy in late 2010 and after that Margaret often flew off to America to visit her? That's carrying fantasy a bit too far, surely. No, that couldn't be it. Anna shivered and stepped, dripping, from the tub. As she towelled herself vigorously she made plans. She needed to go back to the house and read the rest of the letters on the computer and the notes in the box. She hadn't liked to remove anything from the house. She made a mental note to check the legality of that sort of thing. And then there were cupboards and drawers to examine thoroughly. The cremation was to be on Friday next. Harts had heard from the Coroner's. In the meantime she had some reading and more phoning to do and places to visit. She must start making notes systematically, she couldn't afford to mess up the first real job Ted had given her.

Downstairs there was the clattering of plates and Ellis shouting over George's track from Queen. 'No, Pops, I literally, literally, *emphatically* cannot bear it! I'm ill! It's child abuse!' and George turning up the volume on *Fat-Bottomed Girls*. Anna went over and switched off the CD player. They settled down to the meal in silence except for small grunts and the scraping of metal on plate. Faye's seat was empty.

'I'm going to audition for the panto tomorrow, it's Aladdin,' Ellis said spitting flakes of fish.

'Good for you. What part?' Ellis was clearly over whatever it had been.

'Not how it works. You go and sing and read stuff and they decide what part you'll get if you get anything. I should be in though – most boys don't want to do it.' Anna shook out a thought that possibly Ellis was gay. How awful to immediately assume that he was gay just because he wanted to be in a panto at the age of ten.

Not that she would mind, naturally, but it would be *of interest*. That was all. She speared a fat chip and promised herself that she would go for a run the minute she had finished working on her assignment.

'Aladdin! Tales from the Arabian Nights,' cried George. 'The undying power of story incessantly reincarnating down the ages. I read a fascinating thing yesterday about Alexander the Great. Did you know that there are still' – and he banged the table with the blunt end of his fork – 'still villages hidden in the mountains of Kurdistan and Afghanistan where the storytellers talk about Alexander? As though his conquest of the Middle East and the Gordian Knot and all that just happened instead of over two millennia ago! And everyone under the tree or in the marketplace is just as wrapt as when we watch the soaps on telly. Our brains are hard-wired to engage with narrative. Why else would we *pay* to go and see films? We *need* to be told stories. It makes me wild when people say "it's only a story". ONLY A STORY! That's everything, everything. Keats said,' and now the fork was waving in the air, ' "I believe in nothing but the truth of the imagination and the holiness of the heart's affections!"'

Ellis was frowning. 'Why are the people in the villages wrapped up? I thought those countries were hot.' He spoke thickly through a small logpile of chips.

George looked confused and then said, 'No, they can get very cold but - not wrapped up, Ell, wrapt – WRAPT – enraptured, bewitched, transported.' Anna could see Ellis making a mental note.

Perhaps the boy would be a writer, not gay then but sensitive, and immediately chastised herself again.

'Where's mine?' Faye burst through the door as though she hadn't bothered to turn the handle.

'Well, if you'd said when-'

'In the oven.'

'Hey bro what do you think?' Faye wagged her head in front of Ellis on her way to the cooker. She managed to sling her bags and coat on the corner rocker in a seamless movement as she made her way across the kitchen.

'What? Can I have some of your chips?'

'How cool is this?' Faye was wearing earmuffs made to look like reptile hands and on the top of the head band was a stuffed meerkat head with its mouth open.

'Very cool,' said Anna's father, predictably.

'Lame,' said Ellis but Anna could see his eyes narrowing appreciatively. It was quite a stunning sight. 'Let me try it.' Ellis grabbed the creature and stuck it on his head. 'I can't hear anything.'

Faye snatched it back. 'That's the point, it's to go over your headset so you don't get other sounds – nuhh, simple.' She studied Ellis sensing a business opportunity. 'You don't get *ambient* sound. It means sound from the environment.'

'I knew what it meant,' said Ellis, clearly filing that one away in his mental dictionary. 'How much?'

'I can do you one for a tenner if you want, it's my business initiative,' said Faye sitting down with her fish and chips still in the paper. 'I've just got to think of a name for it – my product.' She enunciated the word with conscious irony.

George tried it on. 'I've gone deaf. Wait a minute.' He pushed the earpieces back to behind his ears so that the stuffed claws pushed the flaps of his ears forward. They all laughed. 'Hey, that's great, I can hear much better.'

'You look like a koala bear, Pops!'

'Being mugged by a meerkat!'

Faye's mouth dropped open. 'That's it! The Meerkat Mugger Head Hugger!'

'Junior Apprentice, watch out,' said George.

Faye looked at him with affectionate contempt and rammed another fistful of chips into her face. Anna put her chin on her hand and regarded her daughter. If someone, someone up there, the elves that mixed up genes, had chosen to make a being who was the opposite of Anna and Harry then Faye was it. To these conscientious, gratification- deferring, ideologically p.c. parents was born a hedonist of the first order. Faye let out a satisfied burp. In a way, Faye had been an easy girl to raise. She was rarely out of sorts and only became unpleasant if she was thwarted. Now she was older she was perfectly able to manipulate her family and teachers most of the time by using her impressive social skills so that she rarely was thwarted. Ergo – peace. A kind of Pax Fayana. So far, anyway. As long as she got what she wanted all was sunny. What a lovely-looking girl, though. Anna stopped worrying for a moment and just enjoyed the luxurious brown hair, clear creamy skin and dark, sparkling eyes of her daughter. She could have stepped out of a painting by Renoir although mercifully more warmly dressed. Anna tried not to look at the well-defined shapeliness of her body. They'd got her as far as seventeen without drug addiction, pregnancy, STD, obesity or anorexia. Just hold your nerve, Anna told herself.

'So is this for Business Studies?' Faye nodded, crunching her fish batter. 'How's it all going?'

'Mm.' Faye leaped up, fumbled at the pouch in her top and ran out with her hand to her ear. Ellis grabbed his football and made for the door. 'Mike's,' he said and left. Harry poured himself another glass of wine and went carefully towards the back door. Anna watched him go.

'How's it all going with *you*?' asked George, getting up and gathering the plates. 'First day at big school and so on.'

Anna sighed. 'I thought this case would be easy and I think my boss did, too. That's why he gave it to me since I'm sort of on probation.'

'They're lucky to have you – clever girl like you. Librarian, first-class degree, all that.' George turned on the hot tap and rinsed the plates using the tips of his fingers.

'Thanks Dad, but funnily enough I think it was the genealogy Certificate that did it. I suppose the library thing was good evidence of research skills and an orderly mind, believe it or not,' she grimaced at her father, ' but it was getting so interested in mum's family that led to getting the Certificate and that got me the job at Harts, I suspect. Now I just have to upgrade to the Diploma.'

'You certainly found out much more than I ever knew.' George looked uncomfortable. 'But then, I wasn't with her long.' He pulled down the dishwasher front and started to stack.

'You mean, she wasn't with us long,' Anna said, grabbing the wine bottle and emptying it into her own glass before she stood up. 'It happens, Dad, I've told you before not to feel bad. I hardly remember her, in fact, I don't think I do remember her at all. She just sort of wafts about in my mind from time to time.' Such an easy and tactful lie that it was hardly a lie at all, Anna thought.

'Like a will o' the wisp.'

'Quite so, oh Ancient of Days.' Anna put her arm through her father's and stood beside him for a moment. 'Ashok's written something new? Are you going to put it in one of the mags?'

'I'm thinking of a new magazine. It would be perfect for that.'

'Another one? Why?'

George tipped powder into the compartment, slammed the door and pressed the button. He loved the dishwasher. He turned towards her and propped himself against the wet edge of the unit scratching the hair under his chin. 'I feel as though I'm entering a new phase, Anna. I'm getting ready to launch my Ship of Death as Lawrence had it.' Anna looked at him sharply. 'No, nothing wrong, I'm not ill, but I am sixty-seven and I feel the very cells of my bones turning to look at ... well, I'm not sure. Something beyond, something elusive. I find these days that I like Ashok to talk faith as much as poetry. That's odd for an old Quaker isn't it? But nevertheless it is so. So I want a magazine that won't be about rants or relationships or gritty 'real life' as they call it at all. I want, I suppose, a magazine that collects together and shares poetry about the ghosts that we barely perceive but we know are there. The world beyond and yet entwined with this one. Spirits that weave their lives amongst us and maybe have things they want to teach us. Absent presences.' Father and daughter stood silently for a while.

'I'm going to sit in the garden with Harry,' said Anna. 'It's a beautiful evening and we may not get many more this year.'

Beyond the shed Harry was sitting forward on the mouldy green and grey wooden bench, his empty wine glass at an angle on the lawn. He was staring down the garden towards the big tree which still showed spots of deep red apples in the higher branches. Drifting silently across the grass in the slight breeze were a few gold leaves from next door's silver birch. Anna sat down beside him and tried not to think of the pruning, the grass cutting, the clump separating and the bulbs waiting, aching, in the hut to be planted. The bench squeaked. She leaned back and looked at the sky.

It was always a surprise when you looked up that this magnificent show, this extraordinary work of art, was yet again silently, unnoticed, doing its astonishing thing. A huge sweep of palest turquoise blue wash rose above the rooftops and then, towards the church, lozenge-like clouds glowed pink and gold with purple at their hearts. She tried to remember. Not lozenges, but bread rolls, that was it, the clouds must be alto cumulus stratiformus. She smiled with delight that she had dragged the name out from some small cave in her memory. Little victories. The setting sun had almost gone. There was only a sliver of fire to break the line of the church roof into a blur of brilliance. She raised her glass of red wine to it and sipped. How natural it would be to make a libation to the gods but out of what? Devotion, desire, desperation? What a pity we don't do that anymore. She could do with propitiating something and then expecting it all to be all right.

Harry turned to her, looking her full in the face and said, 'Is there enough money for the family now I'm not working and George only has his pension – are we ok?' She was amazed and delighted.

She turned her whole body to him and smiled with pleasure. It was all she could do not to reach out to him.

'It's fine. I'm getting a decent basic salary and there'll be finder fees soon. Please don't worry.' She waited, holding her breath.

'Only I was thinking that George could probably apply for a carer's allowance. It would help.'

'That's a good idea. I'll put it to him.' She knew they would not be eligible but that didn't matter. She was aware of her heart racing with excitement, her thoughts tumbling over each other. She couldn't just let this rare and lovely moment pass. 'Harry, we love you so much.' He was still looking at her and Anna felt herself burgeon with a joy she hadn't experienced for weeks. His hands with their long fingers and newly cut nails rested on his knees. Could she stroke one? 'So much,' she repeated. So much to say that she could say nothing more in this miraculous break in the clouds so she reached out and put her hand over his.

'When you see my wife,' he said, looking away and firmly removing his hand, 'tell her I can't find my grey socks.'

3

The offices of Hart & Associates were in a converted Victorian bond warehouse near to prestigious canal-side residential developments in the centre of Birmingham. It was known in the business as Triple H - Harts' Heir Hunters. Anna liked the open feel of it and the thick greenish glass plates that made up the stairs. It had been conceived by architects specialising in renovating old commercial buildings as a black-suited, latte and cappuccino sort of place which Triple H let down badly by its employees wearing scruffs and jeans most of the time. Most only dressed in suits to go out on field work. Anna walked up the stairs and through the cathedral-ceilinged lobby into the main office calling a general greeting to the few men and women behind their computer terminals.

It was Steve she wanted. He was in a side office perched in front of a bank of powerful IT equipment. He looked like a large bird of prey, she thought, not because of his features which were unremarkable but because of the combination of his thick crest of dark hair and the vigilant angle of his trim body as he scanned the screens. His eyes seemed to be hoovering information into his brain.

The whole office felt grateful to him that while they got to go out and be private detectives (or whatever fantasy motivated them) he usefully knew difficult technical things they didn't know and was paid to help them. Anna had had little contact with him, why would she given the short time she'd been there, but she had noticed he never condescended or criticised no matter how obvious or trivial the query. She hoped she wouldn't be proved wrong today.

'Hi, Steve. All right?'

He turned from the screen and politely took his hands from the keyboard. 'Yep. You? Help you with something?'

'I've come across something a bit strange and I just wanted to check out the IT angle. On the laptop of a woman whose heir I'm searching for are some emails, well, letters really, in a folder headed with her daughter's name.'

'Yes?'

'There's no email address for the daughter and no emails from her. If she had sent the letters as emails and typed in the address each time (though, why?) would there be any record of that on the computer? '

'Only if you took the hard drive out and analysed it. Very expensive. Last resort stuff. Have you checked the deleted items and the recycling box?'

'Yes, nothing. The letters are affectionate and ordinary and nice. It's not as though she was working as an enemy agent or pornographer or something. Unless they're in code, of course. Joke.'

Anna paused wondering how much of her dilemma to reveal. She didn't want to look completely useless. 'It's just that I can't find a functioning address of any kind for the daughter so far.   It's a bit of a mystery. She's living in the States so no point in looking in electoral rolls here.'

Steve was silent, thinking. 'It's possible that she printed them off and sent them in the ordinary mail. Maybe she preferred to do that and she may have memorised the address. Possibly her daughter doesn't have access to a computer, or at least to the internet. Any chance that she's working or living in some remote location?'

'I hadn't thought of that. I don't know.' This was very helpful. It was a relief to bounce ideas around with someone who understood the problem.

'People are using email less and less for socialising. It's possible that they're communicating on some social networking site. Have you checked if the client or the daughter has a Facebook account or is on Twitter? Does the laptop have Skype?'

'No, I did look for Skype. It definitely doesn't. But because she doesn't seem to use the laptop much I hadn't thought of Facebook.'

Steve swung back round to face the screens. She noticed with amusement that the shop label of his sweater was on the outside.

'Give me her name and I'll have a look. You have Googled her, I suppose?' Anna glanced sharply at his face. No, he wasn't being sarcastic, he was just asking.

'I did, but nothing. Well, unless she's a 70 year-old herbalist living in the Mohave desert or a self-professed genius rockstar by the professional name of Booty.' Steve grunted in amusement.

'Give me a moment.' Anna turned to leave the office and then flattened herself behind the filing cabinet. Steve looked round from the screen and raised his eyebrows at her.

'Ted!' she hissed, 'He's just gone past. I don't want to talk to him yet because I haven't really got anything and he'll only sigh heavily at me.' Steve smiled and went back to the keyboard. He tapped rapidly and then spoke over his shoulder.

'I'll phone you if I find anything. I'm going to try a few things, OK?'

'Eternal devotion.'

'A coffee will do next time you pass. Black.'

Hello Harry, yes, I'm going off my rocker. Thanks for speaking to me yesterday even though you didn't know who I was. Better than the alternative. I'm back at the house, darling. I can't go to Safe 'n' Sound until this afternoon because they've got a donkey coming in or something, anyway an all hands on deck exercise apparently. I haven't really described it to you, have I, the house? It's just an Edwardian terrace but quite nice. It's got quirky little touches here and there like Margaret's made a collage of Donny's baby photos and put them together in quite a humorous way on the kitchen wall. You know how people take hundreds when it's the first one. And then there's a sign up inside the mug cupboard so that when you open the door you see 'If you want to feel rich, value what you have.' Is that Billy Childish? My dad would know. There's a photo of the dog, too, with reindeer ears. I usually don't like that sort of cutesy thing but the dog looked so dignified and reproachful that you can almost hear them screaming with laughter.

Steve from work just phoned. Asked me if I had found her mobile and was it a smartphone? I wonder if it was in one of those boxes that up-himself Coroner's Officer took? If she used the landline for international calls (cheaper isn't it?) then there ought to be a record on the itemised bills if she kept them. That might be in the magic box too. So much for Mr 'You won't need these' thanks very much. It's made me think that perhaps I was right, maybe they just phoned each other and didn't bother with writing. But Margaret *did* bother. There are all those letters. I'm going to look at them now.

Anna pulled open the drawer in Margaret's bedside cabinet to see if there were any other letters but when she drew a blank sat down on the bed and lifted the laptop on to her knees. With the toe of her shoe she pulled on the cabinet door and it popped open. Inside was a printer and some cables. She scrolled to the last letter in the file.

Oh, darling, this breaks my heart. I have to share it with you. It's dated the day before she died at 14 minutes past 11. She must have written it before she went to bed.

Dear Briony,

I don't know what to say to you any more, my dear, darling girl. I'm just sitting here with Bob and a cup of hot chocolate and trying to think what to write.

It's been so long, Bri. I don't want to make you feel bad because I know it's my fault what happened but I am so sorry. Please can you give me another chance? I was so foolish to say anything to you and there isn't a moment that passes when I don't hate myself for upsetting you the way I did. I love you so much my darling and the thought that I may never see you again or see you smile at me over the kitchen table or hug you or share funny things that happen with Donny – I can't bear it. I just can't bear it, love. I feel as if my heart is breaking. You are the last thought in my mind at night and the first in the morning. I even dream of you and you are smiling and coming to me with your arms open like you used to do. If I stop doing things or talking to people then I think of you and I grieve all over again for my stupid, stupid words.

And that's where it ended. Oh, poor woman, how awful, Anna thought. Had they lost touch altogether or was it just that Briony wouldn't come over to England? Maybe that's why there's no address that she could find, maybe she moved and her mother didn't have one. But when did the rift happen? Joan said that Maggie went several times a year to see Briony so it must have happened during the last visit before she died. She would have to see if she could find out when the last flight to Chicago was. All the other letters had been about ordinary things, nothing agonising like this.

Maybe this, this guilt and grief, was what brought on the heart attack? Maybe the thyroid whacked in on overdrive because of the stress and then she just blew a gasket. Her heart broke. Anna couldn't resist speaking out loud.

Harry, she was such a lovely woman – always doing things for other people and animals and she hadn't had such a great marriage. She must have lived for contact with her daughter and grandson. She would never have thought they would go to live so far away and then that Briony would break contact. How easily things get broken, don't they? We know that. Just a few words or a lost address or a faulty gene or being in the wrong place at the wrong time like in a car accident or a bomb or a tsunami. Relationships and people can break up so easily and sometimes they can't be mended. I have missed you so much since you went away. I know, I really do, how Margaret must have felt.

I've got to stop now, sweetheart, because I'm crying into the keyboard and that can't be good. I'll be useless to Briony and you if I'm fried to a crisp. Although to be honest, Harry, between you and me I'm beginning to dislike her. It's so easy to take the hump and go silent when you've got a partner and a child and a whole new life but who did her mother have? I suppose she just wanted to make her suffer a bit. But we all say things we regret, don't we? Of course, she's much younger and probably can't imagine how her mother feels. Sounds like she was a bit spoiled and selfish I think. And, of course, she'll just feel like crap when she discovers her mother's gone and died while she was sticking her nose up in the air being offended.

Anna's phone jingled and she spoke briefly. The comfort of talking to Harry was so great that she had to finish the conversation, she couldn't just leave it.

Just had a phone call from Margaret's solicitor, Ms Khan. Can I go in, they've found something that I need to see. Intriguing. I told them ok but tomorrow because I'm off to Safe 'n' Sound in a bit. Wherever you are this minute, feel me kissing you.

I have to stop this, Anna told herself, this feels so good and it's so wrong.

Only two miles from Mill Lane Anna found herself among fields and farms. Safe 'n' Sound was off a B road and then down a farm track. It was a chill golden day and Anna took her time bumping slowly down the rutted track and taking in the heavily berried hawthorn and elder in the hedges. A hard winter coming or was that a myth? She had read somewhere that hawthorns are magic trees and that some of them house fairies. She should tell George with his new interest in the shadow world – these hawthorns would be prime real estate for any upwardly mobile spirit wanting a spot of R & R.

Was he ok? Was she expecting too much of him? A lot of people his age would be pleasing themselves after forty-five years of work and he'd only had one year of that before coming to live with them. George had needed to earn money in a hurry as a young man and the powerful print unions had made their members the high-earners of the working class so it was at a printing firm he got work before he was even twenty-one. University, for her clever dad, had not been an option. She still only had to sniff an old newspaper for an instant connection to her childhood. He would come home with the reek of it permeating his skin. He had worked his way up to floor foreman but had resisted any more offers of promotion knowing that the increased responsibility often meant irregular hours. He needed to be home at the end of his 7.00-3.00 shift. He needed to be home for his daughter skipping up the street from school oblivious to the sacrifices he had cheerfully made and ready to chatter and complain and demand a golden syrup sandwich like only he could make.

As she got out of the car a roar of barking from soprano to bass burst out. The dogs were clearly allowed to run free in a huge pen bounded by stakes and wire netting. The dafter ones were throwing themselves at the barrier. Beyond them and on the other side of a small paddock was another pen built around an old orchard.

Cats strolled about and lay in the branches taking no notice of the commotion. At the buildings end of the paddock was a brick stable with three stalls and out of one of the doors poked a shaggy brown head.

A grey-haired woman in mud-clumped boots came from an outbuilding at the sound of the dogs. She wore a green polo neck under a flannel plaid man's shirt crusted with tiny grey bobbles and missing buttons at most junctions. 'Mrs Ames?' Inside the extension it was cosy with paraffin fumes and a kettle steaming on a tin tray.

The woman introduced herself as Diane and sat Anna down with a cup of tea. 'We've been like a madhouse this morning. Sweetest little pony but thin as a rake and naturally a bit leery of us.' Not a donkey then. 'She'd been on this patch of mud for weeks and no-one seeing to her the walkers said so they contacted the RSPCA and here she is. We'll soon have her right.' Diane's face glowed with purpose. That's what people look like who do good, thought Anna. They know who they are and why they're here. Not like me, waking up in the morning and wondering what's going to knock me back today and how I'm going to cope when it does. 'I was very sorry to hear about Margaret Clark. It was a shock.'

'Yes, you don't expect a heart attack at fifty-three, do you?'

'She was a grand woman. She'd do anything round here and when she wasn't here she was helping us fund-raise at the shop.'

There was a pause while both women looked towards the door as it creaked open. A black dog waddled in, the grey muzzle and cream fur round his eyes confirming his great age. He made his way slowly over to Anna and sat down regarding her with focussed dignity.

'Hello. Who are you then?' said Anna reaching down to pull his ears. He allowed that but still looked at her seriously as though over his reading glasses. Diane laughed and rubbed her rough hands on her knees.

'Of course, you wouldn't know. That's Bob. Maggie's dog. Poor old boy, he doesn't like it here. It's a bit draughty for him because we're always in and out and of course he's really a family dog. But I'd rather he was here than,' Diane paused, 'you know.'

Anna drank her tea quickly sensing that Diane probably still had a great deal of work to do before the light went. 'Look, Diane, I won't waste your time. I'm really here to see if I can find anything out about Briony's whereabouts. Margaret's daughter. I know she's supposed to be in Chicago but I just can't find an address.'

'That's strange.' Diane leaned forward and rolled her shoulders. Anna noticed that her stripey grey hair grew in a whorl on top of her head like a rosette hamster. It would be hard doing all this physical work at her age, Anna thought. Shoulders aching, knees creaking. Bob might not be the only one with a touch of arthritis.

'Maggie was always going off to see her. It was too expensive for Briony to buy tickets the other way because when you can't carry a baby you have to pay full price for a seat on the plane, don't you? I don't suppose she would have let her mother pay for her, she sounds like an independent sort of girl. Maggie would have wanted to go to help her with the child – you know, give her a break. '

'You don't happen to know if Briony married the father of her child?'

'Not that Maggie mentioned. She didn't really care for him much, I don't think. But they were always Skyping each other, her and Briony. Maggie used to tell us all the little things that Donny got up to at pre-school because he'll be, ooh, getting on for five now. Briony would hold up the laptop and get Donny to show his gran the things he'd made. She was always talking about it. It's a wonderful thing, isn't it, Skype, and free.' Anna made a mental note to ask Steve, could Skype be easily uninstalled? She supposed it could.

'And then, of course, Briony was doing so well at uni, or college I should say. That's what they call it over there isn't it? She probably wanted to finish her degree.' Anna sat up.

'College? Briony is studying?'

'Oh yes. She's doing a zoology degree at one of the universities there. Like her mum, mad about animals. I can't remember which. She might have mentioned which one to Valerie in the shop. Doing very well, anyway. About to graduate I think. Valerie's really upset by what's happened, you know, she was very fond of Maggie. She was asking me yesterday if anyone had heard when the funeral would be.' Diane paused.

'Yes, that's something I wanted to tell you. It's Friday at the Crematorium at 11.00. Can you pass it on in case I don't get to see Valerie before then?' Anna mentally scrolled down her list of missing information. 'You don't happen to remember if Mrs Clark mentioned any other relatives?'

'No, she never did. Her husband's family sound like a miserable lot and didn't bother with her after he died and then, of course, her sister's dead now. I can't just remember when.' Diane broke off and looked intently at Anna. That made four eyes staring at her. 'I find it odd that Maggie didn't have an address for Briony in the house. Or an email address? Have you had a good look?' Anna counted to ten and smiled at Bob who winked at her sympathetically.

'Early days. I'm sure something will turn up.' She stood up and turned towards the door but as she did Bob wobbled to his feet without taking his eyes off her. Even mustering all his restraint and poise he could not stop himself from uttering a tiny yelp of longing.

'He's taken to you,' said Diane. 'You're not after a daft old dog are you?' Bob glanced at her with scorn.

'I'll have a think about it,' Anna laughed, ruffling the dog's back hair. 'Thanks for your help. I'll see you on Friday. Bye Bob.'

The dog sat down heavily with a grunt of disappointment and then collapsed further and put his nose between his paws gazing bleakly into space.

4

Anna found Steve gazing across the city out of the huge lobby window. His sweater now seemed to be on the right way out but his hair was as energetic as ever. When he saw her he turned and she followed him into his office. 'No luck with any of the social networking sites. But I have had a couple of ideas.' Not a man for small talk then. It was a relief.

'Before that, I have a question.' Anna sat on the spare swivel chair next to Steve's in front of his bank of screens and pulled off her coat and scarf. 'How easy is it to uninstall Skype?' She pushed her wind-blown hair off her face where it had stuck in black strands.

'Very. You think they communicated that way and then she nixed it?'

'Could be. But why?'

'In any case with Skype you need a password so you wouldn't have got far even if she had it set up. No, I've been thinking along different lines. Have you thought that Briony might have married and changed her name? Have you phoned everyone in Mrs Clark's address book yet?'

'Yes, I did think of that but so far no-one seems to know. There's no other US number in the book. Of course, for all I know Briony might have come back to England recently but surely her mother would list her under her first name, I mean, not as Mrs Somethingorother?' Steve regarded her steadily. 'OK, I'll slog on with the numbers that haven't answered yet.'

Steve went on, 'If she is still in Chicago she might have married. Especially since she had a son – could have married his father. These things sometimes happen.' Anna glanced at his face but he showed no flicker of emotion, certainly not sarcasm, unless it was very subtle. 'Do you want me to check the register or whatever they call it over there?'

'Yes, please. Can I hang about while you do?'

'Sure.' Steve tapped some keys and then sat back. 'It's Cook County Illinois, isn't it, where Chicago is? Here we are, Cook County Clerk's Office. Wait, they have a private partner called Vitachek which does the searches – it seems like there's a small charge if they give you information... just a minute.' Anna wriggled closer and peered at the screen. 'Marriage certificate, click, here we are. Oh drat.'

Anna smiled at the northern expletive. She realised that Steve did have a slight accent. She recognised it as pleasantly familiar. Staffordshire? Derbyshire? Just like Harry. 'What?'

'We have to have a date for the wedding or they won't tell us anything.' He scrolled around the page. 'Just a minute, it says here, "If you do not have the date you may wish to discuss this in person or by mail with the vital records office responsible."' Anna chewed her finger and thought.

'Try deaths.' Steve tapped away again.

'Same thing. You must have the date of the death. Oh, and with a death it says here that they won't give a death certificate unless you are a relative or can prove a financial interest.' Steve thought for a moment. 'You could write to them saying that you're a probate genealogist etc. but I've just got a feeling that if they know they have to look through five years of records they're not going to do it. Why should they for a resident alien – although if she married she would be a citizen wouldn't she? Even so, I can't see them doing it for you. You could go to Chicago yourself but, quite honestly, Anna, I don't think the size of Margaret's estate would warrant it. You said it was a small terrace house?'

'Yes, and I don't even know whether it's paid off. I really do need to talk to the solicitor. See what the state of Margaret's affairs is.' She straightened her back and got ready to thank him.

'While you're there check the itemised phone calls if there are any bills.'

'Yes, I did think of that.' Anna's phone rang and she fumbled in her bag and found it. It was George. 'When? Does he have his watch on? Stay there, Dad, I'm on my way.' She jumped up and pushed the phone into her bag. 'I'm sorry, Steve, I've got to go.'

'Problem?' Steve had turned from the screens and was giving her his full attention.

'Yes, another missing person, I'm afraid,' Anna struggled quickly into her coat.

'One of your kids?'

'My husband.' She saw Steve's confused look and took a swift decision to tell him the truth. 'He's got Early Onset Alzheimer's.'

'My God, I'm so sorry.' He lifted her bag and held it out for her. 'How long?'

'Just over a year now. He's at the stage where if my dad doesn't keep an eye on him he wanders off and then gets lost and frightened.' She was checking her bag – phone, keys, purse – Steve's eyes were searching her face.

'Look I don't want to hold you up by why did you ask about the watch? Whether he was wearing it?'

'It's a GPS device. We have a receiver thingy at home so if he goes AWOL we just press the button and a map comes up and shows us where he is.' She was ready to go. 'So, if he's got the watch on it's easy to find him. If he hasn't it's like a needle in a haystack. He could be anywhere.' She had sobbed on the last word.

Steve was ahead of her and opened the door.

'Good luck,' he called as she ran down the office and then, more urgently, 'Drive carefully.'

George's face was at the window as she drove up and from the worried look on it Anna knew that Harry was still missing. They spoke briefly and then Anna set off again on foot on a round she knew very well. First she would check the row of shops, especially the laundrette which Harry liked to sit in, and then on to the park where he had been found in the past picking up leaves and putting them in his pockets. Sometimes he would stand outside the gates of the primary school and watch the children, smiling gently. Anna had talked to the head-teacher and reassured her that Harry was completely harmless but Mrs Brick had said firmly that if he turned up she would phone Anna on her mobile to come and get him. Fair enough.

George would be off in his ancient Peugeot in a wider circle checking the temple where he often took Harry to have lunch with Ashok. The mosque, too far away for Harry to find, which was also on George's personal faith tourism circuit was very grand, newly built in marble and gold leaf and Harry was a bit over-awed by it, as was George to tell the truth. He enjoyed going when invited for a poetry reading or to take part in a multi-faith workshop but he didn't often feel like simply wandering in. When they went together he said Harry would sit on the floor (a position George found painful) and gently rock as the recitation of the Koran drifted over them and the men near them stood or knelt or sat in balletic unison. George revelled in the multiplicity of faiths and sects in Birmingham and had found that he was almost always kindly received as a fellow truth-seeker. He'd been interested in eastern mysticism since the old hippie days when he and Anna's mother had bumped their way across Europe and the Middle East in a dilapidated camper van and a cloud of fragrant smoke. He would also check the library and the large supermarket at the end of the High Street.

Anna couldn't find him in any of the usual haunts and phoned George who was equally stumped. She was passing the old church that lay behind the houses at the bottom of their garden when she heard the sound of organ music. The vicar was outside pinning notices on the board by the lych-gate. He wasn't wearing a coat and she could see his breath making little clouds as he panted, shivering.

'Sorry to bother you, but have you seen a man wandering about looking a bit lost?'

The vicar stopped what he was doing and blew on his hands.

'No, I haven't, but there's a chap I don't know sitting in the church listening to the music. He's well-dressed except for his shoes.'

'His shoes?'

'Very comfortable slippers. If I had the nerve I'd wear them all day myself.' He stood back for her to pass. 'Do you want to check?'

Anna walked past him into the church. Harry was sitting in the front pew, quite still, with his head cocked attentively to the music billowing around him. It was *Jesu, Joy of Man's Desiring*. The organist must be practising for a pre-Christmas concert. She stepped outside and phoned George, nodding and smiling towards the vicar. Then she went inside and lowered herself quietly into a seat at the back. The trills and runs of the melody and the rich, complex sounds of the organ were thrilling. The music warmed her like a double shot of whiskey.

She stared at the man she had loved for over half her life, revelling in the chance to look at him as much as she wanted until he might turn and see her. He hated being looked at now, hated being touched, especially it seemed lately, by her. They had slept separately since Anna had woken to find him tense with terror at the foot of their bed. 'If you don't leave now I'll call the police!' he had shouted. That was another phase starting but there had never been a repeat of any violence in speech or action. The weevil that was burrowing into his brain and eating its way through his personality must have taken a different turn. Things seemed to go along much the same for a while and then there was the sudden dropping of a new veil between them. A new chasm had been excavated in his head. He was slowly disappearing into some other world.

But sometimes there were moments of lucidity. Like the time she had given him Ellis' school report to read and he had said, 'Well done, son,' quite simply and naturally. Ellis was brilliant with him and seemed to know by instinct how to cope. When they were having dinner together one night Harry had said anxiously to Ellis, 'Your mother's late home,' when Anna was sitting there at the table but Ellis hadn't missed a beat and replied, 'She phoned, she'll be in soon,' and put another spoonful of treacle pudding in his mouth. Harry had visibly relaxed and then, of course, forgotten all about it.

She had seen Harry and half fallen in love with him before he had even known she existed. She had been walking back from a late lecture through a misty November evening towards her student hall and had heard the sound of a trumpet coming from an upstairs window in one of the old houses that got knocked down for a by-pass a few years later. Cobbled streets shone black and wet in the gaps between circles of yellow light. She stopped and looked up. He was silhouetted in a window with the trumpet raised in a sharp angle from his mouth but she could see even then the straight line of his shoulders and the slim angularity of his body. She remembered feeling something like recognition shudder through her. Then someone must have come into the room because he turned and she saw his face plainly.

She had searched for him for days at the Student Union and then, astonishingly, he was standing right in front of her in the lunch queue. She looked at his back and neck and head just as she was doing now in the church and, perhaps sensing the intensity of the gaze, he had turned and looked right into her with those amazing amber eyes. Lynne, her room-mate, had not been so struck. 'Do you mean that tall skinny one with all the hair? The one that's a bit gingery?' she had said peering at Harry from behind a column in the Union bar. Unbelievable that she couldn't see what a god he was, Anna had thought, amazed. She smiled now at the memory of her indignation. But what had begun with a visceral attraction deepened into love as she got to know him properly. Sitting talking late into the night in coffee bars or walking with their friends through the Yorkshire Dales or listening to him play the battered old grand piano in the studio, she found that here was a person she could respect and admire as well as make ecstatic love with. In just a few weeks they had forged a union that was rock solid. Now that sure-footed Harry was getting lost, slipping and sliding into a crevasse where she could not follow.

Anna got up and walked quietly down the aisle to the front pew. She smiled at her husband and asked if he was ready to go home. So far this had always worked. He would get up and follow her without any resistance. What would they do, she thought, if one day the word 'home' had lost its magic? Not, what would they do, what will they do.

As they were leaving the vicar was hurrying back in. 'You're most welcome any time,' he said, looking from one face to the other. 'Sometimes we need a bit of time-out, don't we?'

Harry said, 'The organ could do with tuning.'

Inside the house there was the unusual sound of George and Faye shouting at each other. Harry sighed and went into the front room where Ellis was playing on his XBox and Anna crept quietly up the stairs to listen.

'You're too young!' George was shouting. 'Think of your mother, she's got enough to deal with.'

'Like you didn't shag everything that moved when you were seventeen? Don't give me that.'

'Totally irrelevant, things were different then.'

'Like you were into drugs and I'm not– like you screwed up and left school and I haven't – like...'

'It's different for girls!'

'Oh that old thing! Why? Why is it different for girls? You are so out of the loop. I can look after myself, you know - if anyone is going to get messed over it won't be me, Pops! I won't let anybody jerk *me* around.' This must have hurt. Anna opened the door to Faye's bedroom.

'What's going on?'

'Oh great!' Faye's face was maroon with fury. She picked up her backpack and stuffed her sweatshirt into it. 'You can't stop me so don't try.'

'Stop you doing what?'

Faye made a twist with her mouth and collapsed like a marionette on the bed. 'Nothing, Mum. Honestly, it's just a party with a few mates. Pops is just being mean.' Her voice had lifted to a childish whine. 'Everyone's going – I'll have no friends if I don't. Please, Mum, don't make me look like a minger.' Anna looked at George who looked at Faye and then at the floor. He never broke a confidence.

'Anyone special going to be there?' Anna said in a soft tone.

Faye, assuming the battle was won, sat up straight, pushed her hair behind her ears and said in a much happier voice, 'There's this fantastic guy I met at the restaurant. He was on one of my tables with some others and when he ordered he just had this great voice, like Russian or something, really cool. I nearly dropped my pad. He's at Birmingham uni doing law. How great is that? He didn't treat me like a kid or anything, he just twinkled his eyes at me and told me about this party tonight. He said I can bring some mates and Trish and Tash are coming. There is no way I'm not going.'

Anna put her back to Faye's bedroom door and folded her arms. She summoned up a firm but fair tone. 'So where is it, and when are you planning to get back?'

'Oh, don't wait up, Mum,' Faye said airily, 'there's no need.' She went back to stuffing her bag. Anna felt a pain beginning to spread across the sockets of her eyes and up into her head. She gathered her resources.

'Faye, look at me, I need to know where it is and I mean an *address*, and I need you to phone me when you leave at *midnight* and you will book a taxi home *now* or you are not going. Have you got the taxi number in your phone?'

'You're the best, Mum!'

Anna and her father made their way heavily down the stairs. He said he hoped Anna knew what she was doing and Anna said that was extremely unlikely but the day had got the better of her and she was making directly, without passing go, for the bottle of wine. As she lifted a glass down from the cupboard her phone rang.

'What?' she hissed seeing a number she didn't know.

'Sorry,' said Steve, 'I just wanted to see if everything was all right.'

'Oh, no, I'm sorry. I thought you were a cold caller, you were just about to get an earful. It's really nice of you to phone and I can report that at this precise moment no crisis is active. One crisis has passed and another crisis (different person) is looming but as of this minute all is calm.' She pulled out a bottle from the fridge.

'Sounds like a good time for a glass of something.'

'My plan exactly. Thanks again, Steve. I'll see you tomorrow.' She clicked the phone off and stood deep in thought for a moment.

At the office Steve had a bit of a reputation. His nickname was Steely Steve because he was said never to show emotion – to have a personality like his computers, in fact. He was not disliked but neither was he one of the chatty gang who hung around at lunchtime together at the neighbourhood pub. Steve went out for a run every lunch-time which made sense considering how sedentary the rest of his day was, Anna thought, but it did mean that he spent most of his work time, at any rate, alone. She didn't know anything about his personal circumstances and there was something guarded about him that made any inquisitive remarks inappropriate. The researchers appreciated his skill and knowledge and certainly didn't want to get on the wrong side of him but noted his air of reserve and backed off. Now, here he was apparently being kind and thoughtful and she pondered it.

5

At Aluminium Fixings Anna was shown into a small room with a few chairs, a drinks machine, a coffee table and a large rubber plant in the corner. The HR manager introduced her to Margaret's closest colleague, Jacqui, announced the reason for Anna's visit and left. Jacqui was almost as short as Anna and neatly dressed in a well-cut midnight blue suit with minimal silver jewellery. Her eyes had stayed wide at the announcement and she kept one hand over her mouth. As soon as she could she crumpled on to a chair.

'I feel awful that I didn't keep in touch as much as I should after Maggie took redundancy,' she said, tears rising in her eyes. 'But my son was out in Afghanistan and he got wounded,' Anna put out her hand. 'He's ok now, thank God, but we sort of lost track of everything else.' Anna noted the simple style and good quality of Jacqui's outfit and the genuine emotion in her eyes. Yes, she could see that Maggie and this woman would get on well.

'Of course you did.' Anna waited. 'I wondered if you knew anything about Briony, Margaret's daughter?' she asked when Jacqui nodded at her to continue.

'Um.' Jacqui thought for a moment. 'Didn't she go to Chicago? I think she had a little boy, didn't she? I did phone Maggie a year or so ago to see how she was. Let me try to remember. She said that Briony was getting married to a very nice man and that everything was going really well. I think she was planning to go out there.' A new man? A different kind of complication.

'Can I just ask something else?' Jacqui nodded. 'Did Mrs Clark chat much by social networking when you were working together as friends, I mean, before your son's trouble?' The other woman looked blank. 'Or would she email you to make an arrangement or did she prefer to send texts?'

'When I knew her she didn't have a computer at home,' Jacqui said. 'You see we're looking at screens all day and quite honestly some of us don't want to be doing the same at home.' She grimaced at the thought of it. 'No, we usually texted each other.'

'On a smart-phone?'

'Oh no! We both have pay-as-you-go! Had, in her case, I suppose, poor Maggie. My husband's got an iphone, and of course my son has, what is it? 5G. No, she and I just used our landlines if we wanted to have a good long chat. Much cheaper than paying for a contract and the sound quality's better, isn't it? We weren't very high tech.' Her eyes suddenly brimmed over with tears. 'Well, we won't be chatting any more, will we?' And now her head dropped and she was weeping. Anna sat quietly by her until she was calm thinking about what she had heard. Another man to whom Briony may well now be married? But no name. And no hint from Maggie in her letters to her daughter of a wedding. It just got more confusing.

Anna drove home as nonplussed as she had been when she arrived. So there should be a phone, a mobile, but it wouldn't help. On the other hand there would be itemised phone calls to the US with dates if Margaret had kept the bills. Thinking of the neatly filed shoebox, Anna was hopeful.

The office of Khan and Partners was on the Bristol Road less than half a mile from Mrs Clark's house. It had clearly been retail premises but was now sporting a smartly etched plate glass window and a very young receptionist who was looking in bafflement at a computer screen when Anna went in. A moment later the inner door opened and she was ushered into a windowless but chic little office. She noted the grey cord carpet and chocolate brown leather swivel chairs, the oversize splashy canvas block mount on the plum-coloured wall and also how young Ms Khan herself was. Still on her training contract?

'Mrs Ames? Please sit down. Thank you for coming in and I hope you won't mind if I ask to see your ID. What I am about to tell you is, of course, confidential and I need to be sure you really are the probate researcher from Hart and Associates.' Anna produced her photo business card feeling intrigued. Ms Khan glanced at it and faced her squarely. 'I'll come straight to the point. I wonder if you have any idea of the value of Mrs Clark's estate?'

'Not really. I don't know if the house is paid for and what outstanding bills there may be.'

Ms Khan leaned forward over the neat folders on her desk. Her darkly outlined eyes held Anna's in a way that commanded attention. 'We're a neighbourhood firm and I know the properties on Mill Lane. They are not high value residencies. We've met Mrs Clark several times - on the death of her husband when we handled his affairs and then in – ' she consulted a file, 'March, 2010, when she paid off the small amount of mortgage remaining and deposited the deeds of the house with us.' That would be the redundancy money from Aluminium Fixings, thought Anna. 'So when the Coroner's Officer left her financial statements with us and we looked through them we were a little surprised.' Ms Khan gave herself a moment to pull out a short list of figures from the top folder.

'Oh?' Anna thought about the re-decorations to the bedroom and bathroom at Mill Lane and her heart sank. Had Margaret overstretched her budget with home improvements and flights to the US? Was there no money left, or worse, was she in debt when she died?

'In her current account there is about £650 and in her savings account approximately £7000. She also has £15,000 in ISA funds.' Wow - lucky her - wish I could say the same. Or, possibly, not so lucky. Anna sighed and sat back in her chair. Ms Khan gave her a tense look. 'She also had in various investments £582,000.'

Anna sat bolt upright.

'What? That's over half a million!'

'Well, assuming the house is at market value the entire estate is worth over £755,000. A considerable sum of money.' Anna realised her jaw was hanging and snapped her mouth closed. But? Her thoughts were racing around but none of them connected. Ms Khan was still staring at her. 'How much success have you had in tracing Mrs Clark's next of kin?'

'There's only the daughter and grandson who live in America.'

'And will she be coming back to settle her mother's affairs?'

Anna groaned inwardly. An estate worth as much as this was good news and bad news. The good news was that her share of the 15% fee would be higher but the bad news was that Ted would now be all over her to get results. 'I'm still tracking her down.' Anna hesitated. 'Can I ask you how she came to have so much money? It may be relevant to my search.'

'I think I can tell you.' Ms Khan put the list of figures carefully back into the top folder and took a document with a different letterhead from another. 'There was a letter from her sister's bank which was acting as her executor, the sister's that is, releasing the inheritance when probate was complete. Her widowed sister, a Mrs Amanda Lewis, who it seems was childless, left all her money to Mrs Clark. The sale of the house in a pleasant part of

London made up the bulk of the estate and then there were some investments.' Again, Ms Khan replaced the document correctly.

'Blimey.'

Ms Khan smiled for the first time revealing perfect teeth. 'Yes.'

Anna remembered what she wanted to ask. 'I really need to look through the bank statements and any other documents you have, Ms Khan. I'm hoping that something in her pattern of spending will help me, like payments to airlines or travel agencies and so forth. Also, do you have telephone bills which are itemised and other invoices?' Anna held her breath and kept her expression as calm and confident as she could.

'I think so.' The young woman frowned slightly as if unsure now of what was permissable and Anna warmed to her serious approach to her client even if she was dead. 'It's going to be quite time-consuming for you, though, and as you see we have limited premises.' Ms Khan considered and then picked up her mobile ignoring the office phone. 'Uncle, it's me. I have the HH, sorry, probate researcher here for Mrs Clark. She needs to go through the box of files and obviously it can't leave the office. Could she work upstairs in the lunch room? OK, thanks.' She smiled again at Anna.

'You can take the boxes upstairs and work on them but it will have to be in office hours, of course, and I don't need to tell you that you cannot take anything away.' No, thought Anna, you don't need to tell me that. Duh, as Faye would say.

'Oh, just one more thing. Did you notice a mobile in the box?'

'No. No, there definitely wasn't one but of course there is still another box at the Coroner's. Jewellery and any other valuables. It could be in there.' Anna thanked her, made arrangements to return to go through the files, and left.

Well, well, well, Harry, what a turn up for the books! Bang goes my idea (and Joan's) that Maggie travelled to America because Briony couldn't afford tickets to come here. No wonder she was so emotional about her sister's death but then you'd think that kind of money would cheer you up a bit. Not that my dad has anything to leave. Poor old George has spent his little all on his shed and good luck to him.

Darling, I've come back to Margaret's house because I'm beginning to realise something. Ted probably will let me go to Chicago now to look for her so I'm going to print off all her letters to her daughter and take them with me just in case she never got them. I've been thinking about that. I wonder if Briony's partner, Donny's father, was funny about Briony communicating with her mother so maybe they had some kind of secret system which couldn't be traced? And then she may have left Karl and married someone else according to Jacqui? Obviously I hope I can find her because we need the money but it's more than that. I feel I owe it to Margaret to find her, to find her daughter and to tell her how loved she was. Yes, I know. A bit close to home.

Anna climbed the staircase to the now familiar bedroom and pulled the printer out of its cupboard. It only took a moment to connect it to the laptop and slot in a small stack of paper. In here she could actually talk out loud to Harry without risking looking as though she was being cared for in the community. She would definitely stop doing it after this.

If I do trace her I'll have to think about whether to give her the last letter, though, the upsetting one I showed you. If she's in pieces over her mother and full of guilt and all that then I may not. It wouldn't be kind. But the other ones would be a lovely souvenir of her mum or am I being sentimental? I'll have one more look through that box of cards, too. I've pretty much done the address book for what it's worth, but there is one thing that is a bit mysterious.

There's a number with no name – just the initials D.C. It looks like a mobile but I can't get an answer or even a dial tone.

Anna sat on the bed and pulled the shoe-box to her, working systematically from the oldest to the most recent. It was good to hear the clunk and clack of the machine in this silent house.

OK, they're all printing off nicely - thank goodness there's enough ink, there must be about thirty or forty of them. I've had another search round on the computer and there's just nothing. I mean, it's as though she hardly used it. There are some airline and travel company websites and there's an ESTA application which you've got to have now to go the States, haven't you? (Mental note, get signed up for one myself.) Whoops, the printer's getting snarled up, just a minute.

Anna put the box to one side and jumped up to clear the jammed paper and re-start the machine.

Oh, Harry, I have to just read you this bit of a letter that fell on the floor. She's telling Briony about a bus journey from Birmingham, dated, er, February, 2012.

You know what I'm like, Bri, I couldn't resist the flowers at the stall near the train station. The one that's at the bottom of the ramp. They'd got everything reduced because it was the end of the day so I bought four bunches of the brightest colours I could find! There were those red gerbera and orange chrysanthemums and some yellow and white asters with lots of dark green with them. They were wrapped up in purple paper so you can imagine what a picture I made! So, I was sitting on the bus with my arms stretched round this lot and my head popping up over them with that mad pink felt hat you bought me and this woman got on and did a double take and said, "Those are nice." So I said what I always say, "We must have beauty." We must, mustn't we, Bri? You and I have always loved flowers, haven't we? There's nothing like them to lift your heart, especially now it's so dreary outside.

Anna lifted her head and smiled.

The more I know about her the more I like her. She doesn't sound like a woman of mystery does she, but she is. All that money but still driving an old Ford and living in a small terrace house.

Look at the time! Must dash off to the crem to do some more sleuthing because if I don't find something soon Ted will be unbearable. I'll have to tell him the value of the estate, I've got no option, but not this minute.

When the hearse bearing Mrs Clark's plain coffin drew up outside the crematorium there was no-one waiting to go in behind it. No previously undiscovered family suddenly appeared to see her off as seen in the movies. Inside the chapel there were about twenty people but Anna decided to stay outside and walk in with Margaret. No-one should have to go on their final journey alone. A cold drizzle had started and Anna pulled up the collar of her black wool coat and wished she had thought to bring an umbrella.

During the short service she glanced discreetly round and identified Diane from Safe 'n' Sound with three resolute looking women and Joan with a small crowd who must be neighbours. Jacqui raised a hand to her but was on her own. There was also a bunch of men sitting together near the back. Little was revealed in the words spoken by the minister and she barely paid attention, watching instead the coffin itself and wondering about Margaret and Briony and what twists and turns their lives had taken that a devoted mother and grandmother was here, about to be put to rest for all time, without her daughter or grandson even knowing about it. What had she said to Briony? It was impossible to imagine this woman being malicious, especially to her daughter. What hasty words might Anna say to Faye or Ellis at some point that would result in a complete estrangement? She couldn't bear to think about it. Hasty words were a bit of a speciality with her. She sighed.

Afterwards everyone milled round outside. There was, of course, no wake or refreshments of any kind but people were reluctant to dash off back to ordinary routines. It seemed disrespectful to the dead woman. Anna went over to the men and introduced herself, asking them what brought them to Margaret's funeral. It turned out they were all bus drivers who had grown to care a great deal for Maggie over the time that she had been cheerfully feeding them.

'Last Christmas' said one, 'we all clubbed together and bought her a massive box of chocolates but we didn't see her for days. Then Bill who drives her route saw her off along a side street and he drove the bus off the main road down there until he caught up with her and gave it to her! The passengers were a bit surprised but nobody minded when he said why he'd done it.' They all nodded and grinned.

'She was golden,' said another. 'Didn't she have family?'

'A daughter in America who doesn't know yet because I haven't managed to trace her.' They tutted and then stamped on their cigarettes and moved slowly away. Diane stomped over in sensible lace-ups and an all-weather parka.

'This is Valerie from the shop,' she said indicating a slim woman with an immaculate blow-dry and a tailored wool coat. 'You can ask her what she knows about Briony.' Having delivered her, Diane went back to the others and Anna wondered how well the two women got on despite their commitment to the same cause.

'I'm so sorry to have to ask questions at such a time,' said Anna noting that Valerie did not look like someone who would easily break down under stress.

'Well, I don't know what I can add. She was a lovely person. She must have worked in the shop for, oh, about a year after she took voluntary redundancy from work.' Valerie opened her bag and took out a small plastic pack of mints. She offered one to Anna who shook her head.

'She did that in 2010, quite early on I think. Could it have been then?' The rain was starting again and Valerie glanced up at the sky, perhaps wanting to leave.

'No, it was definitely in 2012 because we extended the shop to take in some furniture in 2012, April, I think, and that was when she got involved.' Still nothing for the missing year, 2011, Anna thought, the year where there was no useful documentation– at least, none so far.

'So what did she tell you about her daughter? Did she mention the college she was at?'

'College? No, I know nothing about that.' Valerie was clearly debating whether to talk more or dash for the car. She got a fold-up umbrella from her bag and snapped it open, holding it over both of them. 'I do know she had a new man in her life because Margaret said he was a lot better than the first – you know, Donny's father. It was very bad the way he whisked her off to America and then didn't even marry her when the baby came along. They met here at university, you know.'

'Yes.' So that was confirmation of Jacqui's information.

'He was on some kind of exchange scheme and before Margaret knew it he'd persuaded Briony to drop out of her course and go back there with him. Madness, of course, but her mother couldn't stop her. It really upset her, naturally.'

'So, this new man, Margaret liked him? Had she met him herself?'

'Oh yes, she was always going over there. He has a bit of money, too, apparently, and Margaret said he and Briony were going to set up a refuge for horses out in the country.' Valerie looked sharply at Anna. 'Why can't you find her? I would have thought it would be easy enough.' The direct question cut through Anna's attempts to fit together these different versions of Briony's life.

Diane had said that she was a student and there was no man on the scene. Of course, people don't always listen carefully when they're busy and sometimes they hear what they want to. She felt more inclined to trust this version, though, because there was something about Valerie that commanded respect and Jacqui had said much the same.

'Well, oddly enough, there is no address or phone number for Briony that is current that we can find. Did Margaret mention this man's name?'

'Bradley. But not his surname. Why would she tell me that, after all? I suppose she would have done when they got married which was on the cards for later next year.' But hadn't Jacqui said that Briony was getting married last year? Valerie was talking again.

'Such a shame that Margaret didn't live to see that and to see Briony well-settled and happy. I find it very strange that there's no way of tracing her – have you tried Googling?' Anna smiled and nodded politely.

She had got nothing from today except that she felt even more fond of Maggie and more exasperated that there now seemed to be conflicting accounts of what Briony was up to. Why would Maggie tell Diane and Valerie different things or were they all part of one story? Perhaps Briony could do both the horse refuge and the university course and get married. Why not? Perhaps Margaret had only told Diane and Valerie the details about her daughter's life that she thought would interest them. Or perhaps they had only heard the bits they were interested in. And Jacqui had been so distracted by her son's injuries that she may well have misremembered the date of a wedding.

6

Anna drove back to the house on Mill Lane. She climbed the stairs and opened the door to the second bedroom, Margaret's. She picked up the folder of letters which she had forgotten to take with her and was about to leave when she remembered the box of notes.

Sitting on the single bed with its pale blue duvet cover, she spread the notes and cards out in date order. There were at least a dozen baby photos which were clearly the special ones, not to be cut up to put in the collage. Anna looked at them closely, especially the ones with Briony in them. She had seen her face in many frames round the house but in these she thought there was something a little different. The teenage Briony had a plump face with very pale blue eyes, the same shade as the duvet cover, Anna noticed. She outlined her eyes rather harshly with mascara and in the framed photos had her hair falling in well-managed curls about her face. But in these snapshots of her and the baby her hair was straight and rather unattractively pulled back. Was she thinner? Anna remembered grimly how unappealing she herself had looked as a new mother. It was all she could do to get out of her pyjamas and dressing gown by midday.

There was one photo of Briony and Donny with a man, a dark and intense looking young man who was scowling at the camera. There was no name written on the back. Anna lifted her head and stared at the laptop. Why was there no photo folder on it? Surely Briony would have endlessly sent photo attachments?

She picked up an envelope that was much neater than the others as though Margaret had not wanted to look at it more than once. In fact, what was inside was difficult to get out as it only just fitted the envelope. It was another photograph, this time with a much older man and woman who were holding Donny. They had a slightly strange expression on their faces which could only be described as wary. Anna peered more closely. Who had taken the photo, Briony or her partner or someone else? Who were these people? She turned the card over. On the back was written, 'Mr and Mrs Bulowski.'

There was no date but Donny seemed to be about two years old. Anna sat up and straightened her back. Could they be neighbours or Karl's parents, perhaps? She examined his face and theirs carefully. There seemed to be little resemblance but that didn't mean anything. Look at Ellis and herself. No-one would look at his delicate pointy chin and red-brown hair and her oval face fringed with a black mane and guess they were related. Faye took after her father, too, more than her mother. Anna's features were almost obscured these days under her heavy fringe anyway. It was too much trouble to get something done about it.

She pulled her phone out of her coat pocket and called Steve.

He had told her that he was going to look through the Chicago Tribune newspaper archives to see if there were any stories about Briony Clark. A long shot but worth trying since all other avenues seemed dead-ends. 'Nothing in the Tribune,' he said. 'I can try the other papers when I've got a minute.'

'I may have something,' said Anna realising how thin this one word would sound. 'On the back of a photograph there's a name – Bulowski. It might just be possible that this was Donny's father's name. Could you try it?'

'Yep. Will do. Are you coming into the office today?' Anna groaned.

'I have to. It turns out Mrs Clark's estate is worth over half a million pounds. I have to tell Ted.'

'No kidding.' Steve whistled softly. 'You're really going to get some heat now, you know.' Anna stuck her tongue out at the phone.

She tidied away the notes and cards and put the box back by the bed. Her phone rang. It was her father asking her what she wanted for dinner and reminding her to tell the office that she would be late in on Monday because it was Harry's assessment.

'You're going to want a pay rise next,' she said, 'since you've suddenly come over all efficient like this.'

'Cheeky madam. Don't forget it's poetry night.'

She turned the phone off and picked up the sheaf of letters to put in the car. She would have to face Ted the minute she got back and the rest of the afternoon would be downhill so this may be the moment to pop into a nice little cafe she had noticed and pack down coffee and a baguette. She wasn't fat, she told herself, just a little voluptuous and in any case, if she was honest, who was there to care? She resolved again to stop pretending she was talking to Harry.

That way madness lay.

When she got to the office Anna went straight to the Ladies to comb her hair and put on a bit of face-paint since there was no way that she could now avoid a mauling from Ted. She pulled down the skirt of her black suit to tug out the wrinkles and dusted a few rocky road crumbs from her lapels. This was as good as it was going to get. She walked through the main office and was just about to tap on Ted's door when Steve shouted her name. She turned, surprised at the loudness of his voice. Normally he walked up to people and spoke quietly to them, he wasn't a yeller.

'Come here! Now!' he hissed. She indicated Ted's office in a you-know-I-have-to-do-this way. 'No.' He walked quickly towards her and, astonishingly, took her by the elbow pulling her back to his office. Her heels were actually skidding on the floor he was moving her so fast. 'You've got to see what I've found before you talk to Ted.' A few surprised heads popped up from behind flatscreens. In his office Steve pulled up a chair for her and dropped into his own facing her. She fell into the seat gracelessly. He was still holding one arm of her chair and his face was very close to hers, flushed and exhilarated, and for the first time she noticed how well-defined and generous his lips were. Tactile, in fact. She blinked and focussed on what he was saying.

'You gave me the name Bulowski.'

Anna stared at the intense expression in his eyes. 'Yes, it may be the father's name. I mean, Donny's father's name.'

'Well, it became Briony's name, too. She married him.'

'How could you find that out? You don't know any dates.'

Steve was clearly excited by what he knew but she couldn't think what that could be. He couldn't discover anything about marriages or deaths, they had found that out. A warm, slightly spicy scent came from him and Anna fought to concentrate on what he was saying.

'Irrelevant. Just listen to me. I know exactly where Briony is.' She felt her heart start to pound. 'Look at this.' He turned to his main screen and typed rapidly. Then he pulled her chair closer to him so she could read. On the screen was the logo of the Chicago Tribune newspaper. Steve clicked the box 1885-present and typed in Briony Bulowski and a list of articles stretched down the page with the name of the journalist by each one, Carmen Dellio. The subject of all the articles was Mrs Clark's daughter.

'What? Why was she in the newspaper?' For answer Steve clicked open the last article. The headline was "Brit Child Killer Gets Six Years."

'*What?*'

'Read it. Here, sit here,' and Steve pedalled his chair away so she could sit opposite the screen. She craned forward and scanned the lines as fast as she could.

'"Briony Bulowski was today found guilty of the involuntary manslaughter of her son Donny. The little boy, only 2 years old, was brutally beaten by his mother who inflicted injuries which resulted in his death. A majority female jury convicted the dishwater blonde British woman on the single count of second degree homicide, a felony indictment. Juror Moira Thompson said afterwards, "I just didn't buy the stress angle she went for. Who isn't stressed? You don't kill your kid!" Angry scenes erupted outside the courthouse when Mrs Bulowski's defence attorney Stephanie Kukor emerged. The State Prosecutor, Mr Jay Simmons, made a statement on the courthouse steps, "Justice was done today. A little boy who had his whole life ahead of him is dead by the hand of his own mother. She will now feel the full force of..."'

'*Shit*,' said Anna.

'She's in Cook County Jail.' Steve pedalled himself back to her side. 'The largest jail in the United States.' He looked at Anna.

'*Fuck*!' There was silence for a moment while Anna stared at the screen.

'I'm wishing now that I had another sensational piece of news,' said Steve drily. 'In your taxonomy of swear words I'm wondering which one would have come next.' Anna looked at him as if he was crazy.

'What? What are you saying?'

Steve exited the screen, stood up and dragged his coat off a hook behind the door. Then he peeled hers off the back of her chair and gave it to her. 'You can see Ted later. We need to talk this over and decide what the plan is before he grills you about it. This is huge and you need time to think. Come on.' Like a child she followed him dazed by what she had seen.

They picked up the canal towpath and walked briskly towards Brindley Place. It was a calm, misty afternoon and the air was raw but it was better than being inside. Steve didn't talk and Anna was grateful for it because her own thoughts were making quite enough noise for both of them.

So, she had been right the first time, Margaret was living a fantasy because she couldn't cope with the truth of what Briony had done. No wonder her stories to people didn't quite add up, she wasn't the kind of woman who was practised at lying. All those visits, they must have been to the trial and then prison visits. The thought of Briony killing her grandson, the thought that her own daughter could be so brutal would have almost destroyed her.

Perhaps it did. Perhaps the secret knowledge of what Bri had done, which she couldn't share with anyone, had eaten away at her and squeezed her heart so hard that it had burst. Wasn't there some hint that Mr Clark had been violent? Certainly controlling and mean.

These things might be inheritable or learned. No wonder there were no photos of little Donny being older than two. He didn't get any older than two. And what about all Maggie's good works – was she compensating for the dreadful actions of her daughter? Was she trying to prove something to herself?

Anna remembered the pretty but mournful living room. The room which should have been a place to collapse in and laugh and play games and watch tv and chat over huge mugs of tea and plates of toast. A room that should almost never be tidy and should have scuff marks on the walls and even an old apple core or two. That's what Margaret had made it for, wanted it to be. No wonder she spent as much time out of the house as she could.

They found a quiet corner in the Cafe Rouge and Steve ordered for them both. She found it difficult to see the reality around her, the red and cream chairs and the small square tables, unless she made a huge effort. Her eyes were blinded by the dreadful mental image of Briony and little eager-eyed Donny, previously only a smiling face in photos, contorted with rage and terror. Steve tapped gently on the table with his spoon. 'You haven't asked.'

She stared into his face. 'What?'

'The date. The date when Briony killed Donny.' He looked at Anna carefully as though trying to judge how this would affect her.

Anna only paused for a second. The timeline from the last sighting of Donny to Margaret's death was well inscribed on her memory. 'I'm assuming it was in 2011 some time. That was when Margaret started all those trips to the States and it was early that year, well, actually around Christmas 2010, that Joan, the neighbour, last saw Briony and Donny at Mill Lane, at least that's what she thought she remembered.'

Steve looked relieved that she had come to this point in her own thinking. 'Yes, she's already been in jail for nearly two years most of it on remand. But the stories she told at the animal refuge? What about that?'

Anna stared miserably at Steve, phrases from the unsent letters scrolling through her memory. 'She just couldn't cope with it Steve. I've been thinking as we walked here that she couldn't take it in. She had to pretend, at least in her English life, that it hadn't happened. That Briony was fine and happy and Donny was having a normal childhood. That's why there was no email address or mailing address for Briony. The letters I found on the laptop must have been part of the pretence, too. There's a name for it, isn't there, a word psychologists use when you can't cope with a nightmare reality and you kind of block it.'

'Splitting.'

'Yes, that's it. She split. She couldn't go into total denial because she loved Briony and would never have abandoned her so it was like, in Chicago she faced the reality but here, back home, she wrapped herself in a fantasy. She became a mum and a gran like other people of her age. She couldn't bear to tell them what had really happened and perhaps she was right.' Anna thought of the cool-eyed Valerie and wondered how comforting and compassionate to Maggie she would have been if she'd known the truth. 'She must have written real letters to Briony, probably a stack of them, and memorised the address of the Jail rather than break the fantasy by writing it down in her address book.'

Their coffees arrived and they sat silently together sipping them and thinking. 'Ted will want you to go to America now and see her. You'll have the rotten job of telling a woman in jail that her mum, who was really the only one on her side, is dead.'

'Yes.' A small part of Anna's brain noted Steve's compassionate insight. 'Did you read the articles? Did they say anything about the husband and his parents and why she did it?'

Steve took a deep breath. 'It seems that Briony married him not long after she was last seen at Mill Lane. They had had a stormy relationship. Well, it sounds like Karl, the husband, was pretty violent, and he had pushed off but when she came back from England he came round to her apartment and cried and said he loved her and begged her to marry him because he missed his kid and all that crap and she just caved in and did it. She probably had very little money and of course if she worked she'd need to pay for childcare.

She must have been up against it. There wasn't any mention of his parents. She seems to have been very alone.'

'Why didn't she just come home with Donny, do you think?'

'I don't know. Ashamed of not making it on her own, maybe? Maybe she loved him despite his knocking her about. For blokes it's hard to fathom why a woman stays with a man like that.'

Anna nodded and asked again, 'Why did they say she did it?'

'Sounds like everything got on top of her. Very soon after the marriage he started messing her about again. She threatened to go to a women's refuge and he said he'd kill her and Donny if she did and of course she must have had no money to get back to England and probably was too proud to ask her mum. She was getting deep into debt just paying the bills. She certainly was desperate. She'd thrown Karl out but he'd come back the next day and kicked the door down. Donny was screaming, of course.'

'Oh God.' Anna buried her head in her hands.

Steve waited until she sat back so he knew he could continue.

'He beat her really badly and then drove off. The police domestic violence squad took pictures after she'd been booked for killing Donny and apparently she was a mess.' He paused again, checking on her. Anna nodded for him to go on. 'Donny just wouldn't stop screaming. She lost it. She picked him up and yelled at him and shook him really hard to try to get him to stop and his head banged against the sharp edge of a kitchen unit. He was killed instantly.'

'But the newspaper said she'd *beaten* him?

'Journalistic sensationalism. Of course, I'm giving you her version, the one the defence attorney gave. The prosecution made out that she was a violent woman and that Karl and she were always fighting – her hurting him as much as the other way round. That's why he wasn't charged with Domestic Violence even though he didn't have a scratch on him. It's a felony charge in the States. He really laid it on Briony in court – said she was an unfit mother and tried to stop him seeing his son and all that. The jury were mostly women. I'm surprised that none of them took a cold, hard look at him. And there was stuff in the papers about his past – you know, interviews with previous girlfriends saying what a bastard he'd been to them. They can publish all that in America but it was never allowed in court.'

'Not allowed in court?' That seemed incredible.

Steve shrugged. 'The ex-girlfriends would talk to the press anonymously but not take the stand against him. You can't blame them.'

Anna sat thinking. Thousands of miles away a woman alone is pushed beyond what she can bear until she kills her baby, the person who means the most to her. Kills her own heart. Here, in England, another woman whose whole psyche recoils from the knowledge of what the person she loved most has done splits herself in two and the agony of it brings about her death. Two women pushed too far and in different ways, destroyed. What was it someone had said to her about something quite different? "It's a good bridge but it can't bear the weight of the traffic that's driving over it." Neither Briony nor Margaret could bear the weight of the traffic. Who could? The sound of her phone interrupted Anna's thoughts. It was Ellis. She kept her comments short and tried to smile so her voice wouldn't betray her distress.

When she clicked it off Steve asked, 'Everything ok?' He must think we live in perpetual craziness, thought Anna.

'Yes. As far as Ellis is concerned more than ok – "superlative" was the word he used, I think. He's been given a part in the school panto - Aladdin.' She laughed shakily. 'He's bagged the genie.'

Steve grinned and they both relaxed. 'Big role. Good for him.' They got up and left the cafe walking slowly now back to the office. Anna was grateful to him for not telling her what to do next, and for not attacking Briony for what she had done. Come to that, he hadn't even said anything dismissive about Margaret and her comfort blanket of fantasies.

When they got back she touched him lightly on the arm. 'Thanks for what you did.'

He made a dismissive gesture. 'You could have done it yourself. You *would* have done if I hadn't scooped it by getting there first.' He smiled and she noticed that when he did his eyes seemed to be a lighter blue. When this is all over, she thought, I'll take him home to meet Harry and the kids and George. Make him smile a bit more, perhaps.

But, driving home, yet again, she couldn't resist it, she was so mad. Harry had been her best friend for half her life. You can't just stop talking to your best friend even if he doesn't talk back and she desperately needed to get it all out. And in the car she could do it out loud risking the curious glances of other motorists at traffic lights who, she told herself, would assume she was singing to the radio.

You will never believe what happened in Ted's office! I couldn't believe it myself! I went in there calm as you like and told him the whole thing, you know, about the money and how we'd found Bri and all that and he stood there looking out of that damn huge window his office has and saying nothing. Then he turned round and *smiled* at me (bastard!) and said, and I quote, "You've done well, Anna. Not bad at all for your first solo effort. Get all the papers together and pop the file to Karen tomorrow and I'll get Neil on to the job." WHAT? Neil? Senior researcher and all-round fatarse. How dare he! He took no notice of my reaction, of course, just said, "With an estate like this it won't be long before we get competition from other agencies. We'll need to move fast."

The adrenalin was flooding through me and I said sharply, "Actually, no-one else would have the name Bulowski and in any case it's very unlikely that the Treasury listing on the Bono Vacantia site will be up yet." Ha! Not such a bloody amateur you fucker (unspoken). But no, far from impressed he just chuckled (and that's what really got me) and said, "You must realise that more senior researchers are rather quicker off the mark than you and people talk. Mrs Clark's lawyer could have a contact who would slip him or her a sweetener for titbits like this and most researchers wouldn't bother with all that you've done. They'd just go straight to the passenger lists of major airlines flying from Birmingham to Chicago starting January, 2011."

"But they don't give access to information!" I spluttered, getting really cross and red in the face and probably looking ridiculous. "When you've been in the business as long as I have," Ted said, "you get a few contacts. In any case, they could go to the Chicago Tribune website and type in her first name, it's a little unusual, and British woman or something. They'd be on to it in a minute."

I just couldn't think of anything else to say so I asked him to give me until Monday to come up with a plan before he gives MY case to one of his cronies. It's so unfair, isn't it? But I'm going to fight this, sweetie, if I possibly can. Once I've calmed down I'll think of something – I've got to.

7

It was almost dark when Anna pulled up outside her own house. The streetlights were on and there was only a smear of yellowish grey left on the horizon below a spread of dirty clouds.

She paused for a moment, drained by the day. She noticed a man standing in the shadows opposite. There was no bus stop and no reason for him to be there, surely. He looked away quickly when he saw her peering at him and then strolled off. Odd but probably meaningless. She got out of the car and went indoors. In the kitchen sat Harry and her father and Ellis.

'Hey, genie genius!' she said beaming at Ellis. It took a huge effort.

'Yes, I've been telling him about the djinns and genies,' said George happily. 'Even the Koran mentions that we are surrounded by djinns, the unseen spirits who can intervene in our lives for good or bad if they want to or if we make them mad.'

'Oh, don't let's make them mad.' Anna put the kettle on and sat down wearily waiting for it to boil. The warmth of the kitchen and the chatter comforted her.

'Yes, Pops says it's like when you know you've put something somewhere and then it's not there and when you find it you know you didn't put it there, where you found it, well, that's the djinns!' Anna was finding this hard to follow. 'And sometimes you think you see something out of the corner of your eye, like a movement and then it's gone when you look, that's the djinns. Like fairies and poltergeists and all that. I'm going to be one of the unseen...'

'Made visible by the rubbing of the magic lamp!' added George melodramatically.

'Yes, but only because I choose to help Aladdin because he's released me from the evil witch!' Getting the spirit world a bit mixed up, thought Anna.

'It's what I've been thinking about lately,' George said, 'about parallel worlds, the metaphysical. These things sound weird to us because we're so constrained by Hellenic rationalism but it wasn't so long ago that Britain was a magical animistic place of fairies and gnomes and goblins. Green men and forest sprites. Shakespeare's full of it. Queen Mab and all that. They're just other versions of djinns – spirits that live in amongst us and take a great interest in us!' Anna sipped her tea. This was just what she needed, she thought gratefully, after the day she'd had. George's looniness was a balm.

'Talking of spirits who are unseen but move among us,' she said, 'where's Faye?' A tense silence descended on the room. Ellis studied his script. The animation left George and he got up and looked in the fridge for the makings of dinner.

Unexpectedly, it was Harry who broke the silence. 'She was out all last night. She hasn't been home.' He looked at George thoughtfully. 'She's away with the fairies possibly.'

Anna's mood switched in a second. Her thoughts crashed into each other and her heart thumped with adrenalin. 'Why on earth didn't you phone me, Dad?'

George waved a bunch of carrots vaguely. 'I just hoped she'd come back with an explanation and we wouldn't have to worry you. You've got so much to think about already.' Anna was rapidly tapping her phone. Faye's was switched off. She ran to get the phone book but George took it from her. 'I've tried her friends. She spent the night with this Russian chap, it seems. They told me that she's fine and she'll be home later. Try not to worry.' He went for a reassuring grin which ended in a ghastly rictus.

Anna was incensed. 'Thanks for that advice, Dad. I'll do that, then. I won't worry. It's perfectly fine that my seventeen year old daughter is shagging, sorry Ellis, a perfect stranger!' Ellis picked up his script and slid off towards the living room. George banged pans about and started chopping things. Harry was still looking at him.

'She could be playing on the swings in the park, she likes that.'

Anna tried to be calm for his sake. 'Yes, of course, that's what she'll be doing. She'll be back soon.'

Harry smiled, remembering. 'With mud on her knees and one sandal in her hand.'

'Yes.' She ran her fingers through her hair and looked desperately at her father.

George put a glass of wine in front of her. 'Why don't you take this upstairs and get changed and by the time you come down dinner will be ready. We'll deal with Faye when she gets home but right now you need to rest and eat.'

Upstairs in her little bedroom Anna took off her work suit and pulled on some sweat-pants and a mismatched old birdseye blue wool cardigan – comfort clothes. She couldn't be bothered to shower. Lethargy pulled her into a foetal position on the bed, her single bed.

Was Faye completely beyond them now? She had never done anything as bold and reckless as this before. She was sometimes back later than agreed and she sometimes forgot to tell them where she'd gone, but this? Staying out all night with a man she'd only just met and not even bothering to phone them? She could have been in real danger and they would have had no idea where she was – you see it on the news all the time. Apart from anything else it was such sluttish behaviour. Anna recoiled from her own word. She had always known Faye to be wilful and maybe teenage girls do this sort of thing now. Maybe it's normal. Like Briony. Anna curled up tighter into a ball. It could be like Briony all over again. This Russian (Anna imagined him tall and broad, dressed in leather and animal fur with a swatch of blond hair and a beard that looked like a bale of straw come undone) would take her back with him to the Black Soil District or Siberia or wherever and Faye would have a strop over nothing and would stop telephoning them and she might never be seen again. The links between the people you love are so fragile, so easily broken.

Should she be angry with Faye? She probably hadn't the energy, but she realised, too, that it may drive her further away faster. She would have a quiet word with her daughter, woman to woman, about being careful and sensible and *considerate* and tell her she understood, that she had been young once, and that…

'Anna? Faye's here.'

Anna flew down the stairs yelling at the top of her voice, 'How could you do this to me you wicked girl? I'll bloody well ground you for the rest of your life!' and then stopped abruptly.

Faye was standing in the hall holding the hand of a runty looking young man who had a shaved head and a complexion which resembled the corned beef hash Anna's father sometimes made. Faye indicated this scrawny person proudly. 'This is Sasha – it's short for Alexander. He's Russian. He wants to stay for the poetry.' Faye beamed at him, their eyes on the same level. He looked a bit too old for Anna's liking. She breathed deeply, forcing herself to calm down.

'Good evening, Mrs Ames,' Sasha said without smiling but putting out his hand, 'I am happy to meet you.' Faye squealed a little in delight at her darling's grasp of the social skills required from the situation.

Anna tugged the misshapen old cardigan around her and stepped forward and took the hand. 'Come and have some dinner with us,' she said with a hostess smile, 'and afterwards we'll read some poems.' Behind his back as he turned to follow George into the kitchen she pulled her daughter into the front room. 'Why didn't you phone? I was worried sick when Dad told me you hadn't been home last night. Anything could have happened! You are so thoughtless, Faye!'

'Oh, sorry. Tash and I fell asleep on their couch and then it was, like, I forgot.'

'For crying out loud! You hardly know him!'

'Isn't he great?' Clearly the mutual understanding Anna imagined would be engendered by a quiet heart to heart with her daughter where she played the older but wiser and Faye played the grateful innocent was not going to plan. 'His gran, I mean babushka, see how he's educating me, has got a dacha and you say it datcha, not dakka like Mr. Simpson used to when we were doing *The Cherry Orchard*.' She skipped into the kitchen and Anna followed moodily.

Dinner over, Sasha stood up and started to gather the dishes. A ripple of silent approval ran round the room. He turned to face them. 'In Russia we think it not hygienic to wash plates in water in bowl like you. You should not do it this way in dirty water. You should use water which is coming from tap fresh like this.' He took a plate, squeezed some detergent on to it, swished it round and then ran it under the cold tap. He then picked up the next plate. George coughed and indicated the dish washer. 'Lazy and cause environment damage. You use too much of earth's resources in greedy western countries.' Faye folded slightly at the knees, giddy with adoration.

'We'll just leave them for now,' George said diplomatically, 'Let's go out to the shed.'

They arranged themselves on the beaten up armchairs and a recycled bus seat that served for a sofa, Ellis studying Sasha with interest and Faye draping herself across her beloved's bony knees.

Harry sat on his own, his head back staring out of the window at the night sky. He had picked up Faye's Meerkat Mugger Head Hugger and had it on his head set backwards so that the claws folded round the rear of his skull and its tail hung in a curl by his ear.

The effect would have been comical but for his serious expression. Anna carefully sat a little distance from him in her favourite old rocker that had been hers since she was a child and George rummaged among that week's pile of slim poetry books sent to him for reviewing and then stood up.

'I've got some weird sci-fi stuff from Steve Parish up north which I thought Ellis could have to practise your genie spookiness, eh? Here you go. Then, there's a new woman has sent me a collection from Argentina in translation – Christina someone. It's all right, I think. Here you are, Anna, you pick one of those. Faye, I wasn't sure you'd be here but I did think of you when I read the latest collection by Toni Root.'

'Oh yes, I like her,' cried Faye, jumping up and snatching the book. 'She's rude and funny.'

'And then,' George went on, 'there's a brilliant new collection by Geoff Stevens. It's called, '*Sleeping with You and Other Night-time Adventures*' and I thought you might find something, Harry, if you want to join in. No pressure.' Anna stiffened. Would Harry be ok? Would he start to read and then stop and go back to staring out of the window? Would he mix up the words? Would he be upset and sob uncontrollably as had happened before? None of this would matter if it was just the family and Ashok but she didn't trust Sasha not to laugh or comment. She felt a huge surge of protectiveness towards her husband. Probably Faye had told Sasha about him but she didn't want him exposed to anything hurtful. He can still *feel* she thought fiercely, so don't you bloody dare make some smart remark. She looked warningly at Sasha who started slightly but then, misinterpreting her signal, asked to be given something to read. George gave him one of his own most recent pieces simply because it was lying about to hand.

There was a tap on the door and Ashok came in. He was carrying, as always, a chocolate orange and, as always, said, 'One of your five a day!' It was Ellis's job to tap it smartly on the table and Faye's to distribute a piece each. 'Delectalicious,' said Ellis, sucking his slice noisily.

As Ellis started reading, giving the surreal scatter-gun of phrases as much animation as he could, Anna drifted away from the words and into her own thoughts. This was why Friday night was usually so relaxing, you could gently waft in and out of the room like one of George's djinns, there and not there, like Harry himself.

She remembered the scene in Ted's office. She had to find an angle, something that she could do or that she knew that was vital and wouldn't work for Neil. She decided that when this was finished she would go upstairs with her laptop and find out all she could about Cook County Jail. Poor Maggie, how worried and nervous she must have been going out there to see her daughter in such dreadful circumstances, to say nothing of the grief she must have felt over the loss of her grandson. And then, not to be able to talk to anyone about it. You could have seen her driving her old Ford around or standing at a bus stop or on the till in the charity shop and you would have just seen a nice middle-aged woman with a ready smile and a cheerful word and had no clue of the pain she was carrying that would finally strangle her heart. Anna felt tired and a little defeated.

What if she could find no way of keeping the case? Neil would be efficient. He would contact the governor or administrator, whatever that person was called in the States, explain the situation and arrange an appointment with Briony. Done and dusted. But he wouldn't know about Briony and Margaret. He wouldn't know or care what a sweet woman she was and how much she had loved her daughter and grandson. How she had made the tiring journey to Chicago time after time to spend just minutes with her daughter. He wouldn't be able to tell those little stories and tributes that Anna had heard at the crematorium. He wouldn't, Anna thought, sighing, break it to that damaged, ravaged woman *gently*.

Ellis and Faye had read their choices and now Harry was standing up with a book in his hand. He was frowning. On the cover was a picture of a man upside down in bed staring into space, like Harry had just been doing himself. There was an overlay of a section of the cosmos on the photo so that it seemed as though the man on the cover was floating in the sky. Harry began to read the title poem,

> *Sleeping With You.*
> *I want thoughts of me*
> *To sleep with you before I do –*

Anna felt her flesh rise up in goose pimples. His voice was strong like it used to be, the voice that she had loved because it was never bossy, always rich and full, the voice that made the kids in his classes stop talking and listen because they wanted to. She saw Ellis relax his body into the pit of his chair and look up at his father with a little smile. Sasha had started to whisper something to Faye but she put her finger on her lips and turned also to listen to her father's confident voice, so rarely heard now in the house. They miss him, too, Anna realised, wondering why that had never occurred to her before. Harry's voice went strongly on through the poem and then finished,

> *Just murmur my name at midnight*
> *And although I won't hear you,*
> *I will come*

He lowered the book and looked straight at Anna. There was a moment where no-one breathed and then he put the book down gently and opened the door. The meerkat shouted silently at them from the back of his head in a bizarre counterpoint as he went. Anna half rose but Ellis said, 'It's all right, Mum, I've recorded "The Sky at Night" – I'll go and watch it with Dad.' Faye got up and sat on the arm of her chair slipping her hand into her mother's. Still her lovely daughter. Anna shuddered involuntarily and rested her head briefly against Faye's arm willing herself not to cry. If she did she would not be able to stop. Ashok scrambled clumsily across to her and kissed her forehead in an avuncular way.

'Here,' he said, cracking off another section of chocolate, 'you need your vitamins.' Anna smiled at them both gratefully.

'Time for another poem, I think,' put in George tactfully. 'Maybe you would like to read, Sasha?'

Sasha stood, straightened his narrow shoulders and declaimed George's poem in a voice decibels louder than his normal tone. It was a slight poem, unfinished, a bit of a rant about the council demolishing some old cottages to make a car park. Sasha came to the end and looked puzzled. 'In Russia,' he said, and Anna groaned inwardly, 'poems are beautiful. They are about love and death and tragic happenings. They are noble.' George dropped his chin into his beard unsure whether to be amused or annoyed. 'And,' went on Sasha triumphantly, 'they have rhymes and they have music, like this!' He banged a metre on the table. 'Here is no rhymes so here is presented no poem. You should read Pushkin and Akhmatova.'

Ashok, Anna and George regarded the ceiling with interest. Faye looked at Sasha in astonishment. 'You don't have to have rhymes in grown-up poems, Sasha, anybody knows that. Rhymes are for kids.'

'This country is not civilised,' said Sasha calmly. 'Everyone know that Russian literature is greatest in world. I go now.' He turned to Anna and slightly bowed. 'Thank you for nice food.'

Faye leaped to her feet, 'Don't go Sash, it's ok.' And Anna's beautiful, intelligent daughter tripped over her shoes running after him to make sure he was not offended by his own rudeness. After they had both left the adults mimed what they would like to do to Sasha and Anna suggested to George and Ashok that a little something liquid might now be in order.

Anna took a mug of tea in to Harry in the front room and a cup of hot chocolate for Ellis. 'Here you are, darling,' she said tenderly to her husband, setting the cocoa down by her son. She was still trembling inside from the effect of the loving poem and his eyes locked on to hers. It had been so long since he looked at her like that.

"Just murmur my name at midnight and I will come." If only that were still true.

Harry almost snatched the mug from her hand and looked at her coldly, 'Mr Ames, to you, if you don't mind.'

Tonight I'll look up the Jail and tomorrow, thought Anna, I will knock the wind out of that bloody Diploma assignment and on Sunday I'll sort out the bramble patch and how I'm going to keep Briony. The probability was that the weekend would not get any easier.

8

It was fine, in fact it was *good* slashing at the brambles and chopping them up and heaping them in the wheelbarrow. It was just what she needed. She was wearing thick rubber gloves and Harry's ancient and smelly Barbour coat. She inhaled him and the pungent earth and bent and ripped and slashed her way across the patch at the bottom of the garden. November was dry this year and around her lay the wreckage of the summer foliage in shouting yellows and reds. A few nasturtiums were still vivid spots of orange and the rose hips glowed like Christmas bulbs among the yellowing spotted rose leaves. Above was a shifting mass of rolling clouds, low and grey.

She stopped and puzzled over them. Stratus nebulosus breaking up or cumulus humilis breaking down? She smiled at her continuing ignorance. George had bought her a cloud app for her last birthday knowing how she loved to sky-gaze. It was remembering what it told her that was the problem. Ellis and Faye had been in on the plan and had signed her up to the Cloud Appreciation Society. If she needed cheering up she would spend a happy half hour trawling their delightfully casual website.

She hauled a huge stack of brambles to the wheelbarrow and stopped to catch her breath. She was trying very hard and with some success not to think about her tutor's comments on her last assignment. Polite and supportive, they could be summed up as, 'This is crap – try harder or you're out.' She had barely managed to start the next one that was already overdue.

She thought about Briony instead and what she'd discovered about her situation. What was a late assignment compared with what she had to deal with? She put down her secateurs and dropped on to the creaking old bench. She just had to talk to Harry. The man himself was avoiding her as usual. She tried not to vocalise but within seconds was muttering.

You can't believe what it's like, Harry, at the jail. I mean, Cook County Jail. I've been on the website again this morning and you can actually write to some inmates who do a blog. They show pictures of them and the questions and answers under subject headings. Sounds very civilised doesn't it? But it isn't, it's awful, like a nightmare. The filth, the abuse, the hopeless sordid squalor of everything and the noise! Are our prisons like this? You get 15 minutes for a visit, just 15. One of the inmates said he never asks for visits now because he feels so bad when they've gone. I'll tell you if I go if it's really as bad as this, but I feel sick at the thought that Maggie in her sweet-smelling soft jumpers and hair freshly done (I'm sure) would have to face her daughter like this. Yelling down a phone or through a stinking plate glass window. Oh darling, I can't bear the idea that anyone else will tell Briony about her mum. The only kind face she saw I expect. And, guess what? They have male guards! Do we have male guards for women prisoners? Apparently this one guard took out an equal rights action so that male guards could get jobs at female prisons. Men with all the power and captive women with none, it doesn't take much imagination to see what would happen there, does it? I'm so angry and upset. Briony isn't a murderer like a gangster or something – she loved Donny – she was just stretched too far and she snapped. I'm going to have a brainstorm with dad after lunch – see if he can come up with an angle. I would far rather discuss it with you but I know I can't. Not your fault. Love you.

When she went back in the house was quiet. Harry had his Keruve watch on and was sorting small sticks in the front garden. Faye had other more exciting people to be with than her family and Ellis was on his laptop at the kitchen table looking up genies.

'I hope you're not thinking of method acting this part,' said Anna after she'd washed her gritty hands, gingerly sliding her aching buttocks under the table. She licked a pinched finger and wiped the scratch on her arm. The garden was an assault course these days. 'Ok if Pops and I have a chat in here?'

'What's method acting?'

'Don't worry about it – cute and lissom as you are, I still don't think you'll be able to squeeze yourself into an oil lamp.' She caught his expression. 'Two s's.' She reached over and stroked his cheek with the back of her hand which he bore, this time, without complaint. George pottered through clearly on his way to the shed, paused, recollected and sat down opposite Anna. 'I'm sorry to bother you with this, Dad.'

'No bother. I fancy a bit of sleuthing. Did you tell them at work about tomorrow morning?' George was getting untidier these days, Anna thought. He had lost a button from one shirt cuff and had rubbed the collar raw with his beard. She had to be careful not to fuss over him, he hated that.

'Yep. 11.00.'

'Fire away. I'm all ears. No need to check, Ellis, not Faye's meerkat this time.' He settled himself at the table and folded his arms.

Anna told him everything. She told him how Margaret was found, what Joan, Jacqui, Diane and Valerie had said. About the cremation and the tributes. She told him how there were no photos of Donny beyond him being a toddler and how the notes in the box had stopped in December, 2010. How she had found the laptop and the letters and then been told how much the estate was worth. How Steve had tracked Briony down from the chance discovery of the name of her parents-in-law. That she was in Cook County Jail for the involuntary manslaughter of her son. At this point Ellis looked up, shocked. She told them how abused and manipulated she had been by Karl and how he had made things so much worse for her in court.

'And you've tried all the numbers in her address book?'

'Yes. There seems to be no-one close. There's only one that's a bit of a mystery. It looks like a Birmingham number but I can't get any ring tone from it. I've wondered if it was written down wrong.'

'What is it?' asked Ellis.

' 0121 475 4892 and it's labelled D.C.'

'I know what it may be,' said Ellis going back to his screen, 'could be the mum's pincode for one of her cards.'

'No, love, it's far too long, but a good idea,' Anna smiled encouragingly.

Ellis gave her a look. 'Not the whole number, dummy, just the last four digits. DC could stand for Debit Card. Mike's dad does that so he can remember when he's getting money out of the hole in the wall.'

'Oh, right. I'll check with the bank. Thanks, genius.'

'So there are two versions of the last five years?' George asked thoughtfully. 'The version she told her friends and the version that was true?'

'There are three versions, actually. There's also the parallel world of her letters where almost up to the end she writes to Briony as though nothing has happened. It can only be that she never sent the letters and wanted to do it to take some pain out of her heartbreak,' she paused, 'or she was going nuts. I suppose she could have sent them to Briony. But,' Anna interrupted herself, 'she wouldn't have done. In the letters she talks as if Donny is alive. Right up to the end. She wouldn't be so cruel as to inflict that on her daughter, surely?'

'Could you read me one?'

Anna got up from the table and retrieved the folder of printed letters from her briefcase. 'I'll just pick one at random, er, from June 2012 so about over a year after Donny's death.

Darling Bri and Donny,

I wish you were here to look out of the window with me. Bob is in the garden fast asleep with his front paws tucked up on his tummy. It's very hot today and I'm going out in a minute to do the same. But the really funny thing is that the blackbird that lives in the lilac tree is on the lawn too with her wings stretched out right beside Bob! I wish I had a camera.

It's all rubbish in the news. I'm sick and tired of hearing about the deaths in Afghanistan. All this talk of heroes and dying for their country. I don't see any Afghans attacking us. I'm ashamed of my government sometimes. But then, the Americans are even more involved aren't they? I know you wouldn't agree with it.

We had the sweetest little kitten come to Safe n Sound last Friday. Donny would love it. It's very pale grey with darker stripes and the brightest blue eyes! Starving, of course, and frightened but still feisty. It'll be fine in a few days, it's amazing how they recover. The shop is very busy because we've had some lovely donations. I think we might be getting things from friends of Jane – I think she's put the word round to her posh mates. I bought a top myself, I couldn't resist, and there were some smashing things I could have bought for you. But, there's not really any point the way things are. It'll be something to look forward to, my chick, going shopping together like we used to.

All my love as ever, Mum

They're pretty much all like this. This sort of thing.'

George pondered. 'Does she ever refer to anything Briony is doing? You know like, thanks for the photo you sent of you and Donny in the garden or I was interested to hear about your new course at uni?'

'No, she never does. I've read them all now. Why?'

'Well, they sound one-sided.'

'I suppose they do. But...'

'Does she ever mention Briony's real circumstances?' Anna shook her head. 'So they could have been written just for comfort as you say. For Maggie to reach out however ineffectually to a daughter who was beyond her reach. Like separated lovers getting comfort from being under the same moon. They probably are just fantasies of what life could have been. The road not taken and all that. She doesn't sound delusional, though.'

Anna leafed through to the back of the pile. 'This one is different. It's the last one she wrote, the night before she died, although, of course, she couldn't have known that. Listen.

It's been so long, B. I don't want to make you feel bad because I know it's my fault what happened but I am so sorry. Please can you give me another chance? I was so foolish to say anything to you about Donny and there isn't a moment that passes when I don't hate myself for upsetting you the way I did. I love you so much my darling and the thought that I may never see you again or see you smile at me over the kitchen table or hug you or share funny things that happen with Donny – I can't bear it. I just can't bear it Bri. I feel as if my heart is breaking. You are the last thought in my mind at night and the first in the morning. I even dream of you and you are smiling and coming to me with your arms open like you used to do. If I stop doing things or talking to people then I think of you and I grieve all over again for my stupid, stupid words.

And that's where it ends.'

Ellis had stopped pretending to work and was listening with a stricken look on his face. Anna smiled in what she hoped was a reassuring way at him and wondered whether she should have read it in front of him. George was quiet, thinking. Anna noticed how the pink skin on the top of his head was showing through the white thatch in a way it never had before and the other day she had seen how his shoulders had begun to drop and fold forward. It was getting dark and the plopping of fireworks outside was beginning.

'You know what I think?' George announced firmly. 'She isn't nuts and she isn't comforting herself. I don't know what is going on, but you don't write a letter like that to feel better.'

Anna sat bolt upright blinking rapidly. She gathered up the pile of letters and stuffed them back in their folder. 'There is another possibility and I've only just thought of it. Thanks, Dad. First thing tomorrow I'm going to be on that solicitor's doorstep.'

'Don't forget - '

'I won't. But this is something I have to check.' She was almost out of the room when she remembered to ask George about the stranger she'd seen hanging around. 'I think it may be another HH ,' she said.

George was doubtful. 'Why come to your house? You'd think he'd hang round at Mill Lane and talk to the neighbours. '

'I don't know but I don't like it. If I see him again I'm going to confront him.' She thought for a moment. 'Ellis, just go and check on your Dad out at the front, please.' She made the shopping list for Monday and stuck it in her purse. As she walked into the hall to drop off her briefcase ready for a flying start she saw Ellis in the living room looking at the Keruve receiver. 'Ellis?'

'He's gone off, Mum, but I know where he is. I think Pops ought to come with us to get him.'

'Why? Where is he?' She was reaching for her coat.

'At the Elim Pentecostal church off the High Street. We'll go, Mum, you don't have to. It'll be another one to add to Pops' collection, won't it?' He was grinning and Anna felt relieved that he was able to be so light and natural. 'We'll go and get him.'

Anna leaped out of her car as the Khan and Partners' secretary appeared running with the key in her hand fifteen minutes late. Inside, Anna didn't even let her get her coat off.

'Can you give me the Clark Estate box, please? I'll take it upstairs.' The girl struggled with the idea of getting on her high horse since this visit was not scheduled and decided it was too much effort. She pulled out from under her desk a sturdy cardboard box and handed it over to Anna.

The stairs were narrow and steep but the room above the office was just what she wanted. There was drink-making equipment which she ignored and a sizeable coffee table which she knelt beside. In the top of the box were the bank statements held together by a rubber band, the most recent uppermost. Anna removed the rubber band and sat back on a chair to look through them. She started at January, 2011. Her finger flew down the item column stopping at

KLM, Continental, American Airlines. She made notes. So, each time Margaret had flown she'd shopped around for the best deal. No surprise there.

Anna burrowed again in the pile and found the savings account statements from 2010. The first balance was £22,562 which was a bit much for the redundancy pay, Anna thought. Had Margaret cashed in a private pension? There was also a five-year fixed rate bond with a major bank. By the size of the bond this must be the inheritance from her sister and it was clear that she was not planning to nibble into it. With each year the balance in the savings account went down and the amounts transferred to the checking account tallied with trips to America. There were also what seemed to be hotel payments. Below these statements were gas and electricity bills, water and council tax invoices and then the last three years' itemised telephone bills.

The door opened and Ms Khan, looking fresh and poised, came in. 'Hi, how's it going?'

Anna made an effort to be at least polite. 'Fine. Just checking some dates.'

Ms Khan moved over to the kettle and glanced back at her. 'Have you found the daughter yet?' Anna remembered what Ted had said although she thought he had been overly suspicious.

'Making progress,' she said brightly. She hesitated. 'I don't want to seem rude but I am so rushed today and I really need this information.'

Ms Khan waved her coffee cup prettily. 'No worries. I've just come for my caffeine fix.' She clattered down the stairs lightly on her four-inch spikes.

The telephone bills showed, Anna counted them, fifty-seven calls to the USA from January, 2011, to a week before Margaret's death. So Maggie was talking to her daughter on the telephone, then.

Were inmates allowed calls? Some of them were quite lengthy but they were all different lengths of time. Surely the prison would have a set time for calls? She started to copy the numbers down and immediately realised that they were all different. The area codes were different, too, so they were not even to Cook County. Or at least, not all of them. When she had done that she looked at the clock. It was 10.40. Quickly she lifted the remaining documents out of the box and there they were. Right at the bottom were the flight schedules for the last two years. She listened for a minute and then slipped the clipped bundle of schedules into her briefcase. The one on the top was for flights from Birmingham to Indianapolis. In a minute she had replaced the papers and closed the lid on the box.

Five minutes later she was in her car and on her way to the appointment.

9

A light rain was falling as they got to the Queen Elizabeth Hospital and they hurried along the broad pavement outside. George pointed at the posters on the columns saying self-righteously, 'If you must smoke do it in the red shelters,' and grunted. There they were, like bus shelters, packed full of patients on drips and in their dressing gowns puffing away. Anna wondered why this particular form of self-destruction was stigmatised more than the multitude of others that accounted for so many of the hospital's customers.

They exited the huge revolving door into an atrium filled with the delicious smell of fresh coffee as well as light from the three-storey high space and then down the off-white and aqua corridors to the out-patient reception area for neurosciences. They didn't have to wait long and while George elected to stay outside, Anna went in with Harry.

She pulled out a chair and sat slightly behind Harry out of his line of sight. She liked this consultant. He was probably a few years older than them with coppery skin and a square, handsome face. His dark hair was close-cropped and brushed forward in a neat cap and his flesh looked as if there wasn't an ounce of extra fat in it like a healthy animal.

'Good morning,' he said, 'I hope you are both well.' He turned to Harry. 'Now then, Mr Ames. May I call you Harry?' He knew that Harry would not remember him. 'We will be giving you some tests today, some for your physical fitness and some for how good your memory is. I would like to get to know you better.' What a pleasant voice, Anna thought, and how courteous he is to Harry.

She hadn't liked the way the previous man checked things that Harry said with her in front of him as though he was a child. This one had barely glanced at her.

'Yes,' said Harry firmly.

'You were a teacher until recently, is that right?' Harry hesitated. 'You taught geography, I believe?' He knew this, Anna thought, he just wanted to see what Harry remembered on this visit.

'That's a nice pen,' said Harry. 'Is it a fountain pen?'

Mr Shenouda lifted the pen into the air and examined it seriously. 'Yes it is. I prefer a fountain pen to a ballpoint. I know it's old-fashioned but my father gave it to me.'

'My pen has green ink,' said Harry becoming quite animated. 'I like using green ink because it's so positive. I don't like marking work in red, it seems like an angry colour.' Anna smiled, pleased that Harry seemed to be enjoying the conversation.

'What a good idea,' said Mr Shenouda. 'I wonder, do you have any children you could give a fountain pen to?' He waited, smiling a little, for Harry to reply.

Harry considered this gravely. 'I think so.'

'How many children do you have?'

'Er.' This was new. Anna's smile faded and her upbeat mood dulled.

'What are your children's names?' Mr Shenouda continued, trying another approach.

Harry immediately said, 'Faye and Ellis.'

'Those are very nice names.'

'Yes, my wife chose them.' Mr Shenouda looked down at his notes. Harry leaned forward urgently. 'She's not here anymore. I don't know where she's gone. It's a bit worrying really because we get on very well together so I miss her. Do you know where she's gone?' Anna sat rigidly in her chair.

'I'm sure she'll turn up soon,' said the doctor easily, not looking at Anna. 'Now, please will you introduce me to the lady who came in with you?' Harry turned and glanced at his wife coldly and then turned back.

'I'm sorry doctor but I've forgotten what her name is. I think she's been sent by the council to look after me.' Harry glanced back at her again. 'I wish she would go away. She makes me feel – um -' He stalled.

'Well, it's time for your tests, Mr Ames. The nurse will be here shortly and will show you where to go. Is that all right with you or do you have any questions?' Harry shook his head. Mr Shenouda must have pressed a button under his desk because the nurse was there within seconds and smiling at Harry.

'Mr Ames? Please come with me.' He got up and left with her and Anna got up to leave, too, but the consultant came round her side of the desk and sat on the edge of it.

'I'd like to have a word with you, if you don't mind. May I call you Anna?' Anna nodded dumbly and sat down again. He put out his hand to take hers and it was warm and dry. A very nice hand to hold. She would have liked to have held it for a long time. 'You know, of course, that it is the illness that causes your husband to say such things?' Anna wished people would stop telling her that. She nodded. 'But that does not make it any less painful for you, I think. How long has it been that he stopped recognising you - do you remember when it started?'

'It was about two months ago.' Anna was determined to keep to the point and not be emotional. 'He woke up in the night and was frightened to find me in bed with him. I've been sleeping in the spare room since then. But to be honest he was becoming rather aloof with me before that so -' She paused miserably.

'Does he ever know who you are?'

'My father is very involved in small-press poetry publishing and writes a little himself. Every Friday evening we get together, sometimes with other people, and we read bits from various collections and anthologies that have been sent him to review or to publish.'

'How very pleasant.'

'Yes. Well, sometimes Harry isn't able to concentrate long enough to read a whole poem but last Friday he read a beautiful, haunting love poem.' Anna's voice began to waver and she stopped to take a deep breath. 'At the end he looked straight at me with those wonderful eyes, you must have noticed his eyes, and I really believe he knew me – everyone felt it.' She stopped and swallowed. 'But then he just walked away and later he told me off for using his Christian name.' She tried a laugh but it didn't work.

Mr Shenouda took a box of tissues from the desk and handed it to her and it was only then that she realised that her face was wet with tears. He sat down in the chair that Harry had used and again silently took one of her hands in his. After a few moments she took a deep breath and wiped her eyes and he stood up and went behind the desk.

'Mr. Ames has been diagnosed with EOFAD as you know. Have you discovered if anyone else in his family has this disease?'

'We don't know. He was adopted as a toddler.' Anna hated this. The very worst part of all this was the thought that Faye or Ellis may be harbouring this horrible gene malevolently waiting to destroy them. At least Harry had had no idea that this would be his fate. This was the thought she buried deep, deep down and why these hospital assessments were such a minefield. She could just about get through if no-one mentioned this terrifying nice word 'familial'. It was the thought that woke her most mornings with a heart-pounding jolt. So far Faye and Ellis had shown no curiosity about their father's condition and had no idea of the tragic implications for their own lives. Thank goodness for teenage self-centredness, thought Anna. She became aware that Mr Shenouda was speaking.

'I'm going to schedule an MRI scan for him in a few weeks – my secretary will let you know. It's time that we had another one and then we can get a better idea of what's happening. We'll talk again later today when your husband has completed his tests.' He smiled at her in a way that seemed to make his dark eyes both deeper and brighter. Anna's abandoned libido lifted its head briefly to take note but she smacked it down again.

Outside George was reading the newspaper and was just about to start giving his opinion of the editorial when he noticed Anna's face. She sat down beside him and he put his arm through hers. 'Tea, coffee, double scotch?' he offered. She shook her head and they sat in silence together until a nurse came busying along the corridor and halted abruptly in front of them. She spoke to Anna, glancing at George.

'Hasn't this person been seen yet?'

They exploded with laughter and then found they couldn't stop giggling while the nurse disappeared, puzzled, into her office.

Anna was almost late for her appointment with Ted. The assessment had taken so long that she had had no time to eat or even grab a coffee. She was tired, dehydrated and upset. Perfect. She brushed her hair and dabbed her shiny face with powder. The mascara smudges under her eyes fought back when she tried to scrub them off.
She tapped on Ted's door and was let in. Steve was there.

'Don't mind Steve, he's setting up our new website,' said Ted, clearly wanting the really important work not to be interrupted. He rocked back on his heels and folded his arms. He looked a bit like a one of those toy people you can't knock over – they always bounce back. 'Now, give me your pitch. Why shouldn't I give this very lucrative case to our most experienced researcher, Anna?'

Anna's mind went blank.

'Inmates have to request visits,' she managed at last. 'I think I stand a better chance than Neil of her agreeing to see me.'

'Why?' Ted had half an eye on the screen where Steve was working. Triple H was hoping to raise its profile in the Midlands to compete with the prestigious London outfits.

'She's had bad experiences with men.'

'Why wouldn't you just tell the governor or whatever and get him or her to arrange an interview? That's what Neil would do.' He glanced back at her, waiting.

'Because that way she would find out that her mother was dead from some official who didn't give a damn about her! She's all alone in a foreign prison!' Anna burst out. 'The worst jail in America, they say. Her mother was the only caring person she's had for almost two years and now she has nothing.' She paused and tried to calm herself. 'I think we should handle it more gently.' She had an inspiration. 'She might be a suicide risk.'

'Didn't she kill her baby?' Ted came round to her side of the desk. 'She may not be as sensitive as you imagine. She may be bloody thrilled that eventually she's coming out to so much cash.'

Anna was silent. How could she tell him that it was Margaret she was really protecting? Maggie had entered her imagination like one of her father's djinns - a kindly one. Maggie needed Anna to tell Briony about her death in the most tactful way possible. It was almost as though by finding out about Margaret's life and reading her letters to her daughter, Maggie had opened her sore heart to Anna, one mother to another, and was trusting her with the job. She could hardly tell Ted that, he would get a hernia laughing.

'Ted?' Steve had stopped tapping the keys and was looking at his boss in a no-nonsense way, his blue eyes cold. Ted, unused to this confrontational expression from his IT guru, stood up and straightened his tie.

'Steve?'

'I'm doing Harts' mission statement. Did you still want me to use the words 'compassionate' and 'sensitive'? I believe you felt they would be vital to our image?' He raised an eyebrow.

Ted laughed ruefully and relaxed. 'Go on then, Anna, get yourself out to Chicago and do the business. Go and see Sue in accounts and get your expenses set up and *don't waste money*! It's not a holiday, you know.'

'Thank you, Ted, thank you so much.' She could hardly believe it.

'Just move fast and don't screw up.' Ted turned back to the computer screen and smiled at what he saw. 'You're a genius, mate,' he said.

Anna mouthed behind Ted's back, 'Yes, you are!' and ran out and down the glossy green glass stairs.

Back at her desk she pulled the slim sheaf of flight itineraries from her briefcase and spread them out. Like the notes they were in date order. Mrs Clark clearly had a tidy mind. The first ones were from 2011 – that crucial year – and began in February. There were four flights that year to Chicago. Anna checked dates. Yes, Margaret had obviously gone to Briony's arraignment and then must have visited her in prison three times that year. How agonising for her to only be able to spend 15 minutes with her daughter after a 13 hour journey there and another back at huge expense. Of course she wouldn't be allowed to visit more than once a week.

Anna looked at the next year - 2012. This was weird. As well as the international flights, there were internal flights to Springfield, Illinois, and then to Ann Arbor and Lansing, both in Michigan. Quickly, Anna Googled prisons in Michigan and found that there were none for women in either of these cities. So, it wasn't that Briony had been transferred. Why did Margaret go to them? She turned over some more schedules – city after mid-western city and then finally, in October 2012, her last flight to Indianapolis. How odd. This was not what she had expected. Was Margaret lobbying support for Briony, perhaps, with senators or congressmen or whatever they were called? It would be a strange way to do it and in any case they wouldn't do anything for anyone in a different state, surely.

Steve appeared beside her desk. 'All fixed up for the trip?'

'Not really. Sue says I can't go until the end of next week because the flight is £100 cheaper then and accounts won't let me take the more expensive one but that's ok because I need to write to Briony and get her to give me a visiting order. She can reply to my hotel near the jail if she can't email me. I just hope she'll see me this way – through a visit. I hate the idea of the governor telling her.'

'What are you going to say to her then to get a visiting order?'

Anna wrinkled her forehead at him. 'I know you'll think this is wrong and please don't tell Ted but I'm going to say I'm a researcher for an article on British women in overseas' prisons.' She screwed her eyes up further to peer at his response. 'I just can't come out and tell her in a letter that her mum's dead.'

'Up to you,' said Steve, non-committally, beginning to move off. 'Actually, I came to say that if you don't mind giving me a lift home tonight I may have the ideal prop for Ellis and you can pick it up. I only live about half a mile away.'

Anna felt a frisson of curiosity. Yes, it would be *of interest* to see where and how Steve lived since they all knew so little about him, and very kind of him to think of Ellis, of course. It would be rude to refuse and why should she? 'Sounds intriguing. What is it?'

'What do you think?' He smiled at her curiosity. 'It's a lamp, of course. I got it when I was in Teheran.' And then, seeing her expression, he added, 'Don't worry, it wasn't expensive but it is a wonderful thing and totally authentic for the part. Better than some teapot in disguise anyway.'

'I'm always thanking you, Steve,' said Anna and watched his broad shoulders move away.

She couldn't imagine what sort of place Steve would live in but when they drew up and she parked, as instructed, at a smart canal-side development private lot it was still a surprise. 'Mm, pricey,' she said almost to herself and then wished she hadn't. It was already quite dark although still only late afternoon.

'Not too bad for one bedroom,' Steve replied firmly, 'and I can walk to work and town so I only need to use the car for weekend trips.' He seemed different, more tense and less friendly. He set off towards the outer door and Anna winced at her own crassness. She followed him up internal stairs and along a couple of dim corridors and then she watched him unlock his door. It felt uncomfortable.

Although it was, of course, perfectly innocent, there was something about following a man whom you didn't really know into the space he controlled. But it was too late to turn back, it would be rude and childish. He pushed the door open, flicked a switch, and stood back to let her go in first.

Immediately inside was a small lobby with doors off to each side but straight ahead the door was open. The hall switch must have been wired for all the lights and the sound system to come on simultaneously because the room in front of her was immediately glowing buttery yellow, circles of light overlapping each other, and some music, maybe Handel, was sweetly tumbling over the silence.

Anna stepped forward without waiting to be invited and couldn't help a sharp intake of breath. The room was beautiful. It was large and curved with the whole of the outside wall done in panels of glass and aluminium. The floor was warm, honey-coloured wood and there was an oversized deep sofa covered in white linen set against an ochre wall. In an angle of the window wall was a broad recliner and footstool in bruised tan leather with its back to the room looking out towards the lights of the city centre. Beside it lay a book open and face down. There was very little furniture for such a large room but that gave it a spacious, calm feeling that Anna loved.

To one side and set back was the kitchen area done in a rather brutalist granite and steel style that she thought jarred but she could have certainly lived with it. Definitely. She looked round again. What brought the room from designer stylishness to something more special was the presence of rugs. On the walls were rich, jewel-bright oriental rugs instead of pictures. But it was the lamps, she realised, the very contemporary globes of light, that were set low on carved and polished wooden tables that brought up the colours in them so well. She stepped back to the lobby and slipped off her shoes.

'Steve, this is beautiful. Did you do this?'

'Well, yes and no,' he said, moving towards the kitchen area and picking up a kettle. 'My wife chose it and had it decorated but when she left she took everything except the sofa and chair because they wouldn't fit her new place.' He looked around. 'I bought the lamps.'

'But the rugs!'

'Oh, yes, I bought those. She didn't want them, she called them my tourist ethnic tat.' He rolled his eyes at Anna. 'I like visiting Islamic countries, you see. Not out of any ideological sympathy or anything like that, I just think the buildings and the textiles are beautiful. Ancient and beautiful. Some of the mosques I've seen in Istanbul and Isfahan seem to me to be the most beautiful buildings in the world.' Anna looked at him. She had never seen him like this with his face bright with pleasure and talking as though he never wanted to stop. The reserve had completely gone. 'If I could afford it I would buy better specimens but I can't and these are good enough to give me pleasure every time I look at them.' He lifted the kettle off its stand and poured it on to coffee in the cafetiere. The aroma filled the room. 'And then there's the mountains. That's what took me there to begin with. Climbing Mount Toubkal in the Atlas Mountains in Morocco. Anna, you cannot imagine anything more majestic and -' He stopped. 'Well, you've probably been.'

'No, I haven't,' said Anna quietly.

'Sorry, I was getting carried away.' He seemed embarrassed.

'That's ok. I was getting carried away with you.' He brought coffee to her and she noticed that he had remembered from the Cafe Rouge how she took it with a spot of milk but no sugar. 'So you like to climb?' She held the mug carefully so as not to spill a drop on the white fabric and sat as straight as she could on the soft sofa edge. She had no intention of leaning back and keeling over with her legs in the air. It was a hazard of her height which happened too often on untested seating.

'It's a good antidote to the job. Space and fresh air and completely non-cerebral problem–solving. A group of us go out most weekends. There's plenty of good climbing within a four-hour drive of here. Nearer if we're training novices. The Peak District has some great short climbs. In the summer we go further afield. Next year the others will be going to the Andes.'

'Not you?'

'No. I don't go abroad anymore.' His expression shut down further questions.

Anna looked round again. 'I must say, Steve, I'm impressed. I mean, mostly I'm impressed by how beautiful and large it is but also – well, are you always this tidy?' Steve laughed and walked the distance across to double doors set in the lobby wall. He pulled them open dramatically and jumped forward to prevent an avalanche of boots and stuff bags and other very muddy things jettisoning themselves on to the floor.

'See? I just like to walk into a calm place after work. I don't care that my bedroom is usually a wreck and the cupboards are full of stuff.' He surveyed the huge room. 'It looks ok now but you should see it in the summer – when I get home from work it's full of light. You'd never believe you were in the city centre. All I can see is sky. Sometimes at night I turn off most of the lights and sit in that recliner just listening to music and watching the city go to sleep.' He went over to the glass wall and looked out. 'That's why I didn't move after Cathy left.' His voice had lost its joyfulness. Anna didn't know what to say. 'But enough about me. How is your husband?' It was such an abrupt transition that Anna almost resented it but she gathered herself.

'He had an assessment today and it's as expected, really. Everything's a bit worse. He's got a good consultant, though. I'm hoping he'll bring some fresh light. My dad certainly likes him.'

'Oh?'

'Yes, George is a bit of a collector of exotica like you only with him it *is* religion. He looked up the consultant's name on his Blackberry while he was waiting for us to finish and discovered it was Egyptian, well, Coptic to be more precise, so after the feedback he quizzed the poor man about his ancestry.' She laughed. 'He didn't seem to mind. Apparently there's a Coptic church near Birmingham so Dad's been invited to go and sample it. I might go with him and take Harry. It's not really like him at all, not when he was well, but he seems to be going through a bit of a spiritual phase himself. Perhaps he just enjoys the music and the change of scene. I blame dad, of course! Just kidding. It's fine. Whatever makes Harry feel better.'

Steve settled himself next to her at the other end of the huge sofa. She put her coffee cup down carefully on a small table wondering how many minutes white upholstery would last in her family living room. 'How did you first know he was ill? If you don't mind talking about it.'

Anna sighed. 'I haven't thought about it for a while. I suppose it was just over a year ago. It was what decided my dad to sell up and come to live with us so I could work and he could hold the fort. I'm very grateful to him.' Anna sat back slowly and carefully, resting her head on the soft upholstery. The music was slipping into a minor key as though scoring her story. Not Handel. Purcell? One of his lovely sad ones.

'Harry was a teacher. One day he decided to take his class of Year Nine, that's 13 year-olds, to the woods for a field trip. Sounds innocuous, doesn't it? But he didn't send letters home with permission slips, fill out forms for the LEA or even tell the Head. He just walked out of school with them, got on a bus, paid for all twenty-six of them and got off at the Lickeys.' Anna paused. 'They were having a great time, well, most of them were, but you can't do that sort of thing.' She paused again, not knowing whether she was going to laugh or cry. 'What was really bad was that he got interested in some ferns and forgot all about them and came home.

When there was an angry protest from the head and the parents he just didn't care. Shrugged his shoulders and ignored it. So unlike him.' She looked at Steve whom she could see also didn't know how to react. 'Then all sorts of other things came out that had happened at work that had just seemed a bit odd and his GP sent him to be assessed. And here we are. He had to stop teaching, of course.' Anna suddenly felt a surge of pain. 'He was a brilliant teacher. Such a waste.'

'And this was just over a year ago?' Steve seemed to be struck by this. She wondered why.

'Yes. So our lives have changed.' There was a moment of silence.

'He must be very comforted by having a wife like you,' Steve said, smiling at her.

'Not really. He doesn't know me anymore,' said Anna shortly. 'Can I see the lamp?'

It was, as promised, a magnificent lamp, larger than the usual model and burnished to a brassy gleam, interestingly dented and knocked about. 'Ellis will love this. Thank you so much.' She looked at her watch. 'I'd better go, it's my turn to cook.' She looked once more round the softly-lit spacious room glowing with colour and the huge black rectangles of windows pin-pricked with tiny lights. 'I feel as though I've had a mini-break just being here.'

'Any time,' said Steve. Anna looked at his alert face and healthy body and thought, don't tempt me. For the second time in one day she needed to have a firm word with herself.

10

Ellis was doing his homework on the kitchen table, George and Harry were in the shed with Ashok and Faye was, predictably, nowhere to be seen. She rooted among the stack of greasy CDs at the end of the worktop and put on her favourite Norah Jones. Then she pulled some carrots, potatoes and turnips out of the vegetable tray and plonked them on the worktop. Ellis glanced up, 'Ugh, mum.'

She began to peel and chop as the meat sizzled and the aroma of herbs filled the room and he made neat lists of numbers in his maths book. Not all on computers these days, then. She thought about the journeys Margaret had taken to the States and wondered again what could be the reason behind her visiting so many places.

'Mum?' Ellis was frowning at her.

'We're having stew. Get used to it.'

'No, it's not that.' He put his pen down. 'You know last Saturday?'

'Mm.'

'Well, Pops took me to the greyhound racing at Hall Green.' She stopped chopping.

'*Did* he?' Old sod! She didn't want Ellis getting the gambling bug.

'Yes. It was all right but there was something I didn't understand. He had his betting money in his left pocket but he put his winnings in his right pocket. He started off with twenty pounds, 'cos I asked him, and he ended with sixteen pounds twenty in his right pocket. When we came away he was all pleased and got out his money and said, "Look at how much I've won."' Anna smiled. 'But, he hadn't really, had he? He bought me a Big Mac on the way home to celebrate so I said, but you haven't won, Pops, you've lost three pounds eighty.'

'What did he say?' Anna slid the vegetables off the board into a colander and sluiced them under the cold tap. She didn't need to worry about Ellis, it seemed.

'He said it was a win-win situation because if he won he was happy and if the bookies won they were happy and in any case it was all about redistribution of wealth. I think that's what he said. What does that mean?'

Anna swept the chopped vegetables into the pan where the meat was bubbling away. 'It means that your grandfather knows how to take a knock and make the best of it,' she said. 'Don't begrudge him life's little triumphs just as long as you understand the whole picture which you obviously do.' She dried her hands and sat down at the table. 'Actually, you can help me with something if you've got a minute. I'll make herb dumplings?'

'Sure.' His face was thrust forward, the pointy chin and amber eyes making him look like a particularly nice goblin. Could goblins be nice, Anna wondered. Maybe an elf.

'I've found the flight details for 2011 and 2012 up to when Mrs Clark died – you know, the woman whose daughter I'm after - and there's something strange about them.'

'Give.'

'Well, sometimes she only goes into Chicago but then there's internal flights to cities in Indiana and Michigan and to Springfield in Illinois. Why would she want to go there? I've checked and there aren't any women's correctional facilities at any of them. You've just done America haven't you? Can you see a pattern?'

Ellis sucked his cheeks in and then blew them out. 'Easy peasy.'

'Go on then.'

He smiled across at her in glee. 'Those states are all con-tig-you-us!'

She laughed. 'Good word, gene-ee-us.'

He turned back to his maths.

Anna sat back in her chair and looked at the clock on the cooker. 'I don't suppose you can also solve the mystery of where your sister is?'

After dinner was over Anna took her laptop up to the bedroom landline and phoned the US numbers she had copied down from Maggie's telephone bills. They were almost all the switchboards of state administrative departments of one kind or another. One was to the university in Ann Arbor. In every case when Anna asked for details of Briony they hung up. By the time she had finished it was late and office hours were finishing in the US. She got up, pulled on an extra sweater and went to check on Ellis. He was asleep in front of the television in the dimly lit living room. She went in quietly to wake him. Harry reared up out of the sofa.

'Who is it?' he asked in a scared voice. It broke her heart to see him this way.

Anna put on the light. 'It's only me. I've just come to get Ellis up to bed.' They had warned her that this time of night could be difficult for people with Alzheimer's when they're already tired and confused. Harry sunk back down, still wary. How frightening it must be for him sometimes, she thought. Ellis mumbled and moaned but allowed himself to be piloted upstairs. Anna phoned Faye only to find, of course, that the phone was off. She felt drained.

She remembered the calm golden light in Steve's flat and thought about how different he was when he talked about the things and places that engaged him. What had happened with the marriage? She scanned the usual suspects causing divorce – adultery, violence, and so on - and couldn't connect him with any of them. But then, she hardly knew him. She went into the bathroom and filled the bath. At least she could have a bath in peace if Faye was going to go AWOL.

The hot, soapy water sloshed around her breasts and she tucked in her chin to examine them. Not bad considering the neglect they suffered. Why was she thinking of Steve and her breasts in this *contiguous* manner? Ridiculous and pathetic and *wrong*, she scolded herself.

Despite the long day she had had and the hot bath Anna could not sleep. As she heard the church clock strike one she gave up and got up. There was a light on downstairs in the front room. To her relief she saw it was Faye sitting in her favoured lotus position on the floor watching tv and spooning ice-cream from the family-sized tub into her mouth. She supposed she ought to be parental but she just didn't have it in her. If you can't beat them, join them. She went into the kitchen and scooped a handful of chocolate digestives out of the biscuit tin and then made a cup of tea. She took her snack into the front room and curled up in the big chair. Faye grunted at her and continued to suck ice-cream off her spoon and watch the screen. She knew nothing about Margaret's story and Anna's work in trying to find and then reach Briony. She was never at home long enough to overhear any of it and probably wouldn't have been interested anyway. The adverts came on.

'Faye?' said Anna.

'Mm. Don't start, Mum.'

'No, I'm not going to. I just wanted to ask you something.'

Faye uncrossed her long legs and arched her back. 'Yep?' The yoga seemed to be working for her. Anna wondered if she should try it.

'I'm going out to Chicago soon to talk to a woman whose mum has died. She doesn't know yet. There's something a bit odd about the mum, though.'

'All mums are odd, duh.' She flashed a grin at Anna and added, 'What is it?' keeping tabs on the commercial break.

'Well, the daughter was in Chicago all the time but when the mum went out to see her she flew to other places – cities near Chicago. Why would she do that?'

'Shopping?'

Anna smiled. 'Not great places to shop I imagine compared with Chicago.' The ads finished and Faye wriggled herself round to give her full concentration to the screen.

'Maybe her daughter wasn't still in Chicago. Maybe she met her somewhere else. Or she wasn't sure where she was. Maybe they'd fallen out.'

Bingo. Anna almost choked on her biscuit crumbs. She checked all the information she had in her head quickly, like clicking beads. The photo with the name of Bulowski. Maybe Maggie hadn't turned it over or hadn't given it any significance, maybe assuming that Briony would certainly tell her if she got married. If the daughter had completely stopped communicating with her mother and had moved apartment how would Margaret find her? Did Maggie simply not know that Briony was in Cook County Jail? In that case she wouldn't know about Donny's tragic death, the arrest and the trial.

So all the phone calls and the visits to State capitals were to check records maybe? Maybe even search the Missing Persons Bureaux? Margaret would have quickly found through her phone calls that no-one would go out of their way to help her when she had only vague information and for a non-US citizen at that if Margaret didn't know about the marriage. She had started in Chicago in 2011, probably going to the last known address and talking to the tenants and then, if she could find the landlord, quizzing him and drawing a blank. How desperate she must have become, Anna realised, in a strange country and being unfamiliar with how things work but driven to find what had happened to her daughter. Had she checked the morgues and the hospitals, the battered women's shelters and homeless refuges?

Anna pictured her, this ordinary, gentle, kind woman whose heart melted for a kitten, bravely going into the roughest and most dangerous places in one of the most volatile cities in the world asking constantly for Briony. She would have a photograph with her, of course. She may even have had cards printed to hand out. 'Have you seen my daughter and my grandson? They've disappeared. Please?' asked a thousand times a day. But if she didn't know that Briony had married then the name wouldn't mean anything. If she had asked for Briony Bulowski she would have got an answer very quickly, maybe, but not the answer she would have wanted.

What would Anna do if Faye went missing like this? It could happen. They would do anything to find her, but how? What if she was in a foreign country with different laws and procedures? What if it was a different language? What if it was Russia? The police wouldn't take any notice of you, after all, Briony was an adult. Faye would be an adult in just a few months. Anna scrambled out of the chair and lurched across to her daughter, hugging her closely. 'Don't ever go missing, Faye! Even if you hate me don't ever just not tell me where you are! Promise me!'

Startled, Faye reared her head back against her mother's pressure. 'What? What's the matter?' She relaxed. 'Oh, work getting to you.' She turned back to the screen. 'Ok , I promise not to go missing even if I hate you – ok? You going to bed now? I'd quite like to watch this in peace. You're not going to go off the rails as well are you?' The commercial break came on again. Anna felt hurt. Faye had never before been cruel about her father's condition. 'Only you do know that Pops is doing his funeral stuff? He told me that he wants to have a pyre so that he can be burned in cleansing fire and his spirit ascend to the gods. Bonkers.'

Anna smiled at her. 'If he takes Ellis to the dogs again, he'll have his wish a bit earlier than he was planning.' She hugged Faye again. 'I do love you so much, you know.'

'Blimey, Mum, chill.'

Anna walked around the kitchen putting things away and wiping surfaces automatically. She was very tired, but there were still nagging questions. The flight dates had shown that Maggie was in Chicago at the very time that Briony was being arraigned for Donny's manslaughter. Was it possible that Margaret hadn't known, that it was a coincidence? She probably wouldn't have bought the local papers and Briony's case was not that high profile. The story that Steve had shown her which had made the front page was of the sentencing at the end of the trial, not coverage of Donny's death and

Briony's arrest. The killing of a child by its overwrought parent would be too ordinary, too *quotidian*, to be front-page news in Chicago where gang shootings and political scandals were much more likely to sell papers. No-one who had seen the photo of Briony in the paper would connect the thin, anxious face with hair pulled back with the plump and attractive woman in Margaret's photos if that's what she took. And, of course, there was no grandson by then.

Was it possible that Maggie did not know that her daughter was in court for murdering her grandson within a mile of where she was searching? If Anna's theory was right. But why did Briony break off so disastrously from her mother? Was it Karl who made it a condition of their getting back together? Possibly, but he wasn't with her every minute, was he? Briony could have found a way to write or email or telephone. Surely, she was not that ground down by him?

Margaret certainly seemed to feel guilty about something she had said but that was in the very last letter in late 2012. Anna closed the kitchen door quietly and stood in the dark hall thinking hard – putting the timeline together. If she had had no contact with Briony since, at the latest, January 2011, the thing that she said which she felt so bad about was not just before she died, as Anna had assumed.

It must have been on that last visit at Christmas, 2010, and that was why Briony had stopped communicating. So Margaret must have been writing those nice ordinary letters in the computer file to comfort herself but finally couldn't bear the pretence and had to write from the heart even knowing she might never mail that last letter or any of them. What had she said that could turn Briony so irrevocably against her and lead to the tragic marriage and killing?

Anna pulled herself upstairs by the handrail and stumbled into her bedroom missing the hook on the door and letting her dressing gown crumple on to the floor. The narrow bed was a mess of tangled sheets and blankets but she got in and pulled them round her. She remembered the living room at Mill Lane as she had first seen it. She had felt, for all its prettiness and comfort, that it was sad.

As her head sunk on the pillow she remembered Joan and Diane saying how Maggie was always doing things for others. Another way to look at that was that she couldn't bear to be alone with her thoughts and so was rarely at home, couldn't stand to be there because she didn't have the one thing that she and the living room and, come to think of it, most of the house desperately craved

– a family. If she had believed that she had driven her daughter and grandson away then every time she opened the front door the silent house must have rebuked and distressed her. There would only be Bob who would be glad to see her, and the kitchen where she could be busy and feel wanted and useful.

'Maybe...' Anna murmured and was asleep.

11

Do you remember the holiday we had in Florida? I was just dreaming about beaches and shimmering heat and you teasing Ellis to look out for sharks after he'd come out *of the water. You remember the expression on his face? In the dream, darling, you came to me all wet and salty and wrapped yourself round me and we were in a wood somewhere suddenly, you know how dreams are, and you kissed me so sweetly it was like holding a chocolate in your mouth and letting it melt until your mouth is full of it but you can't bear to swallow. I felt your arms round me and your legs pushing against me and we were falling deeper and deeper into piles of leaves and when I woke up I was crying. I miss you so much, so much.*

Anna hurried out to the car feeling groggy with lack of sleep. The air was sharp with frost and she felt her lungs cramp automatically against the chill. As she reached for the door she was suddenly aware of a man beside her. She stepped back, startled. It was the loiterer.

'What are you doing on my drive?'

'I want to talk to you. It's all right.' He made calming motions with his hands which, she noticed, could do with a wash. He was a big man with a huge square head and she couldn't help feeling intimidated as she looked up at him.

She locked the car door from the fob. She was not going to stand close to an unlocked car next to this weird man who could push her into it in a second. His head was wreathed in his condensing breath. She became aware of a smell. It was slightly sweet and very rank. His parka was greasily shiny. She stepped back and faced him. 'Please leave my house,' she said, 'this drive is private property and I have no interest in anything you want to ask me. I'm not giving you money and I'm not donating anything to anybody.'

'Why are you so mean?' he asked looking genuinely puzzled. 'I had no idea you were such a bitch.'

'What?' Anna was shocked. 'How dare you? You don't know anything about me.'

He backed off a little and grinned at her. He was younger than she was and certainly got enough to eat judging by his girth and he towered over her in a way she didn't like. He astonished her by saying her name in a challenging way. 'Anna.'

'How do you know my name?'

'Of course I know your name.' Then he chortled, there was no other word for it and an unpleasant self-congratulatory sound it was. Anna glared at him. 'I'm not here to ask for anything, you paranoid cow, I'm here to tell you something.' He grunted, clearly enjoying her confusion.

'Look,' said Anna as fiercely as she could, 'my father is in the house and my husband and I'm going to- '

'And your son and your daughter who both, as it happens, are late for school by my watch.' This time it was a giggle and, if possible, even more unpleasant. Menacing, in fact.

'Ok, I don't know who the fuck you are but you had better get away from me right now.' Anna had been working her keys through her fingers and now swung her fist up in the air with the points of the keys facing him. 'Back off! I mean it.'

'Ooh, nasty.' But the man did retreat until he was on the pavement. He held up his hands. 'See? I'm not armed.' He laughed again. 'You are going to so regret this when you find out who I am, love.'

'I couldn't give a flying fuck who you are. Just stay away or I'll call the police.' She was trembling with anger and fear.

'And tell them what?'

For a moment Anna wondered if she was still asleep, still dreaming. This sort of thing just didn't happen in your own drive at 8.30 am. Well, it did, but it would be the car they'd be after, not her and her family. She was acutely aware that either Ellis or Faye may come rocketing out of the house at any moment. What did this weirdo want? Was he round the bend or after her for protection money or what? Was he stalking her, or, horrible thought, stalking Faye? Clearly her first theory had been wrong. He was not a competing heir hunter, in fact, he looked unemployable. How did he know about her family? None of it made any sense.

The man gave her a look that would have been indulgent on a more pleasant face. 'That your brother came to pay you a visit?'

'I don't have a brother so bad luck. I'm phoning the police.' Awkwardly, she fumbled for her phone in her bag while still, absurdly, pointing the keys at the man.

He leaned against the gatepost. 'Ah, but you see, love, you do. Your mum is my mum. You know, the one that went off when you were a teensy weensy tot? Well, she met my dad and here I am, your little brother, Len.' He stuck a hand out and began to move towards her again. 'Shake.'

'Certainly not. I don't believe a word of it.'

He began a singsong chant. 'Your dad's name is George, your mum's name is Lena, you were born in Kings Heath, you-'

'You could have found out all that.' Anna was reeling.

'But not this.' He narrowed his eyes. 'Your dad and my mum took off for Katmandou in 1963 in a camper van. They never made it because they ran out of money but they got as far as Cairo. They sold the van and hitched home. Now then, Annie, tell me that isn't true and I'll tell you you're a liar.' He jutted out his purplish chin in an oddly childish gesture.

Anna could hear the sound of voices from just inside the front door. She took a step down the drive towards him. 'Right, this is what's going to happen. I'll meet you tonight at 5.30 at the Corner Café on the High Street. If you've got any proof bring it. But right now you are going to leave this house and if I clap eyes on you again before that time I'll call the police and tell them you're harassing me.' She had not lowered her fist. 'Do not speak to my son or daughter or husband or father. Do you understand?'

The man smiled sarcastically, lifted his hands as though in surrender and made off down the street. Ellis and Faye erupted out of the front door. Faye was yelling, 'Tell him, Mum, tell him! He's got to give me my product back you little shit!'

'Don't call your brother a little shit,' said Anna weakly, lowering her fist.

'Big stonking shit then!' shouted Faye and grabbed Ellis by the hair. With the other hand she pulled off his backpack and unzipped it releasing the Meerkat Mugger Head Hugger and grabbing it. They disappeared round the hedge in a flurry of mutual recrimination. Anna leaned against the car for a moment and then got in and drove off slowly looking around for any sign of the loiterer. He was gone.

There was a package waiting for her in reception at the office. She signed for it, made for her desk, dropped it and went into the canteen area to the coffee machine. She ached to have time to go out and get some delicious Italian coffee but this was as good as it was going to get. At least at this time in the morning it was unlikely that the spout would have the residue of chicken soup in it – always a jarring addition to her brew. Suze waved her fingers at her from behind her screen and she stopped briefly to greet a couple of other workmates but it was a relief to sit down at her own desk and boot up her machine.

The incident with the scary man calling himself her brother had unnerved her. It was, after all, entirely possible that she had half-siblings. She just hadn't ever thought of it. Deep down she didn't really believe her mother still existed. Even though she'd enjoyed researching her mother's family of origin she hadn't thought of her re-marrying and having children. In fact, her mother's family had been interesting. On her mum's father's side she came from generations of jewellers and precious metal-workers all living and working within a few streets of each other on the Soho Road. Anna had been to the Jewellery Museum and been delighted to see some ornate silver presentation plates with her great-grandfather's initials on them. Her mum's mother's side were less settled and harder to trace. Reading between the lines, Anna thought they were probably tinkers or gypsies travelling round various Warwickshire villages but there was too much missing information to be sure. Certainly, as she knew first-hand, her mother had been keener on upping and moving on than staying put so she seemed to have followed the traveller path. Perhaps that was why Anna hadn't thought of her being around this area. She pushed aside the obvious follow-up question that was too painful to contemplate. The so-called brother didn't say she was living locally or alive at all. Anna's heart began to beat uncomfortably fast. *Was* her mother, maybe, still alive? Could she meet her? The thought was so huge that she turned it away.

What did he want from her, anyway, this putative brother? She couldn't see a trace of herself in his appearance. She was small with thick dark hair which tended to rise like seaweed in a neap tide as the day wore on and she had brown eyes whereas he had watery grey eyes and his hair was a nothing brown. Also, he was fat. Despite her chocolate indulgences Anna felt or hoped that she had a Karma-sutra sort of shape – she still had the same size waist as when she was eighteen. Wondering if this was wishful thinking, she chewed her lip for a moment and then, triumphantly, remembered Harry saying just that thing about her one night when he was particularly turned on, so QED. Plus, she had the same healthy-looking skin as Faye whereas that man was an unattractive mix of purple and grey and spots of livid vermilion.

'This is no good and totally unfair,' Anna said out loud staring at the screen. 'Give the poor sod a chance.'

'Give what poor sod a chance?' asked Steve, appearing in reflection in her screen. 'I wouldn't if I were you.'

'Oh, nothing.' Anna turned to him, 'You have no idea how thrilled Ellis is with that lamp. I even caught him giving it a secret rub just in case! He wants you to come and witness his *deus ex machina* moment when he emerges from it by the miracle of digitisation. Can I say you'll come? It's the third Friday in December.'

'Sounds great. What's all this?' Steve indicated the package she had picked up from reception.

'I haven't looked yet. It's from the coroner's office.' She tore open the seal and tipped the contents on to her desk. There was the phone, a modest pay-as-you-go handset (no international calls on that, she imagined) and a small pile of letters stamped 'return to sender – addressee unknown.' There was a note under the Crown crest. '"The enclosed documents were found at the bottom of Mrs Clark's jewellery case and we thought they may be of interest to you. We are also enclosing her mobile phone which was found in the initial house search but mislaid until now. Please ensure that these items are sent on to Mrs Clark's solicitor, Khan and Partners, when you have finished with them."'

'Coroner's Office highly efficient as ever.'

'Just what I was thinking.' Quickly, she scanned the post-marks she could read. They were all from 2011. 'Steve, I've had some new ideas about Margaret Clark. It doesn't affect the trip to the US but it does affect the situation. These letters, the returned ones, are all from the year that Briony was found guilty of Donny's manslaughter and jailed. I rang some phone numbers last night from Maggie's telephone bills and I found the flight schedules and where she was going.'

'And?' Steve had settled on her desk stretching his long legs out beside her.

'This is so counter-intuitive but it could be right. I don't think Margaret knew anything about Donny's death and what happened to Briony. She was in Chicago when her daughter appeared in court but it was a bizarre coincidence. After that she went all over the neighbouring states as though she was searching for her.'

Steve was flicking through the pile of letters and held up an envelope for Anna. 'Look at this.' It was not addressed or stamped but hand-written on it was, "For Briony, in the event of my death."

Anna looked at him and they held each other's eyes for a moment. 'I think you should open it. In fact, I think you have to.'

The flap had been tucked in but not sealed. Anna gently lifted the flap clear thinking about how Margaret might have felt when her fingers tucked it in months, maybe years, ago.

She found that inside the envelope were two pieces of paper with Margaret's neat handwriting on them. She read out loud.

My dearest Briony,

If you are reading this it must be because I have died. More than that, it must be because I have died without ever seeing you again because there would be no need to write this if we were friends again.

When you visited that last Christmas we had such a lovely time to begin with. Do you remember we made mince pies and Donny put a chocolate drop in each one instead of a coin? We played cards and I beat him at Happy Families and he beat me at Snap – it was fun. In the morning he couldn't wait to open his presents and he crept downstairs while we were both asleep. (We had been acting stupid on Christmas Eve and made footprints out of flour pretending it was Santa when we put the sherry and the mince pie out for him. I think we'd had a bit too much ourselves.) Donny came running upstairs and cried, "Mummy, me no mess on Granny's carpet, Santa mess!"

But after Christmas something went wrong. You seemed so tense. Maybe it was my fault or maybe you were just tired, I don't know, but when I heard Donny crying so loudly and then found you had smacked him hard on his little head, I just burst out with what I said. It was wrong of me to say anything, I know you are a very loving mother, Bri, and that you wouldn't do anything to hurt your little boy – it was just a moment when you lost control. I shouldn't have said anything. I should have minded my own business.

But I never expected you to just pack and leave while we were all upset and you were so angry. Why couldn't you have stayed and we could have got over it? Now I'm blaming you when I know it was my fault.

Anna put down the first sheet of paper and went on to the second.

Bri, I just want you to know that I love you very much. I never said a word against your father to you but as you know he was a difficult man and not always kind. It was you who made my life worth living and you who I hold in my heart. My little girl, you made my life so happy and I want you to know that I could not have had a more special or better daughter. No matter what may have come between us, I hope you find this and read it and know that you have my blessing and my everlasting love.

Your mum xxxx for ever

There was silence while they both looked at the pages of writing. Anna slowly folded them back together and put them in the envelope. She thought for a moment and then put the envelope inside a clear film sleeve and then, carefully, folded it into her bag. Steve watched her.

'You're going to give it to Briony.' Anna nodded. There was silence for a moment and then Steve seemed to move away. The next thing she knew he had hugged her and, just as swiftly, he had gone.

Just as well. If he had lingered she might have grabbed him and held on.

Anna began to look through the remaining letters. The first two, as far as she could see the dates, were to Briony at the old Chicago address. Then there was one addressed to 'The Landlord' at that address which had not been opened either. The next one was to the local police in District 3. This had been opened and then clumsily resealed and sent back. Too much trouble so pretend you never got it. The last letter to the Chicago address was marked, hopefully or maybe hopelessly, 'Please forward'. She opened the phone and scrolled through the contacts. There was nothing unexpected and nothing of interest. The Inbox was empty. It seemed as though the mystery had been solved

Anna looked out of the window on to the city ring road with its toy cars constantly and silently in motion. She felt again the gentle pressure of Steve's arm around her and smelled the faint fragrance of him. Don't even think about it, she told herself. Think about Briony and how you're going to tell her what has happened.

Anna could almost feel Maggie pushing her as though she couldn't wait to see her daughter, as though she would be somehow carried by Anna to the very prison bars that held her beloved child. She was getting as bad as her father. Screwy. Anna began to put her desk in order. It was only three days to her trip and she needed to think. She started making a list because she knew that ticking off the items would give her the illusion of being in control when in fact her heart was thudding and her mind careering from one worrying thought to the next.

Harry, I'm sitting in the car outside the cafe and I don't know what to do. I need to talk to you, my darling, so pin back your ears. (I know I have to stop this but I can't – not just yet.) If this really is my brother, well, you know, half-brother, what does that mean? What if I really don't like him when I get to know him better – we certainly haven't had the best start. And when you think of it, he didn't do anything bad, it was me who got scared and startled and threatened him. And what if my mother is alive? What shall I say to dad? Shall I keep it a secret or tell him? I can't bear to tell Ellis and Faye just yet, I know that. But if I tell George (that's if this is genuine) at least I can have someone to talk to about it. Is that fair on him? I have no idea how he feels about her now. He's never had anyone else who really mattered to him so he could still be in love with her. How would he feel about her being with someone else? Or, maybe she isn't? But most of all, I'm skittering around because I can't deal with the idea that I could meet my mother. I – could – meet – my – mother. I know, I know, she may be dead and I shouldn't get my hopes up. But maybe, just possibly, she's sent this brother as a kind of envoy because she wants him to bring me to her. Will she be like Margaret? Is this a weird cosmic parallel? There could be an explanation for everything and she may have been longing for me? The thought is rocking my world and also, ahhh, giving me a cracking headache. Right. Here I go. I love you.

He was already at a table. She struggled to remember the name he had given her. Gone. She sat down and looked at him intently. He seemed cleaner and not so blotchy and he was smiling so maybe she had got his lack of appeal blown out of proportion. He kicked her chair out for her. 'Anna'.

'I'm sorry, I...'

'Forgotten your brother's name already?'

Mentally, her fists clenched. 'Well, I've forgotten your name at any rate.' He bent sideways and picked up a creased plastic supermarket bag. Out of it came a dog-eared brown envelope which he passed to her without a word. The day of the exploding envelopes, she thought. She slid her fingers inside and took out a birth certificate. She read it. 'Is this it?' She laid it back down on the greasy table.

'What do you want?' He seemed affronted.

'Look, I'm a probate genealogist. It's easy for anyone to get a birth certificate. All you do is give the name and the date and the fee and you get one. It proves nothing except that a woman with my mother's Christian name had a son called Leonard and that he was born on,' she checked the date, 'July 26th, 1986.'

He leaned forward and took the certificate from her. 'So you don't want to meet her then? Your mum?' Anna's heart lurched and started banging on her ribs. She tried to breathe.

'She's alive?'

Len seemed suddenly to lose interest and looked around the cafe to the self-service counter. 'You better get a drink or something. These places don't like people just dossing.' Voice of experience, no doubt. She got up. 'Get me a chocolate doughnut while you're there will you? Oh, and another cup of tea – two sugars.' He winked. No, she definitely was not warming to him. But, could it really be that he could take her to her mother? The girl at the counter seemed to take for ever moving back and forwards slowly, chatting with her workmate, not remembering that the coffee should be almost black and making it again. Anna felt her legs begin to tremble with nerves.

Her phone rang. It was George. For a moment she felt guilty as though he had walked in on her secret assignation. 'Dad?'

'Hello, love. Just a word of warning.'

'What? Is it Harry? Has he got lost?' I could go, she thought, I could run out and just pretend this never happened, that I didn't have a sleazy half-brother bumming a chocolate doughnut from me.

'Er. No. It's Faye. Things are a bit tense here and I didn't want you just walking into a minefield.'

'Right. Give it to me. What's she done?' The girl behind the counter had given up even pretending to be interested in serving her. Luckily there was no queue.

George paused. 'It's not what she's done – it's what she's planning to do.'

'I somehow know this is not about her sitting the entrance exam to Oxford to become a brain surgeon,' said Anna grimly, noticing that Len was probing a nostril and then examining with interest what he had found up there.

'You're right there. It's that boyfriend, Sasha. That one that really liked my poetry.'

'Yes, I do remember Sasha. Come on, Dad, stop messing about. Tell me.'

'She wants to drop out of college and go back to Russia with him.'

'No.' Anna threw some money on the counter and took three paces in one second to the table where that man was sitting. 'I'm on my way.' She grabbed her coat, stuck the phone in her pocket and jerked her head at the counter. 'Get your own, I'm out of here. This is my number.' The business card was on the table and she was out of the door before he could close his mouth.

12

At home there was an ominous calm. Anna paused in the hall listening to the house and then made for the kitchen. Faye was staring rebelliously at the microwave where a bowl of popcorn was making its rounds. George was sitting at the kitchen table, head in hands, and Harry was carefully unloading pebbles from his pockets and arranging them in order of size in the frying pan.

'Where's Ellis?' Anna checked.

'Rehearsal.' That was Faye. So, not the silent treatment then. Suddenly everyone shouted at once.

'What are you thinking of?'

'You can't tell me what to do!'

'Let's all...'

'Just shut the fuck up all of you – this is my life! MY LIFE!' Faye yelled. Then there was the inevitable door slam. Anna ran up the stairs after her and just caught the bedroom door in time. She went directly to her and took her in her arms. Faye only struggled for a moment and then broke into sobs. When she had calmed down they sat on the bed. Out of the corner of her eye Anna noticed the half-packed suitcases, one of which was her own best, lying around the room.

'Come on, sweetheart, tell me about it quietly. What's the deal?' She stroked Faye's hair to soothe herself as much as her daughter who raised a mascara-streaked face.

'It's such a great opportunity, Mum. It would only be for a few months – I can easily start uni after that.'

'But what about your A levels?'

'I can catch up when I get back.' Anna was silent. She could see it all made perfect sense to Faye. The ghost of the adventure-seeking Briony strayed sadly through her heart. She was years older than Faye and that had gone disastrously wrong. It was impossible. Faye was too young and Sasha an unknown entity but stating that wouldn't change her daughter's mind.

'It would be an expensive enterprise and I'm not sure we could afford it,' she ventured, desperate for a reasonable excuse to nix the plan.

'Oh no probs.' Faye rubbed the tears off her face and was her blithe self again. 'Sasha's family will pay for everything. They have a house in Voronezh – it's only about twelve hours on the train from

Moscow – and a dacha. I'm learning Russian, I can already count to five. It'll be amazing Mum, and – educational.' It was interesting how educational many of the hazardous experiences Faye yearned for were supposed to be. Anna reviewed her options silently. Faye had a passport and was legally old enough to go against her parents' wishes so there was only one way to deal with this aside from chaining her to the bed – delay.

'I can see you really want to do this, Faye, and I understand how appealing it is to you, foreign parts and all that, let alone the undoubted attractions of Sasha.' Faye simpered. 'But I'm going to have to ask you as an adult to do me a favour over this.' Faye's brows drew together. 'As I told you, I have to go away with my job. I'm going to the States very soon and Pops will have to take care of everything while I'm away. He can't do it on his own. He's an old man and he needs the support of another adult in the house. Please can I rely on you to help him look after your dad and Ellis while I'm away?'

'How long are you going for?' Faye's eyes were narrowed in her am-I-being-conned mode.

'Just a couple of days, I'll be back for Aladdin and Christmas. Ellis would be so upset if you missed seeing him as the genie. Please, Faye, could you stay and help until after Christmas?'

Anna almost smiled as she saw the calculation in Faye's mind. If she left now there'd be no presents, no family Christmas; if she stayed she'd have a great bargaining chip for a breakaway later. Faye loved Christmas.

'I suppose I could. You know, to help out as a favour.'

'I would so appreciate that, love. Thank you. And I'll just take my bag while I'm here.'

'Ok.' And it was over. For now.

The flight to O'Hare was mercifully uneventful. As the plane rose above the early December grey clouds into a glorious sunny blue sky Anna re-read the email from Briony which she had been allowed to send agreeing to be interviewed the following day. She had presented herself as a stringer working for one of the nationals and had made it sound as though Briony's was just one of many interviews she would conduct. In the letter Briony warned that there would only be 15 minutes visiting but said that if it went well she would be willing to write with further information. Her note was brief, no doubt monitored, but well-written. She even seemed eager for the interview. Anna let her eyes rest on the quivering silver wing outside her window. She wondered now if it had been a mistake to lie to the young woman. At the time it had seemed the humane thing to do – to soften the blow of her mother's unexpected death – but now she wondered how Briony would react to her disclosure of her true identity. She felt a knot of anxiety tighten in her solar plexus.

She was too preoccupied to read and it was too light to sleep and in any case Anna felt wired rather than tired. She was uncomfortably aware that the laptop which could easily be reached from under her seat throbbed with a not-even-begun assignment which she had assured herself she would knock together on the flight. Her tutor had been patiently tolerant about the last one but patience and tolerance have their limits. She decided she wouldn't be able to concentrate on it and promptly forgot it.

It had been kind of Steve to drive her to the airport and she had almost been tempted to tell him about Leonard of whose existence her family were still unaware but she had decided against it and felt relieved now that he had not been mentioned. The image of Len's blotchy, sly face rose up on the plane wing and she groaned. It was perfectly possible that he was her half-brother but what a different scenario from those feel-good television shows where families are ecstatically reconnected. She felt convinced that he was not contacting her out of sentiment and there was even a hint of threat about him that alarmed her. What could he want? What could he do to her and her family? Why feel afraid of him? Certainly there was nothing attractive about him but that was no reason to be so wary. She sighed.

In a few days she may meet her mother. Hope leaped inside her and almost against her will she found herself smiling with excitement. But how would George feel about seeing his ex-wife who had walked out on him without so much as a note leaving a small child and a mess of debts? At least she'd never had to deal with divided loyalties, torn this way and that between warring parents. George, for all his dreaminess, had been a lovely dad. Lost and found all round it seemed.

And that thought led to Harry and her smile faded. Every day he slipped a little further away from them as though silently retreating through drifting cloud. Stop it, she told herself. Stop feeling sorry for yourself. Remember him as he was and love him as he is. Suddenly she was furious with him for being ill, for being absent, for being unreachable. Furious with him for not being by her side. How dare he leave her like this when she needed him so much?

The passenger next to Anna nudged her elbow and Anna turned. It was an elderly woman and she was holding out a tissue. Neither woman spoke and when Anna had wiped her eyes and tried to thank her, the woman had put her head back and closed her own eyes in the universal signal which means do not disturb. Anna was grateful.

The terminal at O'Hare seemed made up of endless walkways but at last she was through passport control and customs and at the taxi rank. 'Where to, Ma'am?' It was late afternoon and the winter sun glinted on Lake Michigan as they drove past. The huge muscular buildings rose impressively from Lakeshore Drive in glittering bronze and mirror-glass but Anna was most engaged by the beaches and the marina and lakeside park. Men were playing rugby she realised with astonishment and out on the lake were the bright tippy triangles of sailing dinghies. Then they were under the thundering El tracks of the Loop and horns were blaring and then out into the glossy business district with smart women dressed head to toe in real fur striding down the Magnificent Mile, Michigan Avenue. It was impossible to think of Margaret Clark being in this situation. Impossible, too, to think that this confident, glowing, wealthy city displaying itself along the lakeshore like a fabled queen had in her back skirts a shit-hole like Cook County Jail and that it held behind iron bars the gentle, kind mum from Northfield's tragic daughter.

But for all her fatigue and worry, Anna couldn't help but enjoy the sheer comfort of an American motel. Harts would not have paid any more than they had to and yet there was the huge bed heaped with pillows, a clean, spacious bathroom and by the phone a menu for room service. It was odd not being able to see out of the windows for the thick drapes and dense nets but when she pulled these back she could understand why. Opposite was a wooden fire-escape running the height of a block of apartments so dreary that it was a shock to see a small child perched on one of the balconies. A *wooden* fire escape? But she was too tired to process the thought and instead showered and made her preparations for the next day.

By tomorrow night she would be flying out again and feeling

- what? Relief at a difficult message sensitively delivered or disappointment at a botched job.

Anna stayed awake as long as she could watching endless commercials interrupted by sitcoms but by 9.00 her eyes were closing. It would be the middle of the night in England. She had emailed George from her laptop to let him know she had arrived safely and there was nothing more she could do. To fall into the big bed was bliss.

Anna woke early to Sunday in Chicago. Sunday was the only visiting day and her time was 11.00. She needed to be there an hour early to go through security. From the website Anna knew that the inmates in Briony's medium security women's unit were allowed only two changes of clothing a month. Many women saved their clean Department of Correction outfits of shirt and pants for when they hoped they would have visitors. Anna wondered if she would see Briony in clean or dirty clothes. Dirty clothes would make a point about conditions more eloquently and Briony sounded as though the last thing she wanted would be to give CC Jail a rave review.

Anna had brought her dark suit to wear. It seemed appropriate given the nature of the news she was delivering but she found herself even more nervous about the deception she had practised on Briony. She worried, too, about the narrow window of opportunity she had to see her. It was only this date and only for fifteen minutes. If there was a lockdown for some reason and all visiting was cancelled the cost involved with flights both ways and a hotel stay would be completely wasted and Ted would have more than a few words to say.

She appraised her reflection in the long wardrobe mirror in the hotel bedroom. She was freshly showered, well-rested, and wearing a dark suit which quietly announced authority, she hoped.

Her white jersey top was pristine and the gold rope Harry had given her for her thirtieth birthday lay snugly against her throat. She had brushed her thick black hair up and back and pinned it with a tortoiseshell clip. Her make-up was as subtle as make-up ought to be for a professional woman. She was not, as the Jail had ordered, wearing a bra with underwiring. The image of the pale, frightened woman with the scraped back dirty hair from The Tribune story leaped into her mind and she almost got changed again but decided that she needed clout more than empathy. She had also learned that if a guard didn't like the look of you, arbitrary dress rules would be made up to stop the visit happening. She didn't want to get her pass refused or have her standing doubted so that she wouldn't get to see Briony at all. Anna went down to breakfast.

This taxi ride was very different from yesterday's. When she'd told the driver her destination he looked her up and down and joked, 'Fraud or prostitution?' Then, having ascertained that she was English, began, as if it was a duty to entertain her, to tell her his life story. She barely listened. In her briefcase was Margaret's last letter to her daughter, 'In the Event of my death,' and the email with the apology and the declaration of love and hope. Would this really bring comfort to B though, or just add guilt to the depths of her grief? She would decide at the time whether to give her that.

They were soon clear of the towering skyscrapers of downtown Chicago and into a tangle of tracks, overhead cables, rows of shanty shops and unkempt apartment blocks. Dogs roamed the streets and kids swooped in and out of the traffic on undersized bikes. The driver had centrally locked his doors and as they waited at traffic lights or junctions he impatiently waved aside the figures that loomed towards them hidden in their cowled hoods offering cheap merchandise or a windscreen wipe. She had thought of taking a bus out to Cook County Jail. Idiocy. Steve had told her to take no notice of Ted's caution about expenses when it came to getting about in Chicago. 'Take taxis everywhere,' he had said. 'You may be safe in some districts but even if you are you'll get lost.' Now she understood.

When she arrived the driver handed her his card. 'Don't get a cab from here,' he warned, 'Call me, okay? You got coins?'

'Coins?'

'For the phone. It's a pay phone in there - you won't have a working cell I bet being from overseas.' Gratefully she paid him and got a handful of quarters and dimes. He lifted out her overnight bag and she slipped the strap of her leather briefcase over one shoulder.

Then she turned to look at Cook County Jail, the largest single-site prison in the United States and now the home of poor Briony Bulowski, nee Clark, who was just about to learn that she was entirely alone in the world.

The institute stretched down California Avenue to the right and left. The old, multi-storied Victorian jail was flanked by tall brick walls topped with wire as high again. The visitors' entrance was a utilitarian glass and steel door which Anna made her way towards, her heart beginning to pound. Inside in the reception area were the uncomfortable plastic moulded chairs found now in every corner of the world and people, mostly women and children, sitting around dejectedly waiting to be processed. They glanced at her and then away. The general air of poverty and weariness was almost tangible although several of the older black women were dressed up as if to go to church in suits and hats. There was very little chatting. Everyone seemed to be exhausted. Anna retreated into talking to Harry and hoped her lips weren't moving.

I'm sorry, sweetie, I just can't find anything to lighten up being here. Are our jails like this? I bloody hope not. We don't know, do we, and I suppose we don't really want to know. You just see the prison vans going by with their high square little windows and then you forget. There's a woman over there who can't be more than twenty but she just looks worn out. She's not even in jail, she's just visiting. Do you think Briony looks like that? Oh, she's got a baby under her coat, I wonder who she's seeing? Sister? Mother? Friend? Will she talk to me, Harry, or have I made a horrible mistake lying to her? I bloody wish I hadn't. This place is serious. This is not a place where you trifle with people – not that I thought I was. The road to hell, eh? Oh, they're calling the 11.00 o'clock batch. Talk later.

Ten minutes later Anna was shaking as she was ushered into another waiting room and told to sit.

Well, they certainly know now that I'm not a virgin. That was horrible and demeaning and disgusting. I'll never complain about airline security checks again. Why can't they get one of the machines that scan you? I am so angry and embarrassed and bloody *outraged*. And forget my fond thoughts of giving Briony her mum's letters – they were whipped away from me and locked up with my bags and coat and the gold necklace from you.

Now, we're being let in to the visiting area. Harry, I just can't begin to tell you how awful it is. The noise and the smell. What is that smell? It makes you feel like throwing up. A woman who's visiting saw me gag and just told me that her daughter is an inmate and she says that the loos their side are never cleaned and the walls are smeared with crap and worse and that half of toilet bowls are overflowing with vomit. It must be hell. Can that be true? They were bad enough this side but not as squalid as that. People are shouting at each other through these thick plexiglass grilles that are smeared with spit and stuff and they have to talk to the other person by phone and the phone, oh Harry, the phone is black with dirt and grease and you have to put your mouth right to it. I'm picking it up but there's no-one there yet. Oh, here she is. Briony is there in front of me – hair cut really short and as thin as a wet cat. Wish me luck.

The taxi driver opened the door for Anna, took one look at her face, and offered her a cigarette. She shook her head. 'Mint?'   Yes, something sweet and fresh in her mouth, that would be good. Was the smell on her clothes? She fumbled in her bag with shaking fingers and took out the aerosol spray she had bought at the hotel imagining it would make a nice little luxury gift for Briony. But that was this morning when the world was a different place. She sprayed her hands and neck and inhaled deeply.

'Bad, huh?'

'I had no idea.' She lay back, trembling, against the bench seat.

'No – you wouldn't treat an animal like some of them in there are treated.' He sucked his teeth. 'Worst jail in the US they say.'

Anna stared miserably out of the cab window. And I made it a hundred times worse, she thought bitterly. Her career was over, of course, but it wasn't that that twisted her heart until she almost wept with the pain. She had let Margaret Clark down in the worst way and turned Briony into a screaming demon.

'Same hotel?'

'No. Sorry. I'm going to the airport – O'Hare. Back to England.'

'That's too bad – you should see some sights – I mean, good sights, while you're here. Take in a jazz club – we're famous for the Blues.' Anna thought that the last thing she needed was to hear the Blues. Enough sorrow, enough tragedy and howling pain for one day, maybe for one life.

'Another time, maybe.' Anna thought about the customs form. Purpose of visit: business or pleasure? There should be a third box: cock-up. Shock, and bitter regret welled up and Anna bent her head and wept. The driver tactfully turned up his radio and left her to it.

There were hours to wait at the airport. She went immediately to the toilets and washed her hands and face repeatedly, then she found a small cafe off the main concourse, ordered a coffee and opened her laptop. She stared at the people passing by. There were families with skipping children, smart women tapping along in their heels and dragging fashionable designer luggage, men strolling casually in their expensive button down shirts and loafers looking beef-fed in the American style and they all seemed to be creatures from another planet. Someone laughed. Did they know? Did anyone from this world know about the squalor and despair she had just dipped into? She dropped her head. Who was she to be indignant about anyone else's callousness?

She stared at the screen longing for someone to talk to, longing for Harry to be in his right mind. Impossible to tell George or the children what had happened. She thought about her women friends and realised how long it had been since she had seen any of them. She could hardly spring this on them out of the blue and in any case what would be the point? It was too long a story and too bitter an outcome.

Anna opened her email inbox and Steve's name jumped out at her. Steve. She looked at the time and date and realised that it had only been minutes ago that he had emailed to say he hoped all was well. The thought that he was there at the computer right now, knowing the situation, needing no back story explanation was too much of a temptation. She started to type.

Half an hour later, her coffee cold and her hands trembling, Anna pressed Send and sat back, a shudder running from shoulder to legs down her body. 'Get you a fresh cup, Ma'am?' She nodded. But before the coffee came Steve had replied. 'I'll be at home Monday afternoon. Rest and then come to mine. Don't go into work, Anna, and don't phone them. We'll talk. I know you feel bad but we'll make a plan. There was no way you could have known what would happen, stop beating yourself up. A very large glass of red wine and a hug will be waiting for you and I don't make that offer to everyone! Steve.'

Anna dropped her head and covered her eyes to hide the tears. The email pinged again. It was George telling her all was well and that Harry and Ellis were about to help him build a funeral pyre in the back garden. 'Just practising,' he teased her, 'you don't get rid of me that easily.' Anna closed the laptop and sipped her fresh coffee. Despite her burden she felt a little better. Steve might be able to put it in perspective and there must be some way out – some way that she could make up for the damage she had done. She shifted in her seat realising that she was coming to rely on Steve perhaps a bit too much. Just a friend, just a friend in need she thought, but exactly what was the need and how deep did it go? Enough angst for one day for crying out loud.

There were still three hours to pass before the flight. She got up, gathered her bags, and went to look for a bookshop.

13

It was 9.15 the next morning before she got home feeling gritty and smelly and devoid of any sense of humour, perspective, compassion or sanity. Her body told her that it didn't like being woken up and hustled about at 3.00 a.m. She agreed with it. Please, please, she prayed to any attentive deity, don't let there be any crises. Please just let me get to bed. Harry appeared in the hallway looking crumpled but friendly and spoke directly to her. 'Do you want a cup of tea?' he said.

'Oh, Harry, I'd love a cup of tea,' she moaned, smiling at him. What a nice homecoming.

'I'd make you one but I don't know where they keep the teabags.'

'That's ok. I'll make it, I think I know. I'll make one for you, too.'

'Thank you. I take milk and one sugar in mine.'

'Yes.'

Harry wandered off into the sitting room and Anna leant back against the wall and rested her head. So there had been, against all the odds, an angel passing by to hear her plea because this was the best welcome she could have hoped for and she was grateful. Her husband may not know who she was but the interchange had been a facsimile of normality, a gentle memory of the life they had had, an ordinary moment of connection.

There was a bitter wind blowing down the canal as Anna got out of her car by Steve's block of flats. She was scrubbed clean after her long shower but too disorientated to dress up and put on make-up. In any case, it wasn't a social call and she wasn't in the mood for any kind of frivolity – sackcloth and ashes would have been more appropriate than jeans and a sweater. Nevertheless, as she waited for Steve to answer the door she pushed at her tangled hair in a vain reflex. What, after all, could Steve do or say? In the seconds it took for him to open the door she suddenly realised that she wasn't here for him to solve the problem, she was here because she wanted to be comforted like a scared cat looking for a lap, and that it was a dangerous desire. As the door opened she stiffened and inhaled a deep breath to steady herself.

Inside, the apartment was more humdrum than she remembered and she politely refused the wine and accepted green tea. Steve himself seemed preoccupied and barely glanced at her. It was as though they were both waiting for it to be the right time to talk about what had happened. There was only the recliner chair by the window and the huge sofa so Anna stood awkwardly, not sure where to place herself until Steve came from his bedroom with a bentwood rocker full of faded cushions and placed it at an angle to the recliner. She was grateful to him because this meant that they could talk without having to make eye contact or be turned awkwardly towards each other on the sofa. The rocker was a good size for her, supportive and yet yielding to her need to keep movement going to try to release the nervous tension. She could talk and gaze out of the window if she wanted, not at him. She piled up cushions behind her and sat back. He was, she realised with a small rush of admiration, a tactful man.

'Would it help to tell me again? I mean to talk it through now it's not so fresh?' Steve glanced at her but then put up his feet and looked obliquely out at the canal below.

Anna felt her face still and her heart begin to pound. 'She was so thin, Steve. Her skin was grey, you know the colour it goes when people never get outside, and her eyes just drilled through me when she came up to the window. It was as though she wanted to consume me. She picked up the phone on her side, it was so noisy I can't tell you, and she started talking straight away. No hello or how are you, just launched right into it. The only question she asked was if I was recording. Well, of course they wouldn't have let me take a recorder in but in any case I didn't need one because I wasn't who she thought I was.'

Anna stopped and stared out of the window fighting for control of herself. Steve waited. 'She said there was so little time she would tell me the worst first and then the other things but I must remember everything and quote her and tell the world.' Anna stopped again. 'She's being raped, Steve, by one of the guards, she says it happens every day - every day. A couple of others keep watch while it's happening.' And then Anna couldn't help it, she began to sob in huge wretching gasps. Steve waited silently. 'If she fights him he grinds his knuckles into her spine or bites her breasts – Steve – give me a minute.'

Steve got up and went away. She was only dimly aware that he had gone but in a moment he was back with a box of tissues and a small tumbler of brandy. She drank it and blew her nose.

'The other women don't help her because of her being a child-killer as they see it. They make it hard for her. She says she doesn't blame them because there isn't a moment she doesn't hate herself for what she did even if it was an accident that she killed him she was still shaking him, her baby, her own child. She said the women spit in her food and won't talk to her. There's only one who will who's round the bend and ought to be in a psychiatric hospital. Briony said that this woman would scream all night and sometimes eat her own excrement so they put her in a cell with Briony to punish her. And she's been in there for months, Steve, twenty months. And she's got another eighteen months to do at the very best because she filed an appeal. She was talking so fast, so loud so I wouldn't miss anything, it was like she was firing bullets at me.'

'Didn't the guards try to stop her?'

'I don't think they could hear her, there was such a din, but quite honestly I don't think they'd even care. I mean, nobody cares what the inmates think, nobody seems to care what happens to them. It's like they've been thrown out of the world into this hell where they live like rats.' Anna paused. 'The woman next to her was screaming abuse down the phone at this guy – her husband or partner or something I suppose and he was yelling abuse back. It was a madhouse.'

'And so -' Steve gently prompted. Anna closed her eyes.

'And so I had to break in to stop her, to tell her about her mother. Tell her who I really was,' Anna said slowly, the rush of her words turned to slurry.

'Yes.'

'I yelled that she had to listen to me and then I yelled that it was about her mother and that's when she went mad. She just totally lost it.' Although Anna was staring out of the huge plate glass window she saw nothing of the city beyond.

'What were your actual words, do you remember?' Steve asked quietly.

'I said, "I'm here about your mother," that's all I said. She just became this raging, spitting ball of fury. She shouted "Don't you talk about my mother, you bitch, you fucking cunt, don't you ever mention my mother!" She was drooling, spitting, almost foaming at the mouth. She had her face against that filthy glass, she'd forgotten the phone but I could still hear her. She screamed, "You go near my mother, you so much as think about speaking to my mother and I'll fucking kill you! You don't talk to my mother, you don't have anything to do with my mother you fucking journo bitch," and so on until they dragged her away.' There was silence for a moment while they both took a deep breath.

'So, you never got the chance to tell her who you were and why you were there?'

'No. Time was up and in any case she was gone.'

Steve got out of his chair and moved towards Anna. She thought he was going to try to hug her and thought she wouldn't be able to bear it but he didn't. He put his large warm hand gently on her head, not stroking her hair, just letting it lie lightly for a moment and she was back in her childhood home and it was night-time and she was safe in bed and George was saying goodnight and for a moment resting his hand on her head like a blessing as he did whenever she couldn't sleep. The years and the tension fell away and she felt her whole body and mind relax. She closed her eyes and let the tears come softly through and down her face. Neither of them spoke. After a moment Steve went away again and came back with a fleece blanket which he tucked around Anna kneeling at her feet. It was only then that she realised that she was had been trembling from head to foot.

Steve sat in the recliner and looked carefully at her. 'Are you ready to hear what I've got to suggest?' he asked. She nodded.

'Ted's on Cloud 9 at work. He thinks he can pull off a merger with one of the big London firms he's been trying to compete with and you couldn't pick him off the ceiling yesterday.' Anna looked confused. 'I'm telling you because he doesn't need to know what's happened just yet. He's forgotten all about you. You're entitled to a couple of days' time in lieu anyway because of working the weekend and then we're almost at Christmas and the week's break. What I suggest is that you do nothing for now until you're more up to it and then write to Briony explaining everything. You've done the main thing – you've confirmed she really is Mrs Clark's daughter – so the rest of the information can be sent in a letter. Write it on Harts letterhead so she knows you're telling the truth.'

'But I feel that I have a duty to help her – she thought I would be able to.'

Steve stroked his cheeks. 'I don't see how you can. You don't have enough information and you only have her word so an article would never be published in the press. But she's only got eighteen months to go you said? Well, surely it would give her some hope to know that she's got a good pot of money to start a new life – over here, if she wanted to.'

'The eighteen months is until a retrial but if she gets another guilty verdict she has years to serve. Not in Cook County, of course, but in a prison somewhere.' Anna looked up at him sadly. 'Yes, she'll have money but no mum to come home to.' Steve looked out of the window, his forehead creased with concentration. Anna felt a tremor of affection for him. He'd done his best and she couldn't think of anything that would help the situation either. Not for a moment had he been judgmental or sentimental but only kind and thoughtful. His plan was a good one. It would give her time to recover herself and in a letter she could properly explain and tell Briony how fond she had become of her mother even though she had never met her. She looked at Steve as he leaned forward, his hands resting on his long thighs and his oblong head with its thick mat of dark hair in silhouette against the huge window. He was wearing jeans and a much-washed blue sweater. He looked different, less controlled and more accessible.

'Enough about this,' she said. 'Give me a break. Tell me about something different from work if you don't mind. Did you go up to the Roaches at the weekend or was it too cold?'

He turned to her readily and his smile changed his face so that she felt almost startled by the animation in it. 'Yes, we went. We had some novices with us. We were just roping up and there was a downpour. I've never been so wet, even our armpits got wet! It was sunny when we unloaded the van so we hadn't put our raingear on and then one of those great black cumulonimbus blew up across Tittesworth reservoir behind us and the next thing was a megabucket of water all over us. It was ok though. We just got changed and waited in the van and then in two ticks the sun was out and the rocks dry or at least dry enough and up we went. A trifle cold but you expect that.' He grinned.

'A trifle cold. Mm,' said Anna, smiling with relief at the change of emotional tone, and pleased that he knew his clouds. 'George said it was bloody freezing while I was away and there were you lot scampering over the moraine in your Lycra.'

'More like fleeces and cords I'll have you know but I'm impressed you know the Roaches are moraine, Mrs Ames.'

'Ha! Very condescending! I'm not just a fuck-up, you know.'

She stood up and took the brandy glass and tea mug to the kitchen counter. 'Thanks Steve. I feel a bit more as though I can cope. You've been great.'

He walked with her to the door. 'Remember what I said, don't come in. Just phone Jane and tell her you've got some loose ends to tie up and you'll report to Ted after the holidays.'

'Oh I almost forgot.' Anna turned at the door and accidentally brushed against him. He stepped back as though he had been scalded. She registered the reaction and filed it away to think about later. 'Ellis wants you to come to see Aladdin with us. Wait, I've got your ticket here – no excuses. And we'll be having some supper at home afterwards which you're very welcome to come to as well.' He looked at the ticket.

'I'd love to come to the panto but can I decide on the night about supper?' Anna looked into his clear blue eyes and laughed for the first time, it felt, in weeks.

'Tactful *and* honest,' she said. 'And very wise!'

'I didn't mean...'

'I know. Listen Steve, I really want to thank you. You've helped me out of the Slough of Despond today and quite honestly, things being how they are, I don't know who else could have done. I'm back on my feet.'

Steve seemed to be mulling over what he was going to say next. Then he raised his head and looked her in the eye. 'You tried to be kind, Anna. It went wrong but you tried to be kind and that's rare in my experience.' Then the door was open and closed and she was outside and feeling that for all the neutral tone of his voice and the commonplace words a deeper intimacy now connected them.

Ellis was at the kitchen table with his laptop. He asked about Chicago and she told him what she thought would interest him, nothing heavy. He looked at her expectantly. 'So did you buy anything?'

'Oh no! I'm so sorry Ell, I totally forgot your Cubs hat. Look, I'll get one online.'

'No worries,' said her amazing undemanding son. 'Did you know that Wrigley field was donated by the chewing gum family?'

She looked blank. 'The baseball field, the home ground for the Chicago Cubs. It was donated by them.'

'Not too stuck up then?' Ellis groaned as always at her feeble puns. She sat down by him and used his groan as an excuse to rumple his hair. It was all she could do not to grab him and hold him to her and kiss his freckled face but she knew she couldn't. Such a surreal contrast between sitting at a kitchen table punning and chatting and teasing with a healthy, happy boy and the other reality – the dark side where Briony lived in her body and soul every minute.

'Do you want me to tell you how I'm going to appear, like, whoosh, out of the lamp?'

'Go on then.'

'Mr Shaw, you know, the Physics one, he's had me jumping off a little trampoline while he videoed it and he's going to project that on the stage and then I'll break through the digitised image -'

'Seamlessly.'

'Yes. Well, sort of. He says there's no need for the genie to be bigger than life size, that's just a convention of the narrative that we don't need to use.' Anna hid her smile. Her son was a sponge for a nice juicy bit of jargon. 'So I'll be the same size as the digital me if you see what I mean.'

'Yes, but how will the real you suddenly appear?' Anna leaned her head on one hand realising that she wanted to make this conversation go on and on so she wouldn't have to think, to remember and worry.

'Lighting. I'll be there all the time but then the light will go off the screen and come up on me.' He paused and absently stuck one forefinger in his ear and wriggled it. 'We haven't really got that far yet.' A thought struck him. 'Mrs Wright, you know, who's directing it, had an idea but I don't know if I like it.'

'What?'

'She says that the genie being trapped in the lamp by a wicked witch is like people in prison who get trapped by their crimes – you know, the wicked witch is the crime and-'

'Yes,' interrupted Anna quickly, 'I get it. So …'

'So she wants the lighting lot to do the shadow of bars over the scene and then full light when the genie's free.' Freedom as a trick of the light. If only it were that easy.

'Blimey,' said Anna, impressed despite being startled by the mention of prison. 'It wasn't like this with our school pantos. We were lucky if you could get someone to open and close the curtains at the right time.'

'And if some people remembered their lines,' said George coming into the kitchen and washing his hands. 'I know it's my turn for dinner, Anna, but Harry and I have been outside in that bitter wind for an hour and I'm starving. Let's get an Indian?'

'Yeah!' shouted Ellis.

Anna got up from her chair and went out to the freezer. 'It's all right, Dad, I've got a casserole in here that needs eating up. I'll stick it in the microwave.' She looked at her father in bewilderment. 'You've got leaves all over your trousers. What have you been doing?'

'Funeral pyre,' said Ellis. 'Mike's coming round to help after his homework. His mum said he can have the wood left over from the deck his dad made.' Anna pulled a plastic tub from the freezer and wrestled with the lid. There were some times that she felt George didn't need to be encouraged. The image of Len slid back into her mind for the first time for days. She paused in her tugging. What on earth to do about Len? George looked at her nervously.

'It's only a bit of fun. I'm ok. We could set fire to it to celebrate the New Year or something. I promise not to commit suttee.'

'I know Dad, but it is a bit unnerving. What's Faye been up to while I've been away?'

'Funnily enough, she's been brilliant. And she's got some orders for her Meerkat Mugger Head Hugger from the kids at school so she's been up in her room sewing away. You know what she's like about money. Sasha came over Saturday night but he left again after about an hour and she didn't go with him.' Anna looked at him hopefully as she put the casserole in the microwave to de-frost.

'Do you think she's going off him?'

Ellis muttered from the lap-top. 'Wish she would. He's so bossy and he doesn't even know how to play chess. I thought all Russians knew how to play chess.' Anna struggled between teaching tolerance and wanting to side with him.

'Well, be fair, we don't all know how to play cricket. We'll just have to see what happens.' Harry opened the door. His hair was full of twigs and leaves and his coat was sodden. 'Oh Harry – you're wet. Dad! You didn't tell me he was still out there. Come on, love, let's get you dry.' Anna grabbed a towel from the tumble dryer and rushed towards him. Too quickly. Harry backed off and raised his fists glaring angrily at her.

'Stop it!' he shouted, 'Go and play down your own end!' Anna stopped dead.

Ellis calmly closed his laptop and stood up. 'Dad, I'm going to watch the Eggheads – are you coming?' Harry looked bewildered and then lowered his fists and turned to follow his son. 'I'll put the fire on and get him to take his coat off, Mum. He'll be fine.'

Anna put the towel back in its heap and walked out into the back garden wrapping an old cardigan off the passage hooks round her as she went. The funeral pyre was barely as high as the dustbins. She shivered and looked up to the sky. Through a gap the moon shone pewter bright, edging the clouds with brightness like a child's drawing. She could just make out the shapes of bats flying between their roosts and she could hear the rumble of the distant motorway. Not for one second could she ever forget that in this same world Briony Bulowski was imprisoned by far more than bars.

14

When the doorbell rang Anna was relieved. Her assignment, which was due in two days, was at that stage where she had done the research (which she enjoyed) but now had to knock all the fragments into a structure (which she loathed). Even Jehovah's Witnesses might be a welcome break. But when she flung open the door she was less than delighted to see Len's unappealing face leering up at her. Why was it that he didn't seem to have the knack of smiling? He either leered or smirked. Probably unfair. Possibly not. She noted his sagging jeans rimmed at the creases with dirt.

'Len, this isn't a good time. I've got an assignment due and I'm just getting going on it.' But Len was the sort of person to whom this was as nothing. He came up the steps and put his face near hers. His skin looked like an uncooked burger.

'Mum's worse. I tried phoning your work and they said you were home so that's why I've come.' He peered round her head. 'Aren't you going to ask me in?' He smelled of mouldy laundry and stale body odours and Anna fought the rising nausea in her throat. Was he perhaps sub-normal? If so, she should reconsider all her nasty, conventional middle-class reactions to him, she chided herself. She stepped back and waved vaguely towards the kitchen.

For a large man he could move quite fast and he almost scampered down the short hallway and then stood in the kitchen looking round with satisfaction. She reflected that he did not seem prostrate with distress over their mother, if such she was.

'So what's happened?' She did not ask him to sit down.

'Cup of tea would be nice. For your bro!' He opened his mouth, swung his tongue out and leered again.

'Well, we don't know that, do we? I've only your word for it.' Anna remained standing and folded her arms. 'I'm not saying you don't know my mother because your information is good but that doesn't mean you and I are related. You could have met her in a pub and learned that much. It's not as though we look alike.'

'Your kids don't look alike – that means nothing – unless you've been sleeping around, of course. Are you like that our Anna, eh? Bit of a goer, are you?' Could this be any more unpleasant, Anna wondered, and then remembered visiting time at Cook County Jail. Her scale of the unacceptable had been radically re-calibrated.

'There's only two ways we can verify what you're claiming,' Anna snapped, 'DNA tests or taking my dad to meet your mum. I don't want to do it to him but I think that's what's going to have to happen. I'd have to tell him what you're claiming eventually anyway.'

'Anyone would think you aren't pleased to have a new brother. Bit common am I? Bit beneath you? You need to get over yourself.' He moved to her side of the table in a way she didn't like.

The front door slammed and Anna closed her eyes with relief. 'Dad? In here.' Len took a step back and looked uncertain as George and Harry strode into the kitchen loaded with grocery bags, several of them chinking Anna noted happily. This would be a two-glass evening. George looked at her enquiringly. 'Len, do you want me to introduce you to my father and husband or do you want to leave?' She put as much significance as she could into the words. Harry stared at the stranger and left the room. George looked from Len to his daughter trying to assess the situation.

'Don't need you to introduce me. I can talk for myself,' Len said, looking warily at George who was clearly on standby for some kind of confrontation. 'I'm Lena's kid. Her,' he nodded at Anna, 'half-brother.' George staggered a little and then pulled out a chair and sat down.

'Lena?'

'Your missus. Well, ex. You can't have forgot her.' Len had relaxed now that George was seated and pulled out a chair himself to Anna's annoyance.

'Of course I haven't forgotten her. She's still alive?' George seemed to be having difficulty breathing.

'Only just. That's why I've found Anna - to tell her that her mum's ill and asking for her.'

'You didn't say she was asking for me!' cried Anna, instantly rocked by a storm of emotion. Her mother, her mother whom she had dreamed of and fantasised about all her life was *asking* for her? Her heart pounded in her chest so loudly that she could barely hear Len speak. But was it true? There was still no proof that it was her mother, that Len was her brother.

'Yeah, she is.' Len turned to George. 'She's in the QE. She's on her way out and she wants to see her daughter. It's only natural.'

George was silent. He seemed to have been shocked into complete immobility. Anna thought bitterly that it would have been only natural for her mother to want to see her *before* she was at death's door but she smacked the thought away. Who knew what her mother had had to deal with?

George's voice sounded strangled. 'She's here? She's in Birmingham?'

'Of course she is,' Len said slowly as if to a small child. 'She always has been.' Anna's whirling thoughts froze. She had assumed that her mother had left the humdrum domestic life in the Midlands to travel and explore because why else would she leave? Surely it would have to be something exciting and amazing that would take a woman from her own child? Anna suddenly realised that this was the real reason she had not believed Len. Lena, described by George as a wayward, hippie-dippy, fun-loving mother, would never have stayed in Birmingham. If Len had been half-Masai she might have believed his claim more readily. She had been here all the time? She could have contacted George and seen Anna at any time? She clearly knew where they lived. Why didn't she? The obvious answer was too painful to contemplate. But she had to ask.

Anna tried to make her voice work. 'Why didn't she want to see me before? Or my dad?' George, too, must be feeling awful. Len leaned back in his chair and glanced around the kitchen.

'Ask her yourself.' He craned his neck to look behind him. 'There's no telly in here. I could get you a used one cheap.'

Following his glance Anna saw the time on the kitchen clock. Ellis would be home soon.

'Right. Give me the hospital details and I'll talk to dad. It's been a shock for us and we need to think about it. But you're going to have to go now, Len. I'm sorry to seem inhospitable but we just need some time and I don't want Ellis and Faye meeting you until we understand this situation a lot better. I'm not putting them through it until I know more and I've met your mother.' George was staring in front of himself clearly oblivious to them both so she opened the kitchen door and made an unmistakeable head movement to Len. There was no bloody way he was upsetting the kids like he'd upset her dad. He lumbered up out of the chair and followed her out.

On the front step he turned and regarded her mulishly.

'You got no manners have you? I thought you'd be pleased.' He narrowed his eyes. 'I thought you'd be grateful.' Anna began to shut the door.

'Sorry Len. Just give us time. It's a lot to take in.' They were the kindest words she could manage. 'I'll phone you.'

'She's not going to be around much longer.'

'I know. I'll phone you soon. Bye.'

She shut the door and leaned against the wall. She couldn't yet face her father so she turned into the sitting room where Harry was standing near the window gazing out. He turned slowly to look at her. Anna walked to him and couldn't stop herself reaching out her hand for him and, amazingly, he took it. Wordlessly she raised his hand to her lips and gently kissed his palm as she had done so many thousands of times. He let her do it and then softly pulled away. He looked kindly into her eyes. 'I'm sorry I'm not here,' he said. 'But it will be all right. Don't worry.' Anna stood very still letting the moment sink into her and then smiled.

'Thank you, Harry. Thank you.'

Ellis and Faye burst through the front door and Anna changed gear in an instant and shouted, 'Upstairs the pair of you and get changed! I mean it!' and mercifully they went. She made her way to the kitchen, put her arms round her father and together without a word needing to be said they went out to the shed to talk.

It was the next morning when the house was finally quiet that Anna sat down again to her laptop. Steve had shown her how to work in a split screen from a document map to the body of the text and she was quite seduced by how nicely it happened and how easy it was to flip back and forth. What wasn't so pleasant was the deep conviction that what seemed so orderly with headings and sub-headings and a neat synopsis for each section was actually illusory and the material lacked any real cogency. That was a phrase she heard quite a bit from her tutor. 'Lacks cogency.'

Anna pushed back her curtain of hair and let her mind drift to the moment last night with Harry. How sweet that had been and who was to say that there wouldn't be more such moments? She thought often and longingly of the poetry reading and how he had held her eyes. Even the memory made her viscera clench with yearning for him.

She got up from the table and went over to the dresser to look more closely at an old photo. It was taken when Ellis had been at pre-school and Faye was a leggy, wild-haired girl. Someone had snapped that picture on Porthminster Beach at St. Ives. Faye and

Harry were holding their bikes so they must have just come down from the harbour wall. There was Anna, who easily tanned, looking almost glamorous in her red bikini. Anna squinted her eyes at herself. Not a washboard midriff exactly but in and out in the right places and no embarrassing bulges. She reflexively sucked in her stomach and patted it wondering what she would look like naked now and pushed the thought away. Her hair was rising in the off-shore breeze, much shorter than it was today, but even that looked carefree and happy. Happy hair, hm. Getting soft Anna, she scolded herself and moreover you're sentimentalising the past. But they were happy. Not always, of course, there were plenty of tantrums and not just from the children but mostly, certainly mostly happy.

And so she allowed her eyes to turn to Harry in the photograph. She caught her breath. What a lovely man he was with his coppery, wavy hair and slim, strong body but the main thing was his face. The late afternoon light was shining in his eyes deepening the laughter lines and emphasising the planes of his cheeks and the wide smile. She could almost feel his arms around her like one was in the photo. Sometimes, when she was doing something ordinary like shopping or putting petrol in the car she would find herself near a man of Harry's physical type, a stranger, and she would yearn to ask, 'Can you just hold me for a minute? Can I just touch your skin?'

She had always loved his mouth – his full, crumpled lips. They're wasted on you, she used to tease him, running a finger over their pleats and folds, but he had bequeathed them to Faye. Her eyes found Ellis again and she glanced back and forward between the boy and his father. Fifty-fifty the consultant had said. A fifty-fifty chance with EOFAD . And Faye was equally at risk. She replaced the photo frame gently.

Reluctantly she went back to the table and her laptop but decided before continuing that she would start her letter to Briony. She had been rehearsing it in her mind for a couple of days and was angry with herself for not taking this route the first time. She could have broken it to her gently enough in a letter and then followed up with a visit. Instead she'd made things a hundred times worse. 'Dear Mrs Bulowski,' she typed and her phone rang. It was Steve.

'Are you at home right now?' he asked after checking she was all right. 'Can I come over? I've got something to show you.'

He had not been to her house before but she found she was relieved by his suggestion. His flat had become a little emotionally charged in a way she couldn't quite account for so it was reassuringly normal to have him visit her here in the family home.

When he arrived he tore off his coat without waiting to be asked. He was wearing black cords and a thick plaid flannel shirt.

'Goodness!' cried Anna, 'that was fast!'

Steve smiled at her while he swung off his back pack and pulled out a plastic sleeve with printouts inside. 'Wait till you see this.' He slid the A4's from the sleeve and laid them out on the kitchen table. They were newspaper articles. One was from the Chicago Tribune and the other from the Lakeshore Enquirer. 'I had an alert put on Briony's name just in case anything happened and these came through today.' Anna sat down and pulled the Tribune article towards her. 'The Tribune one was on an inside page, well buried, but the other one is a liberal-owned paper and they've been having a campaign to clean up Cook County Jail. Briony must have hooked up with one of their reporters.'

'Oh my goodness,' breathed Anna, rapidly reading the Enquirer article.

'They probably don't often get someone as articulate as her and with nothing to lose – no family to intimidate, not even a birth American citizen. They must be hoping the British papers will pick it up and shame the administration into doing something. Look, they've made a big thing of her being British until she married Bulowski.'

'Where was this?' Anna asked without raising her eyes from the page.

'Front page – banner headline.'

Anna looked back to the top and read it out loud, '"British Woman Claims Rape by Guard in Chicago Jail – Hell on Earth at Cook County"'. Then she read from further down the article, '"Rat and mouse bites were identified on Mrs Bulowski's arms and buttocks by a medical orderly who remains anonymous..." My God, Steve, rat bites? And look, they've found the ex-girlfriends' witness statements about Karl's previous violence that weren't allowed in evidence in court. This is amazing. When did she do this?'

'She must have contacted them almost immediately after your visit. Maybe you gave her the idea?'

'Mm. I don't think so but it would be a comfort if it was true.' Suddenly Anna threw down the piece of paper. 'Steve – I've had an idea. Don't let's just leave it to chance to see if the British papers pick this up. Let's put it out there ourselves.' Steve stared at her and they held each other's eyes for a long moment but there was only the excitement of rapid problem-solving, nothing more personal.

'Are you on Facebook?' he asked.

'No, but the others are. Why?'

'I'm not either and I don't want to be. I'm just thinking of the options. You could go the old-fashioned way and write to the papers – to their editors – but it's so slow and they might not bother with it. We need to use social networking. Do you have photos of Briony?'

'There's one of her looking lovely and happy at Mill Lane -'

'And there's the one of her looking miserable and haggard in the Tribune from the trial – the one they've published here.' Anna stared at him.

'So we could send the nice photo of her to the Lakeshore Enquirer with a bit of back story –'

'And someone could set up a Facebook page for her and ask for stories from other women who've been in US jails and then start emailing some activists –'

'Just a minute, Steve, about the Facebook thing, I don't want the kids involved in this.'

'Is your dad on it? Would he do it?'

'Brilliant. Of course he would – like a shot. Let's get him in here.'

George was into the blogosphere in two ticks. He knew that his Quaker friends got deeply involved in justice issues and improving penal conditions and his network leaped into life. Then there was a search of blog directories and a slew of possibilities opened up. Two hours later the three of them sat back in their seats and took a deep collective breath. Anna jumped up and pulled a bottle of wine off the shelf above the dishwasher. She raised it at Steve and George and they both nodded gleefully. When she was seated again Anna lifted her glass and made a toast. 'To Briony – justice and freedom.'

'Justice and freedom,' chorused George and Steve and the glasses chinked between them. Steve's phone went. He picked it out of his back pocket, glanced at the screen, excused himself and went into the hall out of earshot. In a few seconds he had returned and was pulling on his coat.

'I'm sorry about this but I've got to dash off. Really sorry.'

'That's ok, Steve,' George said, 'thanks for getting an old man's adrenalin going!'

Steve flashed a quick half-smile and almost forgot to call, 'Bye,' to Anna he was in such a hurry.

15

That evening Anna drove back to Margaret's house and let herself in. It was dark when she got there but she had set up lights on timer switches in the living room and the back bedroom and she was pleased to see that the house was unviolated – unlike Briony. An agent was supposed to be looking after it but Anna had had previous experience of agents so if she was passing she would stop and check the property herself. No-one had thought to ask for her key back. As she walked into the tiny hall there was a barely perceptible change of smell. The very slightest beginnings of staleness and mustiness. It was very cold.

Anna decided that she would come back in the daytime, open the windows and maybe even vacuum. She pursed her lips at the thought. It was not something she did a lot even at home but somehow Maggie's careful tending of her pretty little terrace house deserved a respect that her own untidy house didn't. Thank goodness the garden didn't need attention at this time of year. She walked through the house slowly, noting how differently she now perceived the tidy, stylish bedroom prepared for a lost daughter and grandson.

It all made sense now. Margaret had not known about her daughter's marriage, the horrifying death of her grandson, the trial and imprisonment, and Briony clearly didn't know even now that her mother was dead. She would never expect that a scandal exposed by a minor Chicago newspaper would ever make news in Birmingham in the UK. How desperate Briony's situation was and what a gamble she had taken. Could they extend her sentence if she made trouble? Would she be put through even worse torture inside the jail to try to shut her up? Anna closed the bedroom door and walked quietly downstairs into the sitting room.

There was the photo of Briony in the alcove in a silver frame, a broad confident smile on her face. It was clearly a professional photo and Anna wondered if this had been a birthday present. She took it out of its frame and turned it over. In Margaret's handwriting was the date 2.9.2007 and the proud legend, "Briony at the start of her degree at Birmingham University." Perhaps she planned to have a companion photograph done after graduation. The doorbell rang.

'I thought it was you,' said Joan, 'but I thought I'd better check.' Anna led her into the sitting room as the hall was too small for conversation. 'Are you any wiser?' Sadder and wiser, Anna thought, simultaneously wondering how much to reveal.

'Yes, we know quite a bit now about Briony. Where she is and what's happened.'

'Well it couldn't have been that hard. There must have been some way they contacted each other.' They both sat down, shivering slightly.

Anna looked at Joan's sensible but exasperated face and thought about the social networking storm they were hoping to create. 'I'm afraid it's rather shocking but I know that you care for the family so I'll tell you the facts.' Joan sat forward in her chair and looked at Anna alertly. 'Briony did get married to the man she went to America with but it was an abusive marriage. She tried to leave but he found her and in a tragic accident Donny was killed and she was blamed for it. She's in Cook County Jail in Chicago.' There was a moment's silence. Joan blinked rapidly.

'Did Maggie know?'

'No, she never did. Briony just stopped all communication with her rather than let her mother know what had happened. The time you saw them here, Briony and Donny, was the last time she had anything to do with her mother. She got married just afterwards without telling Margaret and then the violence really kicked off and I've told you the rest.'

'But Maggie kept going to America until just before she died?' Clearly Joan was not a woman to take information at face value.

'I know. She was looking for her. Once the address she had been at was no use she tried going to different cities and then back to Chicago to try to find some trace of her.' They were both silent letting the pain of Maggie's desperate search seep through their thoughts. 'She was actually in Chicago when Briony was being arraigned but she never knew.' Joan dropped her head and impatiently brushed away a tear. She was shivering more now. The room was freezing. She stared at Anna.

'So now what?'

'It's awful in that jail.' Anna decided not to tell Joan that she had been and seen Briony for herself and the terrible scene that had caused. 'And just today something new has happened. That's why I've come – for the photograph.' Joan waited, her fingers interlaced and gripping each other. 'Bri's contacted a newspaper in Chicago and told them she's been raped by a guard. The paper wants conditions at Cook County Jail exposed and Briony is putting herself on the line to do it. My dad and myself' (she felt she couldn't speak for Steve) 'are trying to get publicity to help her through social networking- ' Anna paused wondering if the older woman knew what she meant, 'and I'm emailing them this photo to show how Briony used to look. She looks very different now. I saw her photo when she was sentenced in the Chicago Tribune.' Anna took a breath. 'That's not the same paper that's supporting her.'

Joan's face was impassive, her thoughts turned inward. Anna waited, needing time herself to process the actions they were taking. 'I had no idea,' Joan said finally and there was a tremor in her voice which was normally so firm. 'Poor Briony, she always had a bit of a temper like her dad but she loved that boy and she would never have done such a thing deliberately.'

'She didn't. It was an accident. Karl, her husband, was very abusive and wouldn't leave them alone and there was a terrible fight one night and Donny got caught in the crossfire.' Anna looked at Joan's white face and regretted burdening her with the truth. What could she do, after all, but feel even more upset than she already was. Anna got up and sat down beside her on the sofa. 'I shouldn't have told you. I'm so sorry to have upset you.'

Joan looked at her sharply. 'Of course you should have told me. I was Margaret's friend and I've known Briony since she was a child. I'll tell you what I'm going to do.' Anna straightened her back in shock. She had had no intention of Joan doing anything. Not another cock-up for God's sake. What did she mean? A letter to the Birmingham Mail? A petition from the people at Safe n Sound? She relaxed. Well, it couldn't hurt. Joan was regarding her steadily, checking that Anna was paying attention. 'I'm going to Skype my son in New York. His partner is a well-known civil rights lawyer and he'll know the legal side of things because Bri's going to need some proper legal support if she's not going to get reprisals from those bastards in the penitentiary. They both campaign for Amnesty, too, and they'll have those contacts.' Blimey, Anna thought. 'Give me the details and I'll do it tonight. My Oliver used to look out for Briony. He was like her big brother. He'll be up in arms when he hears. If I give you my address you can email me the links as soon as you get home, can't you?'

Anna threw her arms around Joan and smacked a kiss on her cheek. 'Too bloody right!' she said. 'I love you!'

Joan stood and pulled her coat around her. She looked curiously at Anna. 'Why are you doing this? Why do you care so much? It's not part of the job, I do know that.' Anna thought of her long trip to America, the awful, scalding scene with Briony, her guilt, her feelings about the young woman and her mother and behind all that her worry about Faye and the unknown quantity that was Sasha who wanted to take her away from them.

'Because I have a daughter,' she said. Joan nodded. Enough said.

As though summoned by the power of maternal anxiety Sasha was installed at the kitchen table when she got home. Faye was tripping around the kitchen making eggy bread or 'French toast' as she was calling it. Sasha stood up when Anna entered the room and bowed his head briefly. 'Mrs. Ames,' he intoned, 'Good evening. I hope you are well.'

'Hi Sasha, hello Faye.' Faye flashed an intense look at her mother clearly signalling, don't start. 'So, will you be going home for Christmas?' she said, ignoring the signal and sitting down.

'Is not practical,' said Sasha, 'I will be leaving in May at end of course so no need to return before, for sure.' Anna felt confused and glanced at Faye who was furiously beating an egg and refusing to meet her eye.

'Oh. I thought you might be going away fairly soon?' Faye banged the frying pan down on the metal grille of the hob. 'I thought Faye had mentioned it?' Sasha regarded her coolly.

'That was Plan A. This is Plan B.' Anna had a brief memory of learning about the five-year plans of the Soviet era and repressed a smile. But Sasha had a question of his own. 'You have just travelled to USA?' Anna nodded and put herself on guard. 'To Chicago, I think?' Anna briefly nodded again. Were they in for a diatribe against wicked Uncle Sam? 'I have cousin there. Is great city. He says I should visit and maybe look for work when I have qualified.' This evening was clearly ear-marked for surprises.

'But don't you have to qualify in US law? Surely it's different in each country?'

'Oh, yes, in some fields like criminal. It is different from state to state. I am not studying this kind of law. I am in commercial law – import and export and this law is international.' Well blow me down with a feather, thought Anna, impressed despite this man's salacious intentions towards her daughter.

She got up from the table feeling exhausted and was about to wish them good-night when Faye, getting bored with her unfamiliar role as domestic goddess, slapped two pieces of eggy bread down on two plates and said, 'Who was that man?'

'What man?' Bloody Len, thought Anna. If he's been bothering them, I'll – but then she realised that there was nothing she could do to stop him. 'Who do you mean?'

'Pops said he was a colleague from work?' Oh, Steve. 'What was he doing here?'

'Dad didn't tell you?' Good, she thought. No need to tell Faye and Ellis about the campaign to help Briony yet – not until something had been achieved, if it ever was. No need to open the door on to that kind of horror until there was some hope to counter it. 'Oh, he's the IT specialist from work and he's helping me with a client whose case is a bit complicated.'

Faye's curiosity was unappeased. 'Why come here then? Why not do it at work?'

'You know I'm not going back in until after Christmas. He just wanted to bring me up to speed with some unexpected events.' Faye's eyes narrowed suspiciously. She cut decisively into her snack after zig-zagging it with maple syrup from a squeezy bottle. 'Why are you interested?'

'You seem to feel free to muscle in on my business.' Anna relaxed. So that was it. 'I am an adult you know. All my friends' mothers don't butt in on their private lives and put their mates through the third degree.' Anna thought of the countless conversations she had had with Faye's friends' mothers who, like her, worried incessantly about their daughters and interfered at every possible opportunity. 'You might be old but I've got my life to live and you can't stop me!' She jumped up and got butter from the fridge to make the eggy bread even better.

'Not affecting your appetite then,' Anna said drily, well-accustomed to this kind of attack and barely noticing it. 'I'm off to bed before I commit more mumsy sins.'

Sasha had finished his meal and now stood up. 'No,' he barked, putting his hand out to stop Anna leaving but not touching her. 'This is not how daughter should speak to the mother. This is your mother, Faye, you should respect. Apologise please.'

Anna stood still and waited with amusement for how Faye would respond to this rather tricky tactical challenge. Faye stopped eating and stared at her plate, considering. Anna imagined the options she was scanning: tears at being misunderstood by her beloved when all she had wanted etc.; anger at her mother for getting her into trouble with her beloved etc.; anger at Sasha for daring to criticise her etc. Just as Anna had thought this Faye acted on it.

'Don't tell me in my own house how to treat my own mother!' Faye yelled at him, her eyes blazing. 'Why doesn't anyone mind their own business!' and off she flounced, banging the poor old kitchen door and thudding up the stairs. Quite well-played, thought Anna, she's put him in the position of having to apologise to her if he wants the relationship to carry on. Also, heartening to see that romance hadn't put much of a dent in her spirit - as yet. She raised her eyebrows at Sasha.

'I'll see you out,' she said in a way that meant that access to Faye's bedroom was definitely out of the question, tiff or not. 'Wrap up warm.'

After he had gone the house was silent. Everyone was in bed and Anna got ready to go herself to her little single roost in the spare room. She walked about making a cup of tea to take upstairs, putting out lights and checking the doors. The excitement of the campaign they were starting to help Briony was beginning to fade. What impact could they really have? The woman could at this moment be suffering the consequences of her whistle-blowing. Anna's imagination quailed at what could be happening right now and she shook her head to get rid of the unwelcome images crowding in.

To drive them out she thought of Steve. She stood for a moment in the dark hall looking up the stairs towards the light on the landing. She had known he was skilled and reliable and that he had a sensitive side but today he had impressed her with his zeal. She had not realised that he was capable of passion. Steely Steve? When he had been helping George to get the word out he had been on fire. The blood was up under his skin and his voice had deepened with excitement. Briony was unknown to him and her tragic situation was probably common enough, sad to say, but he seemed completely committed to helping herself and George to fight for her.   He   had taken it on quickly and whole-heartedly and suddenly Anna could picture him gripping the gritty edge of a rock overhang, willing his body to overcome the danger and the difficulty and bravely struggle on.

Anna had noticed how muscular and tanned even at this time of year his arms were as they lay on her kitchen table, shirt sleeves carelessly rolled back, and how strong and shapely his hands looked as they pounced around the keyboard of her laptop. She shook the thought out of her head. It must be late, she told herself – time for bed and oblivion.

16

Ellis had been awake since 6.30. Anna had heard his alarm clock go off, crossed her eyes and gone back to sleep. An hour later she leaped up in bed in a panic. It was the day of the dress rehearsal for Aladdin and she had forgotten the turban. That had been her only job – to create a suitably lavish turban for what the family saw as the star performer. There had been internet searches by George, sketches by Faye (all rejected as more tranny than oriental by the textiles teacher doing costumes) and not a passing thought from herself who was supposed to be actually creating it. She scrambled into her dressing-gown and reviewed the possibilities. Her scarves, some of which were silk and quite colourful, which would be potential contenders, were in a drawer in Harry's room as it was now known.   Harry was rarely an early riser and she didn't want to risk frightening him by dashing in and pulling stuff out of drawers. What could she use for a mount? Fuck, fuck. She padded rapidly along to Faye's room instead.

'Get up!' she hissed, 'I've forgotten the make the bloody turban and it's the dress rehearsal!' Faye groaned and burrowed deeper. 'Wake up! You've got to help me! Faye!' Anna prodded her daughter's rump and then, in desperation, shook her. Faye lifted her head and looked at her mother stonily from under lowered brows. 'I know, I'm sorry, but please help. I can't get to my scarves and he'll be off in a minute. Have you got anything? Anything at all?' Faye groaned again but sat up.

'Bottom drawer, red, turquoise and pink satin.' She yawned hugely and rubbed her eyes. 'Can you see them?' Anna tugged at the jammed drawer and fell back as it sprang open. She scrabbled.

'These?' she asked, holding up a handful of brilliantly coloured shiny fabrics. 'These are your flags from that brownie competition!'

'He'll never know. Doesn't matter anyway. Right, now, tip out the wastebasket – that wire one,' directed Faye before another jaw-breaking yawn opened up her face.

'What?'

'Just do it, Mum. Now then, I'll find some pins. Wait a mo.' She leaped out of bed and rummaged around her sewing machine. 'Here.' Anna gazed at her in bewilderment. 'Oh just let me do it then,' and in what seemed like a moment Faye had bent the wire basket to the shape of a dome, swathed the flags round it and there was a confection of shiny colours. 'Finishing touch – watch and learn!' She tipped the contents of her jewellery box on to the bed and rooted among the pile. Within seconds she'd found a flashing glass clip in the shape of a butterfly that she wore at the back of her hair when it was piled into a topknot. She clipped it to the front of the trimmed basket. 'One more thing –' she was really getting into this Anna noticed with gratitude, 'There!' She had found a string of plastic pearls and looped them around the widest part of the creation.

'It looks fantastic, Faye!'

'Yup. Just sew it up where I've put the pins in or he'll deflate himself and disappear back up his lamp. Now can I please, please go back to sleep?' She threw herself on to the bed, pulled up the duvet over her head and was motionless. Anna regarded her with deep admiration.

'Mum? Mum, I need my turban – I've got to go *now*!' came an agonised shout from the hallway.

'And not a moment too soon!' She hugged the collapsed girl and gave her a big kiss. 'See how I need you?'

Anna showered and dressed in jeans and a warm sweater for the main event planned for the day. George was already on the laptop when she walked into the kitchen and peering closely at the screen, his glasses trembling on the end of his nose. He was clearly firing on all cylinders.

'Look, Anna! There's already been 43 hits on the page we set up about Briony and I've got masses of tweets from Friends about how to help. Some of them are journalists and they've given me their email addresses to send more info.' Anna put the kettle on. It would take thousands to have any impact at all but she didn't want to point that out. 'Some of them on the page are telling their own experiences – it's fascinating. Look this one!'

'That's great, Dad,' she said tipping coffee into the cafetiere, 'I'll have a proper read later and there's another way you could help.'

'Name, it my flower!' he cried gaily. Anna was amused and grateful for the way her problem was energising him. He seemed to have forgotten about Lena but surely that couldn't be the case? He also seemed to have lost interest in his funeral pyre which must be good.

'I'm going to the animal refuge, you know the one that Margaret volunteered for, to see if they can do some networking too for Briony. They were so fond of Maggie. I wondered if you're not busy if you'd like to come with me? Two heads and all that.' She sat down at the table with her coffee pot and mug.

'Well, I'd be happy to.' He paused thoughtfully and glanced at her out of the corner of his eyes. 'We can bring Harry.'

Anna felt a clench at her heart. She hadn't even thought about Harry. Since her abrupt awakening until now she hadn't give him one thought. How obsessed with Margaret and Briony and even, dare she admit it, with Steve, had she become that her own husband had become mere wallpaper in her life. It had been days since she'd 'talked' to him as she had done in her head ever since he had put her from him. What a biblical phrase, and yet one which exactly described what had happened. She no longer existed for him except for occasional flashes of recognition which she may have deceived herself about, but for *him* not to exist for *her* was a horrible betrayal. She dropped her head and stared at the circle of dark liquid in her mug.

'You've had a lot to think about,' said George quietly. So he had noticed. 'Here, check your emails while you have your coffee. I'm going to make us bacon sandwiches. Can't go out on an empty stomach in this weather – I'll get Harry up when they're ready.'

She could not even get her own husband up and dressed now. If she went into his room he jumped out of bed and backed against the wall but if George went he was unafraid and submitted to being helped to wash and dress. It distressed Anna more than she could deal with and she resolutely pushed the knowledge away but as always not before a second of anguish. She had seen programmes on television about dementia where the main carer was always the spouse. What was there deep in the marriage that had turned Harry against her? Had there always been a rift? Had she been kidding herself about the depth of their love? Why was it that she was the first of his family for him to be fearful of and not the last? She took a deep breath and forced the welling tears down. Self-pity would get none of them anywhere.

She pulled the laptop to her and tapped in her own account. Immediately, three messages from Steve jumped out from the list in bold. She read them in time order. The first was telling her about five blogs that might be useful – three journalists from UK national papers, one at Amnesty International and one by an international human rights lawyer based in London. The second was a short piece which Steve had written himself on Briony's situation with links to the Chicago newspapers' stories on her rape claim. He was offering it for George to use. Anna read the blurb carefully. He was good. He had the facts down, of course, but it wasn't just a bulletin, it somehow conveyed the desperation of the situation without being sensational or emotionally manipulative. Anna opened the final email, sent only this morning. It simply said, 'It was good to meet your dad – he's great. And so are you.' She sat back in her chair.

This is the moment, she thought, when it could all change. She felt a stillness in herself. What did she want? What could be possible? What was allowable? There was no doubt that she was attracted to Steve but of course she was. She hadn't had so much as a kiss, let alone sex, for over a year. She would probably jump at any male who was not a relative and still breathing if she spent enough time with him. Well, not Len. But then, he supposedly was a relative, horrible thought. She pondered the quality of writing in Steve's account of Briony's situation in the second email. He was not a person who threw words around loosely. He knew their heft. In a very subtle, very non-threatening or demanding way he was asking her a question in that final email.

Harry and George coming into the kitchen interrupted her thoughts and she watched her husband sit carefully at the table and then very deliberately cut his sandwich into quarters. 'Good morning, Harry,' she said, smiling, wanting an excuse to look at him, hoping he would look at her. 'How's things?' He glanced across at her incuriously.

'Wet,' he said. 'I was wet in bed.' She looked quickly at George who shook his head.

'You were a bit cold this morning. The duvet was on the floor when I went in,' he said to Anna, making his pot of tea, 'no wonder you were cold, Harry.' This was new. They had been told that at some stage Harry would mix up words and the wrong ones may come out. Anna's heart contracted with a spasm of pain.

'I'll put the heating on to background each night, darling, so it won't be so cold for you if it happens again. And maybe one of your thin sweaters to wear in bed. You could even go to bed in your dressing gown if that isn't going to be too hot.' Harry stared at his segments of sandwich in silence. George came to the table with a mug of builders' tea and his own bacon butty.

'Thanks, Dad,' said Anna, pulling the laptop back towards herself, 'that breakfast was a really good idea.' As always she felt defeated and excluded by Harry's refusal to engage with her. 'We're going to an animal refuge later, Harry,' she said to him, 'we thought you'd like to come. It's not far.' Harry glanced up quickly at George, his beautiful amber eyes opened wide in wariness. Wearily she added, 'George is coming. It's ok.' Harry's gaze dropped to his plate and he continued eating serenely. Anna opened the laptop and sent a brief email to Steve thanking him for the information and promising to pass on the statement. She made no reference to the third message from him.

As they bumped down the farm track to Safe n Sound the cacophony of barking started up. Harry, far from being frightened as she had feared, was looking eagerly out of the window at the frantic activity in the dog pound. Anna glanced at the steep wet roofs of the old farm buildings and the mud in the yard and was pleased she had thought of bringing rubber boots for them all. Diane was expecting them and appeared from the stable end with a large haybag slung over one shoulder. A much perkier-looking pony poked its head out of the half-door.

Harry could barely wait to put his wellingtons on before he was over at the dog pound smiling and talking to the animals who greeted him rapturously in the way of all healthy dogs.   Anna watched him while she pulled up her own boots.

She was surprised. His attitude to animals, especially domesticated ones, had come up when the children had wanted pets and he had firmly vetoed the idea. It was hard now to remember why since he was usually indulgent with them rather than firm – it was Anna who had to do the no-you-can't bit. Oh, now she remembered.

He had confessed to her that he found them frightening; he almost had a phobia about pets much as many people would feel about finding rats or spiders in the house. It seemed as though he was becoming a different person who no longer adored her but did now like animals. She filed the thought away to pursue later when she had time to think of what other behaviour was different, not just different, but opposite from before. If there were more things she would ask Mr. Shenouda about them at the next assessment.

George and Diane, against all the odds, got on like a house on fire. His slightly eccentric, poetical, whimsical take on life seemed to appeal to the tough and practical saviour of animals and her straight forward approach to all problems reassured George. Watching them chat together about the refuge Anna realised why. They were both people who had their passions and lived honestly and fully because of them. Unlike herself, she thought wryly, who needed all her energy just to get through the business of life – no passion on the horizon. They left Harry still socialising with the compound's inhabitants and went into the office for a cup of tea.

Anna smiled to herself seeing George glance round appreciatively at the grubby heaps of useful recycled items, the unswept corners and the curling posters pinned into unpainted wood. His kind of place. Diane would probably feel equally at home in his shed and for a second Anna contemplated inviting her to a Friday reading but the thought was dismissed as soon as it had arisen because George was explaining the purpose of their visit. Diane had, of course, known nothing about Briony's situation but was immediately fully tuned to the problem. She was well used to reports of suffering creatures kept in inhumane conditions. When George had finished and she had asked Anna some questions she sat back in her ripped swivel chair and sipped her tea.

'You're forgetting someone in all this – in your campaign,' she said.

'Who?'

'Briony herself. Does she want you to do this? Have you had any contact at all?'

Anna braced herself. 'I did go to see her in Cook County Jail,' Anna said, 'but I handled it badly and she rushed off before I had a chance to tell her about her mother's death.'

'She doesn't know about Maggie?' Diane asked, clearly shocked.

'No, I'm writing a letter –' Anna began. 'I can't contact her any other way. They can't receive emails.'

Diane regarded her intently. 'If you want my advice, don't *be* doing it, do it. Do it as soon as you get back home and send it express.' Anna blinked. 'Don't you see that if the press does take this up they're going to make a big thing of her mother's death because that's the pathos angle – that she was a British citizen and that her mother who didn't know anything about her situation has just died so she's all alone and being tormented in a foreign jail, etc. That's the angle they'll hook the story on. You know how the British press like to bash Americans. Otherwise it's just another US prison horror story and why would anyone here be interested?'

'Bloody hell. She'd hear it in the worst possible way.'

'Yes.'

George laid his hand over Anna's briefly. 'You can get it off today,' he said, 'nothing will have happened by the time she gets it. Even the people we've already contacted, they're not going to move that fast. You can send it express and it should get there within twenty hours.'

'I wasn't thinking,' Anna said, remembering guiltily what had really occupied most of her thoughts recently.

The office door creaked open and Bob waddled in. He sat at Anna's feet and raised his head to give her a serious look. She stroked him and introduced him to George. He looked questioningly at George. George looked back at him. Bob looked from Anna to George and back again and then lumbered to his feet and sat heavily on George's Wellington boot.

'Poor old thing,' said Diane, 'I'd take him home with me but I haven't got room for any more. It's too cold for him here with his arthritis.'

Harry appeared in the doorway. 'There's a lot of dogs out there!' he said approvingly. 'I like this place.' He looked at Diane. 'You've got a lot of dogs. Why have you?' Diane weighed him up.

'These dogs were badly treated where they were. They come here to be well cared for and loved.' She understands, thought Anna, she has sensed his reality. 'We have other animals here, too. Would you like to meet them?' Harry nodded eagerly. They all got up and went out.

The pony looked like a different creature from the matted, bony nag that Anna had seen on the day it arrived. Its coat was still rough with winter thickness but was clean and the flesh beneath was rounded and smooth over the ribs. But best of all were the pony's eyes shining out dark and bright with interest. It snickered when Diane touched its wrinkled black lip. 'Look,' she said to Harry, 'you can talk to horses through their noses as amazing as that seems.' She put her own nose close to the pony's and snuffed at it rhythmically.

The pony happily snuffed back. Harry was transported. He beamed with delight and tentatively reached out to touch the pony's neck. Anna watched him with as much pleasure as he had looking at the pony. Who knew? She hadn't seen him smile so much in months.

As they moved on to look at the cats, who were watching the party out of the corners of their eyes while pretending to be otherwise engaged with washing and napping duties, Diane fell back to be by Anna's side.

'Harry's your husband?' she asked, knowing from the introductions the answer. Anna understood the real question.

'He has Early Onset Alzheimer's,' she said, leaving out, as always, the Familial part of the phrase in a superstitious attempt to make it not be so. 'He never used to like animals – I'm amazed by how he's responding to them – it's wonderful to see him so engaged.'

Diane nodded. 'I don't know about early onset,' she said, 'but we sometimes take some of the older, quieter dogs into nursing homes and there are often residents with dementia. Some take no notice at all and some become very excited and pleased. I'm no expert but I've been told that some hang-ups people get because of bad experiences can disappear with dementia because the association, you know the memory link, has been broken.'

'So Harry might have been frightened by a dog as a child or even a baby and forgotten it in his conscious mind but been left with a fear of animals and that bad association has dissolved?'

'Could be. He's certainly not frightened of them now.' Anna looked for him and saw that he had turned away from the disdain of the felines and moved back with a grin to the dogs who greeted him as a long-lost friend. Bob waddled out from the shed, looked from one to the other of the visitors and made his way slowly across to Harry. Anna and George, it seemed, had not shown him sufficient appreciation.

'Is Bob in pain?' Anna asked, suddenly remembering how fond Maggie was of the dog and feeling bad that she hadn't paid any attention to him.

'He's ok if he's warm enough,' said Diane, following Anna's gaze, 'but this cold wind gets to him. I'm amazed he's come out of the shed. He's usually either in there or in a corner of the barn where his basket is tucked out of the draught.' She nudged Anna's arm. 'Look.' Anna turned back from Diane and looked at Harry again. Bob had pushed his nose into Harry's hanging palm to get his attention and Harry had immediately turned to him and was stroking his large brindled head with a huge grin on his face. Diane turned to Anna and looked her in the eye.

'After all,' she said, 'it's not as though you've got a busy life. A dog would be no trouble.' For a second Anna tensed and then realised she was being gently teased. Diane was quick-witted and had assessed Anna's daily load very expertly, and her joke was a way of saying that she understood. 'Just a thought.' She smiled at Anna in the affectionate way that some older women have. The wrinkles disappeared, the apples of her cheeks shone and her bright grey eyes twinkled. Anna melted. Her mother would have smiled at her that way, she felt, and was then jolted by the recollection that she may, at an outside chance, be finding out whether that was true very soon. She pushed the disturbing but exciting thought away.

It wasn't much longer before they made their way reluctantly to the car and said their goodbyes. Diane had a contact through a niece with a national newspaper's Foreign News section and she thought that Valerie might well be able to stir up general protest through her many church and charitable connections. She would have a word and Valerie might get in touch if she could help. What had happened to Briony was outrageous Diane agreed, but like Anna, her first thought was for Margaret and to try to do what she was not able to do to help her daughter who was in trouble so far from home. Anna hugged her warmly which brought a blush to the older woman's neck and she and George climbed in to the front seats. 'Don't forget,' George told Diane but before Anna could ask what Diane wasn't to forget, she didn't look like the forgetting kind, Harry called out from the open back door.

'Up you get,' Harry was saying. Anna looked across at the back and saw no-one. This was worrying. Diane slipped away from the driving side round the back and Anna saw in the rear-view mirror her expression change from puzzlement to amusement. She beamed again at Anna knowing that she could be seen in the mirror. George, who had twisted in his seat to see what was happening, turned back and raised his eyebrows at Anna. She got it.

'If that's ok with you, Diane, it's ok with me,' she said and after Diane had nodded and laughed they drove off with three hands and one tail waving goodbye.

'What a nice woman,' said George cheerily, 'she's coming to our next poetry evening.'

Anna smiled. 'That's great,' she said, patting her dad on the knee. They drove silently for a while enjoying the sight of winter trees lacy against the grey sky and fields with silver stripes of water in the furrows. When Anna glanced in the mirror, she saw Harry and Bob propping each other up in the back, both with wide smiles on their faces but mercifully only one of them slobbering.

'I haven't forgotten,' George said quietly.

Anna shot him a look. He seemed very serious, even sad. 'What?'

'Lena. Lenny and Lena. Can we talk about it later? What we're going to do?' And the benign mood from the visit vanished. Anna gripped the steering wheel tightly and nodded.

17

Ellis arrived home at 7.00 sweaty and exhausted and in the depths of despair. The dress rehearsal had been a nightmare, he said. He'd forgotten his lines and got shouted at. Aladdin himself had flung out of the rehearsal half way through saying he'd had it with school after his Moorish pantaloons had fallen down and all the girls on stage had instantly photographed this revealing event on their phones. The special effects smoke had been so enthusiastically pumped out by the pupil stage hands that everyone had disappeared from view and rolled about coughing and screaming until told to shut up by Sir who was clearly at his wits end.

Anna was thankful that she had thought to buy a celebration/consolation chocolate cake when she went to send the letter to Briony by express mail. That had, of course, cost an arm and a leg but there was no help for it and given her ineptitude over the whole Chicago visit she could hardly claim it back on expenses. Explaining everything to Ted was a disaster postponed not averted. She looked at Ellis's mournful, grimy face, now faintly tear-stained and produced the cake, a knife and two plates and put the kettle on.

'Isn't the dress rehearsal supposed to be a disaster?' she ventured, hoping this cliché wouldn't be the final straw. 'Doesn't it mean the performance will be fine?'

Ellis regarded her with age-old weariness. 'Not when there's no Aladdin it doesn't.'

'Well – *nil desperandum*, eh?' Despite himself, Ellis perked up.

'What?'

'*Nil desperandum*. It's Latin – it means don't despair.' He considered this, chewing a large lump of cake and letting, in his abandonment to what seemed to be life's inevitable tragedies, crumbs fall where they would. Anna thought about the crumbs littering the floor.

'We have a surprise for you.'

'I think I might have maxed out on surprises for one day,' said Ellis gloomily eyeing the cake and wondering if a second slice might be allowed.

'No - this is a nice one. I hope you'll think so anyway.'

'Ahhh! There's something touching my leg!' Ellis had leaped up from his chair and was looking about wildly. From under the table Bob emerged, muzzle covered with crumbs, wagging his tail furiously. 'It's a dog!'

'If it's ok with you all he's here for a while – the winter anyway.' Anna told him the story but he was hardly listening because he was on the floor with Bob tickling his tummy and pulling his ears and it was hard to say which of them was the more pleased.

Ellis suddenly stopped as a thought struck him.

'What about dad? You know how he is.'

'It was dad's idea – as you'd know if you'd heard a word I said.'

'Brill! Totally brill.' And normal Ellis service was resumed. Anna didn't risk asking about the turban.

She picked up her laptop and went into the sitting room to see if Harry was around. He wasn't so she put it on the coffee table and made her way out to the shed where George was making a great deal of noise knocking together some pieces of wood from the funeral pyre to make a rough kennel for Bob. She doubted very much if Bob was the outdoor type but smiled and approved anyway.

'Have you seen Harry?'

George looked up through a fringe of dishevelled white hair. 'Harry? Oh. I'm not sure.'

'Not to worry,' said Anna airily, worrying instantly, 'he's probably in the loo – I'll just have a look round the house.'

He was not in the bathroom or the bedroom but his Keruve watch was gone. Quickly Anna checked the GPS and there he was, a blip on the High Street. She grabbed her coat and shouting to George where she was going she ran out. It was now bitterly cold. If she took the car she might miss him if he was coming back by the lane and not the road so she ran the shortest way down the lane which cut through the park and on to the High Street. Outside the mini-mart was a group of people standing in a circle and watching as the security guard silently wrestled with her husband. Clouds of condensation steamed the air. She ran up. 'Stop it!' she shouted to the guard, 'He's not well, leave him alone!' but he took no notice.

She pushed through the crowd and yelled again but this time in the man's ear. Harry immediately stopped struggling and the guard, panting, knelt over him and spread Harry's arms out to the side.

'You know him?'

'He's my husband. He's not well. Why are you doing this? For God's sake, what has he done?' The guard, seeing that Harry was calm, stood up and indicated a torn giant box of dog biscuits that was spilling its contents over the pavement. Anna scrabbled in her jeans back pocket and found a ten pound note. She offered it to the guard. He shook his head and wiped his face.

'Can't do it. You'll have to sort it out with the management.'

Anna put out her hand to Harry who was still lying on the ground, a bewildered expression on his face. 'Come on, love,' she said, 'let's just go inside and sort this out. It won't take long. Don't worry.' Harry, still lying flat on the ground, looked at her sternly.

'I'm not going anywhere with you, madam,' he said, 'until I find my dog.' Anna fumbled in her pocket for her phone and avoided looking at the puzzled expression on the guard's face. She then shooed away the onlookers and tried without success to put her folded jacket under Harry's head. People were staring but now the fight was over there wasn't much to see.

Within five minutes George, Ellis and Bob were all there and Harry, who had folded his arms defiantly over his chest, sat up and smiled. While Anna talked to the store manager they fussed over each other and George wrapped a blanket round Harry's coatless shoulders. It was all sorted out in a few moments and they made their way home, Anna trailing behind. When they got home Faye had arrived with Sasha and the whole story of Bob and the shop-lifted biscuits and the rescue and so on was re-told to general hilarity.

As soon as she could do so without comment Anna slipped away to her own room. Once there she half-fell on to the bed and began to sob uncontrollably. Yes, it had all been very funny from their point of view but the look she had seen in Harry's eyes when she held out her hand to him as he lay on the pavement surrounded by strangers was not funny. It happened too often, it happened all the time. Why was he so hostile to her? Why had nothing of their relationship survived when he was comfortable with Ellis and even happy with George? The dog, Bob, had been the final straw. Even a stray dog meant more to him than she did.

She stopped crying and got up to look in the mirror. The sideways light from the lamp made her look even worse. She came to a decision. She brushed her thick hair back and twisted it up into a knot. In the bathroom she rubbed her face with a cold flannel, found some lipstick in the medicine cupboard and put it on. As she ran down the stairs she could hear laughter from the kitchen as Ellis kept up the entertainment by turning the dress rehearsal disasters into a good tale. It was 8.30 on a cold December evening.

'Just going to check Mill Lane,' she announced cheerfully, putting her head round the kitchen door, 'I haven't been for a while and I need to get something. Ok?' George nodded still laughing at Ellis. Anna got into the car and reversed out of the drive. Her head was empty of thoughts, she just drove. Half the houses in the neighbourhood were decorated with strings of lights and some with careering Santas. The tasteful residents had strung tiny white lights among their garden trees but Anna liked the brash plastic deer and the flashing blue icicles. Tonight she didn't even notice them.

When she arrived at Steve's apartment complex she sat in the car for ten minutes thinking. Then she phoned. He was there and yes, she could come up. He opened the door with a pleased smile and waved her in. 'Look,' he said, indicating the mess of papers and books on the floor grouped around the coffee table and his computer and smart phone. 'I've found all this stuff.' She stared dumbly at it all unable to speak. He stepped between the clutter and her eyes, forcing her to look at him. 'What? What is it? Has something happened?'

Then the tears fell again and she grabbed him and pulled him to her. She reached up and took his head in her hands and kissed him full on the lips and it felt so good that she couldn't stop weeping and kissing and holding him. Frantically, she began to loosen his tie, undo his shirt and then, slowly, horribly, she became aware that he was not responding. He wasn't fighting her but he wasn't responding. She let her hands fall and stepped away rigid with shame.

She walked to the window and looked out not seeing anything, wiping her face on the sleeve of her sweater. 'I'm so sorry, Steve,' she said quietly. 'I'm so embarrassed I don't know what to say.'

She saw in the window's reflection that he had come up behind her and then she felt his arms around her, crossing her shoulders lightly, so that they were both facing the window. For a moment neither of them spoke and the tears spilled again, as if they would never stop, down her cheeks. He lifted a warm hand and stroked them away. Then, with one swift, strong, sweeping movement he picked her up in his arms and gently kissed her forehead, rocking her slightly. She felt his power and relaxed into it closing her eyes and letting all thoughts go in the euphoria of being held and cradled. When she was calm he took her to the huge white sofa and sat down with her across his knees, still held in the circle of his arms. She lay against his crumpled cotton shirt inhaling the scent of his flesh and melting into the warmth of his body. Her need was so great that she could not lift herself or say a word. He stroked her hair and she relaxed in the very core of her being. Long moments passed. She could not bear to move, to break this safety and peace.

Somehow he had turned a crazy sexual assault from her into this miraculous compassionate sanctuary. Afterwards, when she was thinking about this moment she had no idea how long they had sat together but eventually he spoke. 'Anna.' She heard her own name from the inside of his chest cavity. She breathed deeply and sat up, reluctantly disentangling herself from him.

'Steve,' she began, 'I'm so -' He put a finger on her lips.

'Don't even think about apologising,' he said. 'I've wanted to take you in my arms for weeks, and when you come to me when you need someone to hold you I'm honoured.' She smiled despite herself at his serious tone. 'No, I am. I feel honoured. But if there is to be more between us I don't want it to be because you're desperate. If that happened you'd hate us both and I would have lost you.' He took one of her hands and held it against his cheek and again she felt the strength and warmth. 'I just want you to know that I care for you very much.'

Anna considered before she replied. 'And I for you.' Then she picked up her coat and went home.

Later, lying sleepless in her bed she thought it seemed like a fantasy, an escapist dream that she had had. How could he have known so perfectly what she needed when she didn't know it herself? She wondered again about his marriage and what had caused the break-up. He seemed on the face of it like a decent, kind and compassionate man but there must have been something. As it was he had handled things so well that they could still see each other but in an even closer way. The wild part of her that had longed for sex only three hours earlier had been completely silenced, at least for now. She had, it seemed, been desperate instead for the kind of protective, nurturing love that a married couple share in crises, not for sexual love, and he had somehow known that and not taken advantage of her passionate attack on him. How often intimacy gets confused with sex, she thought, but with Harry it had been all of a piece. That was then, she told herself, realising suddenly that her tears had, after all, come not from sexual frustration as she had thought, but from grief. Harry. With the realisation they began again.

They had chosen to go for the afternoon visiting time. Faye and Ellis, who still knew nothing about Len's claims, would be at school pretending, together with the teachers, in the last few days of term before Christmas to have real classes. Harry had come along too since he could not be left but was confused when they took a different route in the hospital from his usual visits. Bob was left at home, much to his relief. He was cosily tucked into a huge cut-down cardboard box from the shed which had contained the once-new washing machine and was resting his bones on one of Harry's old sweaters next to the radiator in the kitchen.

Harry stood stock still in front of the unfamiliar lift door and refused to move. George reasoned with him. 'We're going to see someone, Harry, we're going visiting. We're not here for your stuff, we're going to see – well – an old friend.'

'No,' said Harry. Anna and George looked at each other.

Harry stared at Len and then took two steps towards him and pushed him. 'Go away,' he said. 'Get lost.' This was so out of character for the 'real' Harry, as Anna had started calling the memory of him in her mind, that for a second she was disconcerted.

Len bristled and flushed. 'Len, just ignore him,' she said quietly, 'you know he isn't right.'

'He'd better not hurt my mum,' Len said aggressively.

'Of course he's not going to hurt your mum,' Anna snapped back, her own nerves tight as steel hawsers. 'He's just frightened because things are not happening the usual way and he doesn't know who you are.'

'Why don't you put him somewhere?' Len hissed, and it took all Anna's resolve not to smack him right across his fat face.

As they all stood staring at each other the lift doors slid back to reveal a young blonde woman with a stethoscope round her neck and an identity badge pinned to her shapely bosom. Her blouse was cut low and revealed her buoyant breasts. Taking in the group she fixed her look on Harry who was nearest and said with a smile,

'Coming in?' Immediately Harry turned away from Len and

walked meekly into the lift. Anna followed smiling wryly with George who was barely managing to suppress a chuckle. Some things don't get lost, it seemed.

The doors closed and the lift rose. Now that Harry was calm Anna's thoughts careered back to the matter in hand. She felt as though she was reining back a massive stallion of emotion. The stallion wanted to plunge forward and rush her to her mother and weep and hug and talk and be explained to and comforted after the restraints and yearnings of a life-time. But the possibility of a catastrophe, of her being not their Lena, not-mother, not the longed-for one, kept the reins tight and short. What would she say? Would Anna know instantly that this was the one? If she didn't, George would, wouldn't he? It had been a long time. Over forty years. Anna glanced at him and saw in his closed face that he was struggling too.

Her heart started to pound and she felt sweat break out on her back. The polished steel of the lift reflected them in a tense blurred tableau, staring ahead, braced for what was coming. Even Harry seemed to have picked up on the mood and had put his hand on George's shoulder for reassurance. She slid her hand under her father's arm as the lift doors opened.

Len lead the way to the ward and pushed the green button for a nurse. Within seconds the double doors were released and they were walking along a curved corridor. To the left were large single rooms with wide deep windows looking out on to south Birmingham. Through the open doors Anna glimpsed the low ridge of the Lickey Hills before Len stopped and turned to a ward on the inside wall. He didn't speak, he just lifted his hand in an odd, dismissive gesture and stood back as Anna walked slowly in. George mumbled that he would stay outside and come in later. Now that the moment had come he was clearly not coping. There were four beds in the room and only a brick wall could be seen through the window striped with vertical blinds. For a second Anna had an image of a US style jail cell. They stopped in the middle of the room.

In the bed nearest the door was a very old woman with sunken cheeks and yellow skin. She was deeply asleep. An orderly was trying to wake her to feed her and speaking necessarily loud.

'Come on, chicken, wakey wakey. Look it's your favourite. Come on, now. Just a bite. Just for me.' There was no response. Well, thought Anna, at least they're trying. Opposite her was a pale woman about Anna's age. She was awake and sitting up against a pile of pillows, a Kindle propped up on her tray. Anna smiled at her as she lifted her eyes briefly at the interruption they made. She smiled back with her lips but not her eyes. Anna turned swiftly to the next bed which was half-hidden by a privacy curtain. Len pushed past her and walked to the far side of this bed. Anna couldn't stop herself taking a step back. All she could see was the ridge made in the cellular blankets by someone's legs. She stared at them. Only Len's lower back and sizeable bottom could be seen outside the curtain as he bent over the hidden end of the bed. Anna heard him whispering.

'Where is she then? Tell her to come here.' The voice was rough but surprisingly strong. Lena had stomach cancer but the voice told of decades of heavy smoking. Anna swallowed hard and stepped forward and round the curtain. The effort of speaking loudly had made the woman cough and at first all Anna could see was the top of her head as she bent her face to her tissues and struggled for breath.

The hair was dyed dark but the parting showed bright grey. Anna fought down a sob. How piteous to be ill and helpless and have everyone see you like this, ungroomed, with your secret vanities revealed. Then Lena, her breathing calmer, raised her head and looked at Anna. Anna staggered and reached for a chair. Two oval faces with slightly hooded brown eyes and high arched brows gazed intently at each other. Two sets of full lips above cleft chins.

Lena's skin was aged and mottled with illness and her loss of weight had left wattles under her chin and hollows in her cheeks and temples but there was no doubt. This was her mother. They were mother and daughter. This is what I'll look like when I'm old, Anna thought, shocked to her core.

'Mum.' Anna could think of nothing at all to say. The face staring at hers was not smiling. She forced her own face to lift into a semblance of a smile and it felt as though it was cracking.

'Told you!' said Len. Lena turned to him and regarded him with contempt.

'Sod off for a bit, will you? I want to talk to my daughter.'

Her gritty voice was emotionless despite the insensitivity of the words. Len shrugged and pushed his way out of the narrow space between the bed and the wall. As though she was being programmed remotely, Anna picked up her chair and moved it round the bed closer but not too close to her mother.

'How are you?' An inane thing to say to a mother you have just met after an absence of almost your whole life but nothing else came into the void of her mind.

'Dying,' Lena snapped, obviously irritated by this conventional and redundant question. She studied Anna again. 'Yes, you're a looker. Just like I was when I was young. Fabulous bone structure. I could have my pick of any of the men in the club although I have to say that *I* knew how to make the best of myself. I was a dead ringer for Juliette Greco. You know that beat look – all eyes and hair. Not so horse-faced as her, though.' She peered at Anna more closely. 'The natural look does nothing for you – you need a bit of blusher.'

Anna blinked feeling as though she had slipped into some parallel universe. Make-up advice? She felt faint and slightly nauseous. She clung on to the only point of real information that her mother had given. 'Club?'

Lena looked away from her and sighed. 'It used to be a jazz club when I first went there – we had all the greats, it was like Ronnie Scott's, you know, in London, but then the youngsters wanted rock and then disco and it changed. Still lots of laughs.' She brightened. 'You might have been with your mates when you were a kid yourself? Down on Barford Street?'

Anna felt herself to be totally adrift. 'No,' she said faintly, 'I don't think so.' There was a pause and Anna looked round for Harry. She could see him through the ward window next to George. Suddenly she wanted to be anywhere else but here.

'You were probably off at university, weren't you?' There was the hint of an amused sneer in Lena's voice. 'George would have wanted that for you since he was too bloody idle to get it for himself.' Lena made an effort to sit up a little. 'Where is he anyway? I thought he was coming?'

'He'll be here in a minute.' Anna selected the safest one of the swirling questions. 'Did you work at the club?'

'Bloody hell, woman, you seem obsessed with it. I would have thought you'd have something more interesting to ask me after all these years. Yes, I worked there. Len's dad owned it and I was his PA. Well, obviously a bit more than that.' She twisted her lips and narrowed her eyes. 'You don't need to look down on me you know, we did all right. Education isn't everything. I've made a success of my life.'

The chaos in Anna's head began to clarify. In the first three minutes of conversation with her mother in her entire life the woman had implied that her daughter was a drab and a snob and a failure.

Anna stiffened her back and lifted her chin. 'I'm sure you have,' she said, 'and so have I.' She made herself stop there.

Against the odds Lena smiled. The first smile. 'Well, I'm glad to see you've got a bit of spirit, girl. Glad to see you've got a bit of me in you and that you're not all wet and weedy like your dad.'

'Dad is not-' Anna began furiously and then felt a hand on her shoulder.

'Hello Lena,' said George. 'Long time, eh? Give me a minute, love, will you?'

Anna jumped up and was out of the room in a second. She strode up and down the corridor trembling with rage and disappointment. Automatically she checked for Harry but he was staring contentedly out of the large window of an unoccupied single room. No need to ask now why Lena had left her husband and daughter – no mysterious complex psychological diagnosis needed. No ideological crisis. Certainly no bloody existential angst. Lena had been bored with them both. She was just bored with them. Anna realised that she had been waiting all her life for a massive apology, braced for it, ready and eager to forgive and let bygones be bygones.

Or, on gloomier days, she had imagined her mother had had a mental breakdown of some kind, perhaps a victim of the seventies drug culture, and that Anna would rescue her from pitiful self–loathing and restore her with love and nurturing. Bullshit. Her mother had left because she found them boring. Far from self-loathing she seemed self-admiring. And the last thing that Anna had imagined was that her mother would find her abandoned daughter wanting. Would find her dull and conventional. Anna wheeled into the room where Harry was and joined him at the window. 'Bloody good thing you did piss off, you fucking selfish bitch,' she said.

'I'm afraid I'm going to have to give you a detention for that, young lady,' said Harry glancing at her with disapproval. She stared at him and they both looked back at the view. They were silent for a while. 'You can see that place with the trees.'

'Frankley Beeches.'

'Mm.'

George found them. His expression was unreadable. 'Had enough for today, I think,' he said and there was no question implied. They followed him out and walked quickly down the corridor to the lift. Len was coming towards them with a cardboard tray of coffees and plastic wrapped cakes. He stopped and looked startled as the three approached him. George flapped his arms without slackening his pace. 'Another time, Len,' he said gruffly and Len had to leave it at that.

18

The sound of their own front door closing behind them was bliss. Then Ellis called his dad into the sitting room to watch Flog It and George and Anna went on down the hall into the kitchen. Anna made straight for the kettle.

'Um,' said George. She looked at him. There was an expression in his eyes she had never seen before and she turned the tap off to concentrate.

'Dad?'

'Do we have to talk about this? This Lena thing.' It was fear, she realised, fear and a bit of shame, that look in his eyes.

'No,' she said firmly, 'we do not.' His face relaxed and his shoulders straightened. He brushed a strand of crinkly grey hair off his forehead.

'Thank the good Lord for that,' he said. 'I'll be in the shed.'

Anna nursed her mug of hot tea and checked the phone. There was a text from Steve saying, 'How goes it?' She had told him about Len and Lena. She thought about texting back and then checked the other messages. She didn't need to talk to her poor mashed-up dad about the visit but she did need to talk. She pressed his number thinking he would be wrapping things up at work. Only one more day before the week's Christmas break. How would she have coped if she'd had to go in and deal with Ted as well as everything else? She felt a rush of gratitude for his practical thoughtfulness.

'Hi. Ok?'

'Oh, Steve, not really. It was not as you might say, the usual tv script.'

'No.' A pause. 'It often isn't.' Another pause. 'Drink at the Old Hen?'

'I'd love to – really I would,' she sighed, ' but it's Ellis's last night before the panto and he may need a bit of support and I have to cook anyway. You are still coming?'

'Wouldn't miss it for anything.' Anna could almost hear his mind working in the pause that followed. 'I'm always here, you know.'

'I know. And honestly, Steve, that means a lot.' Just hearing his voice made her feel better but she wasn't going to tell him that.

'Oh, what about the Briony campaign? I haven't had a

chance to check the page or emails or anything.' It would be a relief to think about something else. Briony must have got her letter hours ago so she must now know about her mother.

Mothers and daughters. As she thought of Maggie, Anna realised that her fantasies about her own mother had even included her. How wonderful to find that your mother was warm and kind and loved you despite everything. But of course Margaret would never have left her child for the reasons Lena did. Sometimes Anna had even wished she had been dumped on a doorstep as a baby. At least then you knew that your mother must have been desperate and unable to cope in any other way and hoped she was giving you a better life by abandoning you. But Lena had known Anna for three years. She had known her as a person and still walked away. Anna felt both hollowed out and filled with pain. Like a bloody great ulcer. She forced herself to listen to Steve.

'Oh, George has done brilliantly. He gave me his password so I can access what's happening without having to open my own account. It's mainly because of the stories that other women have posted on the page. It's probably because they can do it anonymously though not all of them have. So far there are over a dozen that were incarcerated in the States and three of them, if you can believe it, from Cook County. They're real horror stories. Even allowing for exaggeration it's like the lid has come off a cess pit.'

'But has there been any reaction in the US press? That's what we really need.'

'I can't find any yet and I've got alerts out so I should know when it happens. When you get a chance have a look on the Facebook page and check the links to the blogs and who's tweeting about it. George has put his blog on Technorati so it's getting a lot of exposure. It's happening.' There was a pause. 'Anna?'

'Mm.' She liked to hear him say her name. She remembered how she had heard it echoing in the cavity of his chest as she lay cradled against him.

'Remember. I'm always here. Any time. Try to get some rest.'

She put the phone down but as she pulled her laptop towards her across the kitchen table the door quietly opened and Ellis slid in.

He looked subdued. 'Hi genius,' she smiled at him.

'Mum?'

'Yup. That's me.'

'Are you busy?'

Anna pushed the laptop away again and turned towards him – her non-demanding, polite son. The only one in the world apparently so she'd better make the most of him. 'No, love. What do you need?'

He twisted his face at her.

'Lines?' He offered the grubby, crumpled script.

'Sit yourself down.' Ellis pulled out a chair and sat facing her. She studied his tense foxy face. He was trying so hard to be cool but he was worried sick. She reached out and touched his hand.

'You're so like your dad, you know. When he was a kid.'

Ellis grinned at her and then asked the one question she wasn't prepared to hear from him. 'Will I get what he's got?' No, not now on top of everything else. She swallowed and considered. A scientific explanation? An easy reassurance? Bloody hell.

'Don't know,' she said.

'Ok.' He sat back in his chair and gripped the edge of the table, revving up. 'Start at Act 2, scene 1 because I know it up to there.' As Anna found the page she smiled to herself, amused by how two carefully constructed scenarios that had for so long dominated her thoughts, meeting her mother and how she would explain EOFAD to her children, had been smashed to pieces in one day. No tender reconciliation with the long-lost mother and no shocked and traumatised boy.

An hour later Ellis had relaxed and Anna was thinking about dinner. There was nothing in the freezer and not a lot in the fridge. She decided that after the day she'd had the idea of going to the supermarket and then cooking was just not on. 'I think we all need a bit of a treat,' she said. 'You can choose a takeaway -' Ellis brightened – 'if you'll go outside and take the order from Pops and phone it all in. The menus are behind the pasta jar. You know what your dad likes.'

'Deal! Can I have a pud too?' Nothing like seizing her in a weak moment.

'Go on then. And while you're at it you can order me an ice-cream,' Ellis was almost out of the back door, 'or a sticky toffee pudding.' The door smashed shut. Anna winced. Then there came a crash from the front of the house.

'What's for dinner?' Faye yelled from the hall. 'I can't smell anything.' She rushed into the kitchen and flung bags down in her corner. 'I'm absolutely bloody starving.' Anna stood up and hugged her. She smelled young and fresh and sweaty. 'Mum? What are you doing?'

'Ellis's ordering a takeaway so you're just in time. He's out getting your Grandad's order. We're splashing out and having puds too.' Faye pushed herself out of Anna's arms.

'Oh no, Pops will want Indian and I'm too hungry to wait for all his bits. Ellis!' and off she dashed, her caramel and honey coloured hair flying. Shouting could be heard. 'I won't *want* bloody tandoori when I'm in Russia you idiot! I won't be able to get Triple Delight either will I?'

Anna's smile faded. She sighed and walked slowly out of the kitchen. Harry was asleep on the sofa. She climbed the stairs to the bedroom feeling as though her legs had run a marathon. She hauled on the banister. In her little room she peeled off the day's clothes and pulled old fleece pyjamas from a drawer. So what if it was early. Then she lifted her hair and brushed and brushed it and let it fall softly around her face. She took her dressing gown from the hook on the back of the door and pushed her feet into slippers. When she had changed she went to the make-shift dressing table and scrubbed the apparently inadequate make-up from her face. Yes, it was her mother's. What was the difference, she wondered, between a free spirit and a selfish cow?

She studied the face. When did it start – the way someone was on the inside showing on the outside? She remembered the laughter lines at the corners of her mother's eyes but also the downward drooping mouth. She made her own mouth droop and stared at that. It wasn't good. Maybe her mother had been nervous, too. Maybe the criticism and superficial patter had been a smoke screen. Hard to meet your abandoned child on your own death bed, surely? Perhaps she, too, had been struggling. Anna let her mouth curve back up and stuck her face almost to the mirror glass. 'OK, you old witch,' she breathed, 'We're not done. I'm coming back and you'd better just lump it.'

'So then Sash told me he said to the others in his class,' Faye was announcing as Anna entered the kitchen, 'In Russia students work hard not like here where all you do is play.' She gave it the accent and, Anna noticed hopefully, had a bit of fun with it. 'Of course they all gave him the finger. They know he goofs off as much as they do.' She stood up. 'I've got a test tomorrow – last one. Shout me when the food gets here.'

Anna looked at George. 'Do you think she's going off him?' George held up crossed fingers. She had to tell him. 'Dad?' He looked at her warily. 'I want to go and visit Lena, mum, again. I want to try to get to know her a bit before – you know. Do you mind?'

George sat down heavily at the table. He put his head into his hands and massaged his bald patch with his fingers. When he raised his face and looked up at her Anna was horrified to see that there were tears in his eyes. 'Lena. There's never been anyone else for me. Not really. And she's never wanted me – that's the tragedy of my life. If she hadn't been pregnant she would have been gone the minute we got back from Egypt. She only stayed for you but in the end she couldn't do it. She didn't leave you Anna, she left me.' Anna went to him and put her arms around his bent shoulders. 'It was me that let you down.'

'You've never let me down for one minute,' Anna whispered into his ear. 'And just think what my life would have been like if she'd taken me with her. You saved me from growing up with Len – a fate worse than death, eh?' She could sense him beginning to smile. 'I think it was her that got the raw deal, not me, Dad.' She hugged him tighter. Another thought had struck her. She remembered Lena's calculating, mocking eyes. 'Can you imagine how she would have coped with Harry?'

'Straight to the institution and no messing!' he admitted. 'I'd forgotten how scary she is.' The doorbell rang and Anna rooted for her purse in her bag. 'I think this one's on me,' said George giving her a smacking kiss on the cheek. 'We'll eat to fight another day, my dear.'

That night Anna woke at 2.15 groaning at the red numbers in the darkness. She listened for a moment to see if anything particular had woken her but the house was quiet. It was the turmoil within that had catapulted her back into consciousness. How many things do I have to worry about, she mused. How about a list? It was a short but frightening one: Briony's horrific situation and how she had to help, Harry's deteriorating brain, Sasha spiriting Faye away, Eliot and Faye's potential genetic timebomb, money or rather lack of it, Lena – oh God, Steve. Oh, Steve. No, she wasn't going to think about that.

And she'd forgotten Ted on her worry list. Losing her job would just about put the kybosh on everything. She groaned again.

As if it had been waiting to jump out as the anti-hero from the chorus of the Greek tragedy of her worries, the essay for her diploma which had been due yesterday leaped into her mind. 'Shit, crap and bloody hell,' she said. But it was the only thing on the list that she could do anything about in the middle of the night. She got up, pulled on a sweater and crept downstairs to the kitchen table and the laptop. She opened the assignment document and stared at the daunting split screen. Mm. Maybe check the emails first.

The one from Briony was top of the list. B. Bulowski, Cook County Jail Administration. She sat up and peered at the screen and then clicked the message.

Mrs Ames,

I have received your letter sent by express. I can only assume that you are as incompetent at your job as you are at breaking bad news. Why did you pretend to be a journalist? What possible good could that have done? Your explanation doesn't make sense. I am heartbroken that my mother has gone but I would rather have heard it from a corrections officer than from you. I am totally alone here and in a bad place. I am being bullied and demeaned and I have been repeatedly raped. Now you tell me I am alone in the world. Thank you. You say your job is to look for heirs and connect them with their inheritance. No doubt you get a good fee for this. Well you must know as well as I do since I presume you have poked round my family home that we are not wealthy and I am astonished that your agency would send you to Chicago on a foolish pretence. I will certainly contest it if the expenses for the misguided trip are taken from my inheritance. I shall be contacting them when I am able to complain about your tactics. My mother was a wonderful person and I hope you have respected her home and possessions and have not precipitately disposed of anything without my permission. I do not see that any further communication between us is necessary at this point but when I am released I will be contacting your employers.'

The email was sent with a message which said it could not be replied to.

Anna took a deep breath. Then she quickly brought up the letter she had printed off and sent to Briony. She scanned it and moaned. She had forgotten to say what the estate was worth. Had she not known about her mother's inheritance? She was distressed but not surprised by Maggie's daughter's anger towards her. Every word was true although possibly not the 'sizeable fee'. She'd probably be out of a job anyway by the time Briony stormed in. Her fingers hovered over the keyboard as she was tempted to write a letter in reply but she let her hands fall. There was no point. There was nothing she could say and a reply would be blocked anyway. All she could hope was that the campaign would do some good or at least keep vengeance at bay.

In the corner of the kitchen something was rustling. Anna froze. Then Bob lumbered out of the darkness towards her and sat heavily on her feet. She bent down and pulled his ears gently and stroked his warm head. 'I'm making a bit of a hash of things, Bob,' she whispered. He licked her hand. She brought up her assignment. It was 3.10 am.

By 6.00 the thing was checked and ready for the post. It wasn't brilliant, Anna thought, but it would do. Marine records had never been a strong interest but she appreciated the need to know how to access military data and the factual nature of the assignment had calmed her. Even the sting from Briony's hostile email had eased. What mattered today was only one thing – the success of the genie in Aladdin. Anna closed down the laptop thinking what she would do with three wishes. As Ellis had so rightly pointed out, the first wish should be for a million more wishes. That would just about cover it.

She decided to make everyone a proper breakfast and got up quite composedly to de-frost the bacon before the pounding on the stairs would begin. Four days to Christmas.

19

Harry had been very quiet all day and had been particularly avoiding her, or so it seemed. But he had come along and sat pressed in by Sasha and Faye on either side in the back seat of the car and had not complained. In fact, it seemed that Sasha was the uncomfortable one and Anna noted as she checked them in the mirror that he was trying not to be in physical contact with Harry.   Faye   was   as   usual lolling against her father. Anna was amused by the thought that Faye was probably so easy with Harry because, like her mother, he really hardly existed for her these days except as background. None the less, it hurt that she, his wife, could not have that relaxed contact. It had been a physical pain, the craving for that, but since Steve had held her she thought less about it. Was she using Steve as a surrogate for Harry? Yes. She was. Was it just a coincidence that Steve almost sounded like Harry, coming from the same county? That he was energetic, competent and, let's face it, physically fit and strong? And attractive. No, it wasn't. Was she trying to force her work colleague into the Harry-shaped hole in her life? Despicable. She had only ever made love with Harry. According to national surveys that was some kind of record.

He had known her body so well. He knew the way to arouse her by kissing the soft place under her chin and then sliding down to lick her nipples into rigid cones of pleasure and then turning his whole body and spreading her legs and –

'Mum! The lights were on red! What are you doing?' screamed Faye from the back. George snapped out of his doze and for the rest of the journey Anna concentrated on her driving.

Ellis's school was on its best behaviour. The staff on greeting duties were shiny and fragrant so they must have been home between this and the working day, Anna thought. In fact, everyone was looking scrubbed up and excited. The assembly hall was packed with chairs and she was relieved that as one of the cast's family they had reserved seats near the front. Anna looked round and saw Steve hovering uncertainly at the back. She waved and beckoned. It was a relief that she could introduce him as a major prop-provider and colleague and no questions would need to be asked. She noted the guilt implied in the thought and blushed. She sat him next to George since they had Briony's campaign to talk about together and then put herself between him and Harry who had Faye and Sasha to his right.

She thought about Ellis waiting nervously in the Green Room (aka the gym) and hoped the turban would stay in one piece. Smiling at Harry, she felt proud of the sizeable group they made to support Ellis.

Harry was silent but unusually alert, craning his neck one way and the other to take in the wall displays and the tables set out with refreshments for the interval. Does it seem familiar to him, Anna wondered. The comprehensive school he had taught at was much larger but the atmosphere was fairly similar. She remembered a talk he had given to the community as part of an ecology awareness drive and how proud she had been as he'd presented the dry information with humour and animation. She let her shoulder lean slightly against his but he immediately withdrew and she sat up straight. The temperature in the hall was rising and as the house lights went down and as the curtains parted she was incensed to note that Sasha had inserted his hand between Faye's thighs. At least she was wearing jeans. All faces turned to the stage.

There is nothing like a school show when your own child is involved, thought Anna, smiling idiotically at the opening scene. For sheer enjoyment they beat most professional performances into a cocked hat. You can see the joins in the set and the little orchestra off to one side sometimes play a wrong note and yes, the kids were probably screaming up and down the corridors half an hour ago and some poor teacher was breaking the speed limit to pick up a forgotten instrument but now, now the moment had come, no-one wanted to let the thing down. Aladdin, persuaded back into the production by finding that the phone photos had created a fan club, strode around confidently with a large leather belt round his waist while fresh-faced oldies looked bizarre but eager with their painted-on wrinkles. The director had clearly told them that all old people stoop so they obediently bent themselves over and pottered about oohing and ahhing as though their backs hurt. It was a delight and the best was yet to come with the appearance of the amazing genie.

Some time later, with the heat in the hall beginning to be uncomfortable, Anna became aware of some fidgeting to her right. Faye was hissing at her through her teeth. Anna glared and made a shushing gesture but then she saw Faye's eyes slide meaningfully to her own left. Sasha withdrew his hand. Anna looked at Harry. He was agitated. His face was contorted with anxiety and he was making small sounds. Beads of perspiration were breaking out on his forehead. She looked back at Faye who raised her eyebrows and shrugged slightly meaning she didn't know what the matter was. Harry was now shifting in his seat. They were right in the middle of a row and George, the only person who could really calm Harry, was on the other side of Steve. Anna nudged Steve gently, smiled apologetically, and reached across to George, mouthing, 'Harry?' George immediately leaned forward and peered at Harry while Steve instinctively drew back but looked too.

What was upsetting him? Anna looked back at the stage and there was nothing except a bunch of kids acting and then she saw a tiny wisp of smoke coming from the left side of the stage. It had been a minor part of Harry's job at his school to liaise with the fire service over all productions. She knew that the genie was about to leap out and the smoke would be from the smoke-machine – perfectly safe – but Harry didn't know that. She turned to Harry to try to reassure him but at that moment the stage went dark and then came flashing lights, the astonishing digital projection of Ellis, a huge bang, and a cloud of pink smoke out of which leaped the genie unrecognisable in costume, turban and swarthy make-up.

Harry reared up in his seat and yelled 'Fire! Fire! Everybody out!' and began to lunge across Faye and Sasha to get out. He was panicked and among the chaos Anna, following him, heard the yells and exclamations of the people at the end of the row as he stepped on feet and knocked heads and shoulders with his sharp elbows.

They scrambled after him. But it was not the exit he wanted it was the fire extinguisher against the wall. He was tugging at it like a madman while the production froze and some people in the audience tittered in embarrassment and some complained loudly.

Before Anna could reach him, Ellis was there. He must have jumped off the stage and run to his father. He shouted, 'Dad!' and Harry turned as he approached. Harry stared at him for a second and then let go of the fire extinguisher, grabbed him and held him tightly.

Ellis released himself smiling into his father's face to reassure him, and then turned to the audience and said very loudly and melodramatically, 'Be not afeared! The king of genies is here, freed from the curse of the wicked witch and if you play your cards right it may not be only Aladdin who gets his wish!' He strode forward and pointed dramatically at a large lady in pink. 'You Madam! Tell me your heart's desire and I may grant it if I so choose!' The woman tittered uncertainly. 'Speak up! What is your secret wish? Fame or fortune? What is your desire?' Seeing herself in the spotlight the woman played up to Ellis.

'I wouldn't mind a massive win on the lottery,' she said, and there was a laugh.

'And you, Sir,' went on Ellis to John Bryant, Mike's dad, who he'd spotted near the front. 'What is your dearest wish?'

'Well,' said John understanding the situation and joining in good-naturedly, 'could you magic our Mike into cleaning his room? I'll know you've got super-powers then!' The laughter was louder and the audience's eyes followed Ellis as he made his way back on to the stage and the clearing smoke. There was a smattering of applause. George was shepherding the confused and trembling Harry out but gestured to Anna to stay and watch the rest of the show. Sasha was nowhere to be seen and neither was Faye. There was nothing she could do and Ellis would definitely want her to stay. He had leaped back on to the stage and was facing a dumb-struck Aladdin.

'Aladdin!' cried Ellis folding his arms majestically, 'You rubbed the magic lamp and released me and now I am your slave,' and they were back in the script. Anna and Steve, not wanting to disturb people again, leaned against the wall by the door and watched.

'Great kid,' Steve whispered. 'I bet half the audience think it was deliberate.' Anna smiled at him gratefully but thought not. She could see people muttering behind their hands and glancing at her.

Harry was becoming more bizarre, more unpredictable, and she and George might sooner than she'd hoped have to make some very hard choices.

At the end of the show the genie got especially loud applause and Anna could see that Ellis was thrilled. She waited in the entrance hall with Steve, as all the families were instructed to do, until he was ready to come out and be congratulated and taken home. Mike's dad came past and patted her on the shoulder. 'Great improv, Annie. A star is born, eh?' but his eyes were full of sympathy for her and she knew she didn't need to say anything. She managed a smile. Mike squeezed through behind his dad.

'Hello, Mrs Ames. It was wicked wasn't it? Tell Ellis not to forget his game when he comes round tomorrow.' She nodded and smiled again. Steve turned to her.

'It wouldn't be right for me to come back. Harry may still be upset.' She sighed with appreciation for his sensitivity. 'You've got a lot on your plate Anna.' He was slipping his coat on and looking out at the night. 'See you after Christmas.' Anna put a hand on his arm.

'Come.'

'What?'

'Not now. Come for Christmas dinner.'

He looked uncomfortable and stared at the ground. 'I don't think -'

'Please. I want you to.' He looked up at her with a questioning expression. She tried a shaky laugh. 'My family always behaves better when there are guests.' What am I saying, she thought wildly, why am I asking him this? He obviously doesn't want to come and who can blame him? 'Look, sorry, it's fine.'

'Ok,' he said, still looking puzzled, 'if you're sure.' And suddenly Ellis appeared, makeup smeared and still in his costume minus the turban. The elation seemed to have faded or maybe he was just tired. 'Hey, well done, mate,' Steve said, 'You did the lamp proud.' Ellis, automatically polite, flashed a mechanical smile at him but then turned to his mother.

'Is dad all right? Where is he?'

'Yes he is, but he was confused – thought he was still in charge of fire regulations!' She tried to sound jokey but Ellis ignored that. 'Grand-dad's taken him home, they'll have enjoyed the walk but I'm sure they're sorry to have missed the rest of the show.' She grinned at him. 'You were great.'

'It was fun but it was just a school panto,' said Ellis quietly as though he were forty not twelve. Anna felt the familiar dread squeeze her heart. 'Can we go now and see how dad is?' She turned to say goodnight to Steve but he was gone.

After lunch the next day, the last of the school term, Anna put the dirty dishes in the dishwasher and went to find her father.   She could hear him pounding his computer keys before she knocked on the door. He always treated it like a manual typewriter and the keyboard had to be regularly repaired. 'Dad? Can I come in?'

'Yes, of course. I'm just emailing a reply to that nice Mr. Shenouda.' George was bristling with energy, his corona of white wispy hair vibrating.

'A reply? To what?' Anna cast her mind back to see what she might have forgotten. 'We're not due to see him yet are we?'

'No, but you remember I was asking him about the Coptic Church?'

'Were you? When?'

'You remember – he's an Egyptian Copt just as I thought.'

Anna sat down on a pile of leaflets. She was pleased to see that George was cheerier but irritated, as always, about this nonsense with collecting religions as though they were stamps. 'So?'

'He's invited us all to a service!' George was pink with pleasure. 'It's on a Sunday so we should all be able to go, shouldn't we?'

'I think it might be a bit much for Harry, Dad.' She paused.

'He's getting -' What was the word? Worse? 'He's getting a bit unpredictable. I think we should be careful about putting him through too many strange experiences.'

George glanced at her sharply. 'Why? He was fine at the animal sanctuary, wasn't he, and that was completely new? No, I think it's the quasi-familiar that disturbs him. It was the school atmosphere that set him off at Aladdin, don't you think? And at the hospital it was because he was familiar with it that the change of direction bothered him. No, I think this Coptic Church will be very interesting.'

'Well, you could be right.' Anna sat back and pondered her father's odd hobby. She shouldn't make him feel guilty about it and she tried not to. After all what harm did it do to look for an unknowable supreme being in smells and bells and whistles? Better than drink or gambling (she remembered the greyhound racing adventure), or picking up women. She smiled at him. His confession about Lena being the only one for him all his life had surprised her but when she thought it over it was true. He had had no girlfriends, no lovers that she knew of. Every now and then he would go on a date that some friend had arranged for him but always came back early and shame-faced and refusing to talk about it apart from a vague description of the woman as 'very nice but not for me.'

'Anyway, I didn't come in to talk about that,' she said. 'I'd like you to show me what's happening with Briony's campaign when you've got a minute.' He smiled at her.

'Any more coffee in the pot?'

'I'll make some fresh and check Harry's put his watch on. Five minutes?'

'It's a deal.'

When George brought up the page for Briony's campaign, as they were all now calling it, he craned his neck forward to peer more closely at the screen. His eyes were wide. Story after story was listed, some with photographs and some with links to websites.

'Wow!' As they read, more horror was revealed. It seemed like it was random whether an inmate got a clean, well-ordered prison or a hell-hole. One woman had been taken off in shackles to give birth and chained to her bed while she went through labour.

There were repeated accounts of guards, often working in a group to avoid detection, molesting, abusing and raping inmates.

Eventually George and Anna became quiet, their excitement subdued by the catalogue of suffering. After twenty minutes Anna touched her father's hand. 'I can't take any more of this. Can we go out of it now?' She chewed her thumbnail. 'Is it really going to do any good, Dad? I mean, it's awful, all this, but will it help Briony?'

Anna went back into the kitchen and picked up her own laptop to take out to the shed. She opened her email account and brought up the message. 'Look at this.'

George read the email and studied Anna's face. 'She doesn't know you. She doesn't realise why you did it.'

'I tried to explain, but the road to hell and all that –'

'Did you write back?'

Anna indicated the 'no reply' message. George looked thoughtfully out of the window. 'Don't abandon the idea. She's angry now, of course, because she's grief-stricken and wanting to lash out but letters may be a good idea. Margaret wrote to her didn't she? '

'Letters that were never sent because there was no address to send them to.'

'Yes. But you have an address now.' Anna stared at him.
'You mean send her her mother's letters? That could really push her over the edge.'

'I'm not so sure.' George hesitated. 'I've never told you this but I've found letters very moving and healing myself.' He looked down and traced a circle on the faded old carpet with his slippered foot.

'Letters?'

'You know my dad was killed in the war?' Anna nodded.

'Well, I never knew him, of course. Mum was pregnant with me when he was torpedoed in the Indian Ocean. I asked about him, naturally, but you know how she was with words – she was never a talker. She'd just say things like he was a kind man and then she'd change the subject.' George absent-mindedly tapped his fingers on his latest collection of poetry in proof form which was near the old computer tower. It was as though he was wondering where his own love of language could have come from. The cover was in monochrome; the title, *Absent Without Leave* written in a ghostlike white Perpetua font over an 18th century etching of a brain. 'Well, after she died and I was clearing out the house – you were at university – I found a box of letters. Just an old chocolate box. They were from my dad to my mum. You know, during the war. Before he was killed.'

Anna said quietly, 'You've never mentioned this before.'

'No.' George roused himself from his thoughts. 'They were very ordinary, no big revelations, just what you'd expect.'

'But?' Anna prompted.

'I got a feeling for the man. The tone of them, you know, the way he expressed himself. He was very affectionate but more than that he was funny, well, witty I should say. He knew how to describe things, how to bring ordinary things to life. He loved words. '

'Like you do.'

George reached out and patted her arm. 'Yes.' He was quiet but there was clearly more he wanted to say. Anna waited. 'It was the last letter, the last he ever wrote or sent – it must have been just a day or so before he was blown to smithereens.'   George paused, clearly deeply moved. 'He must have just heard from mum. He knew she was going to have me.' The tears were beginning to well up. 'He was so pleased and excited. He said he wasn't worried about the war now because there would be no honour greater than being my father and he was going to make damned sure he survived to do the job justice.' They sat for a while in silence. 'Letters from the dead, Anna, are very powerful.' He sighed and wiped his eyes and said, 'Let's see what's happening with the blogs.'

As George was bringing his up Anna's phone went and she fished it out of her back jeans pocket. It was Steve. 'I'm just doing it,' she said, 'we're checking who's tweeting dad. The stories on the Facebook page are horrific. I couldn't take too much.'

'I've got news.'

'What? What's happened?' Immediately Anna thought of Ted and that he was on the warpath. Had Briony managed to contact him to complain despite saying she'd wait until she got out? If she lost this job what would they do? As it was they were hanging on to the house by a thread. George's pension and Harry's disability plus Ellis's child allowance would never cover even the bills let alone the mortgage.

'It's front page in the Lakeshore Enquirer and a small article - naturally, they don't want to look like vindictive idiots - in The Tribune.' His voice was excited.

'What? What is?'

'They've picked up on our campaign. And there's some high-profile names involved so Joan's New York contacts must have come through in a big way. Even George's blog is listed but no worries, no-one will make the connection with you through that because the last names are different. It's 7.00 a.m. in Chicago and the story headlined in the first morning news bulletin on Channel 7. The page has had five and a half thousand hits in the last six minutes!' Steve's deep voice was resonating with exhilaration right in her ear.

'Television? What? You're kidding!' Anna joggled her father's elbow. 'Go back to home, Dad. '

Steve said, 'Ironically, it's not so much the abuse and rapes that have got people going -'

'How do you mean?' Anna interrupted, pushing against George and scanning rapidly, her finger on the mouse clicking the link to the Lakeshore Enquirer.

'- it's the rat bites! That's really caught the public imagination. Rats in an All-American jail? But obviously the whole story's out there in a much bigger way than before because, look, they say it in the first column, because of the British campaign!'

'America's shame,' read George out loud, 'British anger at the treatment of one of their own in House of Corrections horror.'

'Steve! They want to get Briony re-located! They're starting a public outcry about Cook County and they want to get her to a decent women's prison to serve out her sentence!' Anna was scrolling rapidly. 'What did The Tribune say about her?'

'Oh you can imagine,' laughed Steve, 'despite Mrs Bulowski's tragic crime, America has always been known in the free world for its sense of justice and decency and something must be done to punish the wrong-doers – that sort of thing.' Anna snorted.

'They're even talking about a Christmas reprieve.'

'Let her out?' Anna mouthed astonishment at George who was watching her face avidly and listening to every word.

'Well, probably not that, maybe commute the sentence. The public loves that kind of gesture if they've taken someone to their hearts and, let's face it, the prison doesn't want to be sued so they'll try to get her to do a deal.'

Anna promised to talk later, ended the call and brought George up to date. Smacking her dad lightly on the back in congratulation she walked outside to clear her head. She sat down on the green lichen-encrusted bench and hugged herself. It was cold but sunny and the sky, when she raised her eyes to her old friend, was Wedgwood blue with tiny balls of white fluff scudding across very high. Cirrus floccus, she remembered, great name. In the distance was the dull groaning of city traffic but nearby, only metres from her, was the piercing trilling of a blackbird. She shivered and smiled and scuffed her slippered feet in the dry leaves blown into a small drift against the bench. No-one could wreak vengeance on Briony now. She couldn't be touched. 'Happy Christmas, Maggie,' Anna couldn't resist saying out loud to the huge bowl of blue above her.

She got up, shivering already with the cold, and went back in the shed. 'Dad? I'd like to thank Diane and Joan, and the others – make sure they know how big it's got.'

'Done.' He was typing furiously with two index fingers.

'Although they are almost certainly following all this themselves.'

'Right. Good.' Anna left the shed and ducked into the house feeling even colder than she had realised. Her teeth were chattering.

She dropped to her knees and wrapped her arms round Bob's thick neck. He was warm and welcoming but smelly. She patted him and addressed him formally. 'It's no good looking like that – you have to have a walk and I have to think about Christmas food much as it's all very exciting about your old friend Briony and all that.'

She unlooped his lead from the hook by the back door. Bob politely wagged his tail but indicated his cardboard-box bed hopefully.

'Nope – we both need the exercise.' She clipped the lead to his collar, struggled into her all-weather green jacket, wrapped a scarf round her neck three times, and made for the hall and the Wellington boots. She put her head round the sitting-room door and smiled at Harry who was sitting passively in front of a chat show.

'Walk?' Harry made no move to acknowledge her. Missing in action indeed.

20

As she strolled slowly towards the park at Bob's pace Anna reviewed the Christmas present situation. She and George had felt that both Faye and Ellis were old enough to know the facts of their financial situation to the extent that money was tight. Very tight.

Faye's job at the Thai restaurant paid for her bits and pieces and nights out and Ellis was generally pretty undemanding but something had to be done about presents and George had had the brilliant idea of Promise Presents.

On Christmas Day they would all (excepting Harry and Bob) give each other a Promise. Anna already knew that Ellis's promise to her would be to clear the front garden of weeds and litter because he had stopped her doing it only yesterday. In addition, they would buy each other something small. The rules were that it had to be from a charity shop of which there were at least half a dozen in the High Street and it had to be under £5. Anna, it was understood, would do the shopping for Harry, too, and George would do Bob. Ellis had the option of making something instead since he was the only one with no income except his pocket money. Anna started guiltily as she remembered Len and Lena. Christmas presents? As Bob waddled off to sniff the latest offerings laid on the litter bin near the park gate Anna decided that she would invite Len to their Christmas dinner and take Lena some cake and mince pies or something. Surely that would be about right? So that meant there would be seven of them for dinner, eight if Sasha came as he probably would.

So what about Steve? No, it would be completely inappropriate to give him a present – but maybe a promise? Anna shoved the thought away roughly. But, it would be good to have him sitting down at the same table as her family. She remembered his unease at the panto and how she had pretty much bullied him into the Christmas dinner idea. Never mind, it should be fine and he already knew George. It would be so great if he became a regular visitor, wouldn't it? She raised her head and stepped out enjoying the sparkling lemon light and sharp winter shadows. Christmas. Even to an agnostic like herself there was something special in the air.

People who moaned had only themselves to blame. It didn't have to be all money and worry and work. She for one, despite everything, was looking forward to it.

Steve's call came at 9.30 am on Christmas Day when she was getting the turkey ready for the oven and George was dodging around her to produce catering quantities of pancakes, bacon and eggs and tea. Ellis was up and dressed and out with Bob and even Faye had got herself downstairs wrapped in her huge pink fleece dressing gown, eyes ringed with smudged mascara and yawning massively. 'Go and get your dad, love,' Anna called to her, massaging chestnuts into sausagemeat, 'He doesn't need to get dressed till later, just make sure he's warm enough.' She flapped her sausage hands at George when the ring tone went. He picked it up from the dresser and pressed the call key.

'Hello Steve! Happy Christmas, mate.' Anna started pushing the mixture into the turkey. Suddenly she felt dull. Steve was going to cancel. 'OK, I'll tell her – see you later.' She raised her eyes to George's face questioningly. 'He's coming for an hour or so around midday but he can't stay for the meal. His mum's just phoned and his dad isn't too good so he's going up early to Derbyshire.'

Anna's heart recovered. 'Right. He was planning on going up to theirs tomorrow anyway. I hope his dad's ok.' George was laying the table and gave her a sideways look.

'You're becoming good friends, aren't you?' he asked. When she didn't reply he went on. 'I'm not saying anything, Anna. I'm glad. He seems to be a decent sort of man. You could do with a friend.'

'Dad, there's nothing going on,' Anna said shortly, wrapping the bird in foil. 'Just leave it.'

It had all been going so well. Delicious smells drifted from the kitchen, Harry and Faye were playing Ellis and Sasha at tiddlywinks which Faye had found in the Heart Foundation and given to her dad. It was perfect for him and he was smiling and flicking the counters with abandon while Faye made up a fictitiously high score and Ellis commentated on the whole thing like a football match. 'And he's coming in to a flick, yes, it's definitely onside -' Sasha whooped and leaped in the air as the counter plopped into the egg cup. 'Goal!' Anna, watching them from the hall door, grinned. It was even possible to like Sasha in this mood despite his hateful plans to abduct her daughter. She went back to the kitchen and poured a festive dry sherry for herself and Steve, not that she really liked it, but tradition is tradition. He had arrived with offers of help to make up for having to rush off later and was peeling potatoes and lobbing them into the pan to par-boil. She got back to the sprouts.

'I don't think it's serious,' he was saying, 'dad just gets a bit moody sometimes. Well, depressed, I suppose – starts remembering things.'

'Christmas is such an emotional time,' Anna agreed, checking the turkey.

'Mm. Have I done enough?'

She checked the pan. 'All this work and you're not even going to benefit – you're a saint.'

Steve grinned. 'How do you know I'm not just making an excuse? I'd just rather have my mum's cooking? She'll have done enough for an army.'

'Ha! Just what I suspected!'

And it was then that her phone rang and the day changed dramatically. It was George in the shed. Anna put him on speakerphone because he had news. He was phoning to say that he'd just seen on the Lakeshore Enquirer website that Briony had had a Christmas Day Governor's reprieve of six months and all she would have to serve would be two more and those in the Edna Mahan Correctional Facility for Women in New Jersey which sounded like a walk in the park compared with Cook County. 'They even have a programme for inmates called Puppies Behind Bars! It's to train guide dogs for the blind!' George yelled down the phone in excitement and hung up.

'Yeah!' shouted Anna and Steve simultaneously and hugged ecstatically rocking back and forth.

And it was at the moment of the hug that Faye showed the just-arrived Len into the kitchen. Len wolf whistled and said, infuriatingly, 'Get a room, why don't you!'

Simultaneously Faye yelled 'What the fuck is going on here?' and Harry and Ellis and Sasha appeared behind her confused by the sudden commotion.

'Faye, it's not -' Anna began. Her face was red with the heat of the oven but she could see in a flash how it would look to her daughter.

'How could you?' Faye screamed, 'With dad in the house! He's still your bloody husband, you know! What the hell are you thinking?'

'Mum?' Ellis's horror-struck face dissolved in tears and he rushed from the room and hammered up the stairs.

'And on Christmas Day of all days,' put in Len, smugly. Sasha put his arms round Faye protectively, as though to shield her from such moral degeneracy. Anna was rapidly drying her hands to go after Ellis.

'Look, you don't understand,' began Steve, who had stood helplessly by shocked by the sudden change of atmosphere.

'You shut the fuck up!' shouted Faye. 'Who the hell are you anyway? Why are you here?' She disentangled herself from Sasha and took three long strides across the room to where Steve was leaning back against the counter top possibly having gone weak at the knees. She shook her finger in his face. 'If you think you can take advantage of our mother just because dad's ill you've got another think coming you bastard! You think you can bribe Ellis with a cheap prop and make buddy-buddy with our grand-dad when all you want is to get into mum's knickers! Well, fuck you, you've got another think coming!'

'I don't want -' Steve began but realised it was hopeless. Faye faced him, her arms akimbo.

'Get your coat and get out,' she shouted furiously, 'and don't come round here ever again, you tosser!'

Anna's protests went unheard and she wanted badly to go after Ellis.

But the surprises were not over. As Steve quietly took a step towards the hall, his head bent and his skin grey with shock, Harry stepped in front of him. Steve raised his eyes and looked at the taller man's face. Anna's husband. The amber eyes were full of concern. Harry reached out and put his hand on Steve's shoulder. 'Are you ok?' he asked. Steve stared at him completely nonplussed. He glanced back at Faye whose rage had disappeared as quickly as it had erupted. She was looking at her father with amazement.

'Yes. I'm ok,' Steve said softly and then added, 'Thank you.'

Harry smiled and patted Steve's shoulder.

'Good,' he said kindly. 'Good man.'

Sasha and Len looked at each other from under lowered eyelids and Sasha sucked his teeth. Len, sensing an ally, made a circling movement near his own head with his finger. Sasha sniggered.

'And you can both shut up,' snapped Faye, rattled by their unexpected complicity and offended by Len's gesture. Ellis slunk back into the kitchen just as George was singing his way along the passageway from the shed.

'Great news, eh?' laughed George raising his fists in a victory salute. 'What a team! I say what a team!' He picked up the sherry bottle. 'I think this calls for a toast.' His expression faltered.

He looked around the room. Everyone avoided his eyes. 'It's true – what I told your mum and Steve just now on the speaker phone, weren't you here?' he said to Faye's blank face, 'Briony is going to be freed early and she's being moved tomorrow to another jail – a much better one – and it's all down to your mum, and this clever chap here!' He looked around, 'Steve?' Steve reluctantly hovered in the hall doorway, his coat in his hand. 'And a few others, like a few *thousand* others! So I think this calls for a sherry all round – you, too, Ellis on this great occasion!' He paused. 'What's the matter with everyone? Aren't you pleased?'

That was round one, Anna thought later. When round two got going poor Steve had mercifully gone. Faye had sort of apologised but was still on alert, Anna could tell. The thought of a seduction had arisen in her mind and was not ready to leave yet. Steve had clearly been very relieved to get off on his trip north all the time insisting that it was fine, he was fine. But Harry, it appeared, had taken to him. For the ten minutes or so that Steve remained, uneasily joining in on the small talk when he was directly addressed, Harry attended to him. There was no other word for it. He brought Steve little gifts – a satsuma from the fruit bowl, a brimming glass of water and then finally, Bob's slobbery rubber bone. It was odd but touching. Steve took all these items gracefully, thanking Harry. Anna had filed this away to think about later when the dinner was done.

Normally, the huge meal took the energy out of the day and the adults gratefully collapsed in front of whatever was on television to doze. But not this Christmas. The pudding was brought in, in flames, as usual. This was Ellis's job and one he loved doing. He heated the brandy in an old tablespoon over a candle flame and then the coup de theatre – the pouring and the match lighting and the licking blue flames. Each year, Anna noted, the blaze got bigger and next year she would have to have a word. The food had been good and the morning's unpleasant incident had been pushed into the background.

Sasha had downed quite a few glasses of wine and was looking flushed and slightly disorientated and Len was gleaming with sweaty satisfaction. She smiled inwardly at her two bugbears.

They weren't so bad. George had congratulated himself too often, too, she noticed and was beginning to steam. Faye and Harry were picking bits off the turkey carcass and feeding them to Bob under the table. She sat back and relaxed as Ellis spooned out the pudding. 'It's wonderful how the poor live,' chuckled George.

'How can you say this is poor?' Sasha jerked into life, not knowing the joke. 'You people in this country have no idea of poor! You live like pigs while rest of the world -'

'Sasha!' Faye warned.

'This big house – just for five people! While poor sleep in boxes on streets!'

'It was a saying,' began George.

This incensed Sasha. His already flushed face turned purple in patches. 'Every time you say it is saying, it is joke, it is expression, like I am stupid! Is not joke. Not funny.'

Len joined in. 'He's right, you know. You lot are very privileged. You should see where I live.'

'See! I tell you.' Sasha was warming to his tirade. 'You stuff yourself while this man, who is family, lives in pigsty with no dinner.' Len was clearly wondering whether to challenge this and decided the ally was worth more than the insult.

'Yeah.'

Anna looked wearily at Len's huge bulk and decided she couldn't be bothered joining in. She smiled at Ellis and crossed her eyes. He grinned and helped himself to more pudding. So, he had got over the Steve incident like the sensible kid he was. Harry arranged his used cutlery in a pattern on the tablecloth and studied it.

'I don't think -' began George.

'No – you don't. You call yourself poet but true poet is person with heart, with soul, not making words about boring.'

'Just a minute -' said George.

'Don't you insult my grandfather, Sasha!' Faye put in unexpectedly, unpinning her magnificent hair and shaking it down her back. 'He's got heart and soul and all that in bucket-fuls.' Anna put down her spoon and folded her arms. Ellis tidied his dishes, picked them up and raised his eyebrows at her. She nodded and he got down, put them in the sink and left the room.

'You are child,' Sasha retorted contemptuously. 'What do you know?'

'Ok, Sasha, I think that's -' George began.

'Child? Child?' Faye moved up a gear. 'At least I don't have to be the centre of attention all the bloody time!' Anna considered this. 'I'm not fucking rude to people!' Anna thought of recent events. 'Especially when you're a guest in this house!' Anna looked at Sasha in whose court the ball now surely was.

Sasha stood up and flung down his napkin. 'No more a guest! I quit.' And off he went, crashing the long-suffering front door on his way out. Anna looked longingly at the coffee pot but that would involve getting up. Harry glanced up at the sound of the door and then rose and pottered out to join Ellis in front of the television. Faye burst into tears. At this George muttered something about the dishes later and made for his sanctuary. Anna got up, patted her daughter's head, filled the kettle, put coffee in the pot and rested while it did its thing. Faye sobbed while Len finished off the pudding and, Anna noticed, the wine. She poured a large mug and made her exit to join the others in what she hoped would be tv zombieland. Bob went to bed in his box.

Harry and Anna were fast asleep at opposite ends of the sofa with their mouths open and Ellis was playing his XBox contentedly when the third crisis erupted. Several things happened, it seemed to Anna, simultaneously. The front door bell rang and there was huge crash from the kitchen. Anna leaped to her feet staring wildly in all directions, Ellis froze with his mouth open looking at his mother and Harry, startled awake, grabbed Anna round the neck and wrestled her to the floor. 'Dad! Mum!' screamed Ellis, 'Stop it!' The door-bell continued to ring and there were yells and shouting from the kitchen. Anna gently but firmly disentangled Harry's arms from her making soothing noises, helped by Ellis telling him it was ok. Harry sat back down white-faced. She was shocked, not hurt. She paused for a moment of indecision and then ran from the room. Ellis went to the door.

In the kitchen it looked like there had been a bomb blast. The long dresser which had been for at least fifteen years the receptacle for all things the family couldn't think where else to put as well as an ancient but pretty dinner service, was almost flat on its face. In falling it had tipped the big kitchen table up at a crazy angle and all the dishes from the dinner, abandoned earlier, had slid on to the floor to add to the mess of broken crockery already there. Somewhere underneath the heap of chaos something was making noises. Faye was by the sink holding a rolling pin in the 'present arms' position and looking, Anna was infuriated to see, as though she was going to burst out laughing at any moment. Bob had felt sufficiently stimulated to lumber from his bed and was regarding the spilt leftovers speculatively.

'It wasn't my fault!' Faye cried the minute she saw her mother. 'It was your sicko degenerate of a brother!' The noises coming from under the dresser grew more shrill. Bob reached out a paw and encouraged a cold sausage towards his mouth. At that moment Sasha, followed as though stuck to him by Ellis, burst in to the kitchen.

'My God! What happen?' Sasha climbed quickly across the upended table and folded Faye in his skinny arms. 'My darling, are you ok?'

'Faye, what happened?' Anna felt that she should be the one doing the comforting if needed. Wrong. Faye, having a moment before been on the brink of hysterical laughter, was now sobbing in Sasha's arms.

'That thing – that fat toad, that piece of shit...'

'Faye -' Anna remonstrated uselessly.

'He came on to me! He actually touched me!' She gave a stage sob. 'Oh Sasha, I feel violated, do something!' Anna sighed and sank on to a chair knowing that Faye was now having a really nice time and would not be in any hurry for it to end. The sounds coming from under the furniture ceased abruptly and there was profound silence for one moment.

The next, Sasha was showing surprising strength for such a skinny frame by dragging away the table and lifting one end of the dresser to peer underneath and yell very loudly in Russian at whatever was there. She wondered what on earth Harry was making of all this but felt unable to leave. Len came into view leg first, dragged out by Sasha but as Sasha drew back his fist Anna leaped to her feet.

'Stop it!' she yelled. 'This is going no further. Stop it right now.' They all looked at her with varying degrees of relief, disappointment and rage. Len scrambled to his feet. He was purple in the face and sweating profusely but seemed to be otherwise unharmed. Sasha stepped back glowering. Faye, Anna noticed grimly, looked just a little shamefaced as well she might. 'So who's going to tell me what happened, Faye?'

'He did, Mum. He did come on to me – I wasn't making it up.' Sasha growled.

'I never, you little bitch.' Len was clearly torn between appeasing Sasha and slapping Faye.

'You said you'd have anything I was offering and it was, like, really gross the way you said it.' She straightened and folded her arms in a decided way.

'I meant the food, you cow. God, the women in your family!'

Len wobbled and then leaned against the wall. For a second Anna almost felt sorry for him despite it all.

'So what?' Anna indicated the wreckage heaped on the floor. Faye coughed and lowered her head sliding the rolling pin quietly on to the work surface behind her. Len rolled his eyes.

'She's mad! She came at me with that thing and I tripped and –'

'OK, this is what is going to happen now,' said Anna firmly.

'You two, Sasha and Len, you've been a pain in the neck all day so you can clear up this lot and not one word will either of you say to me or each other. Do you hear me?' They nodded. 'Ellis, you get the black bags and the cleaning stuff but DO NOT HELP!'

'Yes, Mum.'

'Faye, you will go into the front room and you will calm your father who has had a horrible fright and you will stay there and not leave until I tell you. Any word you don't understand?'

'No, Mum.' She picked her way carefully round the edge of the room and fled into the hall.

Anna fetched herself a half empty bottle of white wine and a glass and then, as an afterthought, added the ravaged but still weighty box of After Eight, and then sat back down on the chair and looked very steadily at the two men. 'When you have finished and this kitchen is spotless, I will have a few words to say and then you will both leave.' They shuffled their feet like kids. 'While you are working you can figure out ways to pay for the damage.'

'But –' protested Sasha.

'Not one word! You,' Anna waved the glass at him, 'need to learn how to behave when you're a guest in someone else's house at the invitation of someone else's teenage daughter who ought to know better, young man.' Sasha looked confused but decided not to press his point.

'I don't see why I -' began Len, looking gloomily at the mess spread out before him.

'And you. You think I don't believe my own daughter? Think again, mister.' A puzzled crease appeared between Len's eyebrows but he took a bag from Ellis and started work.

'Pops is fast asleep in the shed,' Ellis told Anna, handing her more black bags. 'He's somnambulant because he's inebriated I think.'

'I think you're spot on,' said Anna. And that was the third Christmas Day crisis.

When the visitors had gone and Faye had drifted off to her room and the refreshed George was playing yet another game of tiddly-winks with Ellis and Harry, Anna made a cup of tea and climbed slowly up the stairs.

She sat on the little white stool in the bathroom watching the steaming water cascading into the bath and sipping her tea. What a farce the day had been. And yet the moments which came to the top of her mind were not the ridiculous and ugly kitchen scenes or even the pleasure over Briony's re-location and imminent discharge. Instead she pictured Steve tossing potatoes into the big saucepan and chatting easily to her and then the heart-stopping moment when she had seen Harry speak to Steve so kindly and place his hand on his shoulder. Steve's shocked face had almost crumbled at the grace and sweetness of Harry's gesture. What did it mean? Did it mean anything? Was Harry's shrinking brain just firing off random gestures and emotions or was there still, at the core, something left of his goodness, his huge capacity for love, something in his character which might resist the erosion, like granite among sedimentary rocks, until the very end?

She put her hand into her dressing-gown pocket and pulled out her phone. After a moment she put it back again without touching a key.

21

It was a subdued Boxing Day. In the afternoon Anna decided she could put it off no longer and packed tubs of cold turkey and potato salad with a thick slice of cake wrapped in cling film and set off for the hospital. She didn't ask George. This was between her and her mother.

Lena was sucking her teeth and staring out of the window at the brick wall where a few feral pigeons were splashing it with grey and white gloop. She turned as Anna approached the bed. 'Good deed for the day, is it?' Now Anna knew what Faye meant when she said, don't start. She unpacked the food and stacked it neatly along the bed tray. She fetched a plastic cup and filled it with diluted elderflower cordial from a bottle she had brought with her. She laid out two napkins decorated with Santas. Lena eyed the offerings and then poked among the wrappings. 'Doing your Lady Bountiful are you? Visiting the poor and the afflicted? Yesterday was Christmas Day At the Workhouse you know – you're a day late.' Anna pulled up a chair.

'Take it or leave it,' she said evenly. So this was where Len got his cheap cynicism and sense of grievance from.

'No George?' Lena pulled a piece of cake from the slab and popped a chunk of it in her mouth. No, Anna thought, the poor old bugger's having a lovely time today with his old friend Ashok who actually likes him and makes him feel good, not like you.

'Not today.'

'That's a relief. He hasn't improved with age.' Lena chuckled, licking her fingers.

'Oh just stop it,' said Anna. 'I've come to ask you something.'

Lena put her index finger to the corner of her mouth and opened her eyes wide in a musical-hall gesture. 'Oh, now let me think what that could be.' She pretended to think, rolling her eyes. 'Oh, I know. How could I heartlessly abandon my little girl? That's the one.' Anna looked past her out of the window and noticed that the shit from the pigeons made quite a pleasing icicle effect. Almost seasonal.

'No, that's not the one actually. I know the answer to that one.' The answer had been crystal clear after her first conversation with her mother. 'You were bored by us and you wanted something more exciting.' Anna paused. 'They never tell you that, do they? All the child-care experts. That looking after small children is often mind-crushingly boring.'

Lena stopped chewing, regarded her attentively and then must have decided to make a concession. 'It was George was boring,' she said, 'the truth was I couldn't stand him after being cooped up in a little car with him for three months. You were all right but I knew you were better off with him.' This had the sound, Anna thought, of a much-repeated justification. It rolled off the tongue like a dead thing.

'Yes,' she said to her mother neutrally, 'You were right there. I would have had a hard life if you'd taken me with you.' Lena stared at her. 'You see George might have been boring as a husband but he's been a brilliant dad so I did get lucky when you left me, you weren't the only one who got a great life out of it.'

'I didn't say I had a great life.' Lena seemed confused by Anna's composure.

'Anyway, that's not what I wanted to ask.' Anna looked full into her mother's weirdly familiar face noting how the flesh fell and wrinkled and where there were pouches and discolorations. She would look like that one day if she lived that long. What age was her mother? She knew precisely. Her mother was sixty-eight. She thought of Diane at Safe n Sound who couldn't be much younger and yet her flesh was creased, certainly, but firm and rosy and her eyes bright with purpose. Oh well. She sighed. 'I want to know why you sent Len to find me. After all this time. We've been living within a few miles of each other most of my life, it seems, and yet you've never tried to contact me. I looked for you for years but couldn't find you – I guess you must have changed your name without getting married – something like that. It doesn't matter now. So, why did you want to see me?' Anna had spoken all this in the same tone as she would have used for discussing the grocery list. It was not contrived. She felt gouged clean of emotion as far as Lena was concerned.

Lena lay back on her pillows and grinned. 'You can't kid a kidder! I know what you really want. You want the death-bed scene, don't you? You want that precious moment when the long-lost mother tells her teary-eyed daughter...'

Anna stood up and began to pack the containers back into her canvas bag. Lena sat up and grabbed Anna's hand in her own blue-veined one. Anna was startled by the sudden-ness and strength of the movement. 'I want you to look after Len,' she said urgently without a trace of sarcasm. 'He's not right in the head. If I'm not here he'll get into trouble again.'

Anna could hardly believe what she had just heard. Could Lena really be so callous and exploitative towards her daughter? And yet it all made sense. Of course it did. How could she not have thought of this before? She stopped what she was doing and then slowly pulled her hand away. She looked at the old woman lying in the bed, her face slack with fear.

'No,' she said. 'I won't.' Incredibly, Lena's eyes immediately filled with tears. Anna regarded her coolly. 'I'll come each day and see if you need anything until the day you die and then I'll make sure you get a decent funeral, but I will not take on Len.'

Lena tried to rear up in the bed and grab at her but Anna was out of reach. 'He's your own brother! You've got so much and he's got nothing, you selfish troll! How can you be so hard?' Anna bit back the rejoinder that there must be something in the genes. The emotional void she had felt only moments before filled with a raging tornado. She was more shocked and angry than she had ever felt in her life. Slowly and carefully, her hands trembling with rage, she picked up her bags and without a word and without a tear walked and did not run out of the ward.

As she made her way down the corridors and out of the hospital Anna felt extraordinarily alone, as if she was walking across the surface of the moon. Then she realised why. She had no more mothers clustering affectionately around her. All her life she had searched out and carefully conserved mothers. There was the lovely droll and affectionate Judi Dench mother (what a laugh that would give Lena), the fiercer but more than acceptable Germaine Greer mother, there was even Diane and, Anna's heart constricted, Margaret Clark, young enough to be her sister. And countless others. They were all possibilities, all prototypes, all hopeful shapes that one day, maybe, her real mother would fill. They had hovered around her in a kind of spectral host of loving possibilities. Now they had gone. Her real mother had seen them off and there was no hope of them ever returning. Anna missed them so much that it was all she could do to find her car and get in. She sat staring through the windscreen gripping the steering wheel for several minutes willing herself not to cry.

On the way home her hands-free phone jingled and Anna pressed the button. 'I'm so sorry, Anna, but I didn't know you'd gone out.' It was her dad. 'Harry's wandered off again. It shouldn't take long to find him since the roads round here are pretty empty but I thought you ought to know. Sorry. Forgot to check he had his watch on.' Anna felt her heart lurch. She hadn't told George she was going out because she didn't want to have to talk to him about Lena but she should have realised that he would have assumed she was keeping an eye on Harry.

'Where are the kids?'

'Ellis is at Mike's and Faye's gone round to Nicola's house.'

'Bob?' How quickly he'd become one of the family.

'He's here, I'm afraid, so it's unlikely to be the park.'

They made the familiar arrangements – George on foot and she in the car this time and she clicked the phone off. She was coming into their neighbourhood now and she changed down through the gears and began looking quickly from one side to the other, checking the road in front in between. One day this sort of thing would be dangerous – one day they would not be able to find him or he would not come home with them. Nothing can stay the same she told herself for the thousandth miserable time. At some point Harry would be beyond them. Could she ever leave him in a nursing home? Could she walk away knowing that the unfamiliar surroundings and the unknown people would confuse and frighten him? Even though most of the time he didn't seem to know her it was such a distressing thought that she pushed it away. She needed to talk to Mr Shenouda, properly this time.

But first she would have to look in that little plywood box that Harry had stuffed away in the back of his book shelves in the days when he was whole. Harry's adoptive parents had been gentle and quiet people rather taken aback, she sometimes had felt, by the brilliant and handsome chick they had raised. But they had given him the steady care and acceptance that had nurtured him so well – proud of his successes but not too proud, and tender with his disappointments. She and Harry having unknown parents had been yet another link between them. He had told her once that he had no desire to know who his biological parents were because the ones who raised him were the ones he held in his heart. Anna thought of Lena and sighed. Sensible Harry. But the box may hold some sort of clue to any logic behind his new behaviours and no-one else had the right to look in it except her.

George was right, the streets were almost empty. People must be inside relaxing or shopping in the first of the after-Christmas sales. Anna drove as slowly as she dared checking not only the High Street but the little alleyways and lanes off it. She knew that George would go to Harry's usual favourite haunts in order of popularity so she turned instead towards the old parish church where she had found Harry once before. She parked the car and got out. There was sleet in the air and she shivered and hugged her coat to her. What was Harry wearing? She opened the boot and pulled out a tartan travel rug that was kept there as part of their emergency pack.

There was a low light in the church and the door was open so she walked quickly towards it. Inside the air was chill and only muted colours came through the Victorian stained-glass windows. But at the front to one side there was a small chapel – a lady chapel she assumed – and in there a cosy flickering mass of candles made the shadows jump. As she watched more candles were lit so she tried to walk forward silently since there must be someone there praying. Again, like the moment she had wanted to make a libation to the gods, she felt a visceral yearning to do the same. To light a candle, kneel, and in fullness of faith unburden her heart. Not possible.

On either side of the aisle were still the decorations from Christmas Day – great ropes of holly and ivy tied brightly with red ribbon and down by the altar a touchingly crude nativity scene with painted figures in a wooden shed set up on a trestle and draped with plastic grass. She moved forward and looked into the little crib. A stiff baby with rather a startled expression stared back. The animals were in various stages of being knocked about and she imagined the set being taken out each December. Yes, it was corny and crude but part of her wished that she had been in the pack of the congregation yesterday belting out carols for all she was worth.

Harry had always taken the rational view that notions of deity were props and comforting delusions at best and political manipulations to keep suffering people docile at worst. Always fair, he didn't blame religion for wars, pointing out that just as many atrocities if not more had been caused by secular factions. Not being very interested one way or another, she had gone along with him.

George, having been raised as a Quaker, had, in a sort of spiritual rebellion, always been interested in religions with ritual and, as he would put it, poetry, although he still regularly attended meetings of the Friends at Bournville. She remembered him once taking her to a meeting when she was little but she had been confused and bored. Why were people sitting round in silence when they could have been out in the fresh air skipping and climbing and chasing each other around? They had been kind to her afterwards, slipping sugary biscuits into her hand but it had never been repeated.

George would never impose anything on anyone. Unlike her mother who, it seemed, had planned ever since her diagnosis to inflict Len on Anna.

A familiar sound caught Anna's attention. In the side chapel where dozens of candles now blazed Harry was moaning. Anna moved quickly but silently towards him. He was kneeling uncomfortably for his tall frame at a narrow, battered communion rail and was shaking his head and then moaning some more.

Suddenly, with a grab at her heart, Anna knew what he was doing. She knelt down beside him and listened for a moment and then picked up the melody, adding the familiar words. Come all you faithful. Harry was trying to sing a Christmas carol. As she sang the words, his scrap of memory was activated and he joined in where he could. She glanced sideways and had to stop singing for a beat as her breath was caught by the sight of him. The soft yellow light of the candles he had lit gilded his skin and hair and reflected flickeringly in his amber eyes. The candle-light gave him back his youth and he was once again the gloriously alive Harry she had fallen so deeply in love with. Drawn by her look he turned towards her. Please, just don't say anything horrible, she thought. Don't spoil this moment.

She turned back towards the little altar and continued to sing until the end of the verse. Harry had fallen silent.

He stood up then and looked around but calmly, appraisingly. 'I used to like coming to church when I was a little boy,' he said in his old way.

'Did you?' He had never told her that his adoptive parents were church-goers.

'Yes.' He turned and looked penetratingly at her. Anna kept herself still. She wanted with all her body to move close to him and wrap her arms around him and have him hold her and for a moment forget the nightmare that had become their reality. He spoke wonderingly. 'Why is it you? I don't understand. Why is that, that on your head?'

The incoherent question was unanswerable. 'I'm Anna,' she said, 'I'm your wife.' He stepped rapidly back away from her. 'NO!' he shouted, 'Not my wife!' He made shooing movement with his hands to get her away from him.

She walked a few steps up the aisle, feeling physically sick with the rejection. When she could she asked quietly, not looking at him, 'Are you ready to go home? Shall I phone George to come?' He relaxed his shoulders and looked round quickly.

'George? I want George.' And the moment had passed.

At home Faye had returned and was playing her new downloads at full volume in her room. Ellis was still out and after they had settled Harry in front of a recorded documentary, George and Anna switched on the laptop in the kitchen. The Facebook page sprang into life and they spent ten minutes scanning that and then scrolling down the hundreds of tweets but it was the US media that they wanted to see most. Would Christmas have knocked Briony's story off the headlines never to be retrieved? They tried one television network news channel after another and then the major papers. It was still there in the Chicago press but back several pages. The New York Times and The Washington Post had not run it at all.

A planned Christmas Day attack on the Lincoln Memorial in Washington had been thwarted and the media were buzzing with speculation about the would-be perpetrators.

'Doesn't matter,' said George, his wiry beard bristling with animation. 'She's been moved to New Jersey and she'll be released in a few weeks. Job done, really.'

'We should save as much of this stuff as we can,' Anna said thoughtfully. 'We don't know how much of it she's been able to see and I would think that it would make her feel better to realize how much people care.' George scratched beneath his chin.

'I'll see what I can do and if I can't I'll have a word with Steve.' He glanced at Anna. There had been no further word from Steve but then it was only one day after the worst Christmas he had probably ever had. She didn't want to think about Steve. The image of Harry glowing like a mediaeval saint in the candlelight was too poignantly alive within her.

'I'm going to have a rummage among the photo albums,' she said, 'after I've checked my emails.' She opened her inbox and Briony's name appeared. Immediately her heart began to pound as she remembered the previous message. 'There's one from Bri.'

George had got up to make a cup of tea and stood, kettle in hand, waiting for her to tell him what it said. She scanned it rapidly and then astonished herself by bursting into tears.

'Here, let me see. She can't still be angry with you!' George lifted the laptop and read the email.

Mrs Ames, he read out loud, *I've been transferred to EMCFW in New Jersey and on March 3 I'm being discharged and coming back to Birmingham. I will send flight details when I have them and will take a taxi from the airport. Please meet me at the house on Mill Lane with the key or arrange for someone else to do it.*

She had not signed off. He looked tenderly at Anna who had now blown her nose and dried her eyes. 'She has taken the trouble to let you know. It's not an angry email. She must have got the letters from you and her mum and the other stuff you sent.'

'Yes, I hope so anyway. I don't know what I was expecting.' Anna sighed. 'I'll meet her at the airport.' How to tell her dad that although it was a relatively minor one, it was one rejection too many for one day?

'After all, she doesn't know you triggered the campaign, does she?'

Anna smiled gratefully at his concern and stood up. 'Thanks, Dad.' She turned out of the kitchen into the hall and ran up the stairs to the double bedroom which was now Harry's room. She found the box almost immediately. It had never been moved from the time twenty-one years ago when they had come to this house, before Faye was born. It was, as it had always been, tucked out of sight on top of a full set of leather bound encyclopedias, fifty years out of date, on the bottom layer of a sagging wooden shelving unit. She ran to her room and slid it under her narrow bed. Then she went quietly downstairs and into the living room to sit on the floor by the bureau and pull out, one after another, the old albums from pre-digital times. Harry was sleeping on the couch and she was grateful for it.

After an hour she had extracted and dated six photos with her in them, all with different fashions and hairstyles. The current easy to manage straight shoulder-length bob was the simplest style she had ever had. Maybe even severe when she compared it to the more playful earlier ones. Was that what Harry meant? It was true she hadn't thought about new hair or clothes or makeup for months, years maybe.

She smiled as she laid the photos out in date order. The funniest and most alarming was the one from 1991. Good lord. The hennaed frizz leaped from her head in a cottage loaf of wire-wool. She was wearing bright red lipstick and what looked like a coat with shoulder pads on top of a dress with shoulder pads. She looked as though she had no neck. It was a wonder that people hadn't run out of the library screaming but then, they all looked the same. Including the men. She smiled to herself.

Then there was the Afghan hound look-alike from, she checked the date, 1984. Her hair was long and elaborately hot-tongued into ringlets with a fringe that seemed to touch the tip of her nose. How could she have seen out? She remembered what a pain it had been to keep curled. There seemed also to be, if you looked really closely, something stuck in it. Oh yes, of course. They were flowers from the folk festival they'd been to. Anna shook her head to concentrate on the task in hand. It was too dangerous to allow memories to get all stirred up.

The earliest adult photo she had picked out was of when she had gone up to university in '82. She studied it. This is what she would have looked like when she and Harry had met and fallen in love. In the photograph she was standing by the university union building looking shy and proud and wearing a neatly pressed pair of jeans with flares and a plaid cowboy shirt with pearl buttons. A macramé bag was hanging heavily from one shoulder. Pressed jeans!

George must have taken it when he drove her up to Leeds for the start of the first term. She peered closer at the hairstyle. It was much softer than her current unlayered look and was lifted by a breeze into a loose mop. She screwed up her eyes to see better. She looked a bit like a large chrysanthemum on the droop.

Faye slid into the room and folded herself in one fluid movement to sit on the floor by her mother. Could yoga make Anna that lissom? Worth a try. 'Mum. It's after Christmas now. You said.'

Anna's heart sank. 'Ooh! What do you look like!' Faye picked up the wire-wool effect photo and stared incredulously. 'How did you even get it like that? You look like you stuck your finger in an electric socket.' She turned the pages quickly looking for her own baby snaps. 'I haven't looked at this stuff for ages. How cute am I?'

Glad of a diversion, Anna pushed the early university photo at her. 'What do you think of this hair-style?'

'Weird.' Her eyes narrowed suspiciously. 'Why are you changing your hair? Is it him, that Steve?' She glared at Anna. 'Honestly, mum, I cannot believe that you're being like this.' Anna gathered the photos up.

'I'm not being like anything and you're barking up the wrong tree.' Faye looked intently into her face and changed the subject.

'About Sasha – about going to Russia with him?' Her voice had begun to whine. 'You said.' Faye pawed at Anna's arm in an ironic imitation of a puppy.

'Oh Faye.' This was not the day for a conversation with her daughter about going away and leaving her. But, of course, Faye was right. She had said wait till after Christmas as a stalling move.

'Look, it just seems so huge for you to be thinking of this. Faye, I know you'll get mad with me but you're too young to go off to an unknown place with a man you've only just met.' Immediately the image of Briony beaten black and blue, Briony behind bars, Briony raped and tortured hit her like a blow. She gasped.

'Mum,' Faye explained patiently, 'we're much more mature these days than you were at my age. And there's stuff like Skype and Facebook and all that that you didn't have. You'd hardly notice I'd gone.'

Was she being unfair, Anna wondered? Of course it was a bad idea but was she being over-influenced by Briony's dreadful experience? Was there a possibility of putting some limits on the trip, maybe even going with her? She dismissed that instantly. She remembered what Sasha himself had said. 'Sasha said that he isn't going back until Easter, anyway, so there's no rush.' Weak, but the only straw that was floating in the air.

'Oh right, I wouldn't go till then, of course,' Faye said airily as though there had never been any other plan. 'He said it's all ice and mud there now anyway. But I have to get started with visa applications and all that. They're very into documentation over there and I need to learn a bit of Russian, too. I've been doing some online marketing for my meerkats so I can get some money for it.'

'Oh.'

'Yep. I'm even going to outsource the manufacture to Tasha and Nicola to meet the demand.' Anna wondered if Faye's friends were aware that she was planning to use them as sweated labour.

'Don't look at me like that – I'll give them something. Mum, I'm doing it all properly. My tutor helped me with a business plan.'

She frowned. 'Any other mother would be proud.' Anna reached across the photo albums scattered on the floor and hugged her daughter closely.

'I am proud. I just don't want to lose you. Not just yet.'

'I'll always be your little girl,' Faye smiled, a tad condescendingly Anna felt. 'And you've got Ellis and Pops and -' Her smile faltered a little.

'Yes, of course I have, and you must live your life, sweetheart.' Easter was three months away, Anna thought grimly, and anything can happen in three months. She picked up the photo of herself with a chrysanthemum head and tidied the others back into their albums.

22

It wasn't until she walked through the doors of Harts that she realised that she was dreading seeing Steve. It had all been too much too fast. While they had been hot on the trail of Briony and then setting up the campaign it had been purposeful and exciting and they had worked well together but now that was done only the awkward and confusing personal stuff was left. Then there had been the strange experience with Harry on Christmas Day. She realised guiltily that she resented that Harry had been so kind and approving to Steve having only met him once before when he was so off-hand and cold to her, his wife. She realised that this was illogical and certainly not Steve's fault but the feeling remained. And then there was the eagle-eyed Faye seeing something which, for all it was hotly denied, was definitely there – for her, anyway. She had not enjoyed feeling Faye's contempt for the brief moment it had lasted. Had she been sending out signals, right or wrong? Had he? So now what?

'There she is!' Ted boomed, striding down the glass walkway, 'bloodied with her first brush!'

'Excuse me?'

'It's a fox-hunting term,' Steve said, coming out of his office and smiling. 'For the benefit of townies, it means you got your kill.'

Anna felt irritated and surrounded. 'A bit of an unfortunate analogy I would have thought in the circumstances, Ted,' she said huffily.

'Oo, get you,' he crowed childishly. A few researchers had stood up by their terminals and were enjoying the interchange. 'No, you've done very well for a tadpole Mrs Ames.' He glanced around.

'Back to it you lot and work off your Christmas pudding! Meeting for everyone at 2.00 sharp – there's news.' Anna started to walk away. 'Just a minute, Anna,' Ted said quietly, 'I'd like you to pop into the office for a minute.'

Anna was relieved. She had been wanting an opportunity to ask about the timing of her finder's fee. Normally the estate would have been settled and the fee would come in fairly quickly but in this case Briony couldn't do anything legal or financial until she returned and that wouldn't be for weeks. They were just about keeping up with the bills but looming over their heads was always the possibility, no, probability, that at some stage Harry would need professional care and the savings account they had set up for that contingency had been raided again and again. Now there was going to be the unexpected cost of Lena's funeral for which, Anna felt sure, she herself had made no provision. For all her mother's feistiness, the consultant had been clear that she didn't have much longer and that she would soon be moved to a hospice and given only palliative care. Anna decided she would ask about it on the next visit and whether Lena had made a will. It seemed harsh but Anna wanted to be harsh. Damn the woman.

She started to sit down in the big leather chair Ted kept for clients, astutely sized to be larger than his own so they would feel cosseted and valued. 'This won't take a minute,' he said tersely. She stood up. 'I don't want you to say anything, right? *Not one word.*'

Anna nodded, puzzled. 'Now then. I don't know who was the instigator for this campaign to get Mrs Bulowski out of Cook County Jail and away from the crap she was being put through and *I don't want to know.* But, I do want to say this. If ever an employee of this company were to be foolish and wrong-headed enough to compromise our reputation for neutrality and confidentiality by conducting a political campaign that involved social media and network media *on two continents* that employee would not only cease to be on our pay-roll but would also have shot his or her bolt with any of our competitors. And I mean *any* of our competitors. That employee would stink, Mrs Ames. That employee would be unemployable.' He stared at her grimly. 'Do I make myself clear?' She nodded. He opened the door. She left.

Anna retreated to the toilet, shaking. How had she not seen this coming? Of course Ted, with his blood-hound instincts and experience would have picked up on what was going on. He probably regularly checked on the names in all their high-end cases and Margaret, by hanging on to the inheritance from her sister, had slipped into that category. Also, he would have checked to see if the air-fare and hotel expenses had been justified. No-one had said it, but she was still very much on probation. And he was right.

Technically, she never should have got so involved. Her loyalties had been to Maggie and Briony almost from the start and not to Harts.

That was what he was telling her – get your priorities right in future or you're gone. She stared at her face in the mirror. Why hadn't he just sacked her? Maybe because he couldn't prove it, maybe because his quasi-accusation had been an inspired guess and not based on any sure knowledge. She wouldn't even have appeared as a 'friend' of George since it appeared she was one of the world's minority who didn't have a Facebook account. She had never put her name to anything on the web, only George's Facebook page had been referenced and Ted wouldn't know his name unless he had done a bit of sleuthing. Which he might have done, in fact, almost certainly would have done.

This is when I need you, Harry. I'm no good at this conflict thing. OK, we had a few run-ins with the Dean's Office while I was at the library, you know, over staffing and the budget and that sort of routine stuff but there were certainly no ethical dilemmas, no ideological conundrums. She smiled grimly. That would be a good one for Ellis, wouldn't it Harry? You're always so sure about what's right, darling. You were. It's getting harder to talk to you even like this and I'm sorry. I just keep seeing that look in your eyes. As though you're scared of me. You're slipping away, aren't you? I can't even pretend any more. My mothers have left me and now you're going too.

The door opened softly and Suze came in. She looked at Anna's face in the mirror and wordlessly put her arm round her shoulders. 'I don't know what's going on, of course,' she said, 'but well done you.' Anna relaxed and even managed a feeble smile.

'Thanks.'

'Listen, I've got my eye on the sexiest little black number you have ever seen in Zara. Fancy a quick lunch in the Bullring in return for giving me your expert opinion on whether it would get me into Rob's bed tonight?' Anna readily agreed. This was just what she needed, a bit of a laugh with the outrageously sociable Suze and a good excuse not to have to spend time with Steve. Steve. If Ted suspected her own involvement would he also suspect Steve?

Although she didn't want to, Anna decided that she would have to just drop by his office and spend a few minutes seeing how things were.

Most of the morning he had someone with him and it wasn't until she was almost ready to leave for lunch that he was free. She put on her coat and slung her bag over her shoulder as a hint that she only had a moment to spare and walked into his office. He was leaning back in his chair with his eyes closed and massaging one knee. 'You ok?' He swung round.

'Oh, hi. Yes, I just strained it a bit on the Boxing Day climb up Helvellyn. Slipped.'

'Steve! It was sleeting on Boxing Day! Well, here at least.'

'Yes, well, you know.' He looked at her carefully. 'How's things with you?' Anna considered what to say. She could have talked for hours about Lena, Faye, the rollicking she'd got from Ted, and on and on but somehow that seemed wrong.

'Sorry about Christmas Day.'

'Mm. Water under the bridge. I liked Harry.'

'He obviously took to you. How's your dad?'

'Better now Christmas is over. He gets down and then it's really tough on my mother.' Despite her intention to leave quickly, Anna was intrigued.

'Do you know why?'

'Yes I do. He never used to get these black moods but last Christmas my little sister and her husband were coming home from a party and they were in a road accident. Their car was crushed by a truck – driver asleep at the wheel - and they were killed instantly.'

'Oh, my God. I'm so sorry.' Anna hadn't expected this.

'Yes. It was bad. And it's left its mark on all of us.' Steve turned in his chair and gazed out of the window at the grey sky. 'You hear about this type of thing all the time and you think that it's only the people involved who got hurt but it's not. Other people's lives are changed for ever.' He looked so serious that Anna didn't reply. Part of her wanted to step up to him and another part wanted to be away and out of the building. He swung back to her. 'Sorry,' he said, 'too much information.'

'No Steve, really -' she felt foolish and didn't know how to go on.

'Look, I'm glad Ted's pleased with you and I hope you feel pleased with yourself.'

'Thanks. Look, I'd better go. I'm going to the Bullring with Suze –' She hesitated for a moment not wanting to rush off after he'd told her about his sister's death but it was all too much. She just hadn't got it in her to take on board any more emotional freight.

'Fine.' His face froze and then he spun his chair round and tapped a key. The screen sprang into life. 'Have fun.'

They slumped into seats at EAT. Suzanne was clutching a Zara bag gleefully. Anna thought about the photos of herself through the decades. Suze was always right up to the minute in fashion. 'Do you think I need a make-over?'

Immediately Suzanne rallied herself and stared at her friend appraisingly. 'Mm. Well, you've got great hair of course and your figure – well, curves are in – straight up and down is definitely last decade so you're good there.' Anna pondered this. 'What you need is to stop dressing like you're a banker or something.'

'What do you mean?'

'Well, I know you want to look professional and smart but you don't have to wear a uniform, do you?'

'A uniform?' Anna was a bit put out. She had always thought that her work clothes were quite elegant.

'You can wear a suit but it doesn't have to be dark and plain,' Suze explained urgently as though Anna might close down a conversation any second that she'd been wanting to have for weeks. 'You could wear more flattering colours and have a bit of – er –'

'Go on,' said Anna feeling resigned. 'You don't need to be polite.'

'Well, style. Some pleats here, some drapes there, even a peplum –'

'A *peplum*!' Anna repeated. 'With my hips!'

'Well, ok, then, but you get the idea.' Suze examined her again. 'And make-up, Anna, there isn't a law that says you can only use lipstick and mascara. Half the time you don't even bother with that. Your eyes are a really lovely shape, very Kate Moss, but you could just put a bit of shadow -' Anna stopped listening. An image of Lena had sprung into her mind's eye. Lena, her biological doppelganger with her harshly dyed hair and ravaged skin. No, she knew which route she definitely did not want to go down. Is that what Lena had become? Not a role model but a horrible warning?

Even if she was bitterly disappointed and rejected, she didn't have to resort to spite. She became aware that Suze had stopped talking and was munching her sandwich and looking at Anna with fond despair. 'Or if that's too much, just a bit of blusher.'

After work that evening Anna drove home thoughtfully. She felt sobered by the day's events. At the 2.00 staff meeting Ted had been all jolliness and bonhomie, his face creased with shiny excitement, telling them that Harts had secured a lucrative junior partnership deal with one of the top London probate research firms. But, he had warned, they must step up productivity because the work load was going to increase by almost 20% and he couldn't hire new staff until those fees started rolling in. So that was why he hadn't sacked her, Anna thought, he needs all hands on deck. It would be tough in the short term but well worth it, he said. A few of the researchers were earnestly scanning the ceiling at this point knowing who would be doing the sweating and for which managers it would be well worth it. But everyone understood the situation and Ted was for the most part a fair manager and the probability was that eventually everyone would benefit with increased job security if nothing else.

Anna knew she had been within a hair's breadth of losing her job today. In fact, if it hadn't been for this new partnership deal she probably would have lost it. If Ted had looked hard enough he could have made the connection between her and the campaign for justice for Briony. It was more than likely that he knew exactly what she had done. Emotionally she had been all over the place since the trip to Chicago. Astonishing to think that that was only two weeks ago.

The rapidly escalating sexual charge between herself and Steve had been completely out of order and when she thought now of the scene in his apartment when she threw herself at him she blushed deeply. And that awful scene he had had to suffer on Christmas Day with Faye's accusation. She groaned out loud and gripped the steering wheel harder. She'd been behaving like a fool. And then had come the surprise announcement from the loathsome Len, and then the shock of Lena herself, cackling like the wicked witch at Sleeping Beauty's christening, pricking the balloon of Anna's comforting djinn mothers for ever.

No, it was time to put all that emotional crap behind her and get on with the serious business of being the family provider. Soon, if Faye didn't disappear into a Russian black hole, she would need university tuition fees and one day there would be Harry to be looked after. She daren't even contemplate her father not being there. She shook her head and straightened her back. No point in looking for grief and worry before it came. What she had to do now was to get those blasted assignments done and get her Diploma finished. When the new work came in Ted would be looking for the weakest to weed out at the first opportunity. She knew that not all the old-time heir hunters were fully qualified but they'd got experience on their side. She hadn't. She needed that Diploma.

On the kitchen table was a neat pile of post and there among it, tactfully placed down the pile by her sweet-natured son, was her last assignment. In her new mood of gritty determination she pulled it out and scanned the comments. Well, the only good thing that could be said was that she'd passed. She would need to raise her game considerably to get a merit, let alone a distinction.

George shuffled in from the shed followed by Bob. She glanced up. 'Hi. Harry ok? I didn't see him in the front room.'

George crossed to the fridge and pulled out a packet of sausages covered with clingfilm.

'He's gone to bed.' Anna looked at him sharply. This hadn't happened before. Harry never went to bed in the daytime. George shrugged unhappily. They stared at each other for a moment.

'I think we need to have a proper talk with Mr. Shenouda, Dad. I mean before the next MRI assessment.' George cut the links between each sausage and placed them on a baking tray. He pricked each one with a knife and opened the oven door to peer inside.

'I think I'll stick some potatoes in to bake,' he said, 'and leave the sausages for a bit.' Bob waddled over. 'No sir, no pinching them, you're watching your waistline.' Bob turned his eyes away in the exasperated manner of children who know they are being patronised. George went over to the larder and pulled out the potato sack. 'One each should be enough, don't you think?' Anna felt a spasm of irritation. George had been cooking most of his life – why did he feel the need to defer to her? It seemed over-sensitive and was certainly unnecessary. She was hardly going to get huffy about being side-lined in housewifely duties.

'Whatever you think, Dad,' she said a little too brusquely and instantly regretted it. 'Oh, sorry. I'm a bit on edge, that's all.'

George took the potatoes to the sink and began to wash them and pick out the eyes. He bought them from Ashok's wife's allotment together with whatever else was in season. They ought really to be cultivating their own garden for produce, Anna thought, but there was a limit.

'Talk about it?' George offered gruffly with his back to her.

'I just need to really get down to some work this week, Dad. There's going to be a lot going on at Harts soon and I need to be competitive by getting that damn Diploma under my belt.'

'Seems to me you work hard enough as it is,' said George, 'and Lena hasn't helped.'

Anna opened her laptop. 'No. Well, helping isn't really her thing, is it? But I told her I'd go in to the QE every day and I will just to check what's happening.'

'Is that Lena Walker you're talking about?' Ellis was suddenly in the room grabbing Bob's head and waggling his ears. Bob's tail thumped the floor ecstatically. 'Only there was a message on the phone.' Anna and George froze and locked eyes.

'Was there?'

'Yup. She's being moved to St. Mary's Hospice today.' He glanced up at Anna. 'Who is she?'

'An old friend of mine,' said George thickly.

'Oh, ok.' Ellis caught sight of the opened assignment on the kitchen table. 'How d'you get on, mum? I bet you aced it.'

'Sarcasm is most unbecoming,' Anna said, smiling. 'Well, it was a bit boring. Let's see what the next unit is about.' She tapped and frowned at the screen. 'You're not going to believe this.'

'Spill.' Ellis had sat down at the table and propped his sharp chin on his sweaty knuckles while one grubby-socked foot massaged Bob's respectable grey belly.

'Accessing records for subjects incarcerated in adult and young offenders' penal institutions in the UK and selected other jurisdictions in the post WW2 period.'

'How very fortuitus!' Ellis said grinning and chalking one up in the air.

'Or even serendipitous! How's about that? If I can't get a distinction on this I'd better re-train as a welder. Speaking of that -'

'No deal,' said Ellis on cue. 'I'm going to university to be a layabout student and you can't stop me!' Anna playfully cuffed his head since she had been forbidden to rumple his hair. It was an old joke.

23

The rest of the week passed in a dull blur of work at work and then work at home. She and her father talked about whether it was necessary to tell the children about Lena and decided that Faye should be told but not Ellis.

'He's too young and he's too kind,' George said. 'He would want to rush off to see her immediately with a basket of goodies like Red Riding Hood and she'd devour his decent little heart like the bloody wolf.' He sounded very bitter. 'Faye is different and almost an adult. I think she ought to know. If Lena gives her a smart remark she'll get a bigger one straight back.' Anna agreed. She had found Faye furiously sewing and, as undramatically as she could, told her the situation.

'I've got a gran?' She took her foot off the pedal. A half-stuffed meerkat head lolled grotesquely from under the needle.

'Mm.'

'What's she like?'

Anna felt numb. 'Not very nice, actually.'

'Have I got to go and see her? I'm really busy, Mum. I mean, not to be harsh but I don't even know her.' Anna was intensely relieved and mentally stuck her tongue out at the person she now referred to in her head as *my bloody mother*. See? That's how much we care about you.

'Absolutely not,' Anna said, kissing Faye on the top of her head. 'Just wanted you to know.' So that was that, then.

While Anna was so busy George even managed to persuade Faye to cook a couple of meals and Harry was especially quiet and subdued. Anna pushed thoughts of him to the back of her mind and had minimal contact at work with Steve who seemed, in any case, to be avoiding her.

The hospice was, as she had hoped it would be, a sanctuary. The colour scheme was a quiet green and cream, and everywhere the staff and volunteers smiled as they passed her in the corridors. Sensibly, there was a room where patients could smoke. Anna remembered the people on drips and in wheelchairs shivering in the red shelters of the QE to have their cigarettes, and felt sorry for them despite having never smoked herself.

There had been a consultation with the palliative care doctor in charge on her first visit but no surprises. Several of the patients were there on respite care and would be returning to their own homes when they felt well enough but this would be Lena's last stop. The cancer had metastasised from her stomach to her liver and pancreas even before Anna had first seen her. Anna guessed that she had not wanted to see a doctor when the symptoms had first appeared and preferred to self-medicate with quack remedies and internet advice until it was too late. Now she was waiting to die and she knew it. It seemed as though she had given up after she was hospitalised.

On her daily visits Anna sometimes sat by her mother's bed and held her limp hand. Lena was still able to talk a little but made no move to speak or reciprocate the gesture. Anna knew herself to be unforgiven. In a previous life she would have been cut to the heart with guilt to think of her own dying mother wanting something from her which she refused to give. But the attitude from Lena had been too harsh, the entreaty too late and too unmitigated. If there had been even a hint of affection towards herself, Anna thought, maybe she could have considered Lena's desperate demand but her own feelings had been entirely discounted. Why would Lena change just because she was dying? She had never cared for her daughter and didn't now. No. Len would have to just grow up and look after himself for a change. I am not my brother's keeper, Anna thought grimly.

Len himself had not been back to the house since the Christmas Day fiasco. No money for the smashed china had materialised from either him or Sasha and neither had she expected it. It had just made her feel better to ask for it. Sometimes he came to see Lena when she was there and it was clear that he had genuine feeling for his mother and she for him. Anna would watch them together bleakly. Lena would curl her fingers round his podgy hand and they would speak in monosyllables to each other.

'All right?' Len would inevitably ask as he sat down. Lena would get out a whispered grunt. Then Len would place on the tray over her bed a small treat. One day it was a ready-made jelly trifle with its own plastic spoon and on another it was a little toy from the hospice shop, a duck that waggled its head comically. Lena would make the effort to see what he had brought and give a hint of a high-pitched giggle.

Anna was totally excluded. Neither Len nor his mother acknowledged her presence or spoke to her at all. But she had cranked up a drawbridge in her heart and did not allow herself to show any emotion. She tried as hard as she could not to feel it. As she walked out of the hospice each day she trained herself to start thinking about her assignment the moment the automatic doors slid closed behind her. It was no problem to fall asleep at night, she was exhausted, and if she had bad dreams they were gone two seconds after she had woken.

So it was a shock coming home at the end of the week to see the door open and a smiling, rosy, old woman's face greeting her.

Was Lena the changeling mother and this person the real one? Dear me, get a grip, Anna chided herself. Diane? Behind her was George and for a moment Anna had to resist bursting out laughing. They looked just like two garden gnomes. 'Look who's here!' George called out as she climbed the shallow steps to the front door. 'I told you she'd come.'

'And I didn't come alone,' said Diane standing aside for Anna to pass. She was wearing what looked suspiciously like a new pink cardigan Anna thought with interest. She glanced at George. His usually fly-away hair had been stuck to his scalp - with what? Never mind. The effect was touching if odd. 'I've brought Joan – you know, Maggie's neighbour! George says it's all right.'

'Of course it's all right,' said Anna feeling her spirits rise, 'it's great!'

They ushered each other into the kitchen where Harry and Ellis were playing tiddlywinks at the table and Faye was sitting in stunned upright mode next to Joan who was energetically explaining the merits of setting up a Paypal account online for her Meerkat business. Anna was gratified to note that a very nice smell indeed was wafting from the oven. What a great home-coming. Work, Len, Lena were all forgotten. She was with people who cared about her. Well, most of them.

Faye rose from her seat and, making an effort to be polite, detached herself from Joan. She came round the table and grabbed her mother's arm. 'Could I have a word?' she said smiling falsely, and dragged her into the hall. The moment she got her outside and shut the door she hissed, 'Shit mum! Who are all these wrinklies?'

'Faye! Hush.'

'You never know what's going to happen next round here these days! What are these? Long lost aunties or grannies or something?'

'Of course not, and don't be rude.'

'Well, you've got form.' She put on an artificial voice. 'And what did you get for Christmas this year, Faye? Oh, just a rotten nasty old granny who doesn't want to see me and a putrid uncle who tried to chat me up and, oh yes, cheap beads from the charity shop! It was great! Best Christmas ever!' Anna tried to be cross but couldn't be. Faye was flushed and bright-eyed with indignation. *She* could bring someone home who had no compunction about insulting not only the family but the nation of which he was a guest, but Anna had to admit that being related to Len wasn't a nice surprise for anyone.

She drew Faye into the sitting room and explained about Diane and Joan. Faye sniffed. 'Any more surprises coming along?'

Anna knew what she was hinting at.

'No,' she said shortly. 'Don't be silly.' Faye flounced back into the kitchen and Anna followed.

As always, the poetry reading calmed everyone down. Anna was glad that Sasha was not there and that Harry seemed to be relaxed. Ashok's ritual chocolate orange had been passed round held up high to avoid Bob's questing nose. And there was a surprise, too. When George asked whether Joan would like to read she reached into her huge old bag and brought out a neatly bound folder.

'Would you mind if I read a couple of my own?'

Anna was not at all nervous about Joan's reception. She had heard what seemed to her naive, banal and even daft poems read in this space by various guests and friends of George and each one had been greeted with pleasure and appreciation. It was a lovely atmosphere that he had created and even Faye never disrupted it for all her mutterings later. Ashok had already read his latest creation and his work had cast its usual spell with its rich tone and baroque meandering flourishes. You could drift off in your own thoughts and come back and still feel the benefit thought Anna gratefully. No one ever asked anyone's opinion of their work. It wasn't that kind of occasion.

Without preamble Joan started to read. Anna blinked and George leaned forward, his eyes shining. Anna thought back to the first time she'd seen Joan as a little old white-haired woman hanging out the washing in her back garden. What a short-sighted bunch of assumptions she'd made about her! How arrogant she'd been! Not only had Joan efficiently got her son and his partner in New York on board as major players in the campaign for Briony but here she was reading in diamond sharp phrases and gut-wrenching images the most moving poems Anna had ever heard to describe love and loss.

When she stopped there was profound silence in the group. Harry broke it.

'When did you go into my head?' he asked as if he genuinely wanted to know. 'Was my wife there?'

It was unbearable. Anna had to get out. She excused herself and slipped through the creaking wooden door. In the garden there were only small, far-off sounds and a spill of orange light from the shed window. It was cold but she didn't care. She picked her way around the mess of wooden debris George had started to assemble and then forgotten and sat on the cold, damp bench. She tipped her head back to look at the sky. Stars were scattered across it in swathes as though they had been hand sown. Some were bright and flickering insistently like an urgent morse code from outer space. She remembered that, counter-intuitively, the red ones were cold and the blue hot. She searched towards the eastern horizon for Orion's belt and then up to Aldebaran and across to the Pleiades. Wisps of cloud as thin as shreds of rotted net curtain moved slowly across. It was hard to see some of the stars – she didn't know whether she was imagining them or they were really there. One would appear and then vanish as an invisible veil of cloud crossed between them. Anna finally allowed herself to think about Harry.

Was she anywhere in his head? It seemed so. He still knew that he had had a wife. Why didn't he know her in the flesh? What he had said to Joan hinted at such loneliness, such longing, that it gouged a fresh laceration in her heart. Just because he was locked in confusion, retreating constantly from the aggressive attack on his brain, didn't mean he couldn't feel, did it? No one had been able to explain to her his total loss of connection with her and maybe that was because there was no explanation. The disease had taken a certain course. It could have taken another and robbed him of motor skills or anything else. Suddenly, she remembered the box under her bed. She got up at once and rubbing her arms to bring back the circulation, went quickly into the house.

She knew roughly what was in the box. Harry's birth certificate and adoption papers and a few photographs and mementoes. His mum had put the bits and pieces together for him thinking that he may at some stage want to look into his pre-adoption past. He never had. Once, when she was researching her own mother, Anna had asked him if he wanted her to look up his parents but he had firmly told her not to.

She had never revealed to him that she had gone ahead anyway. Then he had become ill and there was no point in telling him – no point in distressing him further. Anna had found out quite a bit about the woman who could have been her mother-in-law, Grace.

She had only been 15 when she had Harry. She had been the daughter of a doctor and was a clever girl at school. Her parents must have been deeply shocked by what had happened even though it was the 1960's. Harry's father was only a few months older. Under current legal practice he could even have been put on the sex abuse register, Anna thought.

The father, Michael Lewis, had become an army cadet and his career was well-documented in military records. He had risen through the ranks to become an NCO. He had been in 2 Paras and had been killed in the Goose Green action on the Falklands in 1982. No records existed of a marriage either between Grace Chilwell and Michael or between Michael and anyone else.

Harry's mother was a grammar school girl and it seemed from the dates that she had deferred her GCE's for a year and then gone on to sixth form and university. Harry had been a short-lived problem. He had been given up for adoption, as was customary then Anna knew, almost immediately after his birth. Grace had studied philosophy at Aberdeen University (getting as far away from her parents as possible?) and had graduated with a first-class degree. Then the records had ceased.

There were only two possibilities. She had died or she had gone abroad. It turned out she had done both. Quite by chance a few months later Anna's eye had caught the name on a book she had processed through inter-library loan for one of the doctoral students. Professor Grace Chilwell, who had grown up and been educated in the UK, had become chair of the Department of Ethics at Melbourne University in Australia. She had written numerous books on the theme of goodness and evil in post-Freudian family systems. Mm, Anna had thought. Was that massive guilt or massive denial or were there far more secrets in the Chilwell family than anyone had suspected? It could hardly be mere academic interest to the woman who had given birth when she was a child herself. Grace had died in a water-skiing accident at the height of her success in 1981. She had married out there but not had children and she had kept her maiden name professionally. Neither parent, Anna realised, thinking about it freshly for the first time in years, had lived long enough to have developed EOFAD. They must have died within months of each other. Had they ever communicated? Had there been a long thread of narrative between them formed from the knowledge of their lost son? Or had they ricocheted away from each other in shame at what they had done in a moment of giddiness never to see each other again?

Anna knelt down and slid out the box from under her bed. It was unlikely it would contain any secrets but there might be something. She was still cold from her time in the garden and she pulled on her dressing gown over her clothes, shivering. She could hear the others coming in from the shed so the readings must be over. Soon she would have to go down or appear rude. A rubber band kept the lid safe and she pulled it off. Instantly it broke, perished by the years of service it had done. Quickly she opened the box and tipped the contents on to her duvet. There was the birth certificate with the parents' names and other details and the adoption certificate dated two years later. So there had been two years before Harry was adopted. Anna paused, wondering why. She hadn't thought about this before. On the face of it he would seem to have been an ideal choice for a young couple who could not have children of their own.

There were also some snapshots of Harry with other children, rather out of focus and crudely coloured; this would have been in the early days of colour photography. She could easily identify him because Ellis was Harry all over again. That was no surprise. She had seen the photos that Harry's adoptive parents had taken and lovingly catalogued over the years of his growing up. She just hadn't seen any this early. She looked closely and noticed that in none of them was he smiling. He was peering at the camera with a look of what was it? Concentration? Anxiety? No, it was fear. He was frightened. What on earth had caused that? She felt her heart beginning to beat uncomfortably fast.

'Are you coming down, love? I'm making us coffee.'

'All right, Dad, coming,' she called down. She shoved the papers and bits and pieces back into the box and slipped it under the bed. It felt as though something dark and menacing had crept into the room, into her head. She pulled off the dressing gown, suddenly far too hot, and brushed her hair quickly.

Faye had gone about her own business and Ellis was at Mike's so it was just the adults settling themselves in the living room in the comfortable old sofa and chairs. George had made a cafetiere and carried it in on a large tray with mugs and a plate containing a lemon drizzle cake.

'I made it myself,' he announced, twinkling at Diane and Joan. 'So you've got to have a piece.'

Anna smiled archly at him. 'Really?' she teased, 'you made it all by yourself?' He blushed and got flustered handing around the plates. It was nice to see him like this, enjoying himself. He must have been cooking all day she realised. So what was all this in aid of? Maybe Faye really had been barking up the wrong tree. As he handed her a plate with a good slice of buttery, lemony cake, she grinned up at him. Unseen by the others he put his tongue out at her.

'George, this is delicious!' said Diane happily dropping crumbs down her new cardie. 'Are you always this good a cook?'

Bob nudged her elbow and a few more crumbs fell his way which he snapped up slobbering on her corduroys.

'Actually he is,' Anna put in loyally. Poor old bugger, give a cheer for the home team. 'And as I didn't have a mother he's been cooking for me since I was three so I think I'm entitled to give him a reference.' Might as well slip a bit of useful information into the compliment, she thought. George looked bashful. They chewed and drank their coffee comfortably together.

'Joan's been showing me how to save all the stuff about Briony,' George said as soon as his mouth was empty. 'I've got it in a folder, well, all that I could save, so it would be easy to put it on to a flashdrive for her when she comes home.'

'That's great, Dad.' Anna looked affectionately at the three of them. 'We make a pretty impressive team, don't we? Once we got going the American penal system stood no chance!' They raised their coffee cups and laughed.

'And Steve, of course,' said George.

'Oh yes, he was wonderful,' said Diane eagerly. 'If he hadn't kept up the entries on Briony's page and listed all the useful websites and blogs it wouldn't have been nearly so effective.'

'And the press releases he wrote – that was him, wasn't it? They were so clear and hard-hitting and what's the word?' Joan wrinkled her brow.

'Emotive?' said George. Anna began to feel uncomfortable.

'He should be here celebrating with us! Why don't you give him a ring Anna? I think we've got a bottle of bubbly somewhere.' George began to get up from his chair.

'Dad, no.' Anna's brain churned. She had not told her dad about the coolness at work. How could she without hinting that there had previously been far too much heat. 'He's not home this weekend,' she lied, 'he's climbing somewhere.' George looked at her more sharply than she wanted for a moment and then let this pass.

'Well you tell him from us that we think he's a knight in shining armour and so will Briony when she finds out all he's done. He's worked his socks off for that girl and I hope she appreciates it,' Diane said and then struck the arm of the chair triumphantly. 'Let's have a party! When she comes home let's have a party for everyone! Us and her neighbours and Steve and everyone at Safe n Sound. It'll be warmer weather when she gets here – we could have a barbeque at the farm! Maggie said Briony always loved animals and Bob could come too. It would be perfect.' And they all talked at once with ideas for how they could make it a special occasion.

Anna smiled and was quiet. She felt awful. It was true what they'd said, Steve had been fantastic. She had been so unfair to him. She had hardly given him a thought for days. It wasn't his fault that Faye had had a go at her about him and he wasn't to blame that Christmas Day had been so fraught. Yes, she still loved Harry but he had understood that. He had been the one holding her off. He hadn't come on to her, it had been the other way round. Her heart filled to bursting. He had been nothing but helpfulness and kindness.

She remembered in a rush him rocking her gently in his arms as he consoled her and dried her tears and how exactly what she needed that had been. He had been gentle and tactful and understanding. She looked at her watch. It was nine o'clock. Would he be at home? Dare she ring him after her coldness all week? The others barely noticed as she rose and slipped out of the room. They had paper and biros and were making lists.

She leaned against the kitchen door and listened to the dial tone. What would she say? He must think she was a silly woman who blew hot and cold over nothing. 'This is Steve – leave a message.' She hesitated for a moment. 'Steve? It's Anna. Well, you know that. I'm so sorry I've been weird this last week. It's not you.' Oh, God, another cliché. 'Steve, please call me.' She waited. Nothing came. She slipped her phone into her pocket, blew her nose and thoughtfully went back into the living room.

They were all sitting quietly staring in front of them and for a second Anna wondered if they'd heard her call. Her dad turned to her. 'We were talking about Margaret,' he said. 'Diane and Joan were comparing the stories she'd told them about Briony in America. So sad.'

'Why didn't she tell us the truth?' Joan said, her voice sharp with frustration. 'We would have supported her, comforted her.'

They sighed. Anna slipped back into her chair.'There was more to it than that Briony had stopped communicating with her.' She paused. She didn't want to betray the extent of Margaret's secret agony even to her friends. 'She thought she was to blame.'

'How could she?' asked Diane, 'It was that rotten man that caused all the trouble! If I could get my hands on him-' Anna couldn't help smiling a little looking at how fierce the older woman had become. She had no doubt that even the bullying Karl Bulowski would have come off worse in any confrontation.

'But she didn't know about that. She could only go on what she knew and she thought that she had said something to upset Briony on her last trip home.' After thinking long and hard about it Anna had not sent that final letter that Margaret had been writing the night before she died of a massive heart attack. What good would it do? 'I suppose she didn't want to tell you because she felt ashamed of herself, crazy as that seems to us.'

'So all the trips to America she told us about. Where *did* she go?'

'Oh, she went to America. She was looking for Briony in any place she could think of – official records in Illinois and nearby states, colleges she might have enrolled in, schools in Chicago where Donny might have gone – just anything she could think of to try to trace them.' Anna paused. 'It's ironic that she had the answer right there in her bedroom.'

'What do you mean?' asked Joan.

Anna explained about the shoe box and the photograph with Briony's married name on the back. 'If Margaret had Googled that name and Chicago she would certainly have found Briony in all the newspaper articles about her arrest and the trial. What a shock that would have been for her. I think the photo had simply never been turned over and I wouldn't be surprised if Maggie had only taken a quick look at it because its envelope was barely creased. Perhaps it hurt her to see strangers with her grandson.'

'Such a tiny thing,' said George thoughtfully, 'it would have just taken her a second to turn the photograph over and put two and two together and all her searches would have been unnecessary.' He stared out of the window from the depths of his armchair. 'But life is like that, isn't it? A moment can change everything. I sometimes think that we are only living one life among countless paths of possibility of other lives we could have lived if we'd made different decisions that keep our actual lives company like wraiths along the way.' There was a pause.

'Sometimes it's not our decisions that change our lives,' said Joan. Her voice was shaking a little with emotion. 'Sometimes it's totally beyond our control.' Everyone sat very still, waiting, remembering the powerful poetry she had shared with them.

In the silence the small sounds of the street came into the room. A couple of teenagers chatting and laughing as they passed the house and the dull whine of a car changing gear as it left the junction at the end of the road. Anna thought of Harry asleep upstairs. Why had he begun to sleep so much? Was it part of the dementia or was something else wrong? After all, just because he had one condition did not mean that the rest of him was in perfect health. Had her father made an appointment for him or not? She needed to check.

Bob, stretched in front of the gas fire, raised his old head and looked at Joan enquiringly. Perhaps he had heard a small intake of breath that meant she was about to speak. Anna pushed her other thoughts away and prepared herself to listen.

'Oliver is not my only son. Was not. We had another son, his younger brother, Howard.' She stopped for a moment as though saying the name had used too much energy for her to continue.

'Twenty-four years ago we came into some money. It was unexpected, from an uncle on my husband's side. He lived in a flat, well, a maisonette, in Hythe in Kent and had a very frugal routine. We used to visit him sometimes when we went to the south coast. My husband was mad keen on sailing and we'd go somewhere in Devon or Dorset and hire a sailing dinghy for the day. We only pottered around the estuaries, never far out to sea, of course.' Joan shifted in her seat and leaned forward. 'Well, we were stunned when he died to find that his entire estate had been left to my husband and that it amounted to over £100,000. We had assumed he rented the maisonette but it turned out he'd owned it for over forty years so of course it was worth a bit. Naturally we were delighted. We hadn't been that close to him and with Ollie about to start university it seemed a godsend.' No-one interrupted.

'Anyway,' Joan went on, 'we put most of the money away but we decided that we would treat ourselves with the rest. My husband was a Forestry Service Warden, we lived in a tied cottage in Shropshire, so he'd never earned much. It didn't matter, he loved his job and we had a good life. It was great for the boys to be out in the country. I had taken a computer technology degree from Shrewsbury College so I set up a little business doing websites for people. I could do it from home.'

There was a longer pause. Anna hoped she had remembered to switch off her phone.

'We bought a boat. It was a 38 foot ocean-going yacht with a cabin that would sleep four. Second-hand, of course. Walter, my husband, was ecstatic. He signed up for a Master's course, you know, navigation and all that, and we had the boat towed from its yard at Portsmouth to a dock on the Tamar estuary. We went down to see it, well three of us did, Ollie was on a school trip, and we spent hours going over every bit of it. It was a fairly old boat that had been reconditioned and it had none of the modern GPS technology. We didn't plan to take it out to sea until Walter had his Master's Certificate.' She paused and sighed so deeply that Anna closed her eyes. 'But that evening it was so calm that he and Howie decided they couldn't resist just taking her out for a sail. Just a little sail down the estuary and then back. There was an engine on her so if there wasn't enough wind, no problem. I'd driven down from home and was tired and there was a three-part drama I'd been following on ITV and I wanted to watch the last episode at the cottage we'd rented.'

She paused for so long this time that George gently nudged her on. 'And what happened?'

Joan looked startled as though she had forgotten that she was not alone. 'They never came back. They never came back. The boat was never found, no bodies were washed up, they just disappeared.'

'Was there a storm?' asked Diane, horrified but fascinated.

'No. It was calm.'

'But -'

'Of course when I reported to the coastguard that they hadn't come back, it must have been around ten when I went to look for them, they got everyone out. You know, the lifeboat, the helicopters, they tried everything. But when there was no sign of them anywhere what could they do? Then the police took over but after only one interview I knew that was hopeless. They kept asking if we'd had a row, if there were family problems. I suppose they thought that Walter had holed the boat out of revenge or something, you hear about fathers killing themselves and their kids don't you? Or, I don't know, maybe they thought he'd taken off to France and was living a new life with a woman there I didn't know about.' No one knew what to say. Moments passed. 'There's a name for it now,' said Joan wryly.

'A name for what?' asked George.

'For when you've lost someone close and you don't know if they're dead or not and you don't know how they died – they've just gone.' She looked at Anna sympathetically. Anna wondered why.

'It's called ambiguous loss. You can't move on, you can't heal, it's like they never really die – they're there and not there.'

Anna looked down at hands.

Diane was sitting next to Joan on the sofa and put her big calloused hand over Joan's neat bony one. 'What do you think happened?' she asked softly.

'I don't know. It's possible that several little things went wrong at the same time. They might have gone a lot further out than they meant to, the engine may not have started when they switched it on, and of course most people didn't have mobile phones then. And then they might have found that the boat had a leak and they were too far out to get help or swim. They weren't prepared for anything to go wrong. Ken wasn't used to sailing such a big boat. It's the only scenario I can think of except for piracy which seems unlikely off the Devon coast.'

Anna's professional head switched on. 'Could you not get a marine archaeology team to look for them?' she said. Joan instantly burst into tears. 'I'm so sorry, I'm so sorry.' Anna scrambled to the sofa and knelt in front of Joan. 'Please, I'm sorry.' Joan stopped weeping and dried her eyes. She took Anna's hand.

'I know that would be the rational thing to do. I know. But to me it would be like grave-robbing. If they're down there I want them to rest in peace. If they're not down there I don't know how I'd cope. Ollie might organise a search after I've gone but not before. He knows how I feel.'

George slipped out of the room and came back with a bottle of brandy and four balloon glasses. 'Medicinal,' he said firmly and poured a liberal shot into each glass. When they were all settled he said to Joan, 'I wondered what it was when you read your poetry. I knew there was something very deep there - something very painful.'

'Writing is all that keeps me sane some days,' Joan admitted. 'This campaign for Briony – it's made me realise how much I'd gone into myself over the years. It was a relief to think about something else, to be honest.'

George raised his glass, 'To true friends and good companions,' he said.

Anna thought she had better say it now rather than wait. 'The party at the farm for Briony's home-coming – it's a fantastic idea and I'm sure she'll love it but I can't be there.' They looked at her in astonishment. 'I can't be connected with the campaign. My boss at Harts told me that if he found I'd been involved I'd lose my job. As long as Briony doesn't make any connection between me and you it'll be ok. And I'm afraid you can't mention Steve either for the same reason.' They were disappointed but once she'd explained they could see it had to be that way.

Anna lay awake in her narrow bed for a long time that night. Ambiguous loss. Yes, Joan was right, she was grieving. She thought about how Harry had looked in the shed when he had asked, 'Have you been inside my head? Was my wife there?' His eyes had been so worried, so vulnerable. And in a heart-beat the other photo of Harry was superimposed – her husband as a little frightened boy staring at the camera, or, she suddenly realised, whoever was behind it.

24

Ellis had come with them to the service at the little Coptic Church in the Warwickshire village. Anna had noticed that he seemed to want to spend more and more time with his father. Could he feel him slipping away? But Harry was having a good day and hummed contentedly in the back seat of the car as they drove through the wet leafy lanes.

George had loved the service and Anna had found that against her will, almost, she had been drawn in to the ancient ritual.

It felt very exotic. The candles everywhere made the gold and silver on the icons glitter so that the painted faces seemed to be living things and the singing from a small knot of men and women was rich and full of poignancy and passion. People came and went, kissing the icons presented on stands near the front and the priest moved backwards and forwards through the curtain which seemed to screen the holiest part of the church. At the end men and women, some of them wearing headscarves, had come up to them and shaken their hands and smiled in welcome. Mr Shenouda had been delighted to see them and had introduced them to his wife and children.

Harry had not wanted to leave. It was the music, thought Anna, and resolved to take him to some short concerts. She remembered that the Barber Institute had lunchtime recitals and so did St. Martins in the Bullring and the Cathedral. How neglectful of him she had become! So mired in her own feelings of loss and anxiety that she had half-forgotten that he was still alive, still able to enjoy things. 'Come on, Dad,' Ellis had said cheerfully taking his hand, 'Bob will be waiting for us.' And of course Harry had got up eagerly and George was able to help him with his coat. They knew how to manage him. Thank God. Anna came to a decision.

She found Mr. Shenouda unloading plastic containers of food from his Nissan X-Trail's tailgate in the car park. 'Picnic?' she said, smiling.

'A christening later!' he replied, clearly delighted. 'A very special day.'

'It was a wonderful service,' Anna said, 'thank you so much for asking us to come. Lots to think about and talk about.'

Mr Shenouda stopped what was doing and gave her his full attention. His skin was almost grey with cold and she noticed that he was probably a little older than she had thought but his expression was warm and focussed. 'What do you want to ask me?' Anna felt flustered.

'It's not fair to talk to you about work.'

'What do you want to ask me?' he repeated softly.

The blood rushed to Anna's face. She took a deep breath. 'Why doesn't Harry know me? Why won't he let me touch him? I'm the only one.' She couldn't stop a catch in her voice. 'I'm the only one in the family that he's like that with.' She gazed up at the brown eyes. 'We were happy. He loved me. And now this has started and I can't bear it.'

As before in the hospital, he gently took her hand. 'It is a little unusual, Anna, although I have seen it happen before, but the brain is a very complex organ. The disease causes breaks in neural links, disconnections between memories, sometimes it can even make false memories. A fairy story character or a monster from a film seen in childhood can become as real as living people. I don't know what's going on in Harry's brain but you must remember that the happy times you had before are the reality. The distance from you, even the antagonism he seems to feel now, is the illness.'

She stared up at him bleakly. 'Yes.'

'But,' he went on, 'I was going to ask my secretary to contact you anyway. I would like to do some further tests before the next MRI and maybe change his medication a little. If both you and your father could attend we could have a proper talk about the situation.'

'Right.' He let Anna's hand drop and turned back to his task.

'And,' he continued, his voice muffled by his exertions with bags and boxes, 'I can introduce you to my replacement. At the hospital.'

Anna's heart dropped down a well. 'Replacement?'

'Yes,' Mr Shenouda emerged with bags and boxes in his hands and tucked under his chin. 'Mr Bellings-Smythe.' He twinkled at Anna. 'With a Y not an I of course.' When she didn't smile in response he regarded her kindly. 'He's very eminent and I will make sure he is completely up to date with Harry's case.'

'But we like you.' Anna thought how childish she sounded and how a bit like an abandoned child she felt. 'Harry knows you.' Mr Shenouda carefully placed all his bundles back in the open boot.

'We have to go,' he said seriously, 'my wife and children too. My mother is a widow and she has become very ill. She needs nursing and she needs us to nurse her. It was always the understanding.'

Anna touched his arm feeling a rush of sympathy for this large, kind man so far from home. 'Of course. But you will be very missed. You've been wonderful to all of us.' And the next minute they were hugging for a brief moment before he picked up his bags and boxes again and hurried into the church.

A few fat drops of rain fell on to her head and she quickly pulled up her hood and walked briskly to their own car where the others were waiting inside. Remembering her resolution, Anna pulled a CD from the glove compartment and put it on. It was Don McClean's American Pie. As Anna pulled out of the car park she glanced at her husband behind her. His eyes were shining and his mouth seemed to be trying to form words. This had been their driving music when they had bought their first car, an old Landrover, and it had been a tape in a player balanced on the dashboard, not a CD, but it might just be that Harry remembered it at least a little.

'Long, long time ago,' she sang along loudly, 'I remember when...'

'Oh no! Help!' Ellis cried frantically putting his hands over his ears. Anna grinned at him in the mirror and cranked up the volume. She was tone deaf and she knew it. It was a family joke that when Ellis was a toddler he had begged her not to sing him to sleep. 'No, Mummy, no sing!' he had wailed shaking his head to underscore the message. 'Daddy sing!'

'....the day the music died,' George joined in resonantly.

And in full voice Harry came in on the chorus, 'Bye bye, Miss American Pie, drove my Chevy to the levy but the levy was dry -' Anna was crying and laughing and singing and when they stopped at a little pub that advertised a 'real log fire' Anna turned to her father as she switched off the engine.

'Moments,' she said quietly, smiling at him. 'We may not have many years but we can have moments.'

'That's my girl,' he said.

As Anna pushed her way through the swing doors at Harts on Monday morning she was resolved to sort things out with Steve. There had been no messages from him over the weekend and she had not felt able to phone him again. He deserved an explanation and an apology and, she smiled to herself, she wanted to pass on the messages from Joan and Diane. Their knight in shining armour! She could imagine him blushing and shy. She dropped her coat and bag at her desk and went off immediately to find him.

'He's not here.' It was Suzanne blithely striding down the corridor. 'London.'

Anna turned away from the locked door to his office. 'Why?'

'The merger, you know, what Ted was on about on Friday – they want to liaise with Steve. They've obviously realised he's the only one here with any real smarts!' She came to a halt and studied Anna's face. 'Seriously, have you ever thought of blusher – just a tiny bit? You've got a lovely skin but this time of year we all need a bit of help.'

'Thanks for that, Suze,' Anna said, 'just what I needed.' They both laughed but before Suzanne could move off added, 'What do you mean, the only one with real smarts? We're all pretty much on a par, aren't we?' She realised she was pushing for information on Steve and her internal moral superintendent thought the less of her for it.

'Oh, of course, you're sort of new. I'd forgotten. Steve came about, ooh, a year ago and he did do a bit of sleuthing but he didn't really like it and then Ted cottoned on that he was really fantastic on IT so he carved out the job Steve has. Turns out he'd been a lecturer at Aston uni before this. Physics, I think.' Anna raised her eyebrows.

'Yeah, I know. Bit of a comedown. He never talks about it but I wouldn't be surprised if he'd had a bit of a marital crisis – you know, something like that. He's not with anyone now unless she's locked in the cellar. When he first came he didn't talk to anyone he didn't have to – that's where the Steely Steve comes from. He's a tad better now – you can have a bit of a laugh with him sometimes. But then, who knows better than us that most people have a least one skeleton in their cupboards?'

Anna flinched but then realised that Suzanne meant their work, not her personally. My family could take out a contract with an anatomy school, Anna thought grimly. She wondered if Steve had come here after the break-up with his wife. If so, it had certainly affected him very badly to make him want to give up a hard-won academic career. She went back to her desk and opened her personal email account. Ten minutes later she pressed 'send' and hoped for the best.

Lena was failing. Anna sat by the bed looking frankly at her mother. Lena was past noticing or caring. The flesh was beginning to recede from the bones of her face so that it appeared beakier. Her hair had been recently combed and lay like strokes of a black marker pen on the pillow. At the crown and down the parting the silver grey had widened to a bold stripe and for a moment Anna tried to imagine her with entirely grey hair. Would that have been better, worse? Her eyebrows, clean of make-up, were sparse and jutting and there were some coarse black hairs by the corners of her mouth and one on the side of her chin. Anna drew back feeling she was being indecently voyeuristic. Lena was now beyond passion, beyond love and sex and excitement and even malice and manipulation. Should she have given her dying mother her wish? Should she have agreed to look after Len? But why? He was not sub-normal, he was not physically handicapped – why should he need anyone to look after him?

Two nurses slipped quietly into the room. It was time to turn Lena and, no doubt, clean her up. Anna got up finding one leg had gone to sleep and limped out of the room. She had already been here longer than she meant. There was something oddly addictive about being at her mother's bedside now that she was comatose. She wasn't sure it was altogether sane. As she left the building her spirits rose and she made a promise to herself to keep future visits much shorter. George had been back only once while Lena was still at the QE and had not talked to Anna about that visit. She had only had to glance at his face on his return to know that questions would be intrusive.

At home there was an unusual hush but on the kitchen table was a note from George. They had all gone to the cinema – her dinner was in the oven. She was starving. She put her plate on to a tray and poured a glass of red wine from the box and then, holding the glass awkwardly with finger and thumb to stop it slipping, she made her way to the living room. The evening news had just started.

Most of it was financial, another indicator had been published with a tiny change in inflation but the press were doing their best to work it up into major news. Her attention wandered until some footage came up of a large red-brick building and she caught the words 'children's home'. She stopped eating and listened.

It was a home in Wales where it seemed that, sickeningly, there had been decades of sexual abuse of some of the children. Only now was the extent of the exploitation coming to light. Immediately the image of little toddler Harry with his frightened eyes sprang into her imagination. It wasn't this home, she knew that, it had been one in Derbyshire, but still. She found the remote and switched the tv off. Quickly, she finished her meal and took the tray back to the kitchen.

She keyed the name of Harry's home into the search engine and three sites came up. She clicked on one and immediately a bright, sunny home page in yellow and light turquoise popped up. Photos scrolled across the middle band of smiling happy children and doting carers. She scanned the options and clicked on 'archive'.

Not only was the home still active but there was an archivist. It seemed that many people wanted to trace the pasts of children who had been abandoned and placed in the Arkwright Residential Home for Children. The page was attractively set up with photos stretching back to the late nineteenth century by the look of the clothes and some description of the history in an elegant copperplate font. But there was also a stern warning. No information about previous residents still living could be given without a face-to-face interview which must be pre-arranged and accompanied by suitable documentation. They very wisely did not want random fishing trips by journalists or anyone else with no valid connection.

Anna clicked on the Contact Us box and wrote her request asking if a marriage licence would be sufficient proof of connection and explaining about Harry's condition. There was a box which asked if there was a particular piece of information the applicant was searching for. Anna thought, yes, what happened to so frighten a little boy forty-five years ago? But she couldn't write that so she asked instead why it had taken so long for Harry to be adopted and any other information about him. Could she visit and speak to the archivist? Maybe look at photos of that time? She carefully did not reveal her professional occupation. She was going to stay very firmly on the safe side of Ted from now on. She pressed 'submit' and sat back.

A creak and a crash announced that the family were back. 'Cool film!' Ellis told her, 'loads of really good SFX! Can I have some ice-cream? Pops wouldn't let us there.'

'Not at £3.50 a go - no,' said George. 'All right Anna? Good day at work?' Anna closed the laptop.

'Why,' cried Faye dragging off her coat, 'can't we go to see films I like? Why does it always have to be stupid boys' films?'

'I don't think that's entirely true,' George said mildly, 'didn't we go to that Anne Hathaway thing last time?'

'Soppy,' said Ellis. 'Oh Mum. Mike and his dad are going surfing to Cornwall at Easter. Can I go?' His skinny arms tensed as he dug into the frozen tub of chocolate pecan.

Anna's heart sank a little. She hated water sports herself but Ellis was like a dolphin. 'I don't know. How much is it? How long for? Not that much!' He had chiselled out half the tub. 'I didn't know you were interested in surfing.'

'How will I know if I don't try?' Ellis said reasonably. 'I'm not sure how much it is but they stay at his dad's cousin's place at Newlyn so it shouldn't be too much. Mr Bryant's going to phone you and tell you stuff.' He grabbed some digestive biscuits to stick into the mound of goo in lieu of wafers and made off to the front room where Harry had gone.

'It's not fair,' said Faye predictably, 'I never get to go anywhere. Spoilt brat.' Anna knew that this was merely a conventional retort and needed no answer. But when Faye sat down at the table with her bowl liberally crowned with chocolate sauce, she became more alert. 'Mum?'

'Yes.'

Faye dropped her voice. 'You know your mum?'

Anna wondered if she should give a truthful answer to that but decided against it. 'Yes.'

'Do I look like her?' She paused with her spoon half way to her lips. This mattered. Anna regarded her daughter's deep tobacco-coloured eyes and clear rosy skin. She was wearing her abundant hair up these days in a loose top-knot and lively tendrils of rich brown sprang glossily around her face and neck. Anna thought of how her mother had looked that afternoon.

'No,' she said. 'Not at all.' Faye's spoon continued to her mouth and she slurped the ice-cream off it with her tongue. That seemed to be the acceptable answer. She decided to build on it. 'I think you probably look like your dad's mum.' Faye swallowed abruptly.

'How do you know?' Anna inwardly cursed herself.

'I was just guessing.' She waited. Faye looked at her steadily.

'Why haven't you ever looked her up? It's what you do, isn't it?'

228

'Dad didn't want me to.' Anna mentally crossed her fingers and waited. In fact, the photograph on the back of Professor Chilwell's book had borne some resemblance to Faye but she had only just put their likeness together. Faye had been just a child when she had done her clandestine research. Faye was quietly playing with the melted mess in the bottom of her bowl.

'Mum?' She looked up at Anna with such frankness and vulnerability that Anna's heart contracted. 'If I do look like her, does it mean that I'll get what dad's got?' Anna reached out and took Faye's hand.

'I don't know.' Faye looked down. 'It's certainly got nothing to do with who you look like and the chances would be very slim but I can't tell you right now that you definitely wouldn't. Darling, I'm being completely honest with you because you asked but please try not to worry about it.'

As soon as the words were out she regretted them and waited for the inevitable storm of retaliation. How could Faye not worry about it? It was what she and George worried about all the time. Whether one or both of the children might develop the disease, how Harry would deteriorate, what they would need to do, how the children might be affected by that, how they could afford proper care, on and on – worrying about it was the ghost in the house, the mischievous and arbitrary djinn that pinched and poked at them in nearly all their waking moments. Now Faye was becoming aware.

She was growing up and it was beginning to dawn on her that she might contain within her that random bad gene that would blight her life. But Faye had not exploded. She was quiet. Anna thought that was almost worse.

'Well,' she said finally, half-smiling at her mother, 'carpe diem, eh?' Yes, Faye was growing up.

Harry was dozing next to Ellis on the sofa. Anna met Ellis's eyes and nodded at his father questioningly. 'He was asleep when I came in,' Ellis whispered. 'Shall I wake him up?' Anna shook her head and went back out of the room to find George. He was in his shed photocopying, making stacks of pages set at right-angles to each other.

'First issue nearly ready!' George said with pleasure. 'I think there's some good stuff in here. Let's hope it brings some different poets out of the woodwork. Probably all old farts like me but that's ok, we have our stories to tell.' He squared off the pile and looked at it with satisfaction. 'It's lucky black and white looks classy – it's so much cheaper.'

Anna relayed her conversation with Faye. 'I was touched, actually. She was very mature.'

'I got an email from Mr Shenouda's secretary today.' My goodness, thought Anna, he didn't waste any time. 'They want to see us all, I mean you, me and Harry. When shall I say?'

'It's got to be in work time anyway so it doesn't really matter,' said Anna, 'but I'd like it sooner rather than later. I had a feeling on Sunday that he had something he wanted to talk to us about. I mean something specific. Just ask for the earliest one, do you think?'

'Will do,' said George. 'Oh, I nearly forgot. I had an email from Joan.'

'Oh, did you?' Anna picked up some waste paper from the floor and put it into George's overflowing basket.

'Yes, it seems events have been moving without us.'

'What do you mean?'

'Joan's been contacted through her son by an American documentary maker who wants to use Briony's case to do an expose of Cook County Jail. I'm pretty sure Briony has already been moved so she couldn't be compromised by it.' He rubbed his chin sorrowfully. 'And of course that guard, that one that was abusing her, is on remand for it so he's out of the way.' Anna was painfully aware that she felt side-lined even though she had asked to be.

'Please be very careful, Dad.'

'We've cooked up a story so that you and Steve don't have to be mentioned. Our story is that Joan's son, Oliver, saw the story about Briony in the Chicago Tribune when he was there on business, recognised his childhood friend and told his mother. She's going to say she and I knew each other through Diane. I volunteered to set up a Facebook page. And it went from there.' Very close shave, Anna thought, very, very close.

'And will the others go along with that?'

'Oh yes. I phoned Diane and she'll pass it on - they totally understood.' George paused and looked at Anna. 'You don't mind not having the glory do you? We all know it wouldn't have happened without you, and Steve, of course.' Anna snorted.

'Wait a minute. If they want to interview you -'

'All sorted. We'll do a little piece to camera by the house in Mill Lane and then to Briony's old school and then into Joan's house for a chat there and then out to the farm to interview Diane.'

'Not here?'

'Definitely not here.'

'I hope they're all up to this, Dad, this is too close for comfort.'

George stood up and rubbed his hands over his tufty head. 'Fun though, isn't it?'

25

Anna went back into the kitchen and began to stack the dishes in the dish-washer. Thank goodness those women were so switched on. We're like the neurons in Harry's brain, she thought. Connect us dendrites up a certain way and you get one story. Make one new connection and you get out on your ear and no job – a very different story. And then make another connection, another synapse crackles, and there's Lena – and you've got dead and dying mothers and missing daughters to make all sorts of narratives out of. If we were celebrities it could keep the red-tops going for days.

She fervently hoped that the American documentary would be forgotten and then berated herself because that was just the kind of high-profile exposure that Briony and women like her needed to right the abuses they had suffered. Wouldn't Len love it if he could claim a connection, heaven forbid? She must tell her dad not to let on to him although he'd probably figure that out for himself. She hadn't heard from Len or seen him for days and despite herself she felt a little unsettled about him. She wiped her hands and pulled her phone out of her pocket.

'Len?'

'Yeah?'

'It's Anna. I just wondered how you were doing.' She could hear the television in the background with whooping noises. A game show.

'How d'you think? My mum's dying.' He was crying, Anna realised, surprised. Not stage crying, not sobbing or weeping, but she could hear that he was choked up and probably had been before her call.

'Len, I'm sorry. It must be horrible for you.' Silence and some muffled noises. 'I could see how much you cared for each other.' A grunt.

'Len.' She decided not to think about what she was going to say next, just to do it. 'Len, I'm sorry we got off to a bad start. Why don't you come round some time? I mean if you want to.'

'Will your mad cow of a daughter be there?' But he was already sounding better, stronger.

'Probably. She does live here.' Anna decided to throw him a bone. 'But on the positive side I haven't seen Sasha since Christmas and I'm hoping that was the last of him.'

'All right then. When?' As they made the arrangement Anna could hear the old truculence creeping back into his voice but strangely, it didn't irritate her. It was a relief. And soon they would need to talk about what he wanted to do about Lena's funeral. Lena wasn't going to last much longer.

Ellis came in and picked up his school bag. 'Can I work down here for a bit?'

'Sure.' Anna liked it when they were both sitting at the big kitchen table quietly getting on with their own projects. She hadn't done too badly on the last assignment despite all the distractions and this one, the last, looked like the most interesting. It had to do with a historical perspective on laws of marriage, settlement and divorce among other things.

When Harry came down, in his day clothes but with his dressing gown over the top, Anna pulled out a chair for him and smiled but he ignored her and went to the fridge and got out the milk.

'Can I get you a drink, Dad?' Ellis offered. Harry smiled faintly at him but shook his head. Anna opened a new document and began typing the title. Ellis jogged her elbow. 'Hey, Mum,' he giggled, 'I've got to do this creative piece on what life was like for the dinosaurs. Can you give me a vox pop on it – you know – personal anecdotes?'

'Cheeky!' she laughed and cuffed him lightly across his hair.

Suddenly Harry was right by them. 'Stop it!' he shouted, 'Leave him alone you witch!' Both Anna and Ellis were shocked into silence.

'No, Dad,' began Ellis, 'she was only -'

But Harry wasn't listening. He pushed Anna and she almost fell off her chair. 'Go away! Leave us alone!' And then he stalked out of the room banging the door behind him. Ellis was almost in tears.

'Mum, I'm sorry. I'm so sorry.'

Anna took some deep breaths. She was badly shaken by what had happened but she wanted to make things better for Ellis. 'I'm ok, love,' she said. 'We know that it doesn't mean anything really. Your poor dad is just mixed up in his head. That's not the real him, you know?'

'I know. Sorry though.' She hugged him and couldn't resist a quick kiss.

'I'll take Bob out if you're all right here,' she said, knowing that concentrating on her assignment was going to be impossible until she had shaken the incident out of her head.

Outside the night air was sharp and she breathed it in gratefully. Bob lolloped beside her reluctantly registering dumb protest. She turned down their street and into the next road for the nearest patch of grass. No need to be out here longer than necessary.

Some young people surged gaily along and passed her laughing and teasing and she felt a momentary pleasure at their light-heartedness but then her own spirits sank. Bob performed his task and she slipped her hand into the plastic bag to clean up. Not a brilliant job for someone feeling rejected and despised she thought grimly.

As she straightened up she heard voices coming from the church across the road. It was the one Harry had wandered into. She liked the sound of the chatting and laughing and realised that she didn't fancy going home just now or walking the cold streets anymore. She strolled through the lych-gate and down the path telling the questioning Bob that they were just having a look. Inside a bunch of adults of all ages were being pretty rowdy, she thought, for a church, down by the 'holy end' as George called it quoting his nemesis, Larkin. Then there was a voice at her elbow and it was the priest she had met before.

'Are you joining us?' He was putting leaflets into hymn books.

'No, sorry. Is the dog all right in here?' When he smiled and nodded she asked, 'What's happening? I'm just being nosy. Are they putting on a play or a concert?' She had noticed the young people who had passed her on the road in amongst the others.

'No. Not tonight. They're just gathering. They'll be off in a minute. It's our turn to be the volunteers for the rough sleepers in the city centre.'

Anna had no idea what that meant. 'They're going to sleep rough? Why?' Some bonding or empathetic stuff she imagined.

He laughed softly. In his sixties Anna thought, glancing at his heavily lined face but still dark hair. He was wearing a thick fleece and sturdy jeans but the collar was still there. 'No, *they're* not sleeping rough. The inner city churches all have their heating on and put out fold-up beds and we go round the streets and along the canals, you know, where people who have nowhere to go spend the night. We just offer them some hot food and a safe warm place for the night. It's been a cold winter even without the snow.' Just then the noise stopped and she glanced towards the front. They were all kneeling and someone was saying something quietly. After a moment they got up and began to come up the aisle towards Anna.

'I'm sorry,' Anna said, 'you probably need to go. I'm holding you up.'

'Oh no. Ruth, my curate, is taking them down and I'll go along later. I have to finish up here. Would you like a cup of tea?'

'No thanks,' Anna said.

'Well, let's sit for a while?' He finished the leaflets and indicated the pew where she and Bob were standing. 'Your dog looks as though he'd be glad to take the weight off his feet.' Anna smiled and sat down while Bob collapsed his whole body on a convenient rug. 'I think we've met before?'

'Yes, I came looking for my husband.'

'He said the organ needed tuning. Quite right – it did.' There was a pause. 'How is he?' Anna thought of how Harry had looked that evening - the anger, the bitterness and hostility.

'Worse,' she said. 'He will only ever get worse.' She was fighting back a welling up of tears and relieved that this man whom she hardly knew neither touched her nor offered any platitude.

'What is it he has?' he eventually asked when she had regained control.

'It's a form of dementia. Early onset.'

He leaned back in the pew. 'Hard on everyone.'

'Yes.' Anna sighed. 'I'm very lucky actually. My dad lives with us now so I can work and he and my kids are just wonderful with Harry. He's sometimes a bit off with me though.' Massive understatement. The priest let this lie.

'What was he like before he was ill? Was it a good marriage?'

'Oh yes,' Anna lifted her head and smiled. 'He was my best friend. They say that, don't they, it's a cliché I suppose but it's true. We were each other's best friends. Not that it was all sweetness and light, of course, but we never held grudges. In fact we couldn't keep up an argument because one of us would just start giggling.' The tears suddenly rose in her eyes and she couldn't stop. 'And it's possible one or both of the children could inherit it. It's just breaking my heart.'

'Yes. I can see that.'

Anna turned to him angrily. 'Why would this happen? He was such a good man, such a great husband and father. What good does it do anyone for his brain to be eaten away so cruelly?'

The priest's head dropped and his hands lay loosely in his lap. After a few moments, he spoke. 'You saw those people going off into the city? The street people they'll offer help to are a mixed bunch. Some may be mentally ill, possibly schizophrenic, some may have been treated brutally as children and fallen into self-harm or prostitution. Some, more and more, may have been living ordinary family lives but spent up to the hilt and when the job went it wasn't long before the house and the family went too.' He looked at Anna carefully. 'Don't mistake what I'm saying. I don't mean that there are people worse off than you. That's not what I'm saying at all. What I'm saying is I don't know why there is suffering like this, often random and faultless when you really look into it. I don't think anyone knows.' He paused and looked at her earnestly. 'But I am convinced we must grit our teeth and believe in goodness. Goodness and love. That's real too and that is what we must hold on to.'

Anna walked home slowly with Bob lumbering and farting gently beside her and thought about Margaret literally breaking her heart over what she thought she had done to Briony and the daughter herself, buckling under the terrible strain of her situation. Hard to believe in goodness sometimes. Much easier to believe in love. She quickened her step. Screw the assignment, she'd make them all a chocolate mocha cake.

It was later, after the cake had cooled and been filled and put away for tomorrow that Anna switched her laptop back on for a final check on her emails. Immediately in bold type came Steve's name and a couple of emails behind it, Briony's. She stared at the two names and decided to open Briony's first. There was no greeting and it got straight down to business.

There's a team from NBC coming to Birmingham to interview people as part of a documentary about what happened to me in Cook County. I have given my permission for them to meet my mother's neighbour Joan McArthy and the woman who runs the animal sanctuary my mother volunteered for, Diane Bell. A friend of theirs, George Walcott, has also been contacted. These three people together with Mrs McArthy's son were responsible for starting the media campaign that led to my transfer to EMCFW which is a very different place from CCJ thank God. I think they are also responsible for my early release date. I believe it was actually Joan's son who knew me as a child who saw the article in the Tribune and alerted his mother who then got the campaign going. I am telling you all this because I do not want you to be involved in any way. It may be that you, as probate researcher, would be contacted by the NBC producers. I do appreciate you sending the letters that my mother was unable to mail but all of that side of things is very painful to me. I want her kept out of the documentary as much as possible. I have put very clear limits on what they can say about her. God knows, I hurt her enough when she was alive, the least I can do is protect her now she's dead. I hope you understand but even if you don't I expect your compliance. B'

Anna replied immediately as it appeared this facility would allow her to do.

Of course I understand and will not be involved with the documentary in any way. Actually, it would be very unprofessional of me in any case as maintaining the confidentiality of our clients is very important. I don't want to get another ticking off for unprofessional behaviour!

Glad to hear things are a bit better where you are,

Anna

She highlighted the last but one sentence wondering whether to delete it and then left it in. As soon as she pressed 'send' she felt she'd made the wrong decision. Oh well. Blimey. News travels fast. She opened Steve's email feeling already shaky.

Hi Anna,

Yes, I didn't understand why you were being so off. Thanks for writing but I still don't understand to be honest. I think we need to talk properly – I mean about several things. I'm free next weekend when I get back from London. I'd like to go out into the countryside

– the London scene is doing my head in. How do people live here? So if you could tolerate a soggy, cold and probably difficult conversation bring your walking boots to Kingswood Junction. It's in Lapworth. I'll meet you in the car park about 9.00. Oh make sure you talk to your dad soon – there are events as they say.

Steve.

Anna took a deep breath and let it out. Anything was better than silence. Yes, it would be a difficult conversation and what exactly would she say? He had clearly not gone for the fudged nuances in her email to him. So what did she want to say? I want you to want me but I don't want to do anything about it? I want you to make me feel I'm still desirable but I love Harry? Ridiculous. Unfair. But all the same her heart was skipping with excitement that in a few days she would see him away from the office. She groaned, closed her machine and banged her head gently on the palm of one hand.

26

Anna had cashed in some flexitime so she could set off for the Arkwright Home after lunch and she was in Derby by 3.30. It wasn't what she expected. No tall red-brick Victorian pile but a collection of bright, modern buildings, almost Scandinavian looking. There were plantings of grasses and shrubs and some winter-blossoming trees. Then, as she made her way following signposts along the pleasantly cobbled path from the visitors' car park to the Administration Department, she saw that the building where it was housed was much older – probably the original orphanage. Impressive slabs of greyish-yellow limestone created a simple symmetry which she found pleasing. She thought of Harts' offices.

This would be such a nice environment to work in. But then she remembered Harry's sad little face.

The receptionist checked her name and looked at her rather too searchingly, Anna thought. She had, as always before meetings, forgotten to check her hair and put on fresh lipstick. Almost immediately a tall, slim woman appeared dressed in a chic dark green fitted dress. 'Mrs Ames?' Anna followed her through a door which had a security keypad and then into a large office one wall of which was made up of filing cabinets.

'Was this building the original home?' Anna asked wondering how many children they had accommodated in what was probably the late-eighteenth century.

'I'm Colleen Dolan,' the woman said putting out her hand, 'the archivist, and yes, in fact,' she looked round, 'this was the dining room, well, the refectory.'

'The other buildings look so modern.' Both women sat down either side of a large wooden desk.

'Oh yes, they are. The Victorian row of houses was pulled down about fifteen years ago – just not fit for purpose and very gloomy.' There was a silence. Both of us are tense, thought Anna, but why is she? Colleen Dolan put on rimless reading glasses and looked at Anna over them.

'You wanted to know about a child who was here in the mid-sixties?' Was she imagining things or was Ms Dolan being deliberately over-formal? After all, she had explained in the email. Perhaps her manner was contrived to deter frivolous searches. 'Do you have the documents?' Anna pulled the slim folder out of her bag and passed it across the table. There was Harry's birth certificate, their marriage certificate, Anna's power of attorney and a letter from Mr. Shenouda testifying to Harry's condition. The archivist examined them closely as if looking for a loophole. Finally she looked up at Anna. 'So Henry Chilwell – Harry as you call him.'

'Yes.'

'What is it you want to know?' She took off her glasses and started fiddling with the earpieces.

'I'd be interested in anything you have about him but I'd like to start by asking how usual it was for a baby like he was when he first came here not to be adopted for two years?' Colleen put the glasses back on and looked down at the papers again. Anna persisted. 'He must have been very adoptable with healthy, bright parents and in good health himself. He was an adorable looking child.' Then she realised that she was actually talking about Ellis.

She flushed.

'It does happen.' Ms Dolan was stalling, Anna realised, it was not her imagination, she really was. Anna remembered the look of interest from the receptionist. She decided to go straight to the point.

'Was there a problem with Harry?' Silence. Anna made a decision – it was time to get tough. 'I really do want to find out anything I can and I believe I have the legal right to do so. There must be a file with details of his time here. Could I see it please?'

Colleen looked at her with what seemed to be despair. 'Just a minute, please.' She pressed a button on the inter-office phone and lifted the receiver to her ear. 'Mr Ainsworth, Mrs Ames is here. She wants to see Henry Chilwell's file.' She listened and replaced the handset. She turned to Anna and sighed almost imperceptibly. 'Mr Ainsworth is the Director of the Home. He's coming down to see you.'

Anna's thoughts raced. What on earth were they up to? Had they lost the file? Or – her heart began to pound – was there something that Harry had been caught up in that they were trying to keep hidden? She remembered the item on the news about the Welsh children's home. The door opened quietly and a large, muscular man came in moving, Anna couldn't help but notice, quite gracefully for his bulk. Rugby player? He pulled another chair up beside Anna and nodded at Colleen who opened a drawer in her desk and pulled out a thick manila file. So they had had it ready but were hoping not to have to produce it.

'Alan,' he said, shaking her hand. 'Henry Chilwell is your husband?' Anna nodded. He had the local accent, a broader version of Harry's own and for an irrational moment Anna was soothed by it. He smiled at her but then his face grew serious. 'How much do you know about his early years? I assume his adoptive parents said something about them?'

'No. No, they didn't.' Anna's moment of reassurance vanished. 'They told Harry he was adopted from the beginning but they didn't say anything else.' Her memory gave a lurch. 'Wait, I do remember his mum saying to me before she died that she'd always been glad that Harry hadn't wanted to go into his background but I assumed that meant looking up his birth parents. What else could she have meant?' Alan Ainsworth and Colleen Dolan looked at each other. Colleen pushed the bulky file across the table to her boss but he ignored it and turned to Anna.

'Something very unusual and serious happened to Harry while he was here.' Anna's heart was racing and her throat constricted. 'I'm going to tell you first and then show you the documents. Is that all right?' Anna nodded. She couldn't speak. Alan Ainsworth leaned his bulk forward a little and rubbed his hands across each other. Then he started to talk. 'Henry was brought here when he was almost a new-born, they did that then. He was put into one of the family units with experienced house-parents.' He paused.

'They were a bit too experienced in a way. I think you could say that they might have noticed what was happening a lot sooner if they hadn't been quite so relaxed about the job. They were only a couple of years off retiring and they'd begun to take their hands off the wheel.' Colleen was watching him with an anxious crease between her eyebrows. Anna felt as though the moments of silence were dragging out unbearably. 'They weren't the only staff. There was a woman in her thirties who was a sort of general helper, and she lived in the house with them and the children. Her name was Julia Smith. She'd got the job because she'd been a nurse before her husband had died and had useful skills.' He paused again and looked helplessly at Anna. 'I don't know how else to put this – she fell in love with Harry.'

'Fell in love?' Anna's voice croaked with tension. 'What do you mean?'

'She was obsessed with him. She was constantly being told off for taking him to her room and neglecting the other children. One night he was found in her bed and she was given a written warning.'

'Found in her bed?' Anna felt cold.

'Yes. The thing was she was frightening the child. The house-parents realised her behaviour was inappropriate but didn't take it seriously enough. It was a supervisor who cottoned on to the fact that Harry would cry when she picked him up or even if she approached him and not at other times. He was too young to talk much, of course.'

'Why didn't they place him in another home? Or sack her?'

Instead of replying, Alan continued. 'Things moved very fast. She was told by the supervisor that she must not have anything to do with Harry and that she would be called up in front of a disciplinary hearing over the incident when she tried to keep him overnight in her bed. That was on a Tuesday afternoon. That night they both disappeared.'

'What?' Anna felt her throat parch. 'What do you mean?'

'The police were called and a background check was done by the home. Now, of course, they're done before anyone's hired but in those days they weren't. People were just interviewed and trusted that what they said was true. And what she said about her husband dying was true, it just wasn't the whole truth.' Anna was beginning to feel sick. More wraiths and shadows and misleading half-truths.

'Go on,' she said grimly.

Alan shifted uneasily in his seat. 'Julia's husband was a violent man and frequently abused her. There was a baby – a little boy. One day when the baby wouldn't stop crying he picked it up and slapped it. The neck snapped.' An image of Briony driven to distraction shaking Donny sprang into Anna's head. She forced it out. 'There was an inquest and the father was found guilty of the child's death – manslaughter, not murder. He served, I think, four years – it's in the file. All that time Julia waited for him to come out. When he did, the first day he was home she waited until he was asleep and then tied him to the bed. When he was secure she woke him, doused him with petrol, and then, hours later, set fire to him.'

'Bloody hell.'

'We have no idea of course what went on in those hours she had him at her mercy.'

'But the police knew she'd done it?'

'After a few moments of setting the petrol alight she ran out of the house to the phone box and called the fire brigade. By the time they arrived the house was a fireball, of course. They may have suspected something, the fire investigators and the police, but he was a nasty man and they were sympathetic to her. That's what I think anyway.'

Anna was processing all this as quickly as she could, trying to push the horrific images to one side so she could get back to Harry. 'She had lost her baby. That's why she wanted Harry.'

'That's what we think. Obviously even back then she would not have been employed if they had known her tragic and violent family life.'

'Poor woman,' said Anna despite herself and half-thinking of Briony.

Colleen intervened. 'Just because someone has had a tragic thing happen in their life doesn't mean they're nice people,' she observed. 'Julia was not a good person to have in a children's home. She was harsh with her discipline and generally feared and disliked by the children. She knew how to be nice when adults were around but after what happened to Harry, the kids told the investigator that they had been afraid of her. Mean little things like pinching where it wouldn't show and threatening to hurt them. She even told one little girl that her mother had taken one look at her and left her because she was so ugly.'

Anna braced herself knowing now that she was going to hear the climax of the horrific episode. 'What happened to Harry when she took him away?'

'We don't know. He couldn't tell us and she wouldn't.' Alan looked sympathetically at Anna. 'It's possible nothing did. Remember, she adored him.'

'How did they find them? Where were they?'

'It was good police work – they interviewed people who had known her when she worked at the hospital. She had a very old grandfather who lived way back out in the Sticks up by Flash on the Staffordshire moorlands in a labourer's cottage. He'd been a farm worker but had become very arthritic and the housework had ceased when his wife died. Truth to tell, he lived in squalor. No phone, barely any running water. You can't believe it, can you, but there were still isolated cottages like that in the 60's. She took Harry there and that's where the police found them both four days later.' There was silence in the room.

Eventually Anna found her voice. 'What sort of condition was he in?'

'Dirty, cold. But no marks on him, no signs of any injury. Very frightened naturally but not starving. She had fed him.'

'What happened to her? She had kidnapped him, after all.'

'Psychiatric prison. She was a very disturbed woman.'

Colleen pushed the file across to Anna and she started leafing through the documents but barely registering what she was seeing.

There were the usual records from the home, court reports, police reports and so on. Anna had almost closed the file when she noticed a photograph in black and white. It was a group with three adults and, she counted them, fourteen children. The focus was not sharp but Anna could pick out a toddler held across the hip of a girl of maybe ten years old. Harry? She concentrated on the two adult women. 'Which one is Julia?' Colleen pointed.

It was only when she was getting ready to leave that Anna remembered the original question. 'Why was he here so long?'

Alan Ainsworth answered. 'His adoptive parents, Mr and Mrs Ames, gave the home the answer to that one. You see when prospective parents came to look at the kids they often picked out Harry but it seems that Julia would tell them privately that, off the record, he had fits and she hinted that his birth mother was round the bend. Most people backed off, of course, but not Mr and Mrs Ames. They must have just looked into his eyes and made up their own minds.'

'Thank God they did,' said Anna sincerely, 'they were lovely people and wonderful parents to him.' Then at the door she thought of something else. 'The place where they found him, the cottage, were there any animals?' Colleen opened the file, found a document and rapidly scanned two pages.

'Yes, dozens of them, apparently. Cats, kittens, dogs and of course, there would have been mice and rats, too, I wouldn't wonder from this description. All living in the most appalling filth.'

Anna buttoned up her coat. 'Thank you for being so frank. You have helped more than you could ever know.' The three nodded at each other and Anna left feeling years older than when she had come in.

In the car she buried her head in her arms on the steering wheel. Oh, Harry. Was that what your mum meant? Thank goodness they never told you. But maybe you did remember what happened in your dreams, your nightmares? Nevertheless, all your conscious memories of your childhood were happy and loving. After a while she sniffed, blew her nose, took out her phone and made a call.

27

When she got home she popped her head round the door of the living room and smiled at Harry, who was engrossed in watching a film about dolphins and ignored her, and then into the kitchen. The sight that met her was the last thing she needed. Faye and Sasha gripped in a fervent embrace. Damn it, she had hoped he was out of Faye's life.

They moved quickly but not quickly enough. Anna had seen Sasha's right arm hidden up to the scrawny elbow under Faye's jumper and his left hand blindly struggling to undo the waistband button on her jeans. Faye's left hand was invisible since she was largely masked by Sasha's body but her right hand was gripping his left buttock. Inside his trousers. Far, far too intimate. The two-second dash started in her head. She could pretend she hadn't seen them, she could then talk to Faye later, no, Faye would deny everything and out-shout her; she could sit them down and talk to them both, no, neither would agree and that would also cause unproductive shouting, probably with the garnish of slammed doors.

She could be direct with Sasha but about what? He was an adult and clearly not doing anything against Faye's will. Faye herself was of consenting age. Her real worry was that Faye was not protecting herself. OK. All runners past the finishing line in the Decision Making Cup. Race over. She'd got her priorities sorted.

'Oh hi, Sasha,' Anna said pleasantly, 'we haven't seen you for ages. OK?'

'Yes, Mrs Ames.' He was clearly ill at ease. She was pleased he was – so he should be. 'I am very good.' No you bloody aren't, thought Anna, you're groping my daughter you louse. She beamed at Faye.

'Darling, could we have a word? When you've got a minute.' Faye was frozen in her what-the-hell's-going-on mode. She produced a counter-offensive.

'Can Sasha stay for supper?'

'Of course,' Anna said, smoothly, 'just check that Pops has got enough to go round. It's his night. But I'm sure you won't mind having a smaller portion if not. He's making lasagne.' Faye loved lasagne. Her pretty arched brows drew together.

'I've just remembered, Sasha can't stay anyway, can you?' He looked confused. 'You've got to get that essay in tomorrow you told me.' He looked fed up. 'And I'm up to my ears. Mocks next week.' Sasha sighed and eased his pelvis away from the sink unit. 'See you later babes?' It was all Anna could do to avoid making vomiting noises.

'Maybe better tomorrow. You're all right seeing yourself out, aren't you?' Was Anna right in thinking that there was a tinge of relief in Faye's voice? The kitchen door closed behind him just a little harder than necessary. Anna put the kettle on and got out two mugs. She could see if Harry wanted anything later and she didn't want to break the moment and give Faye a chance to escape.

'Faye, sit down a moment will you? I want to talk to you about a rather sensitive issue.' Faye was instantly all attention. With the finely-tuned radar of all teenagers to their parents she knew that this was not the tone of admonition. Possibly it was the tone of confession which could be thrilling. Anna carried the mugs to the table and then returned with the open biscuit box and set it down between them. This was tantamount to her mother writing 'friend' across Faye's forehead. In response she delicately picked out a triple chocolate pecan cookie and nibbled it.

'You said something at Christmas that has really made me think,' Anna began. Faye regarded her mother steadily as she munched, mentally scanning all the possible subjects that might now be raised. 'You said my mother didn't want to see you.'

'Well, she doesn't, does she?' Faye spat crumbs. 'Len told me.'

'I know and it's awful.' Anna paused wondering where she got her acting skills from. Oh yes, the Last Chance Saloon. 'It was unkind of Lena but you're a woman now, not a child, and I just want to say to you that if you want to see her – I must warn you, she's pretty out of it - I'll take you.' She paused to give equal weight to each word. 'You can see your grandmother before she dies.' Anna glanced at her daughter appraising the effect. Yes, the drama of this statement coupled with being credited with womanhood had taken hold. Faye was gazing into middle distance prettily.

'Oh, I don't know, Mum. It would be so distressing, you know? She's behaved so inappropriately.' Anna suppressed a smile.

'I know.' She paused, appearing to reflect. 'But then, you see, she hasn't had an easy life. She could have done so much, she was clever enough, but when she had me she was a very young woman. Well,' Anna feigned surprise, 'about the same age as you, actually. Imagine being saddled with a baby and someone who you'd fallen out of love with just when life was beginning to open up.'

Anna glanced at Faye who had paused mid-munch. 'And then she never got back on track. Just a series of dead-end jobs and, Len, of course. Not much of a life. No wonder she was bitter. The last thing she'd want would be to meet a gorgeous young grand-daughter, full of ideas and plans with an exciting life ahead of her free from scratching around for pennies and domestic drudgery.'

Anna's waited.

'I suppose.'

'She doesn't deserve any support from you – I know that. But if you want to see her then that is your right and I'll go with you.'

'Mm.' Faye's hand was creeping back into the box. 'Think about it.'

'Good. Thanks for being so mature over all this, it means a lot to me.' Anna began to get up from her chair. 'Oh, and I'm sure you're taking precautions yourself, darling,' she added as if it was an afterthought. 'I know you wouldn't make a daft mistake like Lena.'

There was one beat of silence and Anna held her breath as she switched the kettle back on for George and Harry.

'Hm,' said Faye maddeningly and left the room.

Two days later George, Diane and Joan had their big break – they were meeting the NBC team. Their fifteen minutes of fame.

Since Mrs Clark's probate had gone as far as it could Anna had been asked to help other staff wrap up as many cases as possible before the onslaught of the new work from the London company. She spent the day peering into her computer screen as passenger lists of shipping lines in the late 1920's scrolled by. She was glad of the distraction. So far there was nothing known publicly to connect her with Briony's campaign. It had been George's Facebook account and Joan and Diane's contacts. The fact that she and Steve had actually instigated it was known only to the five of them. But that meant there was only a paper-thin barrier between safety and losing her job. Someone might do an extra bit of digging. They would only have to find out whose dad George was and the whole thing would blow.

So when Josie in reception buzzed her sounding breathless and saying she had a visitor she felt her stomach clench. She got up from her desk wishing that she was wearing the morale-boosting suit so despised by Suze and not the crumpled slacks and woolly jacket that had only the advantage of being warm.

She knew who he was as soon as she saw him. He was tall with attractively messy hair and dressed in that expensive shabby chic of fashionably scuffed jeans with a close-fitting black sweater.

A black wool coat was hooked over one shoulder by a long finger and on the other shoulder hung a cream canvas bag with tan leather straps. Anna felt very provincial and slightly sticky which presumably was the desired effect. He grinned at her exposing a row of perfect white teeth in an unseasonably tanned face and put out his hand. 'Mrs Ames?' His voice was deep and rich and American.

She pushed back the impulse to apologise for her appearance. Ridiculously reactionary. 'Yes,' she said smiling as glossily as she could. 'And you are?'

'Chad Kovac from NBC – the American television network?' he was still grinning. Why? 'Can we talk? Could I buy you coffee?' He consulted his large and shiny watch, 'Lunch?'

'Actually,' Anna said primly, 'we're all very busy at the moment.' She indicated a stiff and uncomfortable banquette by the entrance. 'I could give you five minutes.'

'Well, I'll take that for now and hope for better things,' he said beaming sexily down at her. She was struck by a horrible thought.

'Would you mind just taking a seat and I'll be with you in two seconds?' She watched him move away towards the bench and when he was safely out of earshot she whispered to Josie, who was making no effort to be unimpressed, 'Don't let anyone else meet him. If anyone comes down into the lobby, especially Ted, warn them off. He's media. I'll get rid of him as fast as I can.'

'He's gorgeous, though.' Josie's pupils had dilated.

'Not my taste,' Anna snapped. 'Don't forget.' She walked quickly back to Chad Kovac and sat down next to him. 'Sorry about that. How can I help you?'

'We're here in the UK to make a documentary about a rather notorious, well, famous, I guess, case in the States.'

'I'm sorry? What would that have to do with me?' Don't overplay your hand, Anna warned herself.

'I believe it involves a client of yours – well, strictly, her daughter.' Chad was gazing straight into her face and Anna knew that look. She had used it herself to analyse useful party's reactions.

'Oh? ' She closed down all expression.

'Briony Bulowski.' He looked searchingly at her. 'You must have come across some of the publicity. Weren't you the probate researcher for her mother's estate?' Anna forced herself to wait for a beat of three seconds.

'Mr Kovac,' she said as coolly as she could, 'the case is not resolved and even if it was all our records are confidential. We pride ourselves on our professional integrity in such matters.' She stood up. 'I'm afraid I can't help you.'

The grin was still there. He gazed up at her squeezing his eyes seductively. 'But I wouldn't ask you for any sensitive information, of course. Just background to Mrs Clark's life here and, you know, how you linked up with Briony? Must be a matter of professional pride, surely? She had cut herself off from her mother, hadn't she? Wouldn't it be great publicity for Hart & Associates that you tracked her down? And,' his grin deepened, 'for you?' No, Anna thought, we don't all want to be in the movies. She was calm now and in control. He didn't have any idea of her connection to the campaign to get justice for Briony.

'I'd like to ask you a question,' she said without a smile. 'How did you get my name and how did you know this company was involved in searching for Mrs Clark's daughter?' His grin slipped.

'I believe Mrs Bulowski herself mentioned it,' he said vaguely, looking at his watch.

'That would be odd,' she said. 'I received an email from her only last week telling me that a documentary was being made about her and with her compliance but that she did not wish me to be involved in any way.' Chad now stood up also forcing Anna to look up at him. 'She expressly forbade me to talk about her mother. Good luck with your film, but there will be no mention of myself or my company by name. Do I have your word?' He nodded a little too casually. Anna sharpened her tone. 'Or do I need to get your promise in writing Mr Kovac?'

He put his hands up as though in surrender. 'I get the message.' He pulled on his thick jacket with its double row of buttons fashionably close together. 'Nice meeting you. If you change your mind, here's my card.' And he was gone. Anna watched him turn into the car park and then went back to Josie. She waited until Josie's eyes had refocused.

Anna placed her hands firmly on Josie's desk and looked her straight in the eye. 'That man's name is Chad Kovac. I want you to write it down. He's a producer for an American network, NBC, and he's making a documentary about one of our cases. He wanted me to talk about it. I told him that we have a strict confidentiality policy and that not only could I not give him any information but he must not use my name or Harts in the film.' Josie stared at her. 'I want you to write that down in the log and note the time he left which was,' Anna looked at her watch, '12.14. Then, if necessary, we can replay the CCTV tape as proof that he was here.' Josie began to type quickly. 'Also, make a note that I recorded our conversation on my phone.' Josie looked impressed.

Anna wished she had thought of that. She was turning into quite an accomplished dissembler, not to say liar what with one thing and another. But who had given NBC researchers the information? Was there, horrible thought, an informer at Harts? And just as the image of a decent cup of coffee and lunch after a quick stroll into the city centre came into her head, Ted emerged from the lift.

'Anna!' he cried brightly, 'Just the person. I've told Mack I'd send him reinforcements so pop up there would you since you're not doing anything.' She went, thoughtfully.

She said nothing to George and the two women about Mr Kovac's visit. They were full of stories about the day. Who had stood where to be filmed and how they'd had to repeat their answers several times to be filmed from different angles. The animals at Safe n Sound had been so overexcited by all the hubbub that they kept having to repeat clips and had finally moved to the other side of the barn where the dogs couldn't see them. At Joan's house, they had asked if she had a key to Maggie's next door and when she said she had, asked to be shown round. She had refused but had to put up with quite a bit of pressure until they accepted that she was not going to give in. They had all been loyal to Margaret's memory. The different stories Maggie had told about her daughter had not been aired – all they had said was that she had been looking for Briony for years after the breakdown of communication but the team knew that already.

'Oh then, at one point,' Diane broke in, 'they asked about Bob!'

'Bloody hell.'

'Briony must have asked them to see what happened to him. I had to think fast – couldn't tell them he was with George because of course they'd have wanted to film him – Bri's mum's pet and all that.'

'What did you say?'

'I muttered something about how the farm was too cold for him in the winter so he'd gone to stay with a friend but she was away visiting family and taken him with her.'

'Good for you.'

They were all in George's shed. He pulled out a whisky bottle and four glasses. 'I think we all did very well – just enough colour to keep them interested but nothing Briony wouldn't want to see.'

'Or me,' put in Anna gratefully.

'Or Steve.' Joan glanced at Anna. 'You both put your jobs on the line didn't you? For Briony.'

Anna laughed. 'I'd love to pretend that I thought it all through very carefully and took the moral high ground,' she said, 'but actually it never occurred to me until Ted, my boss at work, hinted that I'd better not have been involved. Steve probably did weigh it up a bit but -' She was going to say that he could afford to lose his job, he'd soon get another. That was unkind and unfair to both him and to her father who did everything he could to keep the family show on the road. 'But he's one of the good guys,' she finished her sentence lamely.

'Well, no harm done, it seems, and we've had an interesting day with -' they all spoke at once, 'a great lunch thrown in!' They knocked back their whiskies and held the glasses out for more.

Anna made her way back into the house and up to her room. She stared at her reflection in the mirror. It was odd to look so much like her mother, albeit a younger version. Actually, it was spooky if not creepy to see what she would probably look like as an old woman. Minus the dyed hair, of course.

Lena was now incapable of response. On that evening's visit the pretty young doctor at the hospice had taken her mother's hand and said loudly and firmly, 'I'm the doctor, please squeeze my hand if you can, Mrs Walker.' Then she had looked at Anna and shaken her head. 'It's instinctive for people to obey the voice of an authority if they can even when they're semi-conscious but I couldn't feel any pressure. Have you?' Anna shook her head not wanting to explain that even when her mother was fully conscious the last thing she would have done was press her daughter's hand.

28

Saturday morning. Anna woke with her heart already beating fast and a sense of excitement almost palpably in the air. Rather hysterically she paraphrased Mrs Gradgrind in *Hard Times* as she tugged off her flannel nightshirt - there is sexual tension somewhere in the room, but I cannot positively say I have it. She tutted at the thought, pulled on her dressing gown and dragged back the curtains.

The sky was suffused with pink and pale gold with long lozenges of violet clouds. Against it the bare trees and the silhouettes of houses and the church stood out in stark contrast like a mediaeval woodcut. But when she looked down at the gardens and the street she could see that every surface was rimed with silver. Her car looked as though it had been draped in white velvet and the pavements sparkled where the low sun glanced off them. Patches of grass were razor sharp patterns of black and white. A cat appeared on the other side of the street, its fur sticking out at right angles from its skin, shocked by the bright cold. It dashed across the road and skittered up their drive before diving through the dividing hedge.

No-one in the house was up yet so Anna showered and got dressed quickly and then hurried to the kitchen to put on coffee. She pulled butter out of the fridge and popped two slices of bread in the stained toaster. The honey jar was sticky round the lid and she licked her fingers with relish.

While she waited for the coffee to brew she packed a knapsack with tissues and money and her phone. After a moment's thought she pulled out a hairbrush from the big everyday bag she used and slipped that in too. Her dad had been able to give her a four-hour slot to be away from home. Normally she made Harry her priority at weekends since George had been watching out for him all week but today she had been granted a reprieve. She was shocked at the word. Was that what Harry was now, a prison sentence? Was she bored and resentful at being his prime carer for only a couple of days a week? No, the truth was that it had become almost unbearable to be so constantly rejected. She was trying but hadn't succeeded in shutting her physical needs down. All that longing for intimacy and comfort had nowhere to go and her skin craved contact. She knew in her head that Harry had no control over his attitude to her but her body stubbornly wanted him. Her physical self refused to be sedated by abstinence. For a second Anna's anger at Harry leaped up into her consciousness like a frog out of a very murky pool. She furiously rejected it.

She paused in buttering her toast. She had to face the truth that she was avoiding thinking about Harry because she was about to meet Steve. Of course she was not in any way planning to be unfaithful to her husband. Of course not. But to see soon the attentive, affectionate twinkle in Steve's eyes, to feel the nearness of arms that had already held her, just the thought of spending time with him made everything else seem grey. Dangerous and worrying it may be, but she felt more alive this morning than she had done for weeks. Ripe enough to rot off the bough, she thought, exasperated with herself.

Scraping the ice off the car was almost fun. The physical exertion, her breath clouding the air, braced and stimulated her. The sky was lightening and the clouds had changed; very high above there was a drift of mares' tails. Anna got out her phone and lifted it above her. Cirrus Uncinus – harbingers of turbulent weather. Surely not.

As she turned out of the drive she remembered a dream from the night before. The dream had been a variation on her recurring nightmares about dying animals. The common factors were that she had forgotten to feed whatever animal figured in that particular dream and when she realised and rushed in horror at her negligence to check on them, they were in the last stages of starvation. She had always previously woken up at that point, sweating and anxious.

In last night's dream the neglected animals had been in a shed at the bottom of her garden and when she rushed down, having guiltily remembered that they had not been fed, they were heaped up in piles of the dead and dying. A monkey, only fur and bone, was dead with its jaw in a rictus of agony, and other animals were trying to lift their heads and moan. She stared at them through a red mist of horror and guilt. Then she saw the horse. It was large and grey and could barely stand. Its head was drooped down low and it leaned against the wooden wall with dreary eyes cast down. Its flanks were hollow and every rib stood out. In the dream Anna gasped with sorrow and remorse at her neglect. It was too weak. It was dying.

Then, across the little lane she saw a large green field full of succulent grass that waved glossily in the sun. It was not her field and she was not allowed to go in it. But, if she could get the horse over there, she knew that it would survive. She dragged it and it leaned on her, one step at a time, down the path, across the lane and she shoved open the gate not caring whose field it was, what law she was breaking, the only thing that mattered was that the horse would live. As soon as it felt the grass under its feet it raised its head, tossed its mane and in an instant was muscled and young and prancing ecstatically in the meadow.

Steve was already waiting for her at the canal-side car park. A few hardy cyclists were chatting and laughing and rubbing their hands. He was wearing a chunky moss green down jacket and black trousers and a black beanie hat. His chin was deep in a thick grey scarf and Anna wondered how long he had been there. She wasn't late. When they greeted each other she could only see his eyes and nose behind a cloud of vapour. His eyes didn't seem to be smiling but maybe they were.

'Great morning for a walk,' she said brightly, 'there was a brilliant sunrise.' She smiled broadly at him. He stared at her, his hands firmly in his pockets.

'Family ok?'

'Well, as ok as...' but then she realised he wasn't really asking. He didn't want to know details, this was not just a casual subject to chat about and swop anecdotes; he was clearing the ground, politely not saying what he wanted to talk about until he could be sure there were no dramas she was having to deal with. He seemed to be a careful and considerate person and he had warned her already that this conversation might be difficult. The bubbling excitement that had woken her and driven her towards him ebbed a little and as they turned to walk down the tow-path, she became sober. The ancient lock gates at the junction and the black and white ornamental iron-work made a pleasing counterpoint to the bright sky Anna noticed but decided that a cheery commentary was not to be the order of the day. She walked and waited, thrusting her own hands deep into her pockets.

Each bramble leaf and twig and blade of grass in the hedges was edged with frost and the pale apricot skyline pierced through with skeleton trees was reflected in shards where the sun hit the inky canal water. High overhead a delta of Canada geese squawked loudly. Puddles in the towpath cracked as they stepped into them and coots scuttled for safety in the far bank as they passed. Anna was intensely aware of Steve's physicality – his height, his nearness, the male bulk of his body. A couple of times she stumbled trying not to bump into him as the path narrowed and widened and they changed their strides. Before Christmas she might have even taken his arm in a companionable way but now things were very different. She walked in silence waiting for him to speak.

'Anna?' She glanced up at him to let him know she was listening. 'Ted phoned me while I was in London.'

Immediately her thoughts flew into confusion. This was not the subject she had been expecting. Ted? What was going on? Was this whole expedition to discuss work? The disappointment she felt was so keen that she almost gasped. 'Did he?' she asked stupidly, 'Why?'

Steve was looking at the path and not at her. 'He'd got wind of something and wanted to run it past me.' He glanced at her. 'He's heard about NBC doing a documentary on Briony – well, on US women's prisons and all that but she's the main story. They're coming over here to film people involved in the campaign. He was very concerned that there be no link with Harts, no breakdown in confidentiality. He seemed to feel, and he may be right, that the deal with London might be compromised by any connection between Mrs Clark's probate research firm and the campaign to release her.'

Anna thought rapidly. Steve knew there was a link, of course he did, he and she were the link, the instigators, in fact. What was he saying? Had he brought her out here so that there was no danger of anyone seeing them together outside work? No-one over-hearing their conversation? The idea she had had that the walk would be a chance for her to explain her coldness to him, to tell him how much he meant to her, even, she inwardly grimaced at herself, to give him a chance to declare his interest to her, had shrunk to nothing. You mug, she told herself. She forced her mind back to the real conversation.

'Well, I can see that, of course,' she said dully, 'but has he any reason to think there might be? A connection I mean?' Steve glanced at her rather coldly.

'You mean does he suspect or know the truth? That you and I were the prime movers? No. I don't think so. At least,' he flicked his eyes sideways at her, 'not from me.' Anna felt cold. He had brought her here to find out if she had been foolish and careless in any way.

'I could have emailed or phoned to warn you but I didn't want to leave any kind of trail.' *Any kind of trail?* This was getting worse by the minute. If he had emailed her personal address or phoned her mobile the only way he could have been compromised was if she would have betrayed him either deliberately or out of naivety. She remembered how contrary her behaviour must have seemed to him after the Christmas Day debacle. He must have concluded that he didn't know her very well at all, which was only the truth, and that there might be a danger that she could not be trusted to protect their jobs and their reputations.

Anna plodded along quietly for a moment. The day had lost its colour and the air was no longer bright. It was really very cold and she wished that she'd put her thicker sweater on. 'I did know about it,' she said. 'The documentary researchers tracked down Joan.'

'Really?' Steve looked worried.

'Well, it wouldn't have been hard, would it? In fact, they tracked Joan through her son in New York. He's never tried to be anonymous. Then, of course, Joan talked to dad and Diane and acted as the go-between for them and NBC. Obviously they knew about dad from the Facebook stuff.' Anna kicked aside a large pebble and it splashed into the canal. 'They were interviewed last week.'

'What?' Steve stopped in his tracks and stared at her in horror. 'Why didn't you tell me?'

'Perhaps I didn't want to leave a trail,' Anna couldn't resist saying a little bitterly.

Steve ignored this. 'So they know about you?'

'No. I know it's very, very close – literally close to home – but no, they haven't made the connection between me and dad. They were interviewed on Mill Lane and at Safe n Sound and at Briony's old school but that was it. We're not daft, Steve, they all knew how important it was to keep me and you out of it. The four of us talked about it at length.' She could tell from his silence that he was not entirely convinced.

'Well, if you're sure.' Steve started walking again, his hands thrust deep in his pockets. Anna followed glumly.

'There was something else,' she muttered after a while.

He stopped again, turning and looking her square in the face. 'What?'

'One of the producers came to Harts asking for me.'

'*What?*' It was the nearest she had ever heard to him shouting in anger. She felt a shiver of shock ricochet through her.

'A man called Chad Kovac.' Steve was staring at her. 'He didn't know the connection, he'd just got Harts name from somewhere and mine as her probate researcher. Well, Mrs Clark's. He wanted me to give him some background on Margaret and the search for Briony.'

'And did you?' asked Steve incredulously.

'Of course not!' Anna's hurt dissipated and her own anger rose. 'What do you take me for, Steve? I told him that our clients' details are entirely confidential and made him promise not to use the agency's name or mine in any documentary. I made Josie note the conversation in the log with times for the CCTV and I made sure he knew I was serious.' Steve was silent. 'He couldn't have been in the building for more than fifteen minutes.'

'Did Ted see him? Did he know he was there?'

'No, how could he?' Anna was struck by a thought. 'Just a minute, when did you get that phone call from Ted?'

'It was Wednesday afternoon – why?'

'I think I know how Ted got his information. Josie must have told him. She knew who Chad Kovac was. Thank God I made her write down my statement verbatim.'

Steve was still staring at her but his expression had softened. 'I'm sorry Anna, you've handled everything very professionally.' He sighed and grinned apologetically. 'And, to be honest, I don't see how you could have done anything else without making it look very suspicious. With a bit of luck you've saved both our jobs.' He sighed again deeply. 'I was so worried. I should have thought all this through when we were building the campaign but I just wanted so much to help, to do the right thing, you know. Briony's situation was so miserable and she was so vulnerable.'   They continued walking but more slowly, both watching the ground.

If not now, when, Anna thought. 'What I can't quite get, Steve, is why you would be so worried. I mean, ok, if I lost my job and my professional reputation it would be serious, I need to support my family and we couldn't manage on a librarian's wage, but you have such great skills that you could get a job anywhere surely? Here or even abroad.' She was very conscious that she was skating around the information that Suze had given her. She risked a glance at his face and was astonished to see how vulnerable his expression was.

'Two-drink story. Some other time.' Well, that had told her. But at least, she was grasping at straws, there might be another time.

On the other hand, this confrontational, rather aggressive, rather selfish Steve that she had glimpsed this morning when he thought she might have screwed up on confidentiality, irked her. It was a side of him that was new to her and didn't make him more likeable.

A bike whooshed past them from behind startling them both. 'Use your bloody bell!' Anna yelled enjoying the opportunity to shout at someone and Steve laughed.

'There's a cafe up round the next bend,' Steve said, smiling, 'I'll buy you a weak instant and even a soggy biscuit if you can stand the excitement.'

'Sounds perfect,' said Anna evenly, conscious that a new image had been added to her gallery of Steve moments and it was one that would make her more wary in future. She decided not to raise any personal stuff and to keep a much tighter rein on her imagination in future. She felt like a foolish teenager with a crush on a boy who didn't give a toss. Something perky inside her lay down huffily and she realised that her feet were very cold. As they trudged up the incline to the wooden hut advertising snacks it began to rain.

Len was in a terrible state when she got to the hospice. 'Where was you?' he wailed the instant he saw her and shuffled her into the conservatory visitors' room, 'Your dad said you'd gone out!' He sounded incredulous. Anna had put her phone on silent that morning so as not to spoil any precious intimate moment that might occur. So much for that.

'Are you all right? What's happened?' Len's face was flushed and blotchy with emotion and his eyes were wet. An odour of moist and much-worn parka rose around him. At one time she would have been irritated by him but now she didn't feel so heroic and attractive herself. She reached out and hugged him awkwardly; he was quite a bit taller and much wider and it took a bit of negotiating. This brought on fresh tears so she reached up and patted his back and thought, poor sod, he's losing the only person who really loves him.

'It's her breathing. The nurse said,' he choked and swallowed, 'it's changed and that means she hasn't got long. They want to know what I want to do.'

'What do you mean, what you want to do?'

'About staying or going. I could go and they would phone me if - you know - or I could stay, they could make up a bed.' He stared at Anna in horror. 'I don't know what to do.' Anna picked up his large hand and noticed it was trembling and very damp.

'What do you want to do?'

'I'm frightened. I don't want to be there when she - ' He glanced quickly around the empty room and whispered, 'I've never seen a dead person.' Anna genuinely admired his honesty. Most people would just make an excuse of some kind. Come to think of it, she realised, he had never been dishonest with her – just distasteful. Well, get you Lady Muck, she chastised herself wearily.

'That's ok, you don't have to be. They'll understand.' He gripped her hand hard.

'But I don't want her to die alone. It's not right, is it? I mean you shouldn't die on your own, should you?' His whole being beseeched Anna.

The conservatory was full of light and cane chairs with green chintz cushions were scattered in friendly groups around little glass tables. Through the window the garden could be seen, pretty even in winter with its mounded shrubs and sculptures and solid wood benches. She could imagine that each one would have a plaque naming a grateful family or patient. Anna felt very calm as though what would happen next was inevitable and had been all her life.

'I'll stay with her, Len. She is my mother and I would like to be with her when she dies. I am the older sibling so it's only right.'

Anna's imagination stretched forward into the long hours ahead and the moment when Lena would no longer exist which she would witness. She felt peaceful with the decision. Len's hand had stopped trembling and when she looked up at his face his eyes were closed and a single tear was squeezing out from under his lids.

'Thanks,' he said gruffly. They were silent for a moment as people spilled good-humouredly into the room, an elderly man in a wheelchair at their hub.

'Will you say goodbye to her now?' Anna asked him, guiding him out of the visitors' lounge with an arm half-way round his waist, 'If you want to. I'll wait in the cafe for you and I'll phone dad to let him know what's happening.'

Len nodded his big head and wiped his face on his sleeve. She watched him slowly waddle down the corridor and hesitate a moment before entering his mother's room. She smiled at a passing nurse and walked up the carpeted corridor to the small café.

There were CDs to borrow, and drink and snack machines and a pleasant older man slicing cake on to plates in the tiny kitchen area. She lowered herself on to a laminated wooden chair and stared at the small arrangement of fresh flowers on the round table. She gave her emotions permission to hold up their hands and be recognised but there were no volunteers. Drawbridge still in place. Right then, in that case she would phone home and explain and then go back to sit with her mother.

29

By 7.30 she was settled in the big wing chair in Lena's room with BBC Radio 2 playing softly. It was Jo Whiley and Anna felt powerfully grateful for the woman's kind, low voice in between the snatches of music. Could Lena hear? In any case Anna talked to her.

She told her about her life, about school and university and meeting Harry and having the kids. She told her how happy she had been for the most part and how grateful to have a family of her own. She told her how much she had thought about her mother and longed for her and loved and hated her in turn. Every now and then a nurse would pop her head round the door, smile and go away.

About eleven o'clock they came with a fold-up bed and blankets and after they'd gone Anna pushed it close to her mother's bed and lowered it so that they were on a level. She lay on her side, pulled up a blanket over her day clothes and reached out for Lena's hand. The older woman's breath was rasping a little but coming regularly and the sound of it lulled Anna rather than distressed her. A thought struck her. It was the only lullaby she would ever remember from her mother – a gift at last, if only an unconscious one. She gazed at her mother's profile, the flesh almost gone now and only bony ridges and waxy skin left.

Nevertheless this woman had given her birth and deep down she felt proud and moved that it was she who would be the one to hold Lena's hand at the end.

For a few moments she dozed and then was in an instant wide awake. Lena's breathing had changed again. The breaths were harsher and much further apart. Anna sat up and laid her hand on her mother's clammy forehead. Then she kissed it. 'Goodbye and God bless,' she said, wondering at herself. She heard a movement behind her and turned round.

'Is she going?' said George huskily. How long had he been outside waiting?

'I think so,' she said, turning back to Lena. 'Come nearer, Dad. Do you want to be alone with her?'

'Just for a moment,' he said.

She stood up stiffly and clumsily edged round the bed. Outside the room she arched her back and rolled her head to relieve the tension. There was no-one around. She let herself down on to a chair and leaned her head back against the wall. The three of them together. The tiny family together at Lena's end as at her own beginning. She was glad to be there and glad that her father had come too. What had happened in between her birth and Lena's death would finally be laid to rest. The most resilient and powerful djinn, the one that had taunted and seduced her with so many images of loving mothers and fantasies of reconciliation and redemption for most of her life was shrinking back into its lair, robbed of its power to swell and squeeze her heart any more. Lena was as she was, had made the decisions she had made and lived with the consequences good and bad. As we all do, Anna thought. The hot bitter resentment had drained away. Immediately the image of Harry came into her mind. He had not had any hand in his own fate either in his biochemistry or his babyhood. He had done nothing to deserve either desperate outcome. He had been kind, thoughtful, brave and resourceful. He had loved and cared for them all while he could.

These are the gloomy thoughts that come in the dead of the night, Anna mused, and they don't help.

George appeared from Lena's room. He was standing up straight and seemed calm and steady. 'She's gone,' he said. 'You'd better call Len and I'll get the nurse.'

At breakfast they waited until Ellis had gone to school before they told Faye. Anna had no idea how she would take it and watched her face anxiously for a reaction. Would this be the moment that she would break down and wish she had gone to the hospice? Lena was, after all, the only biological grandmother she had whom she could have known if she'd wanted. Faye put down her mug of tea and was quiet for a moment. 'Were you both there?' They nodded. 'Was it ok?' They nodded again thinking of Lena simply and easily ceasing to be. 'Are you both ok?'

'Yes, we are,' said Anna looking at her father. 'We're pleased we were there to say goodbye.'

Faye picked up her mug and drained it. 'Good. I'll be off then.' She got up and hugged and kissed them both and then made for the door. 'Does this mean that we've seen the last of Len?'

'No,' said Anna firmly, 'it doesn't. He's family and we're all going to have to make space in our lives for him.'

'Not me! Not for much longer!' Faye sang and slammed the door behind her.

They didn't have to wait very long before Mr Shenouda appeared at his door, inviting them in personally as he did to all his patients. Between them, Anna and George had compiled a list and they produced it. Harry had been taken away for tests.

'He's sleeping far more than before,' George began. 'He's ready for bed at around nine now and sometimes he naps during the day. He never used to do that.' Mr Shenouda's warm brown eyes studied their faces. His hands were steepled together with his elbows resting on the large desk and Anna noted how his index fingers crushed the soft tissue of his lips. He was good at listening.

'Then there's this thing with language,' she said. He raised his eyebrows slightly meaning that she should explain. 'Sometimes he gets the wrong word. Well, he's done that before but he seems to do it more often now. At least he doesn't notice and get frustrated like he used to.'

'In fact, he's very calm these days,' broke in George, 'but -' he paused and looked miserably down at his hands. 'Not in a good way if you know what I mean.'

Mr Shenouda checked his notes. 'Would you say that his personality is changing? I mean is he behaving in an uncharacteristic way?' Anna and George looked at each other, searching memories, struggling to analyse the daily contact they had with Harry. Anna broke the silence.

'It's more that he isn't himself. He's almost not there. He was always able to be still and thoughtful but now,' she choked a little, 'he's just still. And of course there's how he is with me. You know about that.'

'But sometimes,' added George, 'he'll be almost hyper-active. You don't see that so much Anna, because you're usually at work but in the morning he'll sometimes go hell for leather at something. Like building the bonfire – I couldn't get him to stop that day. It's like all or nothing.' Anna thought about Harry's hands round her throat wrestling her to the floor and said nothing.

'And what about before you knew he was ill? Do you remember any different, non-typical behaviour then?' It had been so long since Anna had thought about that time, the time before the incident at school, before they had realised there was something seriously wrong. A memory from the previous summer flashed into her mind. They had been on holiday in Cornwall at their usual cottage. Ellis had only been about eight and had been horsing around in the water. He loved it when his dad threw him out from his shoulders into the sea. It was a game they often played. Ellis had shouted for Harry to do it again and had tried to clamber up on his back in the shallows but Harry had suddenly pushed him away in a temper and stomped out of the water, up the beach and back to their rental. He hadn't spoken to any of them for the rest of the day and they had all been confused and upset. The next day he had been his normal self and the incident had been quickly forgotten. But there had been other brief incidents, with strangers, when Harry had been rude and angry. She had spoken to him about them, more bewildered than annoyed but he didn't seem to understand what she was talking about.

'Yes,' she said, 'there were a few times in the months before he was diagnosed when he behaved very out of character. He was rude and angry. I'd forgotten.'

Mr Shenouda pushed back his chair, got up and came round to the front of his desk to be nearer to them. 'I want to ask you something which I think you may find difficult but I want you to consider it.' They looked up at him, waiting. 'I would like to test your children, Anna.'

'Oh, no, I'm sorry. I don't think so. They have asked very recently if they may have inherited what their dad has but I don't think they really have understood. I just can't make it that real to them.' She shook her head to emphasise the point. He looked at her sympathetically.

'In the absence of data from Harry's birth parents, we can never have a definitive diagnosis. But we could if the children were tested.'

'What difference would it make?' Anna cried. 'His mind is going – that's not going to change! How could it possibly help for them to know they would have the same thing happen?'

'Might have the same thing happen,' Mr Shenouda amended.

'What do you mean?'

'It's possible that it's not EOFAD,' he said slowly. 'It's possible that it's something else.' Anna and George stared at him.

'And could that condition be treated?'

'It could only be ameliorated a little,' he said gently, 'not cured, of course. Too many brain cells are dying. But,' his voice was very soft, 'it would be good for your children if they could be freed from anxiety since they are beginning to understand what they may be facing.'

'And what effect would it have if they had the test and knew for sure that they would go down the same road?' Anna was shaking with emotion and fear. She stood up and picked up her coat and bag.

'I know you're trying to do what's best but I just can't even think about that. I just couldn't bear to put them through it.' She looked at George. 'I'll see you outside, Dad. Just finish the list, would you mind? I'm sorry, Mr Shenouda, I need some fresh air.'

'Anna.' The consultant was quickly between her and the door. 'I understand. I really do. Just please think about it.' She stared at him, tears pricking her eyes. 'And I want to say goodbye.'

Anna shook her head, remembering. 'I'm sorry. How is your mother?'

'It will be years before she dies and I'm sorry to say they will not be good ones.' The simple statement took the air from the room.

George got to his feet and shook the doctor's hand. Anna also took his hand but as she was reaching up to kiss his cheek the door opened and a small, rather gaunt man came in. He noticed the gesture and quickly looked away.

'Ah, good timing,' Mr Shenouda said pleasantly, 'this is Mr Bellings-Smythe your new consultant.' He turned to his colleague who had gone to the file cabinet without a word. 'This is Mrs Ames, Harry's wife, and her father, Mr Walcott. We discussed his case yesterday.' The newcomer nodded in their direction. Anna couldn't help feeling disappointed and resentful. Mr Bellings-Smythe was dressed in very dark navy with a crisp pin-striped shirt. His hair and face were shades of grey made duller by Mr Shenouda's glossy copper tones. He glanced at them and then spoke to the younger man.

'Children tested yet?' There was an uncomfortable silence.

'They're considering it,' Mr Shenouda said quietly and then, including Anna and George, who were being ignored, 'aren't you?'

The older man pulled a file out of the cabinet and turned to face them. 'Make an appointment with my secretary for next week. Bring them in then. We simply cannot proceed with our diagnostic work without the genetic data.' His voice was nasal and the accent redolent of a top public school. Anna felt herself bridling. He looked coldly at her. 'The children are definitely your husband's, I assume?'

She straightened her back. 'I'm sure you don't mean to be offensive, doctor, so I will take your question at face value. Yes, the children are Harry's.' He turned to go. 'And you should know that we have not yet made the decision to have them tested. We will make an appointment with your secretary when we have considered what is best for them.'

They all left the hospital sadly and silently. How much they had taken the warm and compassionate Mr Shenouda for granted.

Even Harry was more than usually withdrawn and Anna wondered for the millionth time just what was going through his mind. As usual he insisted on sitting in the back with George and when she glanced in the rear-view mirror he was staring at her angrily. Or was it fearfully?

Back at work the atmosphere was frenetic. People were rushing about with boxes and folders while professional movers were organising new desks and IT systems to absorb the extra staff who would start being inducted on Monday and then be ready, in theory, to hit the ground running as the London contract kicked in. Steve was everywhere, constantly advising and insisting and cajoling the installers but all with quiet good humour.

Anna felt very alone. She wouldn't be able to rely on Mr Shenouda to guide them skilfully and tactfully as Harry deteriorated and she wouldn't be able to feel the balm of Steve's companionship any more. She glanced at him as he helped another man to connect a wireless hub. His spiky hair, the colour of charred wood, was sticking up in a jagged crest where he had run his fingers through it so often during the day. She could distinguish the murmur of his voice from the other office noises.

Their relationship had taken a cold that had become arctic. The canal stroll had ended early after half an hour of uncomfortable small talk. She had assumed too much, too quickly. He was a decent man but he wasn't Harry. She was just going to have to grit her teeth and watch her husband fade from her. Even her dad, the one steady source of love in her entire life, had become, not negligent of her, but happily focussed on the blossoming friendship with Diane. Good. Good for him. Her comforting fantasy mothers had, of course, disappeared with the first encounter with Lena. She hadn't realised how much she had relied on them, wraiths as they had turned out to be. Faye seemed as obsessed as ever with the annoying Sasha which was worrying. Since his triumph as the genie Ellis spent more and more time with his friends. Good. Quite right. She sighed and sat down at her new desk noticing with weary resignation that unlike the old one there was no window to gaze out of.

'Bloody bummer, isn't it?' Suze said, slamming two coffees down on the desk and pulling kit-kats from her trouser pockets.

'Welcome to Ted's Sweat Shop.' Anna shook herself out of her dark mood.

'Where are you?'

'Where do you think? Up a corner so I can't see anyone to talk to! Thanks Ted.' She put on a fake American accent. '"No-one puts Baby in a corner!" You can just imagine him moving little paper dolls round on a massive office matrix in his attic and chuckling with glee at how much he can make us suffer.' Anna smiled.

'Bring on the field work!'

'Yeah, man!' and they chinked plastic cups.

'Hey, Anna.' It was Steve. Anna choked on the hot liquid and Suze rose and slid away.

She began to unpack a box. Better to be doing something. 'You've been busy,' she said brightly. 'It's a madhouse, isn't it?'

He stared glumly down at the floor. 'New desk ok?' Anna was baffled. Was this just part of Steve making sure everyone was all right? If so he needn't bother.

'Perfect,' she said crisply. 'Your office?'

'Oh,' Steve said even more gloomily, 'Ted's given me a bigger one.'

'Good for you,' Anna said huffily and then realised she meant it and added more softly, 'You deserve it.'

'Look, Anna,' Steve began and then stopped. She resolved not to prompt him. 'I over-reacted before. You know, at the canal. I was unfair to you.' He glanced quickly at her and then down at the floor again. 'I was really worried. I thought I might lose my job over – you know what.'

'But Steve,' Anna began and then paused. She couldn't let him know she had been prying into his life. Surely a PhD physicist could get a job anywhere? She changed what she was going to say and added, 'I can't afford to lose mine either.'

'I know.' He seemed about to say something else but then stood up abruptly. 'I have to go.' She watched him manoeuvre himself easily between the still jumbled desks and disappear into the corridor. And another disappearing act, she thought. Now you see him, now you don't. He likes me, he likes me not. No need for dandelion clocks. Oh, sod it, she thought. Sod him.

30

At home she found George hovering anxiously in the hall. He had his hat and coat on and was jingling the keys to his ancient Peugeot. 'Diane just phoned,' he said, trying to sound nonchalant, 'she's made a venison pie.' He looked anxiously at Anna. 'With juniper berries.'

Anna pulled off her coat and scarf. 'I should report you to the Buddhists,' she said severely, 'or better yet, your mates at the Jain temple.' George shuffled in embarrassment.

'I never actually-'

'Oh Dad, I'm teasing you. Go off and enjoy yourself. Bring back the recipe and a haunch of venison if she's got one spare.' She gave him a hug and couldn't stop herself from holding him for a little longer than usual.

'Are you all right, love?' George knew his daughter.

'Yes, of course I am. Where's Harry?'

'He's gone to lie down. I should leave him until dinner. There's sausages but remember that Ellis and Faye are out. I've told them not too late back.'

'Well, that says it all, doesn't it? Venison for the lord of the manor and sausages for the peasants, eh?' She pushed him out of the door and quickly closed it against the bitter wind.

The house felt empty. While the kettle boiled Anna stood at the kitchen window looking down the garden past George's shed. So much had happened since that first day in Margaret's house on Mill Lane. It had been a long and increasingly cold winter. She had found and lost a mother. She had found and lost a man she thought would be very special to her. She might be losing her father. Oh stop it, she told herself, and straightened her back and shook her head. Why was she being so miserable? And then she remembered. The dull dread that had hung over her all day had a different cause. She glanced at the clock. In an hour or so Len would arrive. He wanted to plan Lena's funeral with her which was perfectly natural and had to be done. She just hoped he'd had a shower that day. She sighed and opened the fridge door to get out the pack of sausages and then decided to cheer herself up by making a toad-in-the-hole. With mushy peas. Yes. Len might like that and so would she and it was Harry's favourite. Good. Why did comfort food get such a bad press?

When she let Len in she noticed him sniff appreciatively. She smiled and let him pass her in the hall. No miasma of assorted body odours clung to him today so she gave a tentative hug feeling both mean and relieved. In the kitchen she handed him a beer and a bottle opener and checked the oven. The crust was browning nicely and she felt her stomach growl in anticipation. She showed Len where everything was kept so he could lay the table while she searched the fridge for some easy pudding option. If he was going to be part of the family – well, already was really – then he might as well muck in. It had been a long time since the days when she and Harry used to cook together in the big square kitchen trying out new recipes to the despair of the children. She could hear Faye wailing, 'What's *this*? What is wrong with you two? Why can't we have proper frozen stuff like everyone else?'

'So, I'll just get Harry and you can tell me your ideas while we eat. Pour me a glass of water would you?' With her hand on the door knob she added, 'If I'm longer than five minutes could you turn the oven off?'

Anna went into the hall and called up the stairs. There was no answer but then there often wasn't. She climbed up to the landing and turned left towards what had been their bedroom for so many years.

As she approached the door a huge racket broke out. Harry was shouting, screaming, and there was the sound of crashing furniture. Had someone broken in? Adrenalin flooded Anna's body and she flung the door open. It was dark but she could see from the street-lamp that Harry was in the corner of the room with the stool from the dressing table in his hands. He was lunging at something and yelling for it to get away from him. He was frantic and lashing out violently. The chairs were tipped over and the bed was scattered with feathers. There were feathers in Harry's hair and whirling in the air. The window was wide open and the freezing night wind was dragging the curtains into billows. Just as Anna stepped forward the door smashed shut behind her caught in the draught. She called out to him but he was in a frenzy of fear and panic.

Then she saw the bird. It was an owl. The poor thing was frantically beating what was left of one wing to try to escape but the other wing was useless, broken. As it fluttered and staggered at Harry's feet he was lunging at it with the stool which was breaking under the onslaught. Suddenly Anna had a flash of a little boy trapped in a hovel – maybe an outhouse – and the creatures who would appear at night through holes in the roof to terrify him.

'Harry!' She moved towards him quickly, arms out-stretched, her heart full of compassion for him. 'Darling, it's ok, it's just an owl!' She reached out to take the stool. 'It won't hurt you. You're safe with us. Harry just stop. It's me -' Harry's wild eyes swerved from the owl and saw her come out of the darkness.

'No!' he yelled, 'No, no, no, no!' and before she could stop him he had swung at her with the broken stool. She heard her raised fore-arm crack under the blow and then the kick landed in her stomach and she sank to the floor gasping, winded. Harry was howling. It was the most terrifying sound she had ever heard.

Fighting for breath she looked up from the floor and saw him crouching in the corner by the window his head between his knees and his hands covering his ears. He was rocking and howling and sobbing. She began to crawl towards him but nausea and dizziness were slowing her down. Had her head been hit? She couldn't remember – she just wanted to get to Harry and to tell him that he was safe.

Then there was a different noise and the light came on and Len was there. She turned her head painfully towards him to tell him to leave Harry alone, not to hurt him, that he didn't know what he was doing but a black tide rose up and she was gone.

When she came to she was on her back on Harry's bed among the feathers. All was quiet. No one was there. On the floor was the corpse of the poor owl. Its beak was parted and a little blood was soaking into the carpet. The window was closed and the curtains drawn. She moved her body upright very cautiously and found that it seemed to be only her arm that was broken. It hung uselessly by her side hurting badly. She could stand even though a wave of nausea surged through her.

Where were they? What had Len done? He was a big man and it wasn't all fat. If he had hurt Harry she would – well, what would she do? It would have been easy for Len to misunderstand what he saw. He knew nothing of Harry's early years, none of them did. He probably had Harry down as a dangerous lunatic of some kind. She felt a new surge of adrenalin. Had Len called the police? Was Harry confused and terrified at some police station with people who wouldn't understand the situation and treat him like a thug or maybe think he was on drugs? She forced herself forward to the door and pulled it open as another tide of nausea washed through her.

Len was coming up the stairs with a mug of tea. She noticed it slopping over the stair carpet. 'Go back to bed,' he ordered. 'Lie down. You look like shit.'

She clung to the door post. 'Where's Harry? What have you done? '

'Don't worry about Harry,' Len said staring at her.

'He can't help it. He doesn't know what he's doing. He had a horrible experience.' She was beginning to feel faint again and dropped her head. Through the black spots in her vision she saw Len put the mug down quickly and come towards her. She felt him lift her and then the comfort of the bed beneath her. After a few moments she opened her eyes and the blackness had gone. Len was sitting on the bed contemplating the dead owl.

'I can't touch that,' he said fearfully, 'I can't do birds. They give me the willies. Specially dead ones.' He turned to look at her. 'Can George?'

'Where's Harry? What have you done?'

Len looked puzzled. 'What do you mean? Why do you keep saying that? He's downstairs eating his tea. Where did you think he was?'

'I thought you might have ...' Relief took Anna's voice away.

Len regarded her sternly. 'I may not have been to college like you,' he said with hauteur, 'but I do notice things. I'm not stupid.'

'No, of course not. You know about Harry's illness. Of course. I'm sorry.'

'It's not just that. I notice things.' Len turned his face away from her and put his nose in the air. For a second Anna could imagine him as a miffed kid. She suppressed a smile. It felt so good to be lying still. Even her arm wasn't hurting so much now it was supported.

'What things?' she asked, trying not to sound indulgent and condescending.

Len turned to look at her. 'He hates you, doesn't he?' She was appalled.

'What? No, of course he doesn't. How can you say that?'

'He does.' Len stared into space and paused, gathering his thoughts. 'I've noticed that every time you come in a room he gets moody and weird. He's fine when you're not there.'

Anna was silent. Horrified. It was probably true. How could she know? She couldn't see how he was with others. Of course she knew that he only wanted her dad or Ellis to look after him. He could only tolerate being out if one of them was there – or Faye. And he had been so courteous to Steve. He was even relaxed around Sasha it appeared. Faye had said to her, 'Dad's all right with him, why aren't you?' She had known all this, of course. It had distressed and puzzled her. But for Len to come out with that bald statement - for Len, of all people, to have observed what was clearly the truth, what none of the others would say, was monstrous. There was silence for a few moments.

'Here, drink your tea,' said Len. 'I made it horrible like you do.'

'We had a very happy marriage,' Anna said quietly looking at the ceiling. 'We did. This has all started in the last few months. It's part of his illness.'

Len picked up the cup and absent-mindedly began to drink. 'Funny it's only you, then,' he said, wincing at the lack of sugar. He glanced at Anna's white face. 'You ok?'

Anna looked back at him dully. 'No, Len. I'm not. I think my arm is broken and there may be other injuries. Could you call the paramedics?'

Len looked startled. 'What, 999?'

'Yes, please, but first will you call dad and get him to come back home to be with Harry? I may be at the hospital for a while. The number's in my phone on the dresser in the kitchen. Don't phone the ambulance until dad gets here, ok?' Len nodded and got up cautiously skirting the dead bird on the carpet. 'Oh and Len .'

'What?'

'Thanks for doing the right thing with Harry. He's ok now is he?'

'Yep.' Len thought for a moment. 'Do you want some dinner?'

'No. Thanks.' Anna smiled at him. 'Just be with Harry and call dad and have your own dinner, ok?'

When he was gone she lay quietly and stared at the ceiling. It had been months since she had lain on this bed and looked up at the familiar cracks around the light fitting, years since she had thought, I'll get some filler on those tomorrow. What if her hunch about the reason for Harry's fear and hatred was wrong? What could she do then? No point in dwelling on it because the answer was clear – nothing. Mr Shenouda had said that the brain could form false memories and a diseased brain could sometimes make connections which had not existed in real life. His neural pathways would be like the old Land-rover they had in the early days where the gears slipped so much that it was more like waving the stick than slotting it in to a notch. Perhaps the true memories of their life together had been eaten away by the random progression of the disease. Maybe their happy, loving marriage was the bit that got erased. But then, she reasoned, a tear easing its way down the side of her upturned face, how much worse would it be if he was like this with Faye or Ellis? That would be much harder to bear.

A door banged downstairs and there were feet running. Anna composed her face into a smile and waited for George to come to the rescue. St George and the damsel in distress. That was worth a bit of a smile.

31

Ted was trying to contain his annoyance and not doing very well with it. 'Great timing, Anna. Not your fault of course.' He paused. 'Was it?'

'Well, I tripped over in the dark so you could say it was, but on the other hand – pardon the turn of phrase – it smarted a bit so not much fun for me either.' They were hurrying along the main corridor past Steve's office. 'I have had a thought, though.'

Ted put a pretend gun to his head and pulled the trigger. 'Spare me your good ideas, Anna, my heart can't stand it.' They had reached his office and Anna was panting slightly. The cast was quite heavy.

'I can't drive so I can't do fieldwork but I can still be of use.' Ted raised his eyebrows. 'How about I help train the new recruits? Be a kind of mentor. Show them the ropes.'

'And you've been here how long?'

'Come on, Ted. I've done all right. You'll get your cut of Mrs Clark's estate which wasn't small and I've completed jobs for Shelley and Mark, oh, and for Neil, too, actually. In fact,' she said, warming to her pitch, 'it's better for someone who's only just learned herself to train others. I know the kind of things they'll need to know.' Ted pursed his lips and then nodded, his hand on his office door.

'Don't screw up. Keep them on board and happy. We need every one of them.' He turned away from her to go into his office and called over his shoulder, 'Ask Steve to give me a minute will you on your way past?' The door closed.

As George had driven her to work that morning Anna had been thinking about what to tell Steve about her broken arm. He could hardly avoid noticing a great fat cast and sling. She hadn't come to a decision. She opened Steve's door and put her head round it. 'Ted would like to see you, Steve,' she said neutrally and then began to withdraw. Steve swung round on his chair and jumped to his feet. He strode to the door and pulled it open.

'Just a minute, Anna. How are things? Oh.' He stared at the cast on her arm.

'Latest accessory. All the workers who want to irritate their bosses are wearing them this year.'

Steve looked unsmilingly into her face. 'Lunch,' he said. '12.30. I've got my car here. Meet me in the lobby.' Anna nodded and walked away. It was unlike Steve to be so authoritative and she wasn't sure if she liked it. But then, what did she know about Steve and what was typical of him?

At her desk she opened her laptop and checked her emails. There was one from Briony. She always hesitated before opening hers, but it was ok. It was a brief note to say that she had a release date in early March. Anna quickly checked the calendar on her phone. Only three weeks away. She was asking Anna to meet her at Birmingham Airport and drive her to Mill Lane which Anna had already offered to do. 'I could get a taxi,' Briony wrote, 'but I'd appreciate an update on mum's affairs. I want to see Bob as well, in fact, I want him to live with me. I'll email Diane at Safe n Sound and tell her but I'd better settle in and go to the store before he arrives.'

Anna smiled. For the first time Briony's tone was almost friendly and certainly excited and positive. Anna thought of the room Margaret had lovingly prepared for her daughter and grandson. She picked up her own phone and scrolled to Joan's number. She would know what to remove and what to leave.

There was also an email from George. They had got into the habit since the hospital visit of discussing the possible tests on Faye and Ellis by email. George felt it was best to go ahead. They'd have to know some time, he argued, and when better than during the self-absorption of the teenage years when to be forty-five is so unimaginably old that there's no point in worrying about what might happen. Anna wasn't so sure. It was true they had both asked about it so the thought was somewhere in their minds but how would they feel if they tested positive and had to daily watch their own future as Harry deteriorated?

But Anna had had another thought as she lay on Harry's bed waiting for George to come home. If Faye really did go to Russia and stayed there who would look after her if she became ill? Of course there were hospitals but Sasha's family was an unknown factor. Would they be willing to give her the tender all-day care she would need or would she get stuck in an institution? Anna shuddered and came to a decision. With the fingers of one hand she typed a brief note to her father. 'Make the appointment. We need to know.'

Steve didn't drive her back to his apartment for lunch and she was relieved. It would have been too emotional and awkward with their new, cool and wary relationship. Instead he took her to a refurbished Edwardian pub with curlicue red brick exterior blazoned with fancy gold lettering and prettily etched window glass. Inside the floors were richly stained wood and the walls had the original tiles with art nouveau images of flowers. The tables were stripped and scrubbed old pine with glowing amber lamps on each one. A coal fire glimmered in a black-leaded grate and the smell of charring beef laced with garlic made Anna realise she was starving. She smiled at Steve in approval. He led her to a reserved table tucked away in a quiet corner booth upholstered in burgundy leather. But while they waited for their sandwiches there was a tense silence. They had done the small talk about the new recruits arriving while they were in the car and now it was hard to know what to say next.

'Briony emailed me,' Anna began, 'she'll be home in March. Wants me to pick her up.'

'Right.' Steve studied his coffee cup. 'Interesting to meet her. I mean, properly.'

'Yes.' Anna looked round at the other customers half-wishing she hadn't agreed to come.

Steve cleared his throat. 'I had an email too. From my ex-wife. She's in Boston, well Cambridge, at Harvard and it's going so well it looks like she'll be moving there permanently. Wants me to find out about shipping the furniture that's in store. You know, is it worth it.' His tone was neutral and his expression gave nothing away.

Despite her misgivings Anna was instantly engaged. 'How do you feel about her living so far away?' she asked cautiously.

'Oh, it's fine. I mean, I wish her well and it's fantastic that her career is really taking off but we're over.' He paused. 'She's a really brilliant physicist. They're actually lucky to get her.'

'So did you meet at university?' Anna carefully kept in check her knowledge of Steve's academic background. He seemed happy to talk.

'Yes, at Warwick. We were both doing physics but I was always more interested in the technology – you know the application of new knowledge. She was into the theoretical side, more string theory and all that, you know.'

Anna laughed. 'Well, no, I don't. I have heard of it but that's about the extent of my knowledge.' Steve smiled. 'So, um, what did you do after your degree?'

'We both went to Cambridge for our Ph.Ds. It was great once you get used to all the slightly barmy traditions. That was when I got interested in climbing – joined the university club. It was a good way to relax and let a bit of a breeze into my head.'

'So, how did you come to be in Birmingham?' Anna felt that so far this was safe territory. What she really wanted to know was why Steve's wife had left. What had caused the split?

'Cathy got a post-doc at Birmingham uni. It's one of the Russell Group universities and had a professor who was top rank for her field so it was a good chance for her.'

'And you?'

Steve shrugged. 'I knew I could get work of some kind. There are plenty of opportunities in the Midlands - it's a good place for what I'm interested in. There are some excellent innovations in engineering in the area, some real challenges for practical physics.'

He had become quite animated, his eyes shining with enthusiasm. Anna was puzzled. How did this fit with what Suze had said about Steve being at Aston University and now him being the go-to IT man at Harts? She felt it would be too intrusive to ask the obvious question. Instead Steve anticipated her. 'You're probably wondering why I'm at the world-famous centre for technical innovation known in the trade as Triple H?'

'Well...' Their sandwiches arrived. Thick cuts of savoury roast beef between slices of crusty granary bread with coleslaw and salad were packed on to the large oval plates. They both leaned over the table and she sniffed appreciatively. For a few moments they tore into the food, Anna picking up pieces of meat and bread in one hand and not caring how it looked.

Steve swallowed and took a sip of water. 'The best laid plans, eh?' He looked searchingly at Anna. 'Is this boring you? All this me stuff?'

'Not at all,' she answered honestly.

'I did work for a while as a lecturer at Aston teaching which I enjoyed but it's not where I want to be. Ideally I'd like to be in industry. Be helping to make things, you know?' He chewed thoughtfully for a while.

'So why Harts? It seems so undemanding for you. I mean I know you're brilliant with IT but still.' Steve paused and looked away from her. He seemed to be making a decision.

'Anna, I know now that you're discreet. I know from experience that you can keep a secret even when you're being unfairly pressured.' Anna thought he was referring to Briony's attacks on her but then realised he was apologising for his own assumptions. She wondered what was coming next. 'What I'm going to tell you is a tiny bit secret. I mean, if the press got hold of it, it could be a nuisance.' Anna was jolted. She had assumed a personal revelation was coming, not this. 'There's nothing illegal or even unethical about what is going on, quite the contrary, it's just confidential and only a very few people at Harts know about this, well, sideline, I have.'

'Sideline?' Intriguing.

'When I was at Cambridge I was contacted by someone in the government and asked to do some work for their counter espionage unit. It was because I was into applied physics and pretty interested in cybernetics.'

Anna dropped her voice. 'You work for MI6?' She was shocked but there was excitement there as well. Not only did Steve have this rather glamorous string to his bow, it seemed, but more pleasing, he had felt able to share it with her. She didn't seem to be a security risk any more.

He laughed quietly. 'Not quite that hush-hush. And not MI6 – the Home Office. It's not James Bond stuff, Anna. It's industrial espionage mostly, you know, tracing hackers and foiling their wicked plots to steal our secret recipe for Cadbury's Dairy Milk and so on. Life and death stuff.' He grinned at her, finished his sandwich and pushed back his plate. 'And there's something else that suits me about Harts.' He glanced at Anna. 'Ted gives me a lot of flexibility. He knows I sometimes need time off in a hurry but he also knows I'll use my own time to keep up with the work.'

Anna opened her mouth to ask why Steve would need time off in a hurry as he put it when again he forestalled her. 'Enough about me. How's things with you? I want all the crises in order and don't skip any!' She was about to say that her life was not all crises but then realised that, actually, for the last few months, it had been just that.

It was a relief to talk. And he was such a good listener that she told him about her Derbyshire trip. He had heard of the Arkwright Home but no more than that. He seemed keenly interested, nodding her on when she paused and when her voice broke a little he put his hand over hers but then removed it quickly.

She told him about Lena's death and Len's new status in the house. She stopped. Enough.

'Go on,' Steve prompted.

'What, isn't that enough?'

'There's a broken arm in the room that needs explaining, Mrs Ames,' Steve said mock-formally.

'Oh, that.' Anna looked at it as though she was surprised to see the cast in the sling. 'Harry did it.'

'*Harry* did it!' Steve's voice was incredulous. So she told him. When she had finished he put both hands over her rather purplish fingers which stuck out of the plaster. 'Anna, I have to ask this. Is it going to get worse? This with Harry? Do you think he will often get violent?'

'No. I don't. He was badly frightened by a freak event. And then it was me who came. If it had been George he wouldn't have lashed out.' Anna had not told Steve about what Len had said about Harry hating her. That was too painful.

'It's bizarre, isn't it? His attitude to you. I know you well enough, I think, to believe what you've told me, that your marriage was a good one.'

'Is,' Anna said quietly, 'is a good one.' She looked at Steve wondering whether to tell him her plan or whether he would consider it beyond foolish. She decided against it and looked away. Time would tell. She glanced at her watch and got out her purse.

'Now, you may be teacher's pet but I'm not and I need to get back.' She smiled at him. 'This was good. I've enjoyed it. It's a relief to talk and it's nice to know more about your life. Thanks.' On the short drive back to the office they were both silent but the tension had gone.

32

Anna and George had discussed thoroughly how to put it to Faye and Ellis that they were to be tested. The tests themselves were no problem – just a simple blood test and a mouth swab with a few hair samples as back up. It was the reason for the test that would need to be explained. They decided to put the emphasis on it being part of Harry's on-going diagnosis and treatment which was, after all, the truth. But not the whole truth.

They waited until after dinner when Harry was in bed and they were gathered in the sitting room. Faye was draped over the sofa, fingers flying over her phone with ear-buds in and Ellis was staring at his tablet also plugged in to his earphones. What was he looking at, Anna wondered, vaguely anxious. The thick curtains were drawn against the dark and chill and the fire glowed and flickered. It was such a comforting place to be, such an intimate family scene that her heart sank at having to compromise it. She and George had finished watching the Channel 4 news and as he turned off the tv, her father glanced at Anna and she nodded.

'Sorry to interrupt, but could Pops and I have a word?' Two heads turned in her direction. Faye's mouth was slightly open and her stare unblinking in a clear communication that she was only pausing, not stopping her phone activity. Ellis glanced at his tablet wistfully but then set it aside.

'You know your dad has a new consultant? Mr Shenouda has had to go back to Cairo.' Two faces registered polite indifference.

'Well, the new man, who is very highly thought of,' despite being a cardboard cut-out she thought unkindly, 'would like to get some genetic data from both of you to help with your dad's treatment.' Faye registered shock and horror.

'What do you mean, genetic data? Bit sci-fi Mum! What does he want to do to us because you can think again if -'

'Nothing scary or unusual,' Anna broke in, 'just blood tests and cheek swabs, that sort of thing.'

Faye and Ellis looked at each other for one second. 'You want to find out if we've got what dad's got, don't you?'

'Well,' George started, 'it's more to get a better idea of ...' He stopped and there was a moment of silence. Anna waited. Her heart seemed to have risen up her throat.

'Mum,' Ellis said. 'Can I ask you something really important?' His foxy, intelligent face was drawn into an anxious knot. What could she say to reassure him? Nothing. He was so like Harry had been as a child, not just in appearance but character too. Mr and Mrs Ames had always been happy to tell anecdotes about the bright and loving boy at the centre of their lives. Thank goodness, Anna thought, they had died before Harry's illness had manifested itself. She braced herself for Ellis's question. He must be answered honestly no matter how painful that would be for both of them.

'Of course.'

'Can I have some new trainers for going to Newlyn? I've found this really good online outlet for just what I want. Look.' He turned the tablet to her.

Faye bounced upright and pulled out her ear-buds. 'If he's having new trainers I want some Ugg boots. Everyone's got them at college, even Tash and she's only got her mum.'

'You're rich,' retorted Ellis. 'You've got all that meerkat money, you can buy your own!'

'Lot you know! I've run into – um – production feasibility problems.'

Ellis crowed and cracked his fingers at her. 'You got fed up with making them you mean! You said you'd got a full order book – that special one with only one page? And now you can't even be bothered to make those, can you? Tash not willing to be your slave after all? Ha, ha!'

Faye leaped up and grabbed her brother's tablet. 'You cheeky little worm! If I can't have boots you can't have trainers! Mum?' She waved the tablet over her head and studied it quickly, her gorgeous chestnut hair in its loose knot quivering with indignation. 'How much? These are ridiculous! You don't even need them! Mum, tell him.' She looked at Anna. 'Mum?'

Anna and George were smiling at each other. 'The appointment is Thursday at 4.00 so I'll pick you up from school at half three, Ellis. It's your afternoon off so could you be home by 3.00 Faye? Don't be late,' George said, getting up, 'and don't forget that Diane's coming on Friday for the poetry. Hope you're both able to be there but no worries if you can't be.'

Anna got up, too. 'I'll be late home on Friday, Dad,' she said. 'I forgot to tell you.' She began to gather the mugs and glasses to take them into the kitchen.

'Right-oh.'

'Mum?' Ellis was doing his best to be adorable. Faye was glaring, ready for action.

'I'll tell you what. Both of you can come up with ways you can contribute half and then I'll see about giving you the rest but Faye, I'm not lashing out for Uggs and Ellis, no designer nonsense that's going to get stolen. It will have to be something cheaper and less flashy.'

'So mean,' Faye said reflexively, already checking a website. Anna left them to it.

Lena's cremation would be the following week. Len had put a notice in the local paper and had closed the curtains of their flat. Anna had made all the other arrangements as he sat nervously perspiring by her side. George said he had written a poem as a tribute to their free-wheeling salad days. Anna found that she could not process her mother's death. If she thought of it, so many strong and conflicting feelings rushed in that she felt buffeted and beaten down. It was easier not to think about it. Easier to keep busy and have a couple of stiff drinks before going to bed.

Len was handling it in his own way which mostly involved telling Anna endless anecdotes, often repeated, about his mother. She listened with only half her attention but couldn't help noticing that a pattern was emerging. Every now and then she would ask a question to test the accuracy of what she was thinking.

Lena's life, it seemed, had not been the wild-child free-for-all she might have been hoping for when she left her 'boring' husband. Money had been an on-going worry and even when she was working at the club they were often broke and finishing the month with beans on toast every day. The only holiday Len mentioned was a week in a caravan in south Wales with his mother and father. This was the source of many of the anecdotes. One week in thirty plus years. If Lena was flush for some reason she would go shopping, not take Len out anywhere. He was not allowed at the Club, naturally.

As he talked Anna began to build up a picture, not of a spoiled over-indulged favoured child as she had assumed, but of a very lonely and rather neglected one. One time, after a third repetition of a story from the Welsh holiday, Anna asked Len if he kept in touch with his dad. He had continued to chop carrots the way she'd taught him and without missing a stroke said, 'Croaked.'

Anna was learning more about her brother's life. Len had had jobs. He had been a warehouseman for a sportswear shop in the centre of Birmingham but it turned out that they had paid him less than minimum wage in cash and when sales dropped he was shown the door. When Anna asked why he had not taken them to a tribunal Len had looked shifty and made an excuse so Anna assumed he had also been drawing benefits.

His favourite job had been working as a cook in a fast-food franchise. (The question popped into her mind of how often he had washed his hands before picking up the raw burgers and she wished it hadn't.) He liked the company, the joking around and the routine of the job. He was planning to start a chef's course at the College of Food and Technology but it had all come to an abrupt end.

One day when things were slow he was asked by the manager to clear the tables in the outside eating area and wipe them down. He had always routinely checked any cigarette packets left behind in the hopes there might be one tucked away un-noticed so when he saw a pack lying on a vacated table he turned his back on the occupied tables and quickly flipped the lid. There were no cigarettes but there was a twenty-pound note. He hesitated for one moment but then slipped the pack into his apron pouch and finished wiping the table. On the way past the bin he threw the carton away.

He had just got back from the toilet where he had slipped the note into his wallet when the manager called him to his cubbyhole. Anna could have finished the story for him but she let him do it. The 'customer' had come back, had demanded the carton be retrieved from the bin, had sworn there was money in it and Len had been given the sack. If Len had been more sophisticated, if Lena had been more vigilant and kicked up a stink, things might have turned out differently. But as she asked a few questions Anna felt she was getting the picture. Unused to a regular job Len had often been late; co-workers had complained that he didn't wash and smelled bad; sometimes he 'cheekily' filched stock. Clearly he had been set up and, truth to tell, Anna couldn't really blame the manager. Len equally clearly still believed that he had been the victim of an injustice and that anyone stupid enough to leave money about shouldn't be upset about losing it.

Since then there had been nothing and Len had become used to being on benefits. Television was a big part of his day but he had done the shopping for himself and Lena and was a surprisingly useful source of information on where to get the cheapest of just about everything. On market days he would drift around the Bullring happily with his plastic bag clutched in his hand looking for bargains in the books and the DVDs and on non-market days he would do the same in charity shops. He did have friends. People like himself who for one reason or another had never quite climbed on board the mainline train or had fallen off it. On fine days they met in one of the city centre parks and if it was wet in the Central Library. If they had just got their benefit cheques they would spend the afternoon in a pub. Anna got the impression that during these sessions of conviviality they would come to a consensus on what needed to be done to set the world in general and the foolishness of British politicians and football managers in particular, straight.

But it had been only last week when Len had stopped talking endlessly, moaning and boasting alternatively, that she became aware of another side to him. He had gone into the back garden for a smoke and she had been putting some laundry away upstairs when she heard faint music. When she opened the back bedroom window she was astonished to see Len sitting heavily like a toad in his big coat on the mouldy bench playing a flute. Playing it beautifully. The sweet plaintive sound of the melody rose like a miracle from the damp, cold garden. What was it? Danny Boy. Another window opened and Ellis's head popped out. His mouth was open in amazement. She closed the window and ran down the stairs and outside.

Len had quickly slid the flute away inside his huge parka as she approached. 'I wasn't doing it loud,' he said defensively. Anna sat down beside him and hugged his arm.

'Len, it was beautiful. It was really lovely. I had no idea you could play like that.' He jiggled his mucky trainers in the leaf mould on the ground. 'When did you learn?'

'One of mum's boyfriends. From the club. Cal. Calvin. He was good. He played in America once in a tour. Not the flute, that was just what he liked messing about with, he played the saxophone. He give me this.' He was pink and trying not to smile. 'I know some others.'

'Have you had your smoke?'

'Yep.'

'Come in then, come into the warm and play for us. Ellis's been listening too.'

And it became a regular thing. Most times that Len visited after that he would bring the flute and after dinner they would all stay around the table and listen to him play. Sometimes it was a folk song and sometimes a theme tune from a soap opera or a film. It didn't matter. He had learned them all by ear and his playing was almost always perfectly in tune. As soon as he finished he would say, 'That was crap,' and whoever was there would tell him, no, Len, that was really good and he would dip his head to hide his smile.

And so, little by little and easing herself out of her prejudices Anna was beginning to grow fond of Len. She often thought of the dying Lena's fierce grip on her arm and her demand that her daughter look after Len. But she was not doing this for Lena. The same burgeoning affection could not be applied to the ubiquitous Sasha. Far from his relationship with her daughter cooling down as Anna had hoped, it seemed to be heating up.

33

Len had never been to a funeral before, not even to his own father's who had died at a hospital in Spain. Anna whispered to him that they should wait outside the main room for the hearse to arrive so they could go in with Lena on her final journey. They had dispensed with following cars since Lena's body was coming from the funeral director. There was a waiting room just inside the porch area and they installed themselves there sitting on the edge of their seats.

Harry sat next to Anna. She could hardly believe what had happened. She still couldn't take a full breath when Harry was near. George leaned forward from his chair on the other side and smiled at her.

Ellis alerted them to the approach of the hearse and they went out into the wind, the clouds scudding and jostling in a huge lively sky. The tall cypresses were bending and creaking and Anna felt a new chilly sensation on the back of her neck. They stood in a little group waiting for the men to lift Lena expertly from the car. A young woman was in charge. She was tall and well-built and had a pleasing, reassuring air of calm competence. She alone wore a top hat but far from looking odd it looked quite regal. Anna tried not to think about the last time she had seen Lena and what might be in the coffin. Instead, she took her father's arm and Len's hand and led the others inside.

There were a few mourners in the seats, Anna guessed neighbours, and a woman she recognised as a volunteer from the Hospice. The minister did what he could with Lena's life but it was George's poem that evoked the dead woman as only he had known her. He wrote of her beautiful dark eyes and irrepressible sense of mischief, of her sitting under an olive tree in a Marrakesh souk sharing Berber mint tea with a seller of false teeth, both giggling with the effort to make themselves understood. He wrote about how he had woken at dawn in their camper van outside Tripoli and discovered she was missing. He had found her walking along the beach as the sun rose, rimmed in gold, with the dazzle of light from the water rippling over her body and the breeze lifting her black hair into a whirl around her head . She had turned to look at him, held out her hand and smiled. It had been the most beautiful moment of his life.

Then it was Len's turn. As the coffin waited to be rolled away into oblivion he stood beside it and pulled out his flute. During the planning there had been all sorts of half-serious suggestions about what he should play but he had looked reproachful at all the 'fun' ideas. Now, as the words of the committal prayer finished, Len lifted the slim instrument to his lips. Across the cheap lacquered surface of the coffin and across the rows of empty seats to where the small gathering of Lena's rejected family sat, heads bowed, came the pure clear notes of the Last Post. It was completely inappropriate and just right. Lena's life had been a battle and she had, in her own unsentimental terms, fought it to the end.

None of Lena's neighbours or bar staff from the Club showed any interest in coming back to Anna's house for the wake and she was glad. She unlocked her car and got into the driver's seat. She dabbed again at her eyes – Len's bloated figure tenderly lamenting his mother had moved her in a way that Lena herself never had - and waited for the car to fill up. She knew George had brought his, too, so there was plenty of room. Diane had been tactful in not coming herself. This was the end of a very long love affair for George and without anyone saying anything, everyone knew it. How deeply someone is loved, Anna thought, has nothing to do with the worthiness of that person. It has everything to do with the size of the heart of the person doing the loving. After a moment she looked in her rear view mirror to see Ellis and Faye getting into the back seat of George's car and Len into the front. What was going on? Was she supposed to drive home alone from her mother's funeral? Hot tears sprang back into her just-dried eyes. She got out of the car.

Harry was standing by the passenger door. Her breath stuck in her throat. She stared mistily at him. 'Can I come in your taxi?' he asked, smiling. And so it was with her husband beside her that Anna left her mother's funeral. She pushed the button for the CD and let Don McClean fill the car with the gentle acoustic sounds of Winterwood, '*No one can take your place with me, and time has proven I am right...*' She couldn't sing because her throat had closed with emotion but she could hear Harry humming the familiar love-song, their song, beside her - '*we are like birds in winter woods.*'

She had taken the photo of herself on the day she had started university with her chrysanthemum bobbed hair and showed it to the stylist at Get Ahead. Ellie had looked at it hard. 'Why?' she said.

'Your hair's beautiful. And it's the fashion now to wear it long and straight.'

'And I want highlights,' said Anna. I want very thin ones, just a few round the crown to lighten it up, ok?'

'Foils in the halo?' Ellie corrected.

'Yes, that.'

When she was handed the bill Anna gulped.

The photograph of Julia Smith had shocked her. It was blurred and the image was small but it could have been herself. Severely cut black hair hanging down each side of a heavy fringe so that the face was almost obscured. Everyone complimented Anna on her hair because it was thick and, for lack of interest in blow-drying and teasing on her part, glossy. She had not given a moment's thought over the last year to how she looked apart from wanting to be professionally turned out for work. When was the last time she had seen Ellie? It must have been over a year ago. Faye had trimmed the ends of her hair around Christmas but had refused to take off more than a few millimetres. Faye wanted her to grow it even longer and put it up in a French pleat or a bun, 'like those cool women on Mad Men'. 'As if,' Anna had retorted, 'should I get a pointy bra as well?'

Mr Shenouda had been right, it seemed. There was a monster from Harry's childhood she reminded him of. More than that, she had become that monster to him. But the monster was not from a fairy-tale or a scary film. He had met her in real life and she had taken him prisoner. The woman everyone trusted, who was in charge, who smiled when other people were around, who spoke kindly to him, that woman who could turn into a witch in a heartbeat if he ever allowed her to be alone with him.

Last Friday night she had walked into the kitchen to a chorus of disapproval. 'Mum!' Faye had wailed, 'What have you done! Bloody hell.' Ellis had twisted his mouth sympathetically and offered the only positive thing that he could think of, that it would grow out. George had nearly dropped the casserole dish but recovered quickly. 'Takes years off you, love.' She didn't care.

'Where's Harry?'

'Taken Bob down the garden.'

She made for the back door. 'I'm serving up now!' George warned, 'don't disappear!'

I don't want to disappear, thought Anna, I want to appear. She pulled her new coat closer around her in the chilly breeze and felt her short hair lift and tug at her scalp. She remembered that feeling. She remembered the windows permanently wound down, stuck in a rusty groove in the crumbling Landrover and Harry driving as they rattled their way along mountain tracks and unmade roads up in the moors near Leek to the campground. It was their honeymoon. They had no money. It didn't matter. They yelled every song they could think of over the juddering, grinding engine noises and they had just got to Christmas carols (in August) when they crested a ridge and Harry stopped the car. At once there was a break in the clouds and the sun lit up the broad valley and the silver lake spread before them.

They had got out of the car and stood on the very edge of the escarpment. Harry had put his arm round her and gently turned her face to his. The sun made a wedge of golden light across his bright hair and amber eyes. 'I will love you all my life,' he had said simply and he had kissed her. The huge heaped boulders of ancient gritstone stood around like witnesses.

Anna could see them at the end of the garden. Harry was throwing sticks for Bob and she noticed with a pang that his movements were becoming awkward. Bob didn't care. He was only pretending to run for them anyway. He had his arthritis to consider.

She walked down and waited in a patch of light from the shed window, watching them and smiling. She had bought a new coat. Instead of the severe but practical black she normally wore this one was scarlet. And to go with it she had bought a gaily striped scarf of purple and orange. Faye and Ellis would have to wait a little bit longer for their boots and trainers. They would always need new things. Harry must come first this time. If her gamble paid off. If it didn't, they were over £200 down and she'd have to go round looking like an advert for a retro kids programme. She called to him.

Harry turned and saw her. For a moment he stood utterly still, staring as though he couldn't believe his eyes, as though she were an apparition. She moved very slowly towards him so as not to alarm him. 'Harry?' He didn't move. 'I've come to find you.' She put out her hand. 'Dinner's ready – it's liver and onion with bacon. And mashed potato. Will you come?' And as simply as that he had grinned, walked towards her and put his hand into hers.

As they walked back in, Bob more than ready, she looked up at the tumbling sky, the first stars already visible above the roofline of their house winking as the clouds passed over them. If there is anything, anyone, any being or cosmic whatever making this happen she thought incoherently, then, well, thank you.

From then on Harry wanted to be near her as often as he could and seemed comforted by her presence. She could hold his hand, sit close to him on the sofa, even have the bliss of putting her head on his shoulder. Ellis and even Faye had relaxed and she realised that for them, too, the strange hostility towards her from their father had been distressing and bewildering. Harry was more peaceful, too. Sometimes he would gaze at her for minutes at a time and she would see the love there and smile and offer her mouth to be kissed. This must be how people feel when they fall in love and then one of them has to go off to war, she thought. This joy made exquisite by the approaching separation. Except in this case the loss would be inevitable. The void left by Lena's rejection was shrinking and she could just begin to put the shock of her mother's attitude to her in perspective. It would take years, she knew, to get over completely. But for some of those years she would have Harry.

After the funeral, when Faye was out with Sasha and Ellis was in his room doing homework, she told George about her trip to Derbyshire and what she had discovered. He shook his head repeatedly thinking of the misery that Harry must have suffered.

'Are *you* all right, Dad? After today?'

George sighed. 'Yes, I am. In a way it's a relief. I could never, you know, never think about anyone else before because part of me still believed that one day she would come back. Daft isn't it?' He laughed bleakly. 'She was here all the time. Just didn't give a stuff.'

'Dad -'

'No, she didn't. No use sugar-coating it. She got over me the minute she walked out of the door, well, many minutes before in fact.' He took off his glasses and laid them down on the arm of his chair. 'You know the woman you met? Hard, selfish, sarcastic? Well, she was always like that. I just didn't want to remember it. I wanted to remember those moments, you know? The moments, as T. S. Elliot said, that are "in and out of time".' Anna thought of her own multitude of timeless moments, and in particular one on a

293

Staffordshire ridge twenty-five years ago and one much more recently. She nodded.

'I think a little something may be in order,' George said, getting up.

'Oh,' gasped Anna, 'what a happy thought. Bring it on, my good man! In fact, bring the bottle.' She lay back in the deep armchair smiling and letting her whole body relax.

The front door crashed shut and the living room door crashed open. Anna struggled to get up to protest.

'That fucking bloody arsehole shit!' Faye shouted. 'I could kill him if I could bear to touch him!' Anna found she hadn't the energy to protest about anything so she sank back. Faye rarely needed prompting to reveal all when she was in full cry. 'You know those tests? Those tests we did on Thursday last week? To see if we'd got that whatsit that dad's got?' She was not expecting an answer so Anna didn't give one. 'Well, I just told that moron about them and do you know what the fucker said?' Anna dumbly shook her head. 'He said, he said, in that stupid voice, "If you have bad genes you don't come Russia. No good for babies." Can you believe it? How bloody dare he? Why am I not allowed to kill him and roast his nasty little balls? No, roast his balls and then kill him!'

During this tirade George came in with a bottle and three glasses. He filled Anna's and passed it to her silently before filling his own. The third he set down quietly on the coffee table next to the bottle.

'As if I wanted to go to stinking Russia, anyway,' I said. 'He told me tonight that everybody lives in these nasty concrete block flats and his family only has one bedroom and his sister lives there too! I mean, where would we sleep?' Anna noted the plural pronoun without surprise but with some dismay. 'Do you know what he said? "On kitchen floor of course. It is normal." On the fucking kitchen floor, I said, are you joking or what and then he said what he said about the tests! Can you believe it?' Anna felt her daughter may have strayed a tad into melodramatic invention but was in no mood to correct her. Faye was sufficiently incensed not to notice the third glass. Anna gently pushed it out of sight behind a box of tissues with her toe and mock-frowned at her father who was looking as cheerful as she felt.

Faye turned to the mirror over the fireplace for consolation. She tugged at her heaped hair to pull it up a notch and blinked at herself. 'I'm telling Tash,' she decided and was gone.

George raised his glass to his daughter. 'It's a black cloud,' he said.

'That has no silver lining,' Anna agreed and they both drank deeply.

34

'Whoa!' Suze said when Anna skipped into the office the next day. 'Wait a minute, turn round, yes, I can see what you're doing here -' Anna laughed. 'What I don't know is *why?*'

'I like it,' said Ted passing by. 'Add a few inches of shoulder pad and I might be tempted.'

'Poor old man,' teased Suze, 'I bet you watch boxed sets of Dallas!'

'Come up and see me some time,' Ted gave Anna an exaggerated wink. Then, dropping the facetiousness, 'No, I mean come and see me - now.' Suzanne rolled her eyes and Anna trotted behind Ted's broad back scanning her memory to discover what she might have done or not done. When they were both in the office he stepped behind her and closed the door. 'I've been checking the log in reception,' he said. 'Why didn't you tell me that guy from NBC was here?'

Anna's mind went blank. 'I don't know,' she said truthfully. 'I just assumed you wouldn't want the publicity. Confidentiality issues and all that.' Ted banged his head with an open palm.

'Of course I don't want the publicity! But you didn't have to keep it a secret from *me!*'

'No, I suppose not.' Anna had been so careful to keep all compartments separate so that she and Steve would not be exposed that she had not thought it through. She should have gone straight to Ted and told him what had happened and how she had dealt with it. 'Sorry.' Ted stared at her for a moment and then turned away to his desk.

'Don't let it happen again. I want to know everything that goes on in this place. But you did the right thing I've got to admit, although that log entry of Josie's wouldn't hold up in court. Sounds like you scared him off.' Anna was so relieved she was on the point of telling him not to worry, that it was all over, that the interviews were done and Chad Kovic was back in New York when she abruptly realised that she wasn't supposed to know that and snapped her mouth closed. 'Now then, how long to that cast coming off?'

'Couple of weeks, I think.' With luck, before Briony got back.

'Right. Well, you're doing ok with the new intake. They seem to like you and they're picking things up fast enough so that'll keep you busy for now. I may have a nice juicy little job for you after that but you'll need to have all your wits about you. I need Steve here when I tell you and he's in London for a couple of days so it can wait.' Anna immediately thought of what Steve had told her. Could it be connected to that?

'So that would be the one with the pay rise?' she said dead-pan. Ted laughed.

'Off you go, mop-head – I'm not that smitten with your new hair-do.'

It was strange to be back in the house in Mill Lane. Joan came in with her and they both paused for a moment in the hall. There was no musty smell, the air was warm and Anna was glad that she'd persuaded the agent to keep the utilities connected.

'Come and see what I've done and tell me what you think,' said Joan leading the way upstairs. Anna opened the main bedroom door. Yes, there was the picture of Briony and Donny but Joan had moved it to a less dominant position. In its place she had put the picture of Margaret with her arm round Briony as a little girl that had hung in the second bedroom. The cot was gone and all the toys and books suitable for a child. Anna was relieved. Now, the bedroom could have been Maggie's – there was nothing to show that she had been waiting for years, in vain as it turned out, for her daughter and grandson to come back and had created a quasi-shrine to them. Anna had not sent Briony the last letter that Margaret had written but she had kept it. She had sent instead the letter found by the Coroner's Office 'In the Event of my Death' which was meant for Briony to read. They made their way back downstairs. At the front door Joan turned to face Anna.

'She will find out, you know. Who you are.' Anna had wondered the same but didn't want to dwell on it.

'I hope not, Joan. She seems pretty volatile, understandably, and I don't know how she'll react. She might go off the deep end and tell people, complain, and then I could lose my job.'

'But why would she? You did her a huge favour.'

Anna sighed. 'I handled the Chicago visit very badly. She was furious and she can barely be civil to me now even in emails. I've done what I can – sent her mother's letters – and she's asked me to meet her at the airport and bring her here but I just don't know how she would be if she knew. It's not just me, Joan, it's Steve's job on the line too if it all came out. She might even be thrilled and phone Ted to congratulate him on our work which would have the same result.' Anna chewed her lip. 'The problem is, I don't know her. I don't know what she's really like. I can't take the risk at this point and let's face it, there's no need. She'll want to see Diane to get Bob back but otherwise, why would she have any contact with any of us except you, as a neighbour?'

Joan took Anna's hand and chafed it gently between her own slim, warm ones. The two of them were much the same height.

'Well, I know the truth even if she doesn't. You were doing it for her mother weren't you, as much as for Briony?'

Anna laughed. 'At the time I got the case it looked as though my teenage daughter was going to dash off to Russia with a totally unsuitable man. Let's say, there were resonances!'

Joan shook her head at the thought. 'Changed her mind then?'

'Oh yes.' Anna looked thoughtful. 'But it was a near thing. I've had enough missing people in my life, Joan, and so have you so I know you understand why it was important to find Briony if possible.'

Joan looked round. 'Yes, this is a peaceful house now. You did well, Anna. Even if Bri never knows it, we all do and we love you for it.' Anna was astonished to feel her eyes fill with tears. 'As long as Diane and I are alive you'd better get used to being plagued with mothers.'

'I think I can get used to that,' Anna said huskily. 'Do you do ironing?'

'Don't push it,' said Joan opening the door.

These days Anna felt giddy, like a girl again. Each day on the way home from work she thought of little treats for Harry. Yesterday she had brought down the old photo album from when the children were small and the two of them had sat close to each other on the sofa. She had pointed out a skinny, tousle-haired Ellis with a long string of seaweed he had found on the beach grinning for the camera.

When she next pointed out a field and the tent they had that year he said, 'Sand!' as though the word had been slow in making its way from his brain to his mouth. Then there was Faye proudly riding a neighbour's pony. 'She nagged us so hard to get her a pony, she even woke us up at 5.00 on her birthday to ask if we'd bought it, and then a month later it was boys. Just like that.' Harry had looked hard at the photos, his forehead furrowed with concentration and then quickly glanced at Anna's face. Sometimes a broad smile lit him up as he remembered and then Anna felt her heart grow huge. It was all she could do not to hug him and kiss him but if she did he sometimes seemed uneasy so she only allowed herself to stroke his arm and hold his hand. She had not moved back into their bedroom. It was his place now.

She had downloaded his favourite music to the MP3 player and he wandered around the garden with Bob humming and picking up twigs and leaves and then dropping them. But each day he needed to be shown the device again and how to put in the earphones. She knew George was worried. He had been so delighted when Harry had changed towards her, but now, seeing her joy in being with him, getting a response from him, he had grown concerned.

'Go easy, Anna,' he had advised. 'We can't know what might happen. What the next, er, phase may be.'

'Dad, I can't think about that. Let me just have now for as long as it lasts. OK?'

It was true, there was a continuing decline. Harry was not as he had been except for passing moments. He was sleeping more and sometimes he was hard to reach. The wandering off had stopped but only because he had less energy. Still, he was able to go out with them for a walk in the park as long as they took it slowly and let him stop and examine things. For Anna all that mattered was that she had entered the circle of people he trusted, people he felt safe with. Only now could she fully admit how agonising it had been to be rejected and yes, Len was right, hated by him. An unlikely bond had grown between him and Len. Probably because of the music, Anna thought.

They didn't talk or even take much notice of each other but when Len went outside to smoke Harry would often go too and mooch around the garden while he played the flute. A thought occurred to her and she decided to talk to Steve about it some time.

A steady barrage of bulletins was coming from Briony. She had decided that as well as writing her tell-all book she would re-enrol in Birmingham University to study criminology. Privately Anna thought it may be a bit too soon for that but she was pleased that she was planning and thinking of the future. Briony was well aware that the window for applications was closing.

I know what courses I want and I've talked to the Admissions people but I have to get the application in quickly so could you pick up the forms for me and see if there are any documents I need that won't be at the house? My A level certificates and birth certificate should be there and they've got that all on record from before anyway but could you check?

Sometimes Anna felt resentful of Briony's tone. She was being treated as a lackey. She was never thanked for what she did and the 'requests' were clearly orders. She was finding it easy to believe that Briony would be pig-headed over leaving her course to flit off to America with Karl. Perhaps she was her father's daughter and more like him than her kind and gentle mother. She began to think that she would need to set limits on how much she would do for Briony after she got home and then chided herself for her meanness. It was a good thing that Anna had made it clear from the start that she would not be at the celebration at the farm as planned by Diane and the others. She was certainly not in danger of being invited by Briony herself since Joan had told the young woman all about it and Briony hadn't mentioned it to Anna at all. That was ok. Much easier and safer that way.

As Anna browsed the supermarket shelves looking for a treat for Harry, she realised that it would be good to arrange something for herself to be doing that day and then, with a rush of delight, realised she could go somewhere with Harry. George could enjoy the party and not have to worry. Ellis would be in Cornwall and Faye had forgotten all about Briony anyway and would have her own social plans. She would need to think about it because in a week Mrs Bulowski, nee Clark, would be back. Then she had an even better idea.

When she got home Ellis was moodily checking his phone. She knew what the problem was. He was upset about Bob. How to explain why Bob had to leave them? She and George had puzzled over it. In the end the best explanation was the truth, or a version of it. Bob's owner had been abroad and had not expected to come back but plans had changed and she was arriving soon, desperate to be reunited with her loved old dog. Again, Anna had the uncomfortable feeling of people who should be kept apart being far too close for safety.

'Are you sure she really wants him?' he worried, 'She went off and left him before.'

'No, she really does,' said George. 'She told Diane that she was looking forward to seeing him more than anything.'

Ellis rubbed Bob's head and hid his face in the black fur. Anna and George looked at each other. 'I always wanted a dog,' Ellis mumbled, 'but Dad would never let us before. Does he have to go?' He raised a flushed face to Anna. She made a questioning face at her father who would have to bear the responsibility most of the time.

He looked resigned. 'Well, there is a new puppy at the farm.' He didn't get any further.

'A *puppy*!' Ellis had leaped to his feet so suddenly and shouted so loud that Bob had uttered a rare yelp of surprise.

'But, not till you come back from Cornwall,' George warned. 'It will be your dog to look after and train and it wouldn't be fair to bring it home and then disappear for a week.' Anna realised that her father was ahead of her and had already been thinking about this – maybe even discussed it with Diane. A wave of gratitude to him washed over her.

'Yes! Yes!' Ellis was almost burbling with joy and then the barrage of questions started. George put his hands over his ears and shook his head. Ellis chased him round the kitchen, Bob now barking with excitement, until George gave up.

'I'll tell you what,' he panted, 'why don't you come out with me after school tomorrow and meet him? Would that shut you up?' Ellis nodded and sank down into a chair dazed with anticipation.

'What will I call him?' he wondered out loud and George took the opportunity to slip away to his shed.

It was later, walking in the park with Harry, that Anna was reminded of her earlier idea. Harry rarely took any notice of other people these days but there were exceptions. The evenings were lighter and around the trees strong green fuses had appeared from tufts of yellow winter grass. In the shelter under the hedges around the park there were drifts of snowdrops. Anna noticed them with mixed feelings. In her childhood they would never have survived. They would have been wrenched up by grubby little hands to make posies, or just thrown around with that delight in destruction that some children take. Now they were left unmolested. Children were never seen in the park on their own any more. A vigilant adult was always on hand scanning for threat.

There was a bench near the central picnic area where they had formed the habit of stopping. It was still chilly and Anna snuggled down into her cheery red coat. Harry sat for a moment but was then up again and examining a discarded sandwich carton with shredded lettuce stuck in it which was skittering gently across the trestle table. She almost called out, 'Don't touch it,' as you would to a child and stopped herself. She noticed his hair needed cutting and decided that this time she would do it herself. She snuggled into herself with pleasure at the prospect. A cyclist in full biking get-up pedalled up to the area and braked. Harry stopped watching the carton and looked at him with interest. The man carefully leaned his bike against a tree and pulled a bottle of water out of his back pouch before sitting down next to Anna. Harry went straight to the bike and stood looking at it. The cyclist watched him warily, glugging the water. Anna was just about to say something when Harry swiftly, more swiftly than she had seen him move in ages, pulled the bike upright and swung his leg over the cross-bar.

'Whoah!' shouted the cyclist jumping up. 'Get off my bike!' Harry looked around as though not sure where the sound was coming from. Anna jumped up too.

'Harry,' she called. 'It's not your bike.' She ran to him just as the bike's owner was about to punch him away from the expensive machine. 'He means no harm. He's not well,' she tried to explain, 'he used to love cycling.'

'That bike cost over a thousand pounds – get him off it!' the man ordered, but dropped his fist.

Harry looked upset and confused. 'It's my car,' he said.

Anna went put her hand on his arm. 'No, it isn't, darling. Your car is at home. Shall we go and get it?' Harry reluctantly got off the bike and the owner watched grimly until he could pull it away.

'Thanks mate,' Harry said to the stony-faced man, putting out his hand. He had a wide smile on his face. There was an awkward moment.

'He won't bloody bite,' Anna said quietly, 'you can see he's ill. Just shake his hand for God's sake.' But the cyclist only glowered at Harry and then quickly mounted and rode away standing on his pedals. Harry watched him go wistfully. 'Come on,' she said, 'it's a bit chilly, let's see what dad's got for tea.'

35

Steve opened his eyes wide when he saw Anna's hair. 'Blimey,' he said, 'You look fantastic!'

'Everyone hates it,' she smiled, 'well, almost everyone.'

'No, I really like it. You look, er, jollier.'

Anna raised her eyebrows. 'And that's a good thing?'

'I was frightened to death of you before, Mrs Ames, you looked like you might have a spotted fur coat in the closet!'

'What? Are you saying I looked like Cruella Deville? You don't know the half of it.'

Things were so much easier now between them. The old tension had gone or at least was on a manageable simmer setting and it was a relief to be able to chat and tease without putting every word through analysis. Nothing had been said but Anna guessed they had both decided to let explanations lie. They were in the bleak office canteen staring resentfully at the coffee machine.

'Oh blow this,' Steve said, 'let's just break out and get a proper coffee.'

Anna glanced at her watch. 'Tell you what, give me fifteen minutes to send a couple of emails and I've done all I can for today. Ted owes me some time for that fiasco yesterday.' One of the new recruits had calmly driven them both into a bus. No one was hurt but it had taken hours to sort out with the police and quite a lot of fast talking from Anna.

'OK,' said Steve, 'Come and get me when you're ready and you can fill me in on what happened.'

Anna turned and began to walk away quickly but then called back to him, 'Will do. I've got a favour to ask, too.' She flashed a smile.

'Why am I worried?' Steve called after her.

Just as she was pressing the send button for the second email and thinking about a quick call home to check on Harry, Steve strode into the main office and up to her desk.

'I'm sorry, Anna, I've got to be somewhere.' She looked up at him, surprised. His face was drained of colour and he was shaking slightly. He seemed desperate. It was such an abrupt change from the care-free man she had been laughing with only minutes earlier.

'What's wrong? Can I help?'

'No. Look I've got to go.' He began to walk quickly away and then broke into a run almost knocking Suzanne off her feet as they collided at the door. He briefly apologised and was gone.

'Something you said?' Suze asked Anna.

'No. He just had to be somewhere suddenly.' Anna gazed at the space he had left. What on earth was going on?

'Somewhere?'

'I don't know.'

Suze pulled up a chair and sat down. 'I told you that hair was a frightmare,' she said winking at Anna. 'Now look what you've done. Spooked Steve.'

Anna leaned on the rail and stared, like the others, into the distance. The large window giving a distant view of planes and a grey dawn sky was at least better than a brick wall. Her arm was aching a little with the drive here, the first since they had taken the cast off. She glanced longingly back at the little coffee bar only metres away but the flashing screen said that the plane had landed and passengers were in the baggage area. At least the sky was beginning to brighten and it looked as though it might be a fine day. She glanced to either side of her. A man was holding a still-sleepy toddler in his arms and rocking gently to and fro. She wondered who he was meeting and if it was the child's mother, what the story was, where she had been. Nosy, she thought.

A flight from Germany had landed at much the same time so as the first class and carry-on luggage passengers emerged she amused herself by trying to work out which flight they had been on. They were mostly smartly dressed business men and women. Anna had wondered whether to wear her black or scarlet coat and decided on the former. More and more she was feeling that she would need all the props she had at her disposal to weather this encounter with Briony. What a change from six months ago. Then she had seen the young woman as a poor victim, which of course she had been in many ways, who would be in need of the kind of motherly hug Maggie would have given her. Anna had wanted to be the one to pass that on. Now, she wasn't so sure. The last email had contained new information.

I'm sure you remember that NBC are making a documentary about my experiences which I hope will raise public consciousness of the issue of the treatment of women in American jails but I have asked them to delay airing it on the network until after I leave the country. I do not want to be called for television interviews and become a travelling freak show. In fact, I don't want to be recognised at all. Because of this and for other obvious reasons I've gone back to my maiden name and will be travelling under it. It is still the name on my passport anyway.

Fair enough. Anna had wondered whether to make a placard since her change of hairstyle but just couldn't see herself standing there with it. Instead, she had a piece of card in her slim briefcase which she could get out and wave if needs be.

There was a hiatus in the flow of passengers. Anna thought again about Steve. What could it have been that took him away like that? It was the second time he had rushed away from her but he had also made that mysterious reference in the pub to needing time off in a hurry. A connection flashed into her mind but it took her a few seconds to locate it. A man rushing off without explanation and looking worried – oh, yes, it was Mr Rochester in Jane Eyre and he was rushing off to attend to the shenanigans of the mad wife in the attic. She smiled at the bizarre thought. Steve's wife, ex-wife, was far from mad and living in New England. The flow of passengers began again but these were hauling luggage. Some people were struggling with heaps of bags and yet looked from their deep tans and sandals as though they had only been away on holiday. She stood up straight and examined the stream of bemused, tired people.

Once again she marvelled at how much data the brain can process in just a second or two. Afterwards she couldn't decide how she had recognised Briony. Would it be the young, nubile, pre-USA girl or the haggard, scrawny version who had spat at her? Neither, of course. Briony Clark had re-invented herself. It was the combination of an alert, intelligent expression, a slim, soberly dressed figure, a determined stride despite the long flight and of course the blonde hair cut now into a sleek chin-skimming bob. She was dragging by its wheels only one large case. She scanned the waiting line and zeroed in on Anna almost as quickly. They both walked either side of the barrier to where it opened up into the concourse.

Anna smiled and held out her hand, 'Ms Clark. Welcome home.'

Briony took the proffered hand and shook it briefly and rather painfully firmly. Anna was very glad she had not gone for a hug. 'Mrs Ames. I hardly recognised you. Please, call me Briony.'

They began to walk towards the exit. 'It's the hair. My children hate it but my husband likes it.' How good that felt, to be able to say that about Harry. Such an ordinary statement and yet bursting with pleasure for her.

It soon became clear that Briony was very much in earnest about writing her expose of the conditions in jail and almost immediately began to tell Anna more. Edna Mahan had been much better than Cook County but still, since the zero tolerance of drug offences had come into law, very over-crowded. 'I've been reading official reports,' Briony said striding energetically through the car park, 'and there's a Human Rights Watch report from 2003 that says that, "Prisons are now the largest mental institutions in America." That was *before* zero tolerance.' Anna wondered if she had been working all night on the flight over. 'And,' Briony went on, installing herself in Anna's car, 'nearly three-quarters of the women in jail have been sexually and/or physically abused. Most of them had their first sexual experience between the ages of eight and ten! And they lock *them* up!'

On the drive to Northfield Anna felt she needed a change of subject and talked Briony through the details of her mother's estate. She already knew the facts in broad brush terms but it was good to have something practical to base their conversation on. She couldn't help glancing at the younger woman every now and then. Briony was looking around her with interest and as they sped along the M42 she took a deep breath and said, 'Oh - fields. And sheep. I have missed this so much.' Anna smiled at her. 'My own country,' Briony said, her pale blue eyes moist and shining, 'my home.' There was a pause. When Anna glanced at her again she saw that tears were about to spill.

'I'm so sorry about your mum,' Anna said quietly. Briony was silent, struggling for control. 'My own mother died not long ago.' Anna realised that she had now made two statements that would seem commonplace to her passenger but were huge to her. Is this how we accommodate our joys and sufferings? Telling them and re-telling them, coining them again and again, making them ordinary? Part of the common lot. Quotidian.

'Sorry to hear that,' said Briony taking a tissue out of her large leather bag. 'How old was she?'

'Sixties,' Anna said. Briony blew her nose and there was a pause.

Briony had given instructions for the house to be aired which, of course, Joan had already seen to and when they drew up outside the terrace she was there waiting. She stepped forward as Briony got out of the car. 'Welcome home, dear,' she said, giving the tall young woman a very quick hug. 'I'm not going to chat on because I know you must be tired but I'll just see you settled and that you've got everything you want.' The sudden droop in Briony's shoulders showed how much she needed that tactful care. Anna helped her with her case and put the folder of documents into its side pocket.

'Phone me if you need me,' she said, moving towards the car, 'I've put a Harts card with my extension number in the folder. Good luck, Briony, I hope all goes well for you.' She had not added her personal mobile.

Unexpectedly Briony came back out from the porch and hurried towards her. 'Just a minute.' The two women looked at each other. 'I want to say something.'

'I'm sorry I messed up in Chicago,' Anna said, having planned not to mention it at all.

'But that's what I want to say. I sort of understand why you did. You chose to come all that way to tell me face to face about my mum and that was the only way you could think of to get to me without tipping me off.' They searched each other's faces, both willing to let the past go and wondering if they could.

Anna smiled ruefully. 'That was the plan.'

'I know. Honestly, I do. And since then, well, you've been very supportive. I just wanted to say that I am grateful despite coming across as a psycho the last time we met.' So, in the end, they did hug and meant it.

She had only just fastened her safety belt when her phone rang. She rummaged in her bag and pulled it out. It was her father.

'Anna? There's been a phone call from the hospital.' Anna's stomach clenched and she felt bile bite her throat. 'They want us to go in this afternoon at 3.00 to talk to that new chap. Smythe-whatsit.' There was a pause.

'OK,' Anna whispered.

'I think they've got the results of the tests.'

'Yes.'

'Are you all right?'

'Will be. I'll meet you there, shall I?' Anna put her phone away and sat very still. What she was going to hear in just a few hours would determine the rest of their lives – all of them. For a panicked moment she wished she had never agreed to the tests. She might not even be alive when Faye or Ellis - Faye *and* Ellis - would be fifty. Who would be there for them? Who would watch out for them and calm their fears and make their favourite meals? A surge of blackness hit her. When she could think again she looked at the car clock. It was not even 9.00 yet. Somehow she would have to find a way to get through the next six hours.

Steve seemed rather distracted when she popped into his office but she could see that he was inundated with work. On his desk he kept a tear-off pad with the day's 'To Do' list and a cheap biro ready on top. In the past she had teased him about this and asked why he didn't use his phone or another device to keep records but he had said, 'I'm a pragmatist – I do whatever works and to scribble stuff down is quicker usually and it's there all the time by my laptop to remind me.' She glanced at it and saw that the writing was densely packed.

He winked at her but didn't close the window he was working on. A subtle hint. 'I won't keep you, Steve, I can see you're busy, but I just wanted to tell you a couple of things. Briony's home and I think it's going to be ok. She's full of plans for university and finishing her book and she didn't even hint at keeping in touch with me now that she's got all the documents and contacts she needs.'

He looked at her curiously, 'What's she like?'

Anna reflected. 'Sharp. But not hard. She's no fool. But she's got a soft side too. She's so glad to be back in England and there's no doubt she's grieving for her mother so being at the house where she grew up is bound to be emotional. She actually apologised for how she behaved to me when I visited her in Chicago.'

'You're kidding?' Steve smiled properly now. 'Feel better? Guilt monkey jumped off your back?'

'Yes. Well, about that, anyway.' She turned to go.

'You said a couple of things.'

'What?'

'You said you had a couple of things to tell me. What's the other?'

309

'Oh.' Anna's heart lurched again. 'Dad and I have to go to the QE this afternoon. They've called us in - that new consultant, something Smythe or Smythe something. They must have the results of the tests on the children. I can hardly bear to think about it.' She wished so much that it could have been Mr Shenouda. He would have known how to talk about it, how to comfort or celebrate. This man, from what she'd seen, had no empathy at all.

Steve stood up and gave her a brief hug. 'Fingers crossed, eh?' She nodded dumbly. 'I'd like to suggest lunch but I just can't do it today.'

'That's ok. Quite honestly, I don't think I can eat anything anyway.'

'I haven't forgotten that you wanted to ask me a favour, Anna. I should be done with all this by tomorrow night if I keep at it. Do you fancy a walk on Saturday morning? I'm desperate for some fresh air. We don't have to go far – perhaps walk the ridge on the Malverns? On a clear day that's as good a walk as any and we could be there in under an hour.' She hesitated, thinking of George needing his own time away from Harry but then remembered that Ellis was playing in a local league on Saturday morning and her dad always took Harry to his games.

'That would be great.'

'But, Anna,' Steve was already sitting back down to his terminal, 'phone me tonight if you can? Either way it's a big deal, I know that.'

'Of course. Thanks.'

36

Being in the QE public area was like being in an airport for the second time that day, Anna thought. She looked round the vast lobby restlessly for distraction. George and Harry were coming in by train and she would drive them all home afterwards. The children had not been told. Time might be needed to prepare them and there was, of course, no urgency. In fact, if the news was bad she knew she would want to put off that conversation as long as possible. She thought back to dinner last night and had to breathe in sharply to stop the tears rising. Faye, her infuriating, wonderful daughter, had been in a sunny mood.

'Mum,' she had said beguilingly, 'You know Friday night?'

'Well, yes, of course. What do you want?'

'You know Pops likes new people to come along - poets, you know?'

'Mm.' Anna continued to fork spaghetti into her spoon but ratcheted up her listening skills. 'You want to bring someone?'

'He's not like that bloody Sasha,' Faye said quickly. 'He's sensitive and kind and really nice.'

That was quick, Anna thought, pleased. 'Bring him to dinner if you want. Diane's coming so it would make a special occasion of it.' She could do a roast. It would be easy and a bit special. Maybe bought cheesecake for afters with clotted cream and tinned peaches?

Faye dimpled prettily and wiped sauce flecks off her cheeks. 'Thanks, Mum, I'll tell Pops. Len's not going to be there, is he?'

'I doubt it,' said Anna, 'he seemed bored last time. But – if he is, play nice!' Faye got up to leave and was at the door before Anna called, 'What's his name, this friend?'

'Justin. He's so cool.' She was in the hall when she added, 'Oh, and Mum, he's a vegan. He might bring some people.' And then she was off.

Anna mentally revised the menu for Friday in light of new information. Did vegans eat pasta? Berries, not cheesecake? Maple syrup? Would this be the new normal? Faye, falling for someone for eternity and then falling out of love again as easily as changing her clothes. She loved her so much. And it wasn't just her rich and glossy looks, her fresh skin and slender frame. It was her energy, her vitality, her exuberance that made her glow. How could Anna give her the news that would inevitably dim that shining light? And Ellis

– full of earnest plans and urgent tasks. He was only a boy. A 50/50 chance they had said. But then a new diagnosis had been mentioned. Better? Worse? She remembered the priest's words. 'We must grit our teeth and believe in goodness – and love.'

'Sorry to keep you waiting,' George panted. 'The train was a bit late. But we've still got a few minutes. Pop to the loo, Harry?'

Harry shook his head and George rushed off.

Harry looked around. 'I come here sometimes,' he said neutrally.

'Yes.'

'Is it a space station?'

'Looks like it, doesn't it?' Anna said. 'But no, it's a hospital.'

Harry looked worried. 'Will you have to put your head in one of those things trains go down?' he asked.

'A tunnel? The MRI? No. I'm fine. We're all fine. We're just here for the doctor to talk to us.' Harry lost interest and looked around vaguely. A rowdy little group of soldiers in combat fatigues approached laughing and talking loudly. They'd probably been to visit a wounded friend, Anna thought, and were letting out the tension and fear. Harry moved protectively against her a little as they approached and then, to her joy, took her hand. She squeezed his long familiar fingers and smiled up at him. George found them and they set off down the wide hall to the offices of Mr Bellings-Smythe in the Neurosciences wing.

The man was wearing the same dark suit and crisp shirt. Well, not the same, Anna thought pointlessly, he probably has a wardrobe full of identical ones. She had the ridiculous image of him being dusted off and put to bed in a cellophane packet at the end of the day. Her brain was skittering foolishly. She forced herself to pay attention. George was leaning forward slightly with his forehead furrowed in concentration and she knew he would be worried he may not hear everything. He resolutely refused to have his hearing tested. Anna had a small notepad in her lap and was holding a pencil which was quivering slightly.

She took a deep breath and then another one. Only Harry was unperturbed. George had had the foresight to bring the MP3 player and had set the device up for Harry before they had been called in. Anna could hear very faintly the familiar sounds of Space Odyssey. Good choice, so that's why Harry had thought they were in a space station. Concentrate, Anna, for goodness sake.

Mr Bellings-Smythe looked over his half-glasses at them and then glanced at his computer screen. 'We've had the results of the gene tests on your children, Faye and Ellis.' George and Anna waited tensely. 'Before I discuss them with you, I will explain something about the demented brain.'

Oh goodie, Anna thought resentfully, because we'd never have thought to research that for ourselves, would we? As the consultant talked, going over ground that was already horribly familiar to them, Anna tried not to tap her feet or shuffle with impatience. There would be no point in telling him they knew all this; that would only antagonise him and, to be fair, there may be people who had not be able to do their own fact-finding and would welcome this overview.

'So, dementia in general is caused by one of three faulty genes,' he continued. 'But for an accurate diagnosis we must also look at the area or areas of the brain which are affected. Normally the onset of any of the dementias would be in older people. The incidence rises sharply when patients are in their eighth or ninth decade. Harry's case is clearly unusual.' Anna looked across her husband, who now had his eyes closed, at George. He was having as hard a time as her with this mini-lecture. Neither of them interrupted.

'In most cases of early-onset dementia like Harry's the cause is an inherited gene. His parents could not be tested because he was adopted.'

Anna could bear it no longer. 'Doctor – we don't want to seem rude, but we know all this. Harry has been seen here for months and all of this has been thoroughly gone into. We are desperate to know about our children.'

'Ground control to Major Tom,' Harry murmured, rather appropriately Anna thought. She gave him a quick smile and was rewarded with a twinkle in his eye.

The consultant looked at her soberly. 'I am building to that.' He cleared his throat. 'You must understand that I cannot know what has been explained to you before. Mr Shenouda and I have discussed Harry's case very thoroughly and I agree with him that Harry has been mis-diagnosed.'

Anna and George leaned forward. 'Mis-diagnosed? You mean, he hasn't got dementia?' Anna's thoughts raced wildly. What other disease could account for Harry's erratic memory and crumbling reason? Was it psychiatric? What on earth could it be?

Was it – her heart pounded – curable? You read all the time about a simple intervention that had saved someone who had suffered misdiagnosis and they recovered totally. A major nutrient or hormone deficiency? Or could it be that it really was a grossly under-active thyroid and the test results had got mixed up?

Mr Bellings-Smythe seemed puzzled by their reaction. 'Oh, no. Mr Ames is demented. He has dementia. It's the form of dementia that is in question.' Anna's shoulders slumped and the notepad slipped to the floor. The blood beat in her ears. She picked it up and tried to control her emotions. 'That's why in the absence of parents we needed to test his children.' George and Anna waited. 'If I can just show you this.' He turned the computer flat-screen towards them. A cross-section of a brain with coloured patches came into view. 'These are the areas of Harry's brain that are affected. These are the frontal temporal lobes,' he tapped his own temples, 'and this is the hippocampus in the median area. I'm sure you are aware that much long-term, declarative memory processing goes in this area which is connected to the cerebral cortex. You will see that the areas which show up in green on this view are largely in those areas. Other small centres are starting elsewhere but the origin of the dementia seems to be here.'

Harry spoke, startling them all. He, too, was looking at the screen. 'This,' he said, whirling an index finger near the top of his head, 'is it catching?' There was a moment of shocked silence.

'No,' the consultant said calmly, 'It isn't.'

'Oh, good.' Harry lost interest and got up to look out of the window.

'So, what does that mean?' Anna was finding the strain almost unbearable and she knew that George would be feeling the same. At least the man's clearly enunciated words were easy to hear.

Mr Bellings-Smythe folded his hands on top of the file on his desk and leaned forward a little. 'On its own the location would simply flag up a possible alternative diagnosis from EOFAD. Together with the test results from your children we think we can be sure.' There seemed to be no air in the room and Anna noticed a red mist rise in her vision. 'There is a rare type of early onset dementia called Picks Disease. It usually manifests in fairly bizarre behavioural changes but not always. Harry's inertia and fatigue which sometimes alternate with hyper-activity as you mentioned to Mr Shenouda is a characteristic. Inappropriate social behaviour is also a possibility.' Anna thought of Harry taking the dog food from the supermarket and trying to ride off on a stranger's bike. And, it was 'inappropriate behaviour' that had flagged up the problem in the first place. Taking a class off and then abandoning them and seeming not to care. She couldn't help remembering him trying to strangle her and breaking her arm but that was for different reasons, maybe?

'So?'

Mr Bellings-Smythe finally turned away from studying the computer screen and looked directly at Anna. 'Your children did not test positive for any form of dementia.'

'Oh God!' Anna cried, 'Oh God,' and burst into tears. George was frankly sobbing, too. The next thing she knew was Harry kneeling at her feet and staring at her face with deep concern.

'Are you ok?' he said.

She cupped his anxious face in her hands and kissed him lightly. 'Yes, my darling, I'm ok. These are tears of happiness. Of relief.' He looked unconvinced. 'Mr Bellings-Smythe has just given us some very good news.' She looked past Harry at the dapper, grey-haired man who was watching the scene without expression. Poor sod probably got sent off to a boarding school at the age of seven, she thought, and learned not to wear his heart on his sleeve. It doesn't mean he hasn't got one. 'Thank you,' she said, 'I'm sure you can imagine what this means to us.'

A faint smile lifted the corners of his mouth. 'I have children and grand-children,' he said quietly. 'I think I can imagine a little of how you feel.' Harry sat back down beside Anna and her father, took her hand in both of his and closed his eyes beating time to the music in his head with his foot.

George was the first to collect his wits. 'So what does this new diagnosis mean for Harry?'

The doctor paused before he replied and closed Harry's file. 'I'm afraid his life expectancy may be less than we had thought.' Anna's mood immediately deflated. Give with one hand, take with the other, she thought. But still, surely it would be years and years yet. She just couldn't bear to ask. 'We want to take him off his current medication because it could be counter-productive,' the specialist continued, 'but also we would be grateful if he could take part in research. The etiology of non-inherited frontal lobe dementia is a mystery to us at present. If he and you, of course, would be willing. It's a rare condition and we can learn a great deal from further research.'

'I don't know,' said Anna, instinctively recoiling from the suggestion of Harry being used as some lab project. 'We wouldn't want him to be upset.'

'No, of course not. And this is not the time to discuss such possibilities. We will talk again at your next routine visit.' He stood up. It was over.

Anna stepped forward and put out her hand. If it had been Mr Shenouda she would have hugged him until he couldn't breathe but she still wanted to show how grateful she was to this self-contained but dedicated doctor. These clever men and women, she thought in a wave of gratitude, who work so hard to make lives better. 'Thank you so much,' she said. He looked slightly bewildered as though thanks were not expected or of relevance and she warmed to his lack of egoism. 'You have made our futures much brighter.' He nodded and opened the door for them to leave. Out in the waiting area anxious faces turned towards him. What had been for them a life-changing revelation had been for him a small part of a working day.

Faye and Ellis burst into the kitchen together that afternoon both convulsed with giggles.

'What?' Anna asked, kettle in hand.

'You know that kid that was Aladdin in the panto?' Faye gasped. 'That one that lost his trousers – same age as Ellis?'

'Yes. What?'

'You know Tash's sister, Nicola?' Anna nodded.

'Who's *fourteen*,' added Ellis significantly.

'Yes.'

'Well, he's only asked her out!' Faye dropped her jaw dramatically. 'I mean, she's *fourteen*! And his chat-up was to send her a text with a photo of his bum! Can you believe it?'

Anna put the kettle on its stand and reached for the biscuit tin. 'So what did she say?'

Ellis broke in, 'She texted him back saying he was a bit old to expect her to change his nappy!' He and Faye did a high-five. Anna made their tea and they all sat down at the table.

'We had some good news today,' she said as easily as she could.

'Mm? Faye's cheeks were bulging. Ellis was getting his tablet out of his bag.

'Yes. We saw your dad's doctor and he gave us the test results from when you both went in.' They were instantly still and attentive, but Anna went on quickly, 'You're clear. Both of you. You have nothing to worry about.'

Faye gave Ellis a small push, 'Obviously didn't check for the geek gene then!' He stuck out a tongue covered with mushy ginger snap and Faye made puking noises. Five minutes later they had gone about their business and Anna put on her coat to take Bob for a walk and indulge in some very deep breaths of fresh, cold air.

At dinner that night Anna and George were quiet. They had planned fish and chips knowing that the children would be pleased and that either way the result went at the hospital neither of them would want to cook. Harry was tired and left as soon as he had finished his food to go to bed. Anna joined her father in his shed.   They sat for a while in silence, sipping their coffee.

George tapped the pile of his latest collection. *Absent Without Leave.* 'This lot. I didn't realise until after it had been printed that my poems in here are full of ghosts.'

'Ghosts?'

'Yes.' He took off his glasses and rubbed his nose. 'Well, more mirages, really. Shimmering illusions. Worse and more stupid, regret for those, grief and longing for those things, those people that turned out to have no substance. I should have called it Djinn and It.'

Anna smiled. 'Lena? Mum.'

'Lena, who never was what I wanted to believe she was, yes, but not just that. Other selves I could have been, other paths I could have taken.' He looked out of the window into the night sky. 'All my life I've been searching for meaning. And now I'm old and I've got to stop living in a dream world of possibilities. This is it. I have to make sense of the ordinary life I've lived, not dream of a life I might have had.' Anna was quiet knowing that easy assurances of how wonderful a dad and grandfather he was would not help. 'You can't pack your Ship of Death with might-have-beens. You must pack it with real memories, real moments of joy.'

Anna moved closer and put her arm through his. 'And will there be enough?' He patted her hand and smiled. She smiled back.

'Can you hang around a while to make some more provisions for your ship, please?'

'I'll think about it,' he said gruffly.

37

Anna went up to bed thinking that she must be exhausted but found that she was wide-awake. In fact, it was impossible to even imagine getting to sleep. It was too late to phone Steve, so she texted him and sat staring out of the bedroom window at the night sky.   There were no stars but as her eyes became accustomed to the dark she could see layers in the clouds and every now and then a gleam of moonlight as the strata of wadding momentarily shredded apart.

Her mood was running around on a hamster wheel. The kids are all right! Up! Harry's life may soon be over – down. Harry knows me and likes me! Up! Dad is feeling his age and how could I ever manage without him? Down. And so on.

The phone on her bed rang. It was Steve. 'Great news, Anna, I'm so pleased for you.' There was a pause and she could hear a telephone and voices in the background. He was probably watching a late-night movie. 'How are you feeling?'

'Wired. He gave us a new diagnosis for Harry, too.' She talked him through it.

'You must feel really scrambled.'

'I do. I can't even imagine sleep.' There was another pause and a voice sounded much closer, clearly in conversation with someone else. 'Steve, are you at home? I can hear a television I think.'

'No. I'm not. Anna, there's somebody I want you to meet.' He sounded tense and shaky. 'I was going to tell you another time about this person but maybe it would be a good idea to do it tonight. I mean, for you two to meet.'   Everything in Anna's head went silent. She could feel her heart thudding and registered that her mouth had gone very dry.

'Who is it?' she asked, angry with herself for croaking the words.

'Will you come?'

'Where? Where are you?'

'It's a little way, I'm afraid. In Worcestershire. I'll give you the post code. I know it's unfair to ask when you're dealing with all that's happened today but it would clear up some stuff between us which I think I need to put straight. I didn't want to tell you before when you were so worried about things. Will you come?'

And so, ten minutes later there was a note for George on the kitchen table and she was on her way through almost deserted streets to pick up the M5 out of the city. Why would she have assumed that he did not have a woman in his life even though his wife had gone? After all, he had never made a move on her - she had initiated all the passes. No wonder he put her aside that time in his flat. If there was someone else, why had he not told her months ago? It would have been so easy for him to just mention someone and that would have set things straight between them. Instead, furious with herself for it, she had allowed herself to believe that they had more than a friendship; that his eyes held more than affection when he looked at her.

Too much, she thought swinging too fast round a container truck, today has been too much. Yes, it is selfish of him to drag me out on this errand to meet his special someone. Yes, it is. She had been so keyed up about the children's tests and then the news about Harry made the pit of her stomach ache. She should have been left in peace before a new bombshell burst. He said he couldn't tell her before because she had been so worried about the children and, she realised now, all of the events that had erupted in the last few months. Ever since she had known him it seemed her life had lurched from one drama to another. First it was the Clark case with all its twists and turns and then Len and Lena and her death and today the good-news/bad-news fairy had struck again.

She felt as though she had been driving for ages. She glanced at the dashboard clock. It had been nearly half an hour since she had left home even though there was hardly any traffic. She felt so resentful towards Steve that she almost stopped and turned the car round. She had left the motorway and miles of dual-carriageway and was now on an empty A road. She remembered how he had been when he thought she might have spilled the beans over the media campaign. Cold and suspicious. Now he was expecting her to drive off into the blue because he needed her to meet someone. Selfish.

As she drove slowly through yet another village the satnav told her to turn off down a minor road. What on earth is this, she wondered? All she could see in the darkness were the shapes of isolated houses, quite large ones, and every now and then her headlights would pick out an old farmhouse right on the road before she quickly dimmed them. So whoever this person was, she was probably pretty well-heeled. Great. Or, did Steve have another house which they shared? After all, Anna had no idea how much his Home Office 'sideline' paid. What a fool she'd made of herself after all. As if the disillusion of Lena wasn't enough.

Now she was being told that she was at her destination. A driveway made an opening in a thick hedge and she unwillingly turned into it. Ahead of her was a substantial house with many windows lit up dramatically in the darkness of the countryside. She drew up on a gravelled forecourt, switched off the engine and sat for a moment gathering her thoughts for whatever lay ahead. Might as well get it over she told herself grimly and remembered to put a brush through her hair and fluff it up a bit. Make-up was out of the question.

As soon as she pushed her way through the stained-glass panelled front door, the collar of her red coat turned up round her ears against the cold outside, Steve was there.

'Are you ok?' She nodded, not able to trust her voice any more. 'Do you want coffee? Tea? Are you hungry?'

She shook her head. What on earth was going on? He was, in fact, already hurrying her along a corridor. Was it a hotel? She glanced from side to side noticing oil paintings and glass cases. While they ran up a wide staircase with a polished wood banister she tried to calm herself, empty her head of questions and force herself to breathe normally. Whatever it was that Steve was going to reveal may be upsetting and disappointing but nothing could take away the deep joy and relief of knowing that Faye and Ellis were ok.

Then they were walking so quickly along an empty hallway that Anna almost bumped into Steve when he stopped at a door and tapped gently on it. He turned to Anna and raised a finger to his lips and then beckoned. She followed him in.

The room was a complete surprise. Not a hotel but a medical ward? A nurse sat at a small console in the corner of the room, her face up-lit from the monitor in front of her. She was making notes from the screen but paused for a moment to look up at Steve and smile. She was beautiful. Anna guessed that she was maybe in her early twenties with the soft facial moulding and perfect skin of youth. Her eyes had lit up when she saw Steve. Her pale golden hair was pulled back into a loose bun. The same style that Faye liked. A ministering angel, indeed.

There was a crash trolley in the corner and just one bed in the room. A dimmed light shone above it and there was a small shape under the blanket. With a start Anna realised that it was the person in the bed and not the nurse that Steve had gone to. She was very tired. Her mind was moving too slowly for all this. Steve beckoned her forwards to the bedside.

A young child lay still on the bed. It was not clear whether it was a boy or girl because the head had recently been shaved and only a short re-growth covered the skull. As the tiny ribcage rose and fell Anna could see that there were electrodes attached to the chest, their different coloured flexes coming out from the body like tent stays. The child seemed tethered to the machine as though without the cords and cables its weightless frame would float away. The skin that she could see was very pale, so pale that blue showed through where the veins pumped and the eyelids were as translucent as a baby bird's.

'Oh,' she breathed. She glanced at Steve.

His face was transfixed with tenderness. But there was something else, much sharper, in his expression and her mind moved slowly to identify it. Anxiety. Well, of course. How could anyone look at this child who was clearly seriously ill and not feel worried?

If the child was known to him, then he must be frightened for its safety. But who was he or she? Steve had told her months ago that he and his wife had had no children. The child was too young to be from a previous relationship but too old to be from a new one, surely? She put all that aside. Here was a child whom Steve clearly loved who was probably fighting for its life.

Slowly and very carefully she made her way round to his side of the bed. She came up softly behind him and felt for his hand. As soon as he felt the touch of her fingers he gripped them and kept hold. Then he turned his face away from the unconscious child and looked at her. The blue eyes burned fiercely but as she held his gaze they softened and the flesh of his face lifted almost imperceptibly into something approaching a smile.

He flicked a glance towards the door and she moved back and carefully made her way out ahead of him, nodding to the lovely nurse as she passed. When he had quietly closed the door behind him and they were both out in the hallway he caught her hands and brought them up to his chest.

'I couldn't explain in words. I had to show you.'

They drove separately back to his flat and then sat for a long time on the huge white sofa with the panorama of the sleeping city spread outside the wide window, talking. There had been three people, not two, in the car accident which had killed his youngest sister and her husband. Their two-year old daughter, Alice, had been badly hurt but, thanks to her car-seat, not killed in the collision. Her skull had been damaged though. A piece of bone had dented in to her brain and partially fractured - but she was alive.

When she had been born Alice's parents had asked Steve to be her guardian in case anything ever happened to them. It was a routine precaution that many families took. Of course, nothing was expected to happen. But when the unexpected, the hypothetical, became a tragic reality it had put Steve and Cathy's relationship to the test. The child, at best, would need hospital care for many months if not years and after that might need special care and attention for the rest of her life.

Cathy had thought about it very hard. She was fast becoming one of the rising talents in her field and loved her work. She had never really even considered having children and knew that if she committed to this one then Alice would have to be the centre of their lives. They would possibly not be able to travel or work abroad which meant she would have to turn down research posts in top universities. She would become resentful and bitter. She was not a callous woman but she was a clear-eyed one and decided she couldn't commit to Alice. For a little while they had talked about compromise, about her being free to follow her career path and Steve staying in Birmingham to be near his niece. But the problem was more than a practical one. As they had talked it all through they had discovered how very far apart they were in values.

So, sadly, they had agreed to part. That had been just over a year ago. Around the time, Anna realised, that Harry had been diagnosed. Now he heard from Cathy from time to time but they had very little to talk about any more. She was puzzled that he had stepped down from his academic post but Steve felt it would be unfair to the students and the other faculty if he often needed to leave work at a moment's notice. He had to be on hand to give permission if a new medical procedure was suddenly needed.

His forward thinking had been appropriate as events turned out. Ted knew the situation and was happy to trade-off flexibility against Steve's skills. So that was why he stayed at Harts, Anna thought. Cathy felt he was wasting what should be the most productive years of his life for what may well be a lost cause. He felt that he was living his life in the only authentic way he could, by fulfilling his promise to his sister, to Alice's parents (and her grandparents), to love and watch over the little girl who was going through so much for as long as she needed him. And as time had gone on and he had watched her bravely struggle with pain and mischievously play him up when she felt well, he had come to love her even more than he had before, for herself, not just out of a sense of duty.

It had turned out that the depressed skull fracture from the accident was only the start of a long and painful process. There had been several operations to pick out the pieces of bone from the brain and repair the damage and for a while it had looked as though Alice would make a straight-forward recovery as was normal. That was the first time she had come to this old house in the country which had been converted to a neurological rehabilitation centre.

But then she had started having fits. Steve had dashed into the Children's Hospital ICU to give permission for emergency surgery and a blood clot had been found and removed.

Again, the hope was that there would follow a period of increasing recovery and that the little girl would finally be able to leave the rehab unit.

But there had been another major setback when the seizures began again. This time scans revealed that an abscess had formed at the site of the second surgery and Steve had spent hours pacing the hospital corridors in an agony of worry for his little niece. It was this latest surgery that she was now recovering from in the country house, pumped full of antibiotics and very ill indeed. This had been why Steve had rushed away from Anna earlier in the day. The unit doctors had been alarmed at a spike in Alice's temperature and had called him but it had almost immediately begun to normalise again. He had been at the unit ever since to watch over her but it had remained steady and the little girl had fallen into a natural sleep after he had read her a story.

Anna remembered the pallor of the child's skin and the little fluttering eyelids. She put her arm through Steve's and held his hand. So this is what he'd been coping with all the time she'd known him. This was why he had no plans to go abroad on his climbing trips.

'But why isn't she in Children's Hospital now?' she asked.

'I know, I was surprised, too. Apparently, it's more efficient to treat these serious head injuries in a special unit that draws from a wide area. It's a bit difficult for family who don't drive or haven't got much spare cash for extra petrol but it's a way of spreading medical resources better. You know, specialist nursing and all that. This kind of complicated head injury is quite rare.'

'And will she recover fully?' Anna asked quietly, wondering if the question was too harsh.

Steve sighed deeply and leaned his head back on the cushions. 'I don't know. No-one does. Time will tell.' They were both silent. There was no need to spell out the possible outcomes. 'But, I did wonder about something.'

'Mm?'

'When she's over this and living with me I'll need a proper house, you know a family home.'

'Yes, of course. What are you thinking?'

He hesitated. 'I don't know how you'll feel about this but I liked what I saw of Ellis's school. They seem to really care and the work on the walls was amazing.'

'Oh, it's a great school. And they both did well there.' Anna was beginning to smile.

'So, maybe, if you didn't mind, you know - I could get somewhere in the same neighbourhood?' His voice became nervous. 'Only if you didn't mind, of course.'

'It's all right, Steve, house prices are going down anyway, you couldn't lower the tone much more.' He ruffled her hair and laughed.

They had talked so long that they saw there was a faint change on the horizon as dawn approached. Anna got up and flexed her legs. She looked affectionately at Steve who rose and wrapped her in his arms. They hugged for a long moment. Then she yawned and pulled on her coat. 'Have a nice walk on the Malverns,' she said, 'I will not be among those present.'

'Neither will I,' said Steve, 'not today anyway.'

'If you feel like it you could come to Ellis's game later on. Dad will be there and Harry.' She stuck her fingers into her gloves. 'Stay for lunch with us if you like. Dad was asking about you last week and saying it would be nice if you came round.'

Steve was crumpled with tiredness. 'Sounds good. Fresh air without the exercise.' She smiled and opened his door to leave.

'Anna?' She turned as he came up to her and again put his arms around her. 'Drive carefully. Thank you.' The kiss was light and warm and she returned it. It felt easy. It felt right.

38

The field was a choppy sea of mud. Twenty-two grimly determined boys were battling it out with sharp cries and red, sweaty faces. Families were grouped along the touchline stamping their feet and yelling encouragement. They were mostly on a nodding acquaintance with each other and it was only a rare parent now who, over-invested in a child's prowess, jumped up and down screaming directions. That tended to happen much more with the younger children and, two pitches across the park, Anna could see and hear tots being given the drill sergeant treatment by their nearest and dearest. She and George had developed the practice of clapping and cheering Ellis's good moves and ignoring the other kind.

Ellis was tall for his age but skinny and not a natural footballer for all that he loved the game. She could see that in time he might move towards tennis and cycling like his dad had. She made a mental note to take more of an interest in his activities and maybe go on some longer bike rides with him. She would have to be mother and father to them now. Why had she not realised before quite what that would mean? George was great but he couldn't do the very active stuff any more and it would be up to her. She made a resolution to get her own bike serviced and see if Ellis would be interested in joining a tennis club if they could find one they could afford. At least Faye didn't need support in that area. Years ago George had taken her to an after-school yoga club and unexpectedly she had liked it and kept up the classes. Swimming had been her child-hood sport of choice but in later years she'd given it up like most of her friends, not wanting to get her hair wet.

Anna glanced to her right. Harry and Steve were standing together and when Steve gave a shout for Ellis, Harry did too. She had been right. Harry looked so much more alert. He must have been missing male friends of his own age so much but was not able to articulate it.

Cycling friends had dropped by in the weeks after he had been put on sick-leave before the diagnosis meant that he had to give up all ideas of work. But as time went on and Harry's memory became more and more erratic it had been hard for most of them to keep coming. The basis of their friendship had been all about cycling. What routes needed work or would be a new challenge, the condition of their bikes, the social evenings with other members of

Sustrans. It was hard for them to chat with someone who not only didn't share their experience but sometimes wandered out of the room as they were telling an anecdote. One friend, Mick, had remained a loyal visitor. He didn't try to talk about the passion they had shared, he just chatted about things Harry could relate to. What the weather was like that day, what was growing in the garden and so on. He never asked questions that would challenge and embarrass Harry. Anna had been so grateful for his easy, thoughtful approach. But, he had been promoted to a top managerial position in the main branch of his company which was in Glasgow.

Teaching friends had tried briefly to support him but it was the same there. Their socialising at work had almost always been about the amusements and frustrations of the job, the madness of the latest political initiatives, the idiosyncrasies of the kids and some good-natured teasing. Harry quickly lost all context for that kind of conversation. One by one they had become bewildered that a colleague who looked just the same as he always had could no longer follow a line of thought, couldn't remember most people they mentioned and who sometimes didn't even remember the visitor himself. And there was another thing. What had happened to Harry was frightening. Increasingly Anna saw the fear in visitors' eyes.

Over the last year since he had had to stop work, Harry had increasingly lost tenses. Now, the future and the past were almost gone and it was only the present that existed for him. Familiar routines and faces had meaning for him and sometimes he would surprise them by mentioning something from the past, something that had happened before the onset of his illness, but most of the time he lived in the now.

Faye and Ellis had understood this almost instinctively and never asked him questions he couldn't answer. They had been told about his condition once the diagnosis was made and given some simple idea of what their father was experiencing. Anna remembered the first time Ellis had really grasped the situation. It was last summer. They had been spending a few days in St Ives in the cottage. They were getting ready to go down to the beach. Ellis had grabbed a couple of life-jackets from the store the cottage kept for visitors and, in high excitement at being at the seaside on a perfect sunny day, called to his father to bring the inflatable and the pump. Harry had looked around himself in complete confusion. The inflatable dinghy was at his feet but he couldn't put the word and the object together. 'What?' he had asked Ellis.

'The inflatable – look – it's there right by you!' Ellis had said and then stopped and put the life-jackets down. He had stood stock still and looked at his bewildered father. Then he walked the few paces back and lifted up the slack rubber. 'Will you bring this, Dad?'

Harry had nodded quickly and the transition was made. From that moment on it was Ellis who looked out for his father, not the other way round.

A yell from George brought Anna back to the present. Ellis had, against all usual practice, scored a goal. He looked as stunned as anyone else. Anna jumped up and down and whooped and saw that Harry and Steve were doing the same. Ellis glanced towards them and flicked them a grin until he was inundated, in the approved Premier League manner, by the bodies of his team-mates. Anna wandered across to join Harry and Steve for a minute. 'Brilliant!' Harry grinned at her in the old way and she grinned back. Steve was smiling at them both.

When play resumed Steve turned to Anna. 'You wanted to ask me a favour?' He looked severe. 'Now might be the best time, Mrs Ames, before I hazard your lunch.'

'Ha! Watch it! You should count yourself honoured,' Anna laughed. She nodded towards Harry who was watching the boys play. 'Actually you're doing it already but I did have a plan. It's for next Sunday when it's Briony's party at the farm. Unless you're going?'

Steve shook his head. 'Meeting Briony would be a bit too close to the edge of our carefully constructed scenario, I think,' he said, 'Why, what are you thinking?'

The game was over and the boys who had families there made their way to them, calling to each other as they did. Anna noted the warning signal in her son's eyes and instead of hugging him gave him what she hoped was a manly nod of approval. It was what Steve was doing. She must learn from him about what was expected from a dad. Odd thought. Suddenly a rush of warmth engulfed her. She was not alone any more. Harry was walking off towards the trees in the opposite direction from where the car was parked. She opened her mouth to call him but before she could Steve had sprinted the distance to catch up with him and was clearly saying something. When they turned back to walk the right way, both men were smiling.

Anna was very glad that she had some flexitime hours in hand. What should have been the simple business of getting Ellis off on his break to Cornwall had become frenetic. At 2.30, after the early end-of-term final assembly, Mike's dad had found that his car had two flat tyres. Anna had done the school run while John Bryant phoned his breakdown company and had the car towed into the tyre dealership. While this was happening Ellis spun into a state because she had forgotten to wash his favourite hoodie, the one with the Despicable Me logo which was apparently indispensable for the trip.   The delay over the tyres at least meant she had a fighting chance of a quick-wash followed by a tumble dry. If it was still damp he would have to drape it over the seat or something. It turned out that the tyres were studded with nails, deliberately driven in. Start of the holidays, Anna supposed, and in among her annoyance felt sad for kids who didn't have the chance to go surfing and decided to get their kicks in less acceptable ways.

Finally, two hours after they should have set off the car was loaded and on its way. Anna turned back to the house to see Len's bulky form lumbering up the road. Oh, well. She waved at him and waited for him to come up. 'All right?'

'No, I'm bloody not,' he moaned breathlessly. 'There was no heating on the bus after I had to wait twenty-five minutes for it to turn up. Then there was these two old ladies next to me on the back seat must have had half a pound of talc on each of them. I couldn't breathe.'

'Mm,' murmured Anna, now well used to Len's overture of complaints. She usually allowed him about five minutes before she cut him off but decided that food might take his mind off his injustices a little sooner. 'Staying for dinner?'

He regarded her with interest as they mounted the steps to the front door. 'What is it?' She had given up being offended by such directness – in fact, it was quite refreshing. Len said what he thought without any subterfuge.

'Vegetable lasagne.'

'What?' He regarded her with horror. 'Why?'

'Faye's bringing a friend for the poetry and he's a vegan. He might bring friends.'

'Fuck,' said Len dismally, halting on the top step as Anna opened the door. 'Have you got anything else?'

'Bacon sarni?'

'Go on, then.' As they stepped into the hall a shout came from behind them as George and Diane got out of his battered car. Len dropped his voice in a rare moment of diplomacy. 'I don't have to stay for his poetry thing, do I?' Like it's the price of a bacon sandwich, Anna thought with amusement.

'No. You can get off after dinner, dad won't mind.'

'I've got a gig, anyway,' Len added bashfully, 'Nine o'clock tonight.'

'A gig? What sort of gig?'

'They wanted a tin whistle in the band down at The Horse and Jockey near me. You know, that folky one?'

'No, but go on. Do you play the tin whistle?'

'I asked them if a flute would do and they said they'd give it a go.'

'You'll knock 'em dead,' Anna said.

Len regarded her solemnly. 'You're all right, Sis,' he said.

Anna glanced round the group. Ashok had seemed a bit huffy about the presence of Diane for the third time in a row at their sessions. It was true, George had seen much less of his old friends from the temple and the mosque since Diane had come into his life. What Anna privately called his meaning-of-life friends. She wondered whether to have a word with him but couldn't think what to say that wouldn't be condescending or bossy. He should be allowed his own social skirmishes, she decided.

Joan had said she was too busy making goodies for the party to come tonight which Anna regretted. She was becoming very fond of Margaret's neighbour. She was sensible and intelligent but also had a wise deep-heartedness that Anna appreciated. She was what George called an 'old soul'. She was fond of Diane, too, but these days Diane was becoming almost girlish in her behaviour towards George. The tough, almost gruff woman Anna had first met had been transformed into a much softer version. While George was sorting out the poems for them to read Anna leaned sideways towards her.

'How did it go with Briony picking up Bob?' she asked.

Diane gave a snort of laughter. 'It was definitely a Heathcliff-Cathy moment except that only Bob was moving in slow motion.'

Anna giggled. 'He did recognise her then?'

'Yes.' Diane reflected. 'I was a bit relieved to be honest. People always expect their pets to have missed them but sometimes they don't. And Briony's been away years. I was pleased as well for Bob because I think he was a bit offended about coming back to the farm after yours.'

'Mm. I felt awful dropping him off,' Anna said and then quickly added, 'Not that it isn't a great place.'

'No, I know what you mean but it was only for a day and a night and he was with me most of that time.'

'Shall we start then?' said George, slightly nervous and excited as always before a reading. 'Can I welcome Justin to our group and also Taylor and – er –' he consulted his notes, 'Mel, friends of Justin from university, I think?' He looked over the top of his reading glasses and beamed at them. 'Taylor, have you brought some of your work?' He raised his eyebrows at a large and hairy young man. 'Would you like to start us off?' There was a ripple of good-natured laughter.

'Oh, I'm Taylor,' said his petite girlfriend perched like a pixie on a high stool. 'I know it's a weird name here but it's real common in the States. Yes, I would like to read a couple if that's ok.'

'Just a minute,' said Ashok, fumbling in his bag. 'You will need your vitamins!' He tapped the chocolate orange sharply on his chair arm and passed the foil package on. The young people laughed and Justin grinned at Faye and nodded. He seems ok, Anna thought. At least he isn't bossy and arrogant. In fact, she might have to stick up for him against her feisty daughter once she'd got over the sweetness and light phase. What was it someone had called romantic love? A period of mutual deception. Anna crunched her segment of chocolate as she discreetly watched Harry lounging on the almost collapsed old bus seat alongside her. Were his eyes brighter these days or was she just imagining it?

As always, the reading of the poems worked its magic. By degrees an intimacy grew between the young poets and the older ones. Three generations, some of whom had been strangers to each other only minutes ago, were drawn into each other's innermost thoughts and feelings. To George there were no such divisions in poetry as 'good' or 'bad' or acceptable or unacceptable style. He was as happy for someone to rhyme as for someone else to rap. Free verse was as interesting as a villanelle. He only cared about honesty and love of language. Anna, half-listening, laid her head back on the squashed vinyl and realised that for the first time since Harry's initial diagnosis over a year ago she felt at peace. A good feeling.

Ashok stood up and told them that his first reading would be an extract from a translation of a very old poem – a thousand years old in fact. Later he would read his own work. He was dedicating it to his old friend George. As he read the beautiful words the group were hushed, relaxing into the mood. He finished with Khayam's famous quatrain:

A Book of Verses underneath the Bough,
A Jug of Wine, a Loaf of Bread – and Thou
Beside me singing in the Wilderness –
And Wilderness were Paradise enow.

Ashok read the familiar words as though they were a blessing. The young people seemed enthralled and when he had finished Ashok generously passed the translation to them to borrow. Anna understood the dedication. He was saying in his tactful way that he understood about Diane, about what it meant for George to have her in his life, despite his twinges of jealousy.

Later, when the readings were over, Harry had fallen asleep and the others crept out quietly to have supper in the kitchen. Faye was hosting the second half of the evening for her friends and Anna knew it wouldn't be long before the four students would be curled up in the front room with snacks and drinks and a stack of DVDs. George and Diane rose rubbing their bottoms and pulling down their jumpers. They were starting to behave like an old married couple. They nodded at Anna and left, too. Only Ashok remained.

Anna smiled at him noticing how the finely-grained wrinkles made a darker web round his eyes. How old is he, she wondered. He had been in their lives for so many years entertaining and comforting. 'How is life treating you, Ashok?' she said, almost whispering. 'Are you ok?'

He chuckled. 'Life is treating me much as I have treated it,' he said. 'But yes, I am.' He looked at her gently. 'And you, Anna? You never complain but you've had it tough.'

'Oh, I'm all right,' Anna said, reaching out for the slim brown hand. 'In fact, I'm better than I've been for a long time.' She reflected for a moment. 'My head is clear now. And there are only real people in my heart. People who when I smile at them, they smile back at me. Well, usually.'

'That's a good place to be.' He got up slowly as the old chair creaked and gathered up his books. 'I'll go and put the kettle on if I may.'

'Of course. We'll come in just a minute.'

He understood that she wanted to be alone with Harry. Softly, carefully, she began to stroke his hair. It had been so rich in colour when they had first met and even now there were points of bright auburn among the duller brown that gleamed in the yellow lamplight. His head was turned slightly towards her, the dark eyelashes making a deep shadow on his cheeks. Her fingers barely touching his skin, she caressed the curve of his eyebrow, the tender soft pouch of flesh on his cheekbone, the deep groove from nose to mouth. His lips. And miraculously, as her finger lightly moved, while he was still sleeping, his lips puckered slightly and she leaned over and, as softly as a moth, kissed him. She leaned back. It was enough.

Later, when the kitchen was empty again and a subdued murmur came from the front room, Anna got out her laptop. This was the last assignment before she would be fully qualified and she wanted to make it a good one. But before she started to edit what she had already written she opened her email window. There were a surprising number of work emails but then she remembered that she had left early. Normally these would have been dealt with by now.

She opened each one and noted that they could wait until Monday but there was also one from Ted which she had left until the end. His email style was appalling. Why was it, she wondered, that competent business people felt they could get away with anything if it was an email?

missed u at the office i need to see you about job so firt thing Mon ok

She emailed back to confirm and realised that she was actually looking forward to being called to his office. That was a first. It wasn't just a job to pay the bills any more – it was beginning to feel as though she belonged, as though this was something she could really be good at. Immediately she snorted at her own wishful thinking. Probably Ted had lined up a difficult case from the Treasury List which no-one else would take on. Never mind. The front door closed quietly and moments later George came into the kitchen unwinding his scarf. He had taken Diane home.

'Ok?' she asked. 'Cup of tea?' He nodded and she got up to put the kettle on.

'It was good tonight, wasn't it? It was great to have those young people there and Justin's stuff is quite impressive, isn't it?' He was fizzing with pleasure. She looked at him a little more quizzically.

'Dad?'

'Mm. Are there any of those crumpets left?'

'In the cupboard. You haven't been to the temple lately, have you? I was just wondering.'

He looked at her sharply. 'Did Ashok say anything?'

'No, of course not. I just wondered if you were thinking of including Diane when you go off God-bothering in future.' She gave him a teasing wink.

He emerged from the cupboard clutching a packet of crumpets re-sealed with a washing basket peg. 'No,' he said, 'I probably won't.'

'Oh why, Dad? I thought you were getting on so well.'

He waved the packet in the air. 'Well, that's the thing, you see. We are.'

'What do you mean?'

George stood motionless for a moment, the crumpets dangling from his fingers. He looked pink and a little sweaty. 'Well, I don't need to, do I? Bother God, I mean. I've found what I was looking for. It's all about love isn't it? It's so simple. It's all about love.' Anna took the packet out of his hand and went to the toaster so that he could not see her face.

39

By the time they left the Uttoxeter by-pass the sun was glittering on puddles in the fields and a mist of bright lime green drifted through the trees. Spring. There wasn't a cloud in the sky and Anna hugged herself with delight. She had decided to sit in the back with Harry so he wasn't left on his own and he was looking around with as much pleasure as she was. It had been months since they had been out of the city together. Every now and then she would point things out. It was fun to see the tiny new-born lambs wobbling around their mothers, the bright new growth of grass stippling the dun colours of winter ground cover.

There was just one moment of panic when Harry spotted some cyclists riding along a canal towpath and tried to open the door as they sped along at 60 mph. She grabbed him in time and heard Steve discreetly click the child-locks on. For a moment he had looked startled by her action but when she smiled, he relaxed and forgot the incident.

Anna glanced at her watch. Back at the farm Joan's son and his partner would be firing up the barbeque ready to start grilling in an hour or so. The dogs would go crazy with the smell. It would be pandemonium. She wondered if Briony would take Bob and thought she probably would. And somewhere among the crowd of wildly barking animals there would be the puppy. He was a funny-looking little thing, a motley mix of breeds with a square shaggy head far too big for his body and a spotted short coat. Ellis had looked into his huge brown eyes and both of them had fallen in love.

An hour later Steve pulled into the almost empty little car park and turned off the engine. 'Coffee?' They crunched their way over the gravel to the famous Roaches Tea Rooms but Harry hung back wanting to look at the view.

'Would you order cappuccinos for both of us?' Anna called to Steve, joining him.

She stood by the dry stone wall that bordered the property with Harry and they gazed over the dropping fields to the expanse of Tittesworth Reservoir glinting below them. A patchwork of random green shapes edged with grey stone was spread out in the sun. Harry turned to her. 'Are we going to run there?'

'No,' said Anna, 'we're going to have coffee and then we're going up there.' She turned Harry round and pointed up to the ridge behind the restaurant. Harry's face lit up. Anna took his hand. 'It's the Roaches. It's where we used to bring Faye and Ellis when they were children.' She almost asked him if he remembered but had trained herself not to do that. 'We all loved it, didn't we?'

Harry nodded. He was staring at the scarp edge above them, boulders heaped untidily along the rim. 'Terminal moraine,' he said.

'Yes. Yes, it is.' Of course, it had been Harry who had taught her the geological term. 'Let's go and get coffee and then walk up there.'

'Is the driver coming?'

'Steve? Yes, he's coming.'

'Good.'

The path up the side of the hill to Hen Cloud zig-zagged through heather and bilberry and was liberally sprinkled with sheep droppings. Then there was a scramble over some rocks on to the ridge. They all turned with the same instinct to look at the magnificent view. The sky was huge and deep blue, only the merest wisps of an old con-trail drifting high above them in a chalky diagonal. Beyond was the broad valley and the reservoir and beyond that woods and more fields. A skylark was piping above them and Harry whirled around and stared up to try to see the bird, just a tiny speck in the clear air. By their feet amongst the cracks in the limestone pavement were dots of white flowers, only visible this close up, shivering on their short stems in the breeze.

Harry threw out his arms in an uncharacteristically dramatic gesture. 'We must have beauty!' he shouted, 'We must have beauty!'

Three browsing sheep shot off away from them. Steve and Anna laughed with delight at Harry's exuberance. Anna remembered Margaret. That's what she had said when the woman on the bus had noticed her massive bouquet of flowers. 'We must have beauty.' Anna stared into the huge space and wished Maggie peace.

They made their way along the ridge path, edging between rocks for a while and then out into a clear stretch where they could stride out. Anna put herself last to keep an eye on Harry. When was the last time he had walked any distance at all? She couldn't remember. He had been physically fit when the illness had first shown itself but that was over a year ago. The centre in the brain responsible for motor coordination was in the cerebellum, she knew that, but a great deal of processing went on in the frontal temporal lobes and she had noticed that Harry was becoming a little more awkward in his movements. Sure enough, after twenty minutes he stopped and she stopped too, calling to Steve to alert him. Harry had sunk down on to the pillowy turf.

'My legs don't want to go,' he said baffled.

'Let's all take a breather,' said Steve kindly, walking back to them. 'It's so great just to be out here.' They all sat down and stared at the view.

'Is this where you were telling me about, where you teach novices to climb?' Anna asked, her short hair whipping around her face in the wind.

'A little further back where the rocks are heaped up. Yes,' said Steve.

'I thought so. We used to laugh at you,' said Anna, teasing. Steve looked startled.

'What do you mean?'

'When the children were younger we used to come up here a lot. They would run off and scramble up the rocks in their trainers in among the serious climbers in all their gear with their ropes and crampons and all that.' She grinned. 'Two kids could out-climb all of you lot!'

Steve pretended to be offended. 'Well, anyone can climb mountains in *trainers*,' he scoffed. 'It's doing it on a rope that's hard. Besides,' his blue eyes sparkled at her, 'you know that half the fun of sport is the kit.'

'Ha! I've always suspected it!' Anna laughed.

While the tone was light he asked, 'How much further shall we go do you think? Just a quarter of a mile or so along here is something I'd like to show you both.' Anna looked at Harry. He stood up.

'Should be ok,' Anna said, 'let's just see how we go.' For the first few steps Harry stumbled a little but then recovered and strode on quite quickly. Naturally his muscles would be unused to the exercise they were taking. Anyone would need to tone up. Anna's own legs were quivering a little with the unusual climbing they had done. To Steve, of course, what they had done so far would be like walking a few metres down the road to the post-box for her.

As they went on she looked past Harry to the other man, his dark hair rising in the wind to form a ragged crest. The Other Man. Well, hardly. But there was what Victorians would have called 'an understanding' between them now. An understanding that they were no longer alone struggling with the random tragic events that had swept up those they loved and changed their own lives for ever. Of course the future was unknowable and could not be planned for except in the most tentative, pragmatic way. There would be many hard things ahead. But they had each other to lean on and there was also the now, the present, and that could be full of life and love and moments like this of pure exhilaration.

After a while Steve stopped and grinned back at them. The sun caught his flushed skin and turned his blue eyes to sparkling crystals. Not Steely Steve now, Anna thought happily. 'Look! Come off the path a bit and see!' They walked a few yards and there was the surprise. It was a perfect little tarn, a pool fringed with reeds and reflecting the shining sky. A freak of nature. A little pool on the roof of the world like an oasis tucked away in the desert. 'A real blessing for travellers and shepherds,' Steve said, 'and the wildlife, of course.' Secret places, moments in and out of time, unexpected blessings. What was it Blake had said? 'Catch the joy and kiss it as it flies.' Yes. There would be worry and tragedy enough but there was also this. 'The water's sweet,' Steve said. 'You can drink it.' He knelt down and cupped his hands under the wind-rippled surface.

Harry immediately knelt beside him, intrigued. 'Here you are, mate,' Steve said, lifting his cupped hands to Harry, 'taste it. It's lovely.' And Harry did, dipping his head briefly to taste the water.

Anna turned away, her eyes full of tears.

They all stood up and gazed ahead. 'Shall we go on again or turn back?' Steve asked.

'Go on!' insisted Harry, 'We should go on!' He began to walk back to the path.

Anna looked at Steve. 'Let's go on together, then, shall we?' Steve put his arm around her shoulder and hugged her to him. 'Fine by me.'

Harry glanced back at them standing together. 'Come on, kids,' he shouted, 'come with me!' And they did.

Thanks

I've been very fortunate in my friends and family in the writing of this trilogy. I am especially indebted for expert advice on genealogy to Catharine Stevens who rarely hesitated more than a few seconds to answer complicated questions and who never snorted with contempt over simple ones. Her knowledge and breadth of experience is truly impressive. Any idiocies in this area are my own. Also, my thanks to Jeremy Plewes for his advice on medical matters. Even when presented with convoluted criteria he would unerringly describe just the condition the narrative needed. I am also deeply grateful to Terry Quinn and others who read the unpublished manuscripts and who, through their vigilance, saved me from embarrassing errors of all kinds. And, with deep appreciation for their support, I want to thank my sons who have been unfailingly interested and encouraging as I've woven together these stories.

Geraldine Wall has lived and worked in the UK, the USA and the Cayman Islands and now lives in Birmingham.

Email: geraldine.wall@blueyonder.co.uk

Made in the USA
Monee, IL
09 February 2024

53110011R00204